Tree-House Comix Proudly Presents

DOG MAN
FOR WHOM THE BALL ROLLS

WRITTEN AND ILLUSTRATED BY DAV PILKEY
AS GEORGE BEARD AND HAROLD HUTCHINS
WITH COLOR BY JOSE GARIBALDI

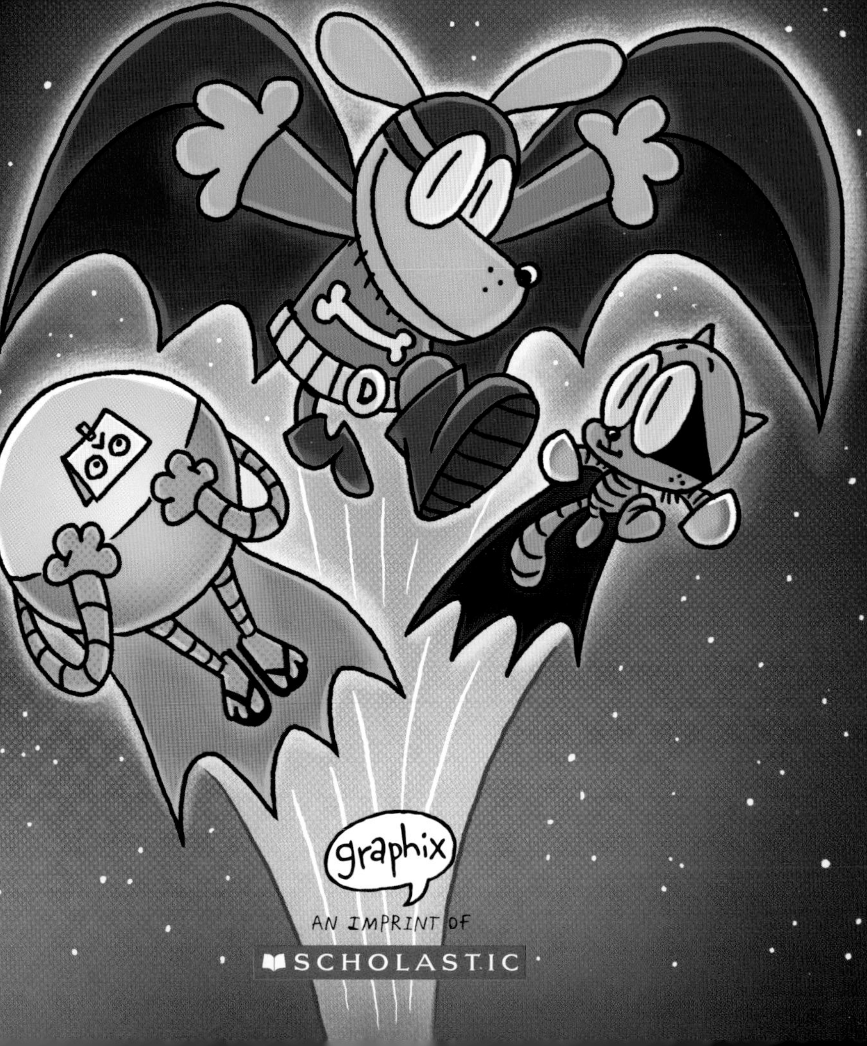

graphix
AN IMPRINT OF
SCHOLASTIC

FOR CHARISSE MELOTO, WHO INSPIRES US ALL TO DO GOOD!

Library of Congress Control Number 2019932354

978-1-338-23659-0 (POB)
978-1-338-29094-3 (Library)

10 9 8 7 6 5 4 3 2 1   19 20 21 22 23

Printed in China   62
First edition, September 2019

Edited by Ken Geist
Book design by Dav Pilkey and Phil Falco
Color by Jose Garibaldi
Color flatting by Aaron Polk
Publisher: David Saylor

CONTENTS

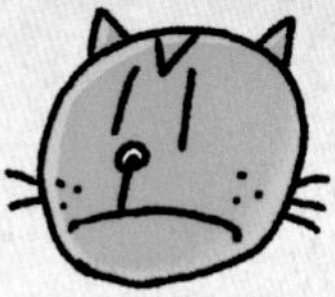

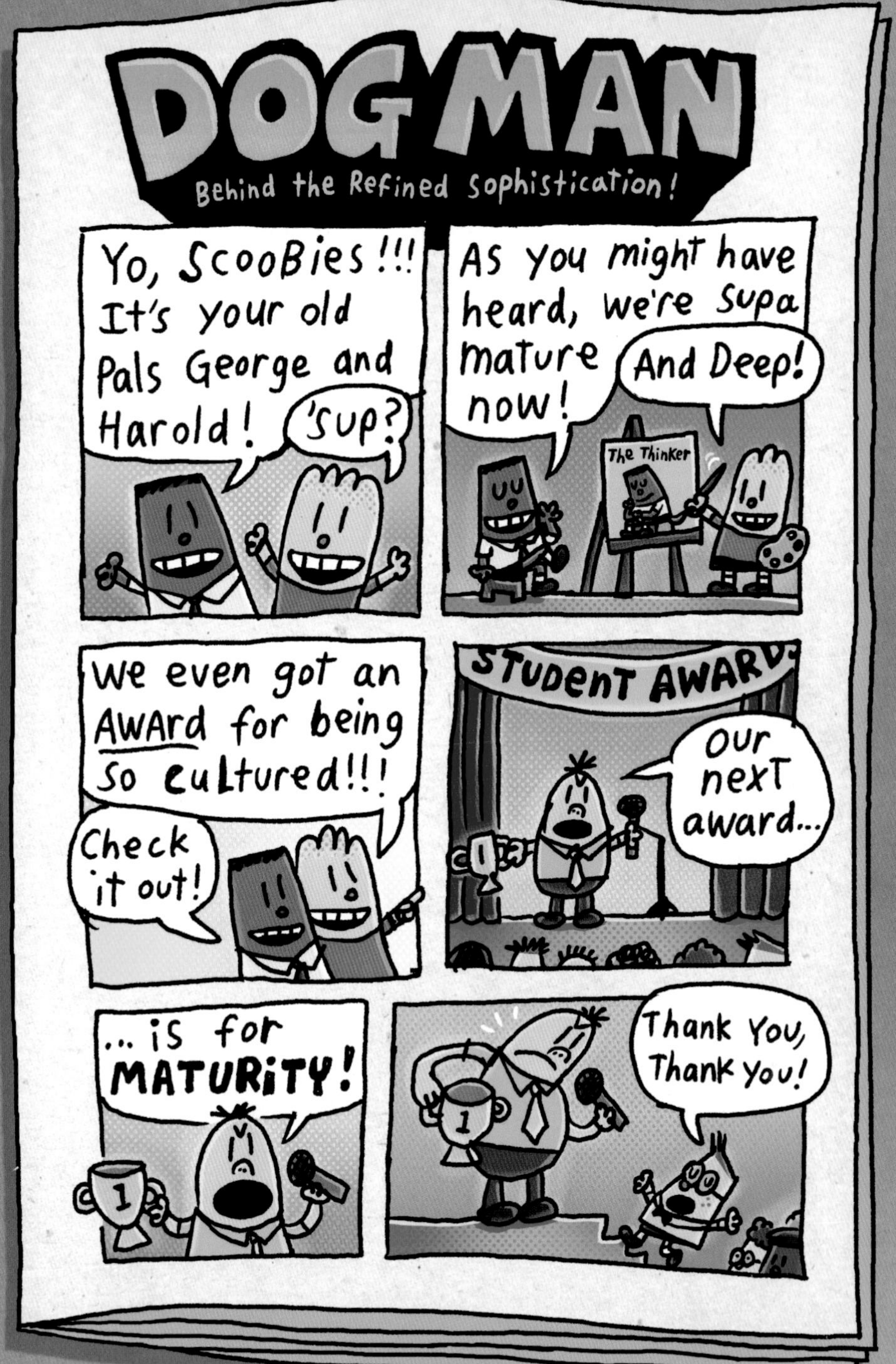
DOG MAN
Behind the Refined Sophistication!
Yo, Scoobies!!! It's your old Pals George and Harold!
'Sup?
As you might have heard, we're Supa mature now!
And Deep!
The Thinker
We even got an AWArd for being So cultured!!!
Check it out!
STUDENT AWARD
Our next award...
... is for MATURITY!
Thank You, Thank You!

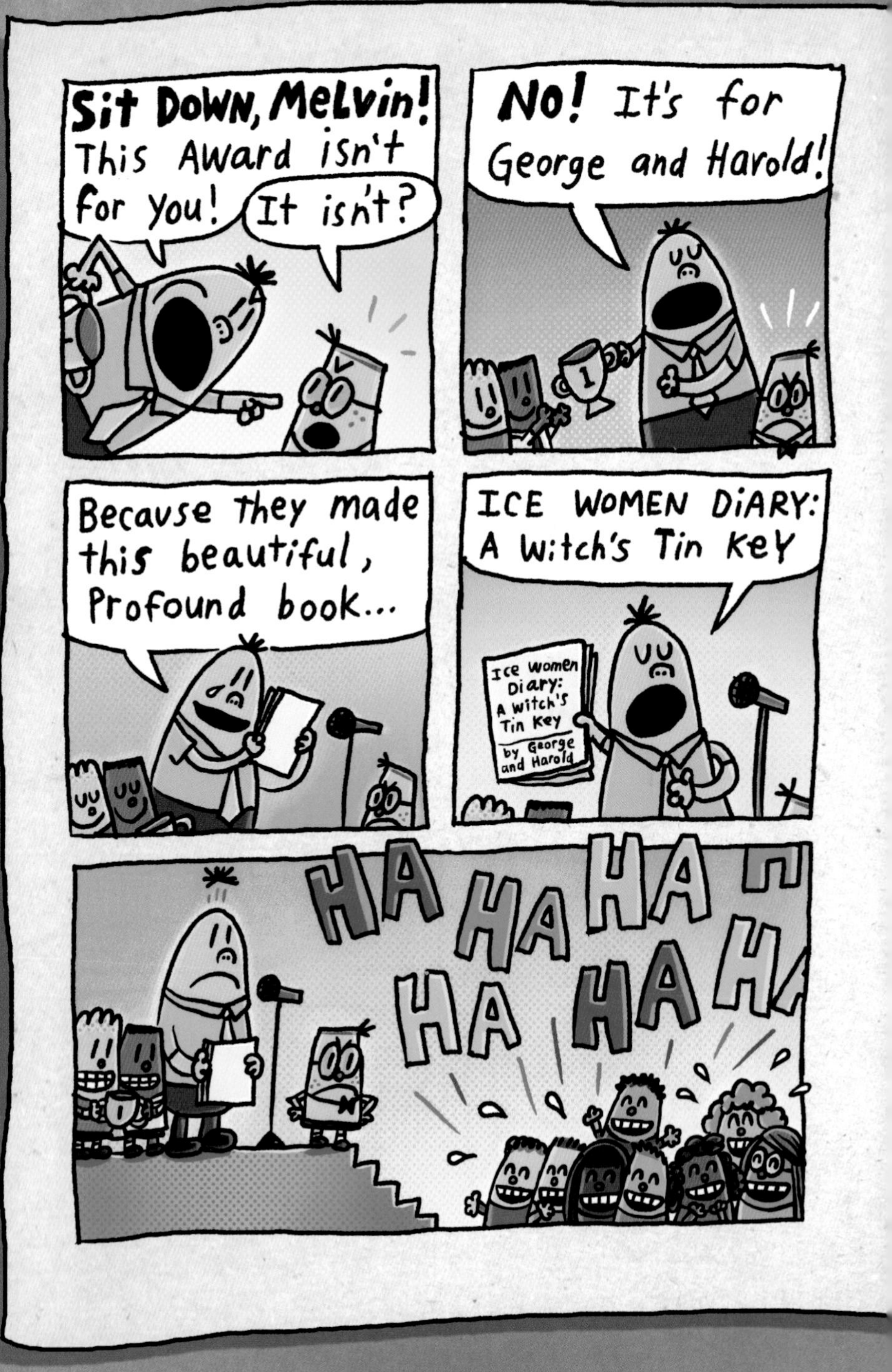
Sit DOWN, MELVin! This Award isn't for you!
It isn't?
NO! It's for George and Harold!
Because they made this beautiful, Profound book...
ICE WOMEN DiARY: A Witch's Tin KEY
Ice Women Diary: A Witch's Tin Key
by George and Harold
HA HA HA HA HA HA HA HA

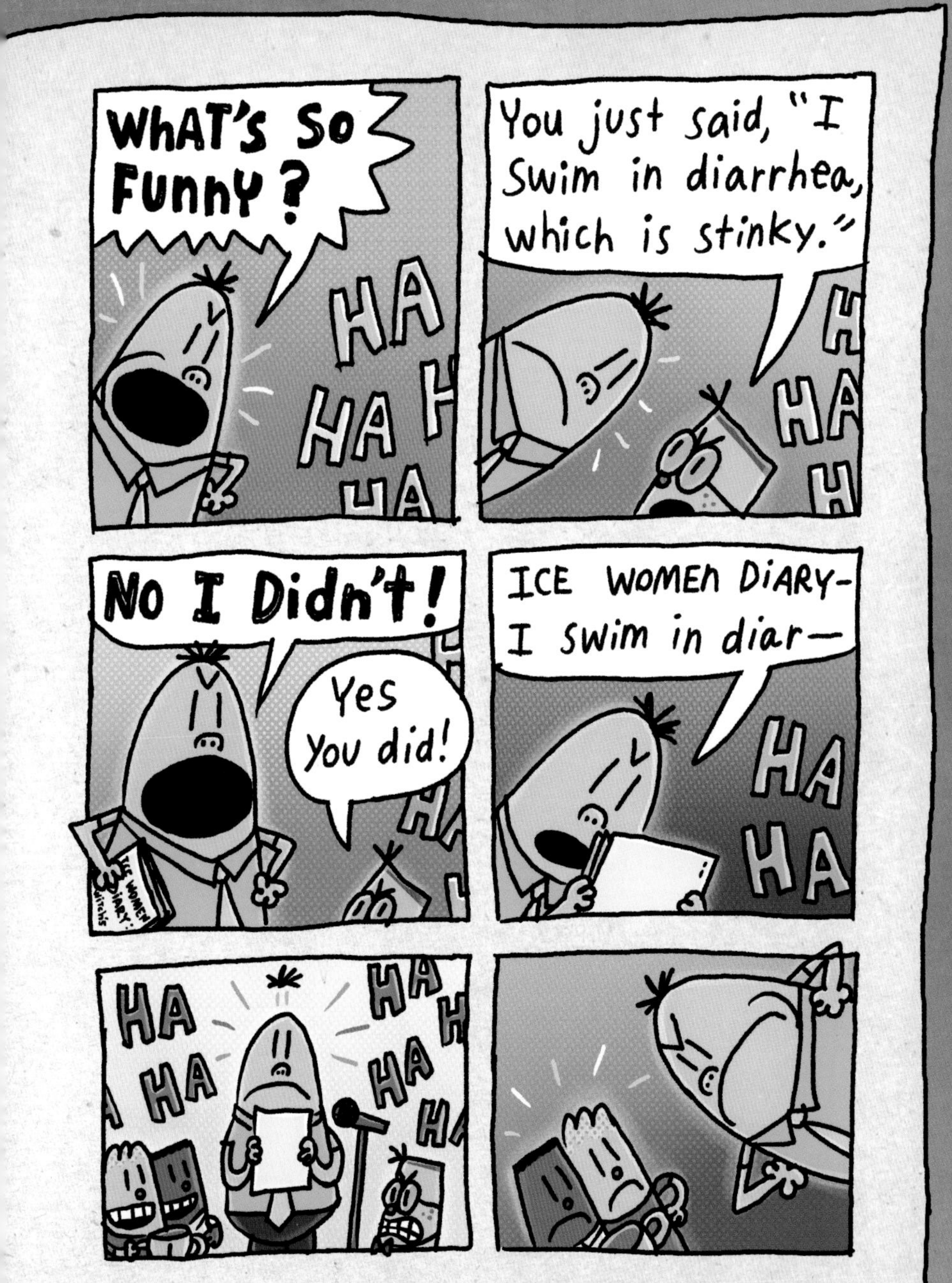
WHAT'S SO FUNNY?
HA HA HA
You just said, "I Swim in diarrhea, which is stinky."
HA HA
No I Didn't!
Yes you did!
ICE WOMEN DIARY-
I swim in diar—
HA HA
HA HA HA HA

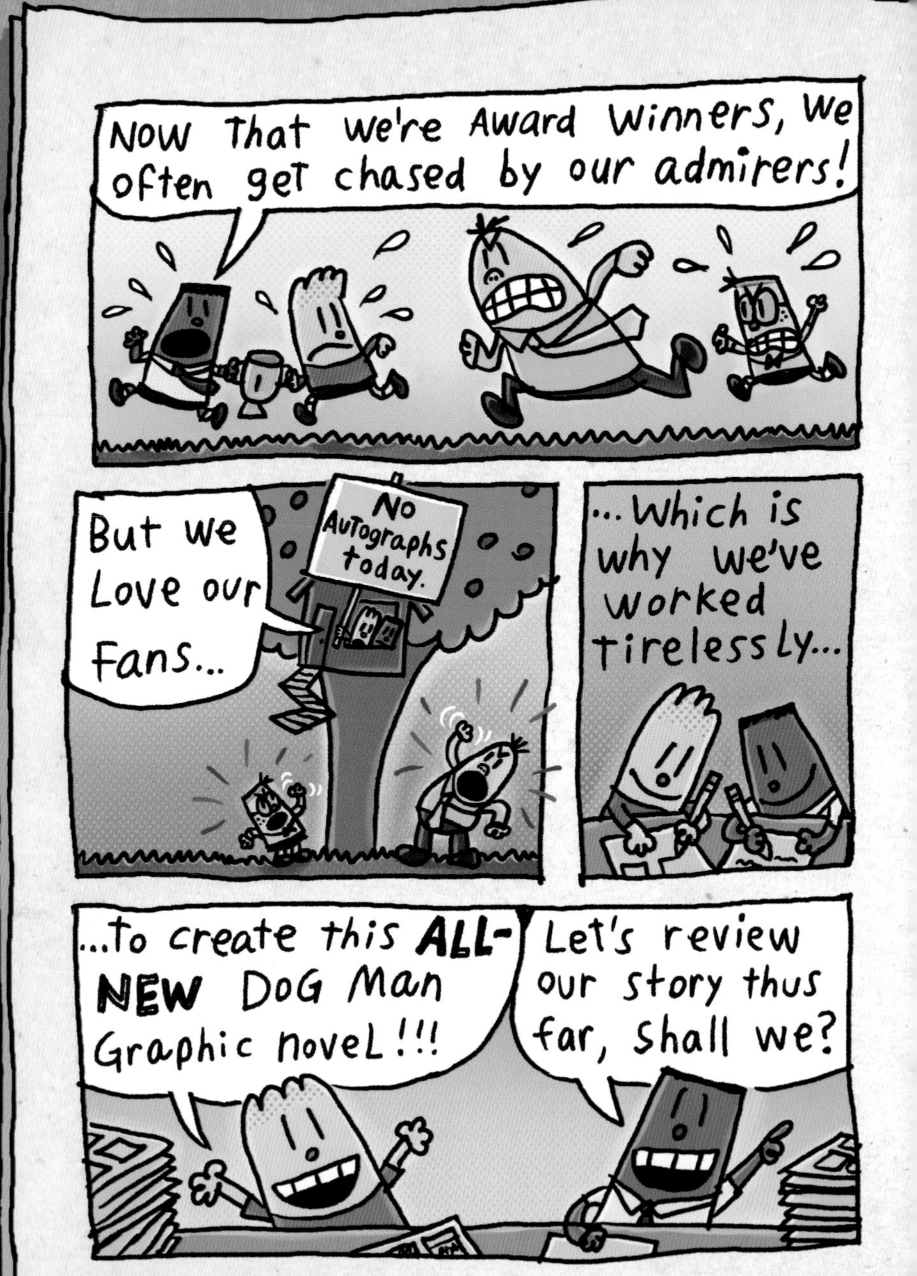

NOW That we're Award Winners, We often get chased by our admirers!
But we Love our Fans...
No AuTographs today.
...Which is why we've worked Tirelessly...
...To create this ALL-NEW DoG Man Graphic noveL!!!
Let's review our story thus far, Shall we?

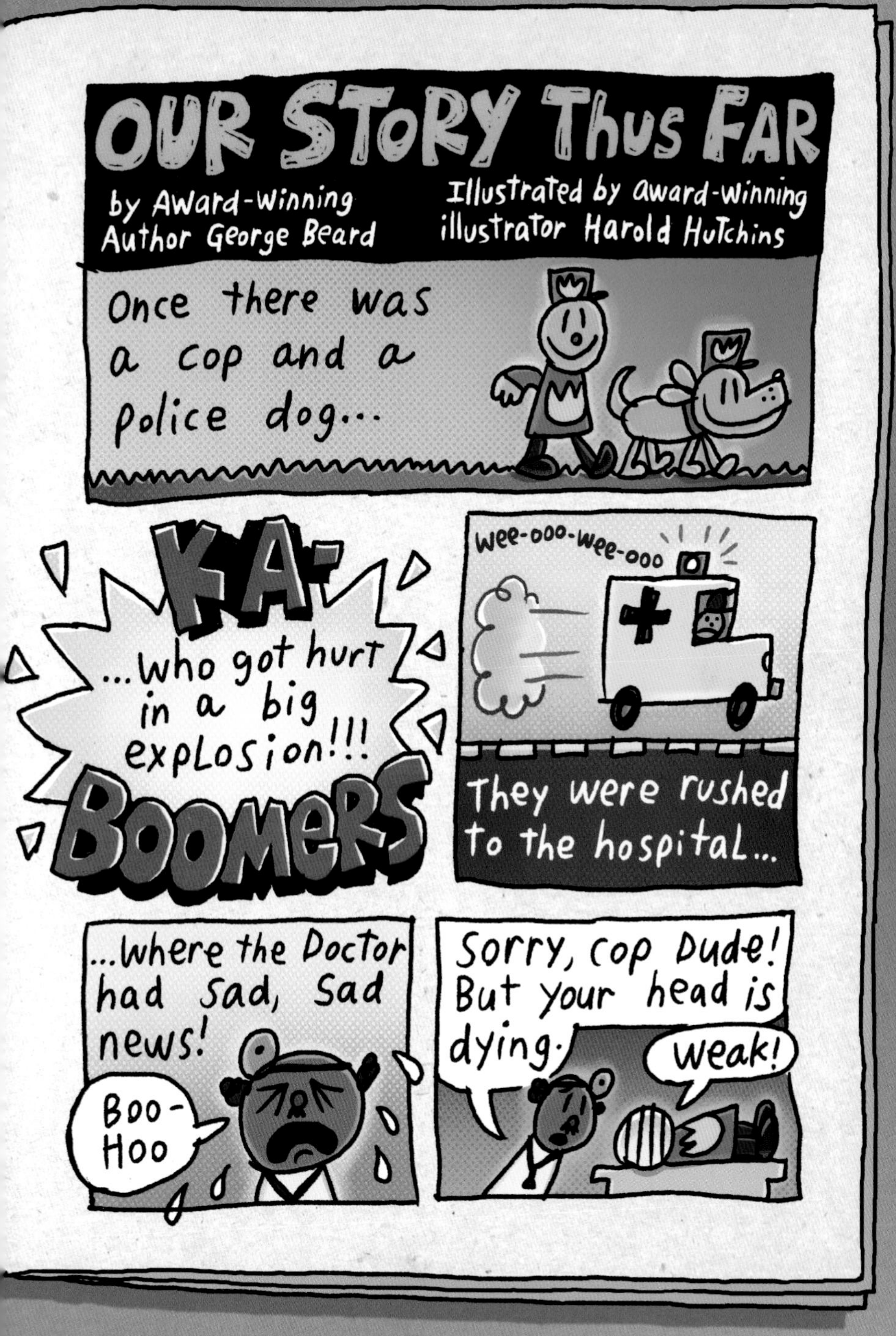
OUR STORY Thus FAR
by Award-Winning Author George Beard
Illustrated by award-winning illustrator Harold Hutchins
Once there was a cop and a police dog...
KA-
...who got hurt in a big explosion!!!
BOOMERS
wee-ooo-wee-ooo
They were rushed to the hospital...
...where the Doctor had sad, sad news!
Boo-Hoo
Sorry, cop Dude! But your head is dying.
Weak!

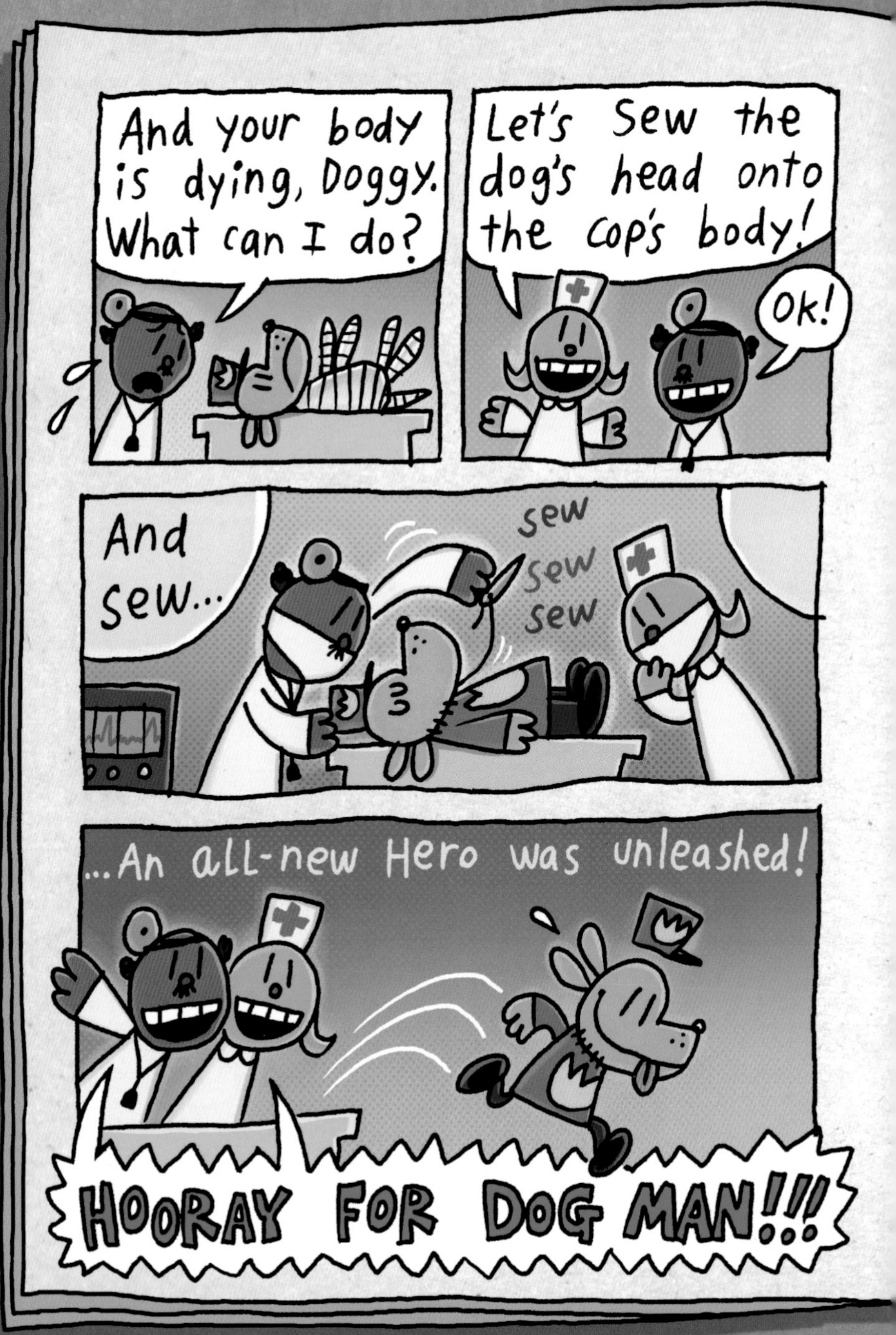

And your body is dying, Doggy. What can I do?
Let's sew the dog's head onto the cop's body!
Ok!
And sew...
sew sew sew
...An all-new Hero was unleashed!
HOORAY FOR DOG MAN!!!

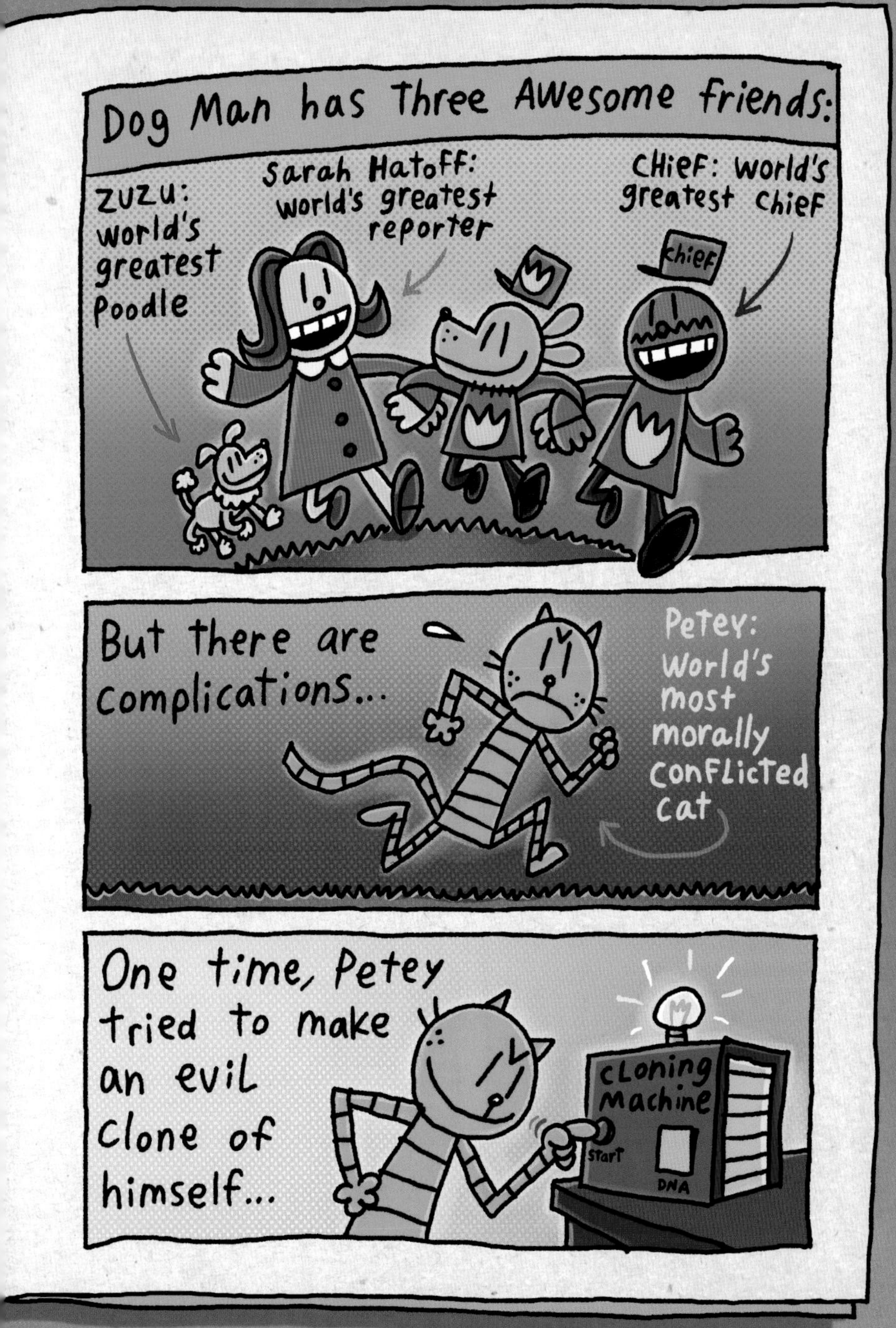

Dog Man has Three Awesome friends:
ZUZU: world's greatest Poodle
Sarah Hatoff: world's greatest reporter
CHIEF: world's greatest Chief
Chief
But there are complications...
Petey: World's most morally conflicted cat
One time, Petey tried to make an evil clone of himself...
Cloning Machine
Start
DNA

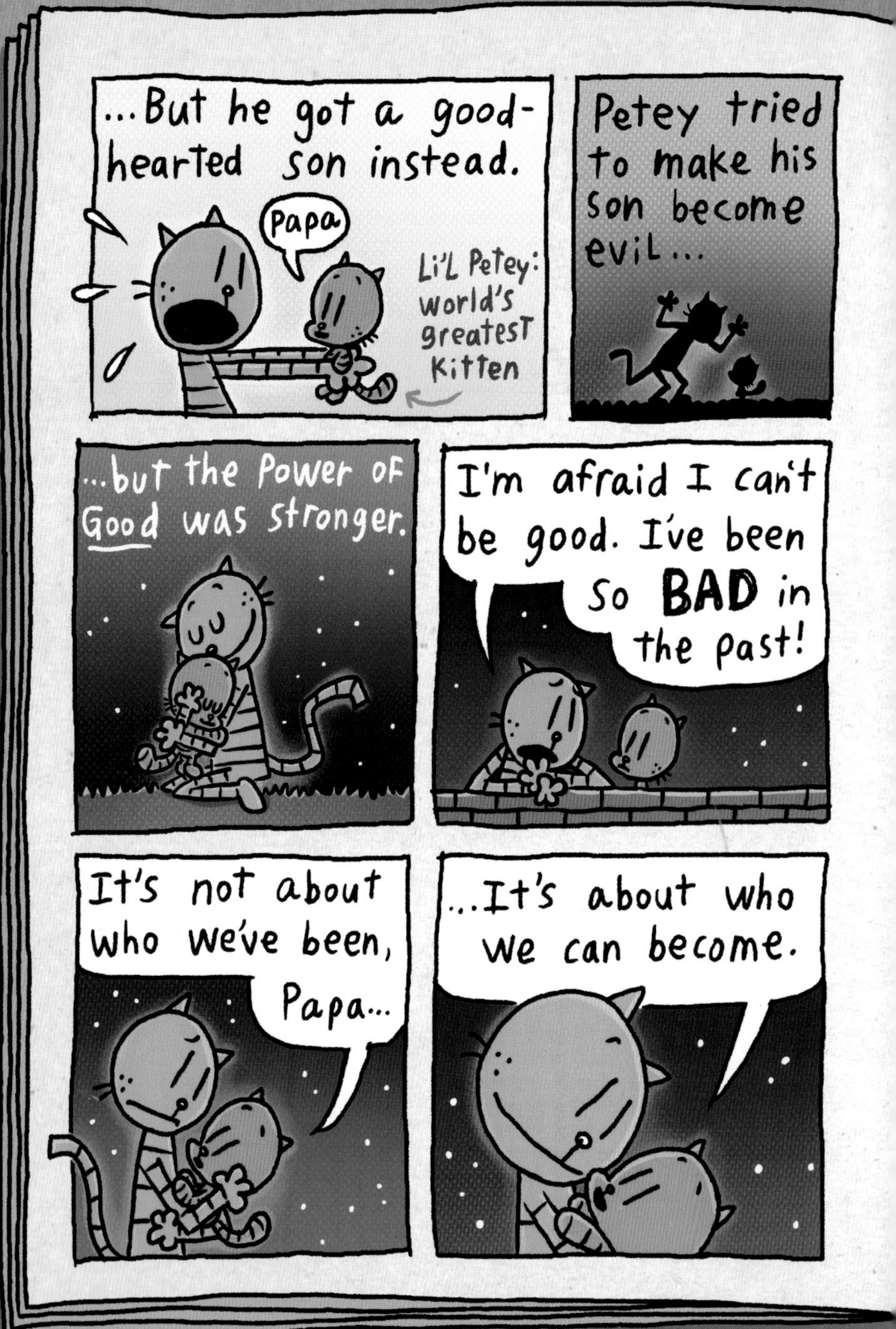
...But he got a good-hearted son instead.
Papa
Li'L Petey: world's greatest Kitten
Petey tried to make his son become evil...
...but the Power of Good was stronger.
I'm afraid I can't be good. I've been so BAD in the past!
It's not about who we've been, Papa...
...It's about who we can become.

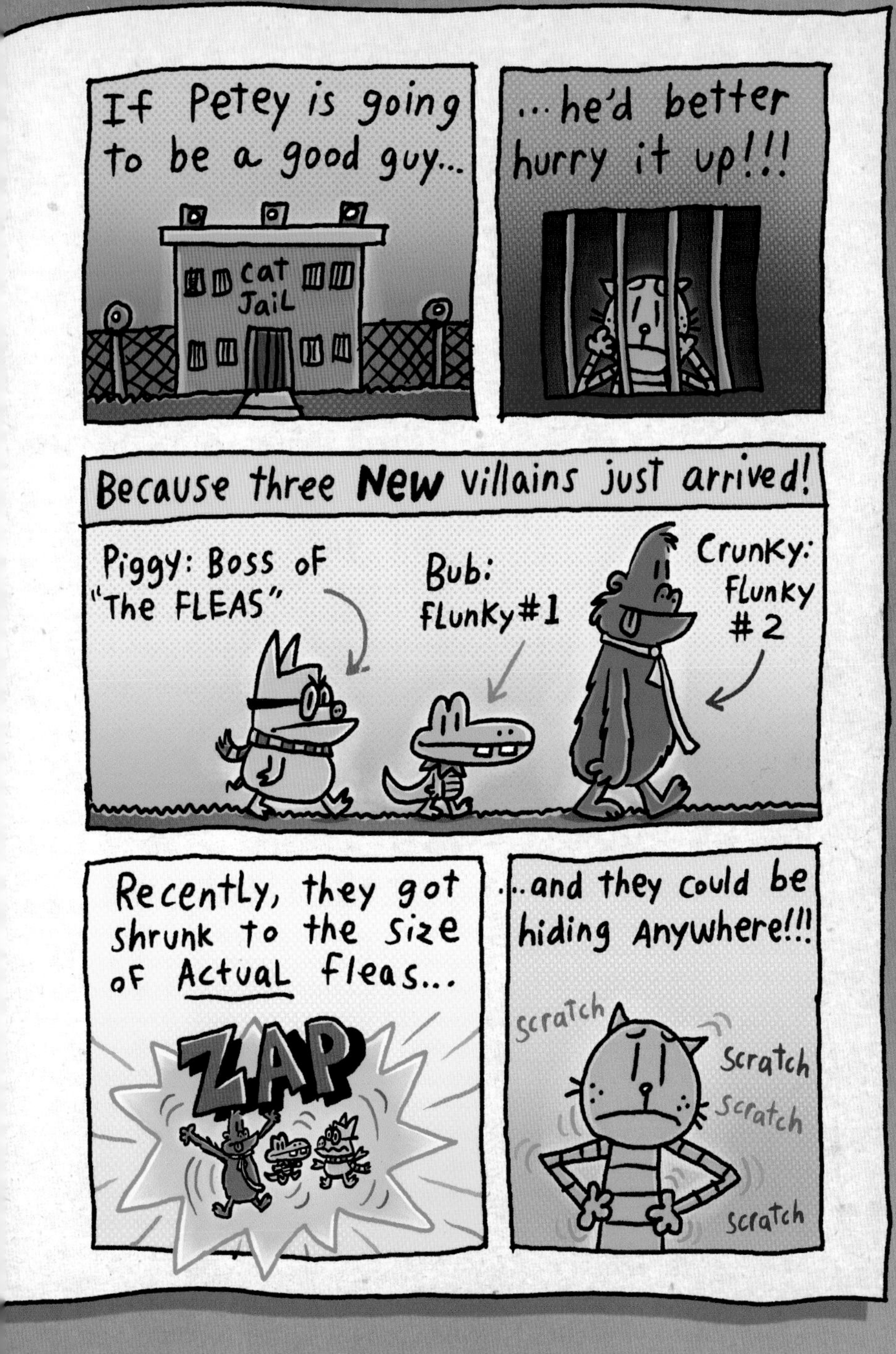
If Petey is going to be a good guy...
Cat Jail
...he'd better hurry it up!!!
Because three New villains just arrived!
Piggy: Boss of "The FLEAS"
Bub: Flunky #1
Crunky: Flunky #2
Recently, they got shrunk to the size of Actual fleas...
ZAP
...and they could be hiding Anywhere!!!
scratch
scratch
scratch
scratch

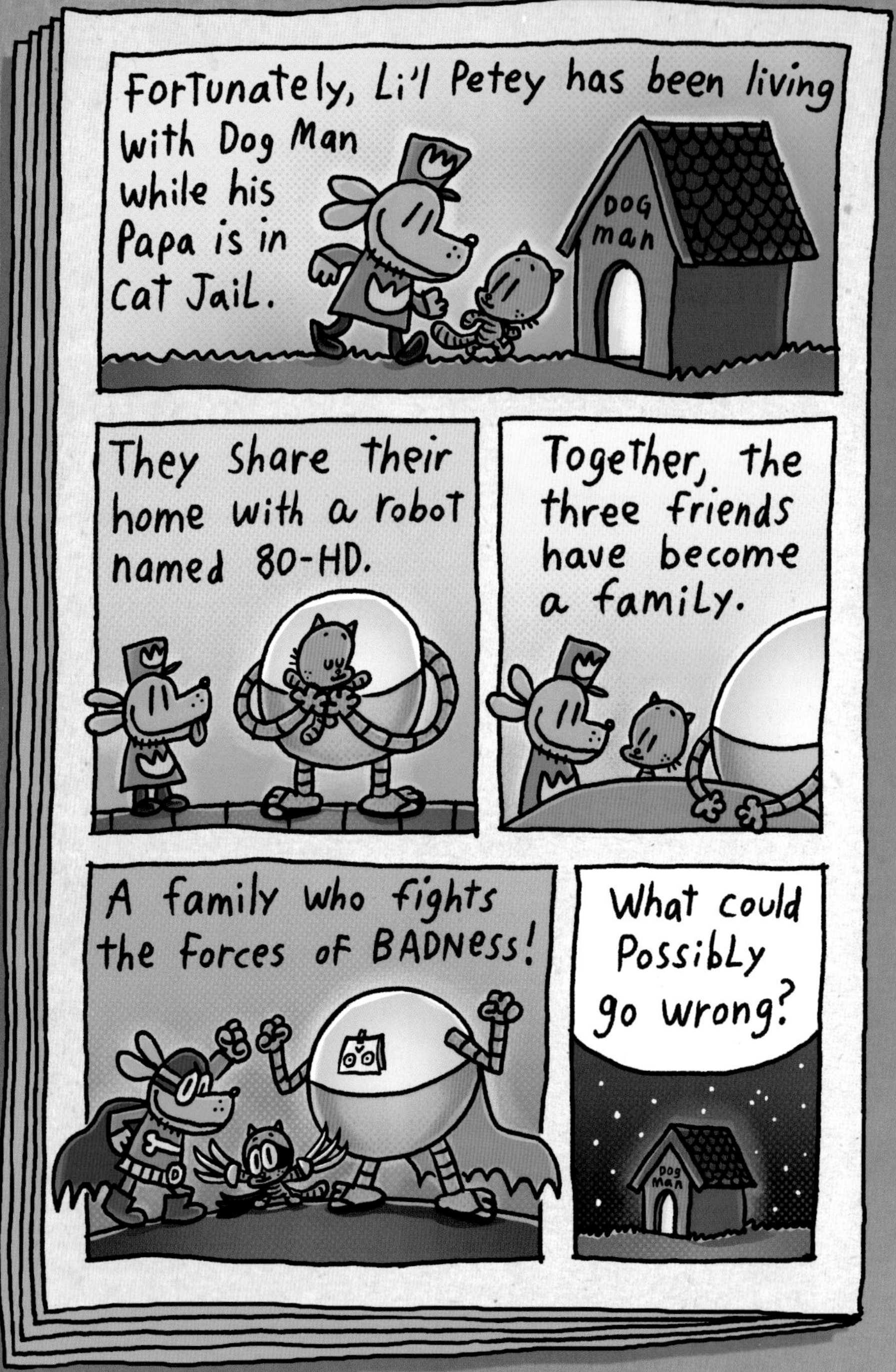
Fortunately, Li'l Petey has been living with Dog Man while his Papa is in Cat Jail.
DOG man
They share their home with a robot named 80-HD.
Together, the three friends have become a family.
A family who fights the forces of BADNESS!
What could possibly go wrong?
DOG man

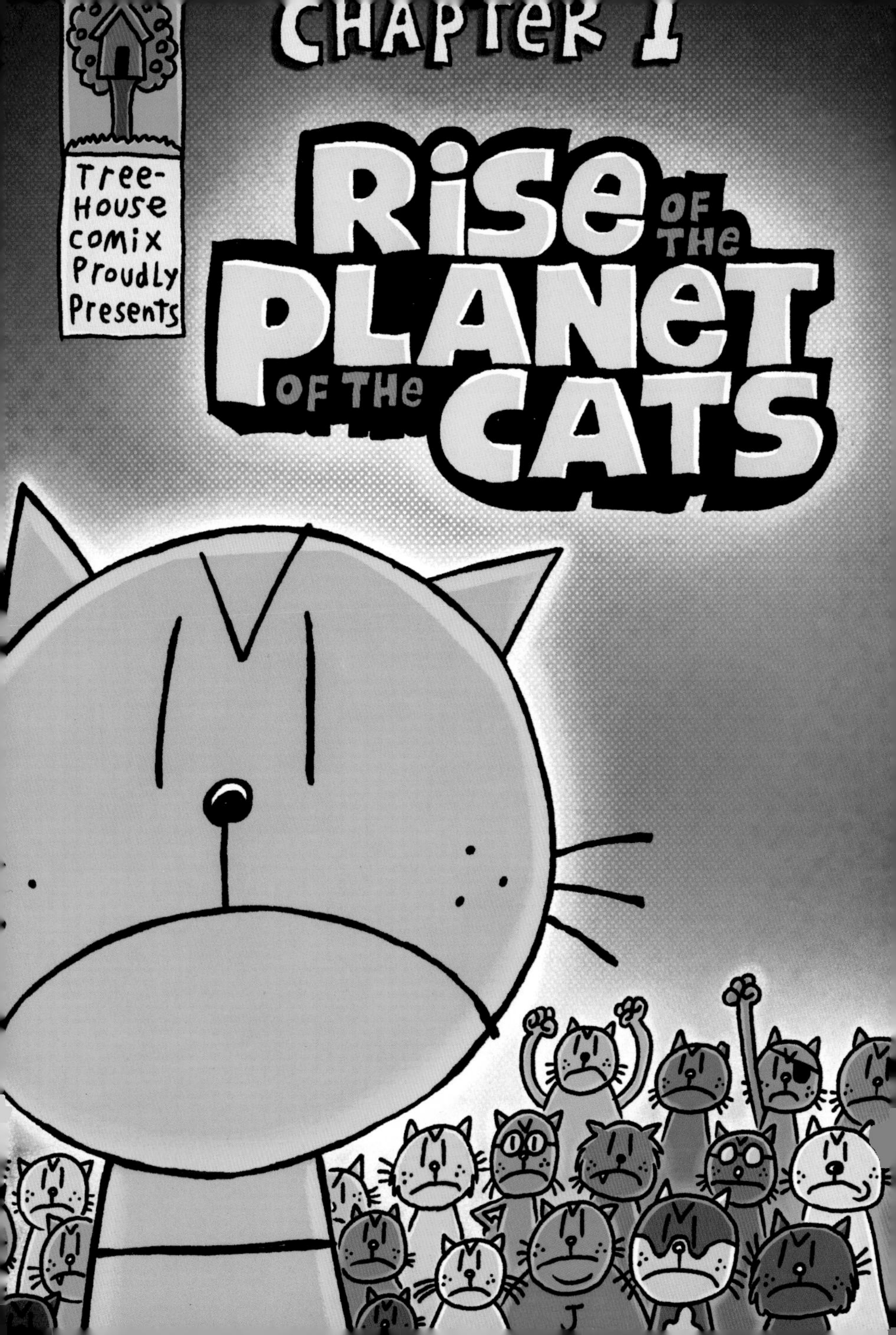
CHAPTER 1
Tree-House comix Proudly Presents
Rise of the Planet of the Cats

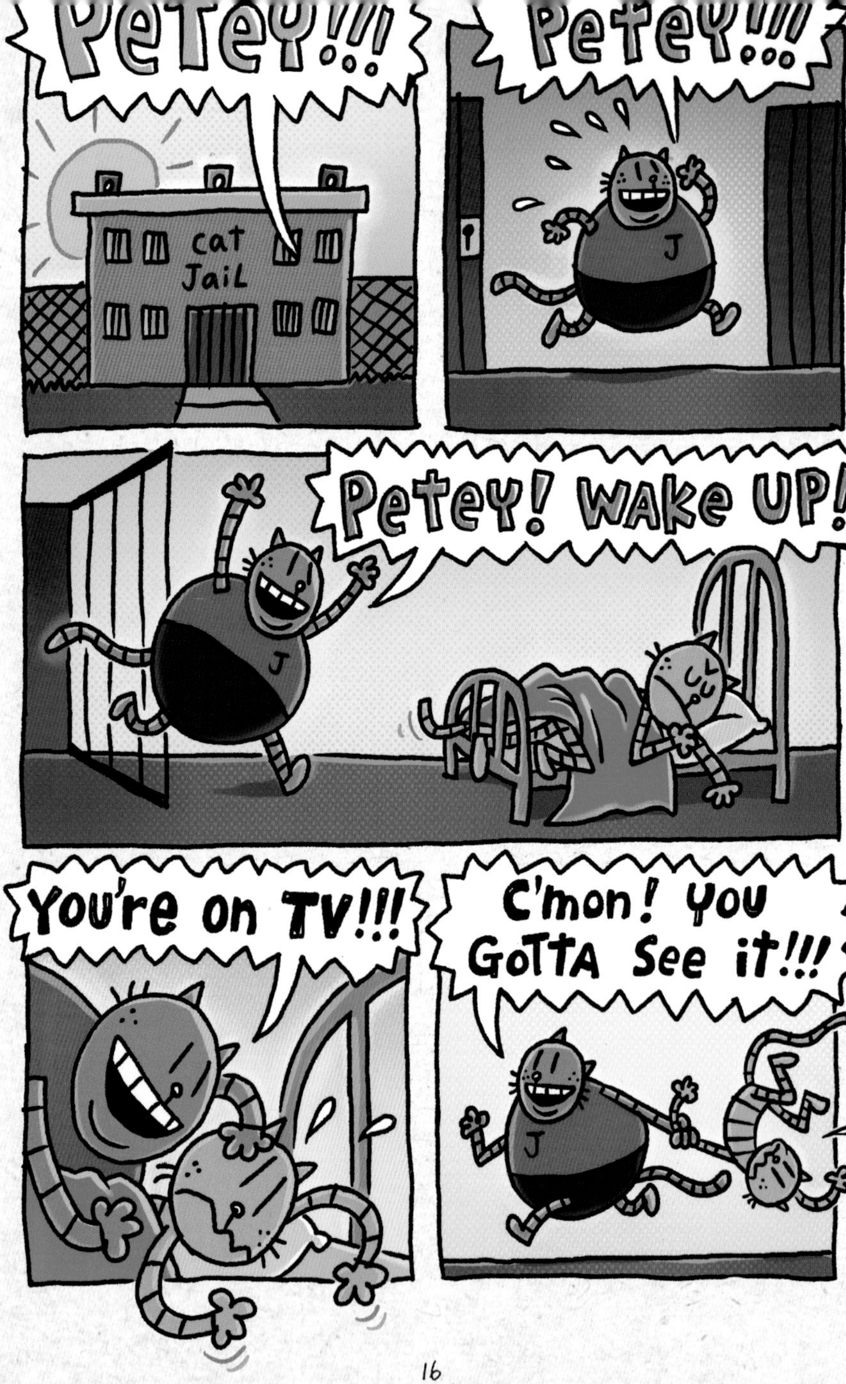
PETEY!!!
Cat Jail
PETEY!!!
PETEY! WAKE UP!
YOU'RE ON TV!!!
C'MON! YOU GOTTA SEE IT!!!

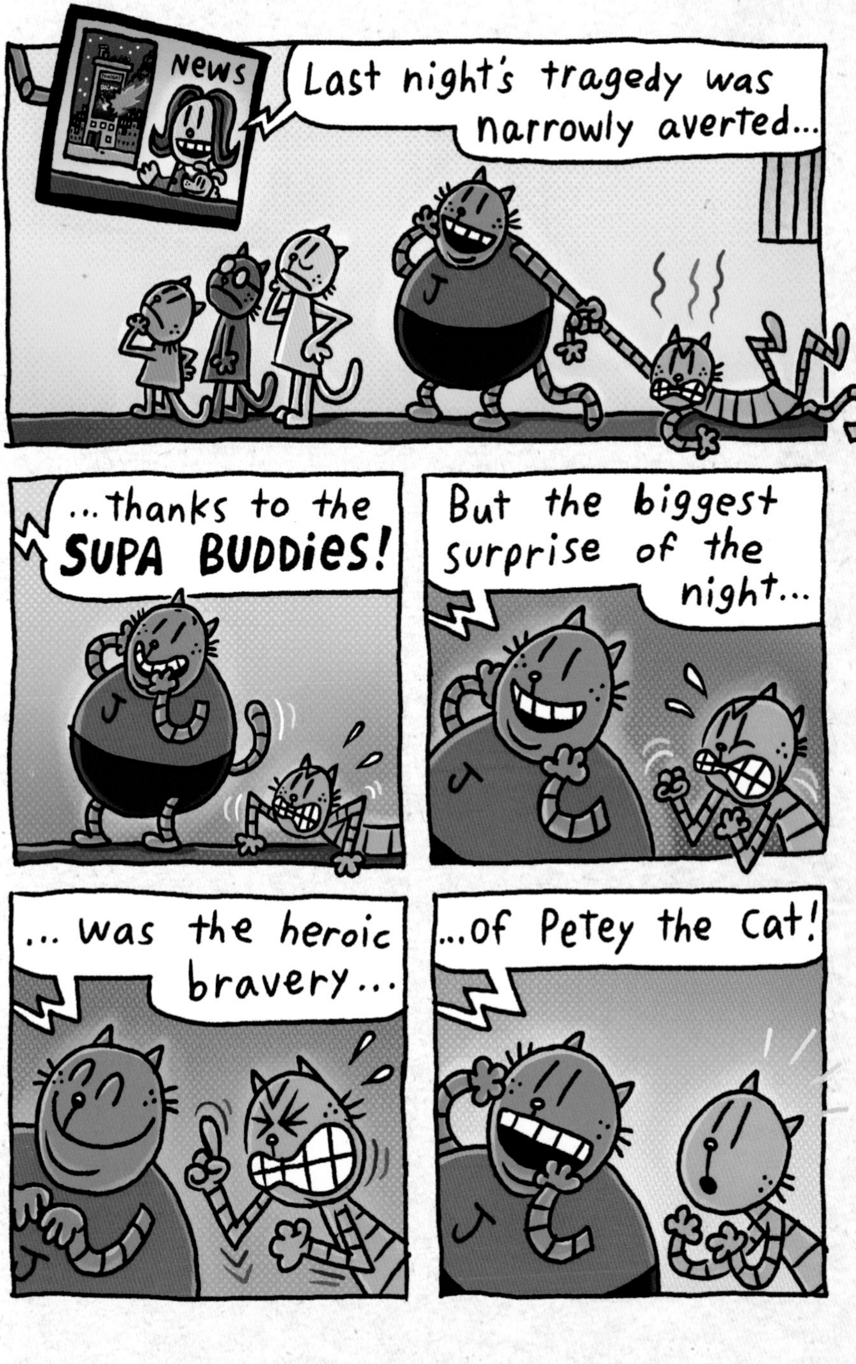
NEWS
Last night's tragedy was narrowly averted...
...thanks to the SUPA BUDDIES!
But the biggest surprise of the night...
... was the heroic bravery...
...of Petey the Cat!

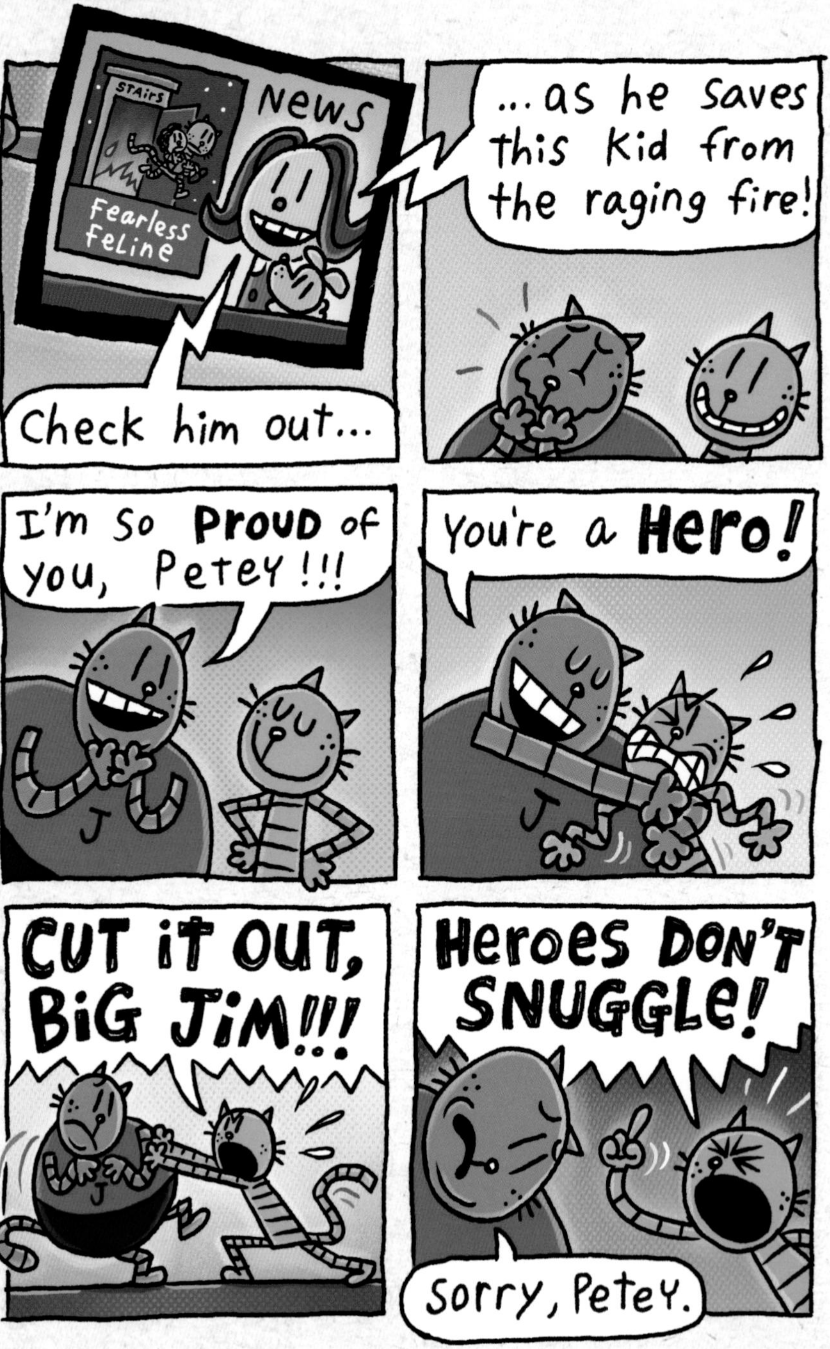
STAIRS
Fearless Feline
NEWS
Check him out...
...as he saves this kid from the raging fire!
I'm so PROUD of you, Petey!!!
You're a Hero!
CUT it OUT, BiG JiM!!!
Heroes DON'T SNUGGLE!
Sorry, Petey.

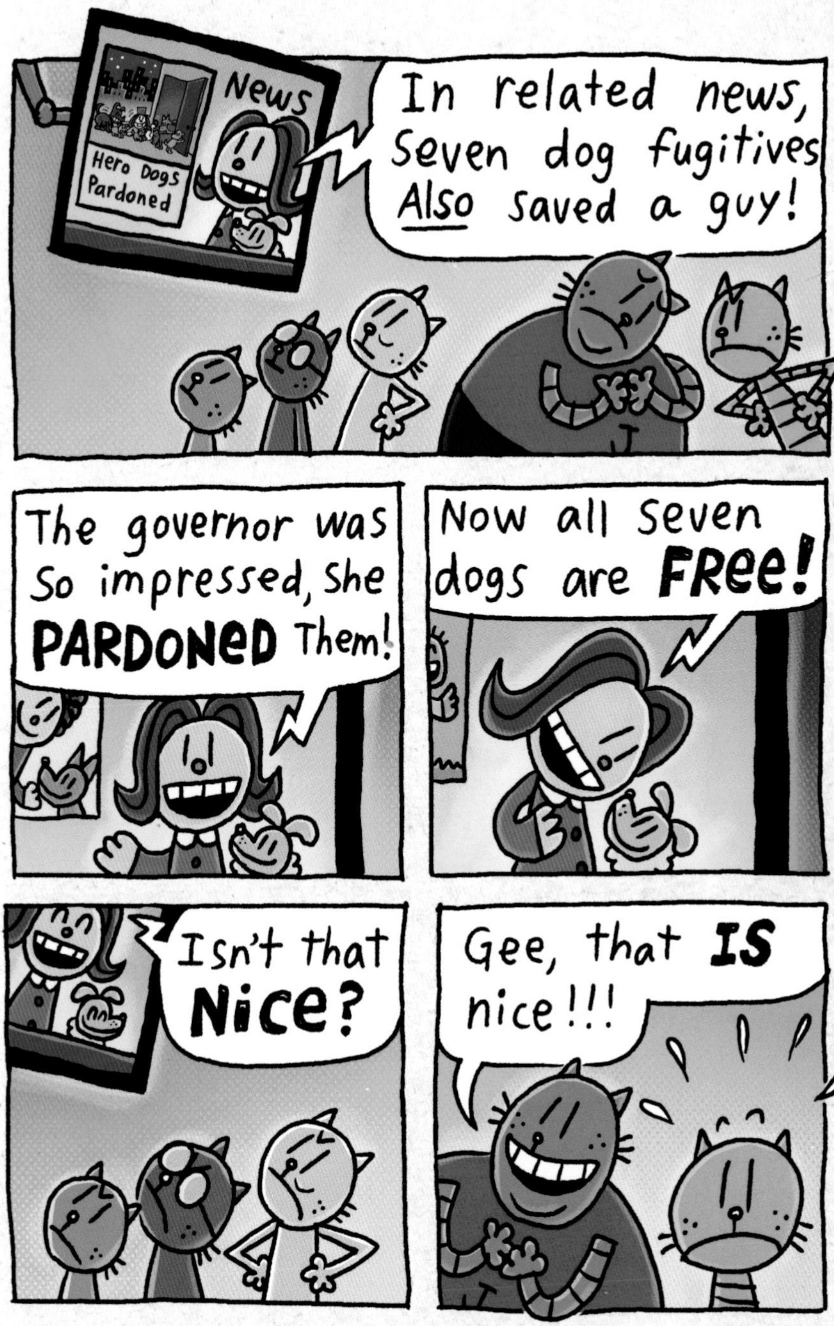
News
Hero Dogs Pardoned
In related news, Seven dog fugitives Also saved a guy!
The governor was So impressed, She PARDONED Them!
Now all seven dogs are FREE!
Isn't that Nice?
Gee, that IS nice!!!

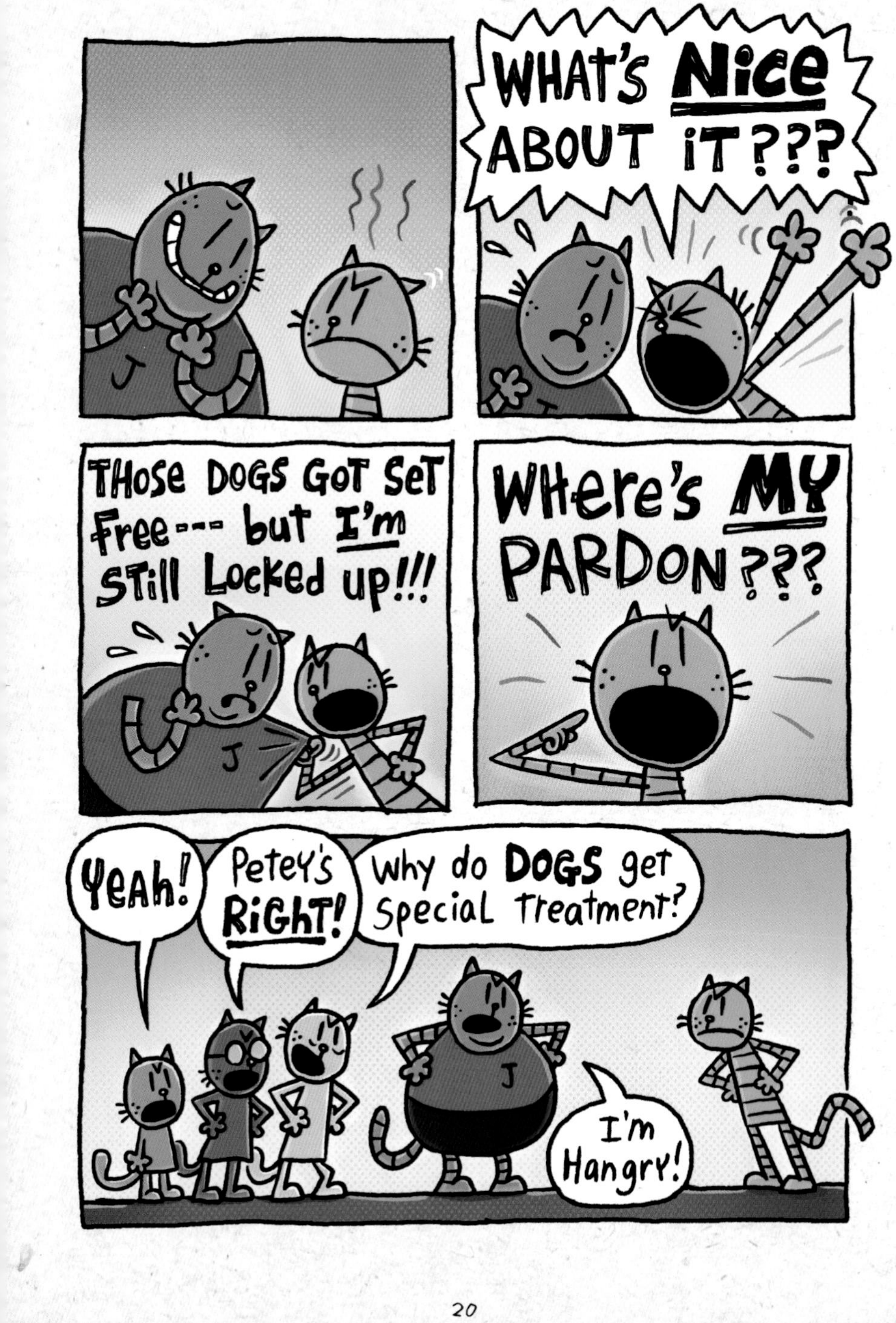
WHAT'S Nice ABOUT iT???
THOSE DOGS GOT SET Free--- but I'm STill Locked up!!!
WHere's MY PARDON???
Yeah!
Petey's RiGHT!
Why do DOGS get Special Treatment?
I'm Hangry!

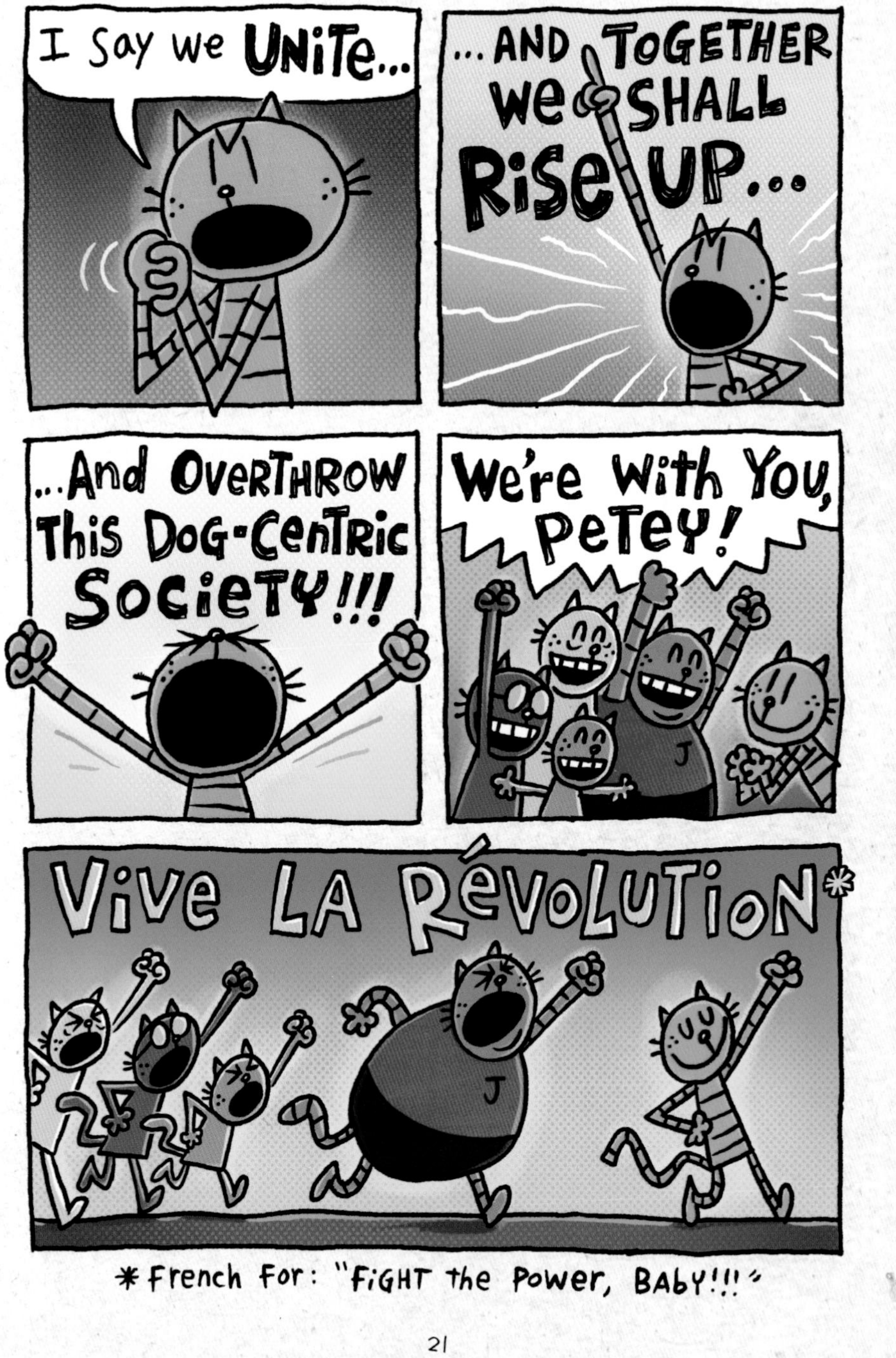
I Say we UNiTe...
...AND TOGETHER we SHALL RiSe UP...
...And OverTHROW This DoG-CenTRic SocieTY!!!
We're With You, PeTeY!
ViVe LA RéVoLUTioN*
J
J

* French For: "FiGHT the Power, BAbY!!!"

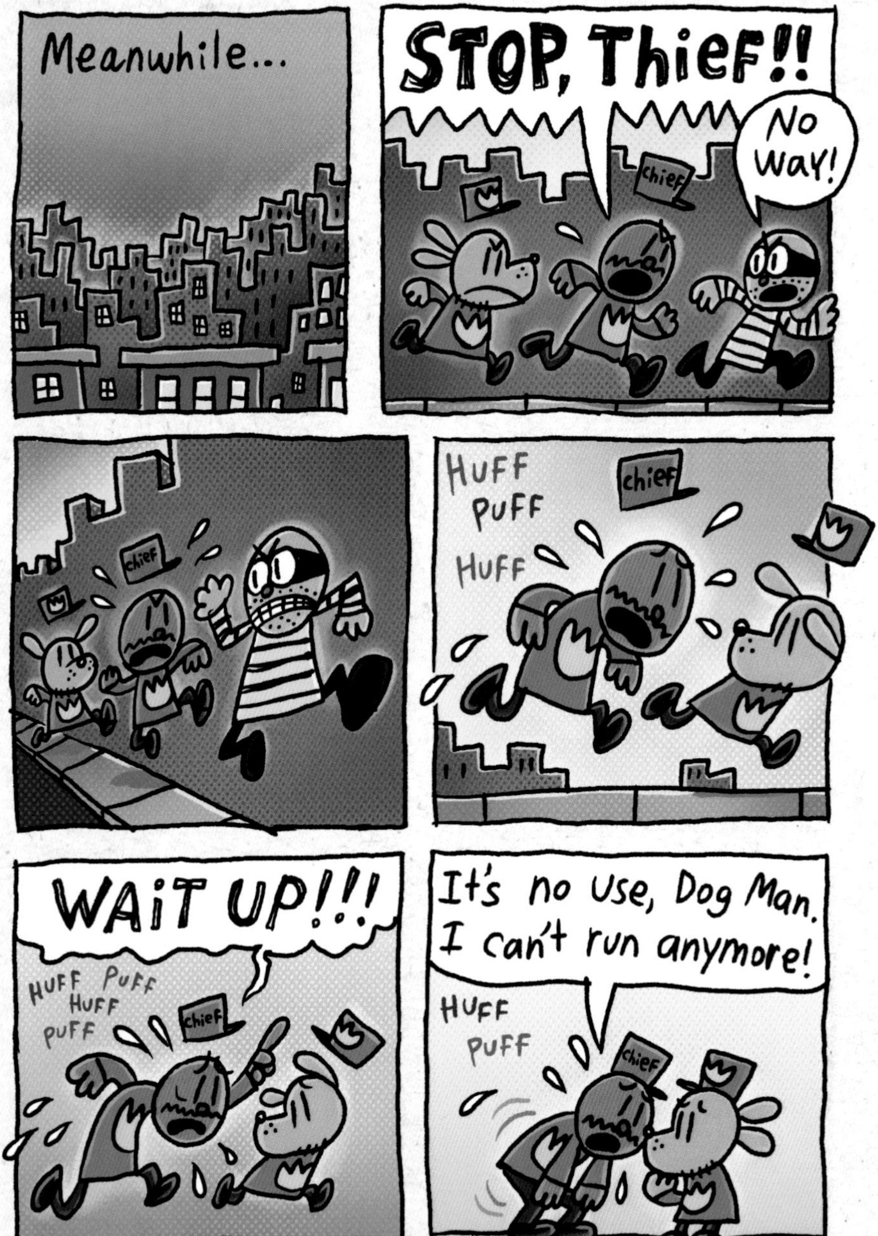
Meanwhile...
STOP, Thief!!
No way!
chief
chief
HUFF
PUFF
HUFF
chief
WAiT UP!!!
HUFF PUFF
HUFF
PUFF
chief
It's no use, Dog Man. I can't run anymore!
HUFF
PUFF
chief

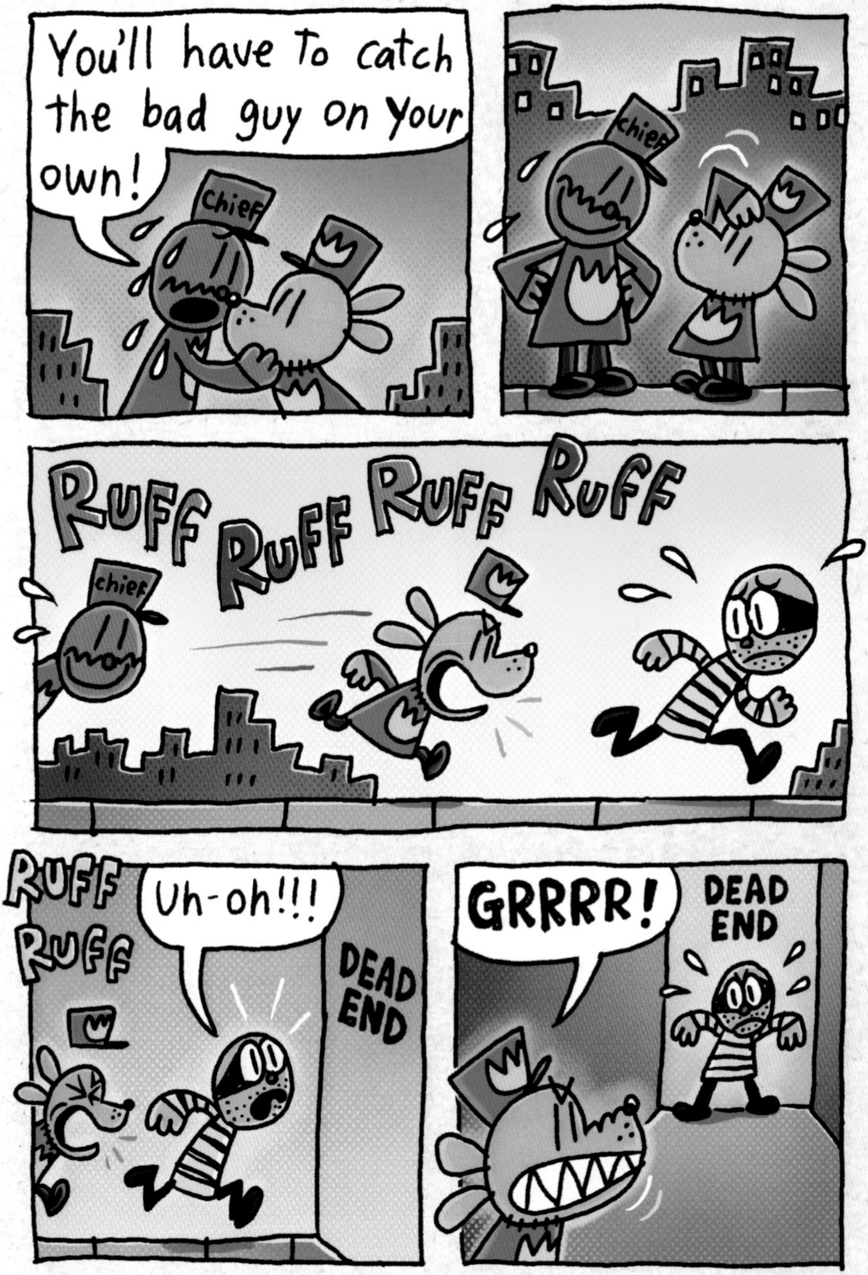
You'll have to catch the bad guy on your own!
Chief
chief
RUFF RUFF RUFF RUFF
chief
RUFF RUFF
Uh-oh!!!
DEAD END
GRRRR!
DEAD END

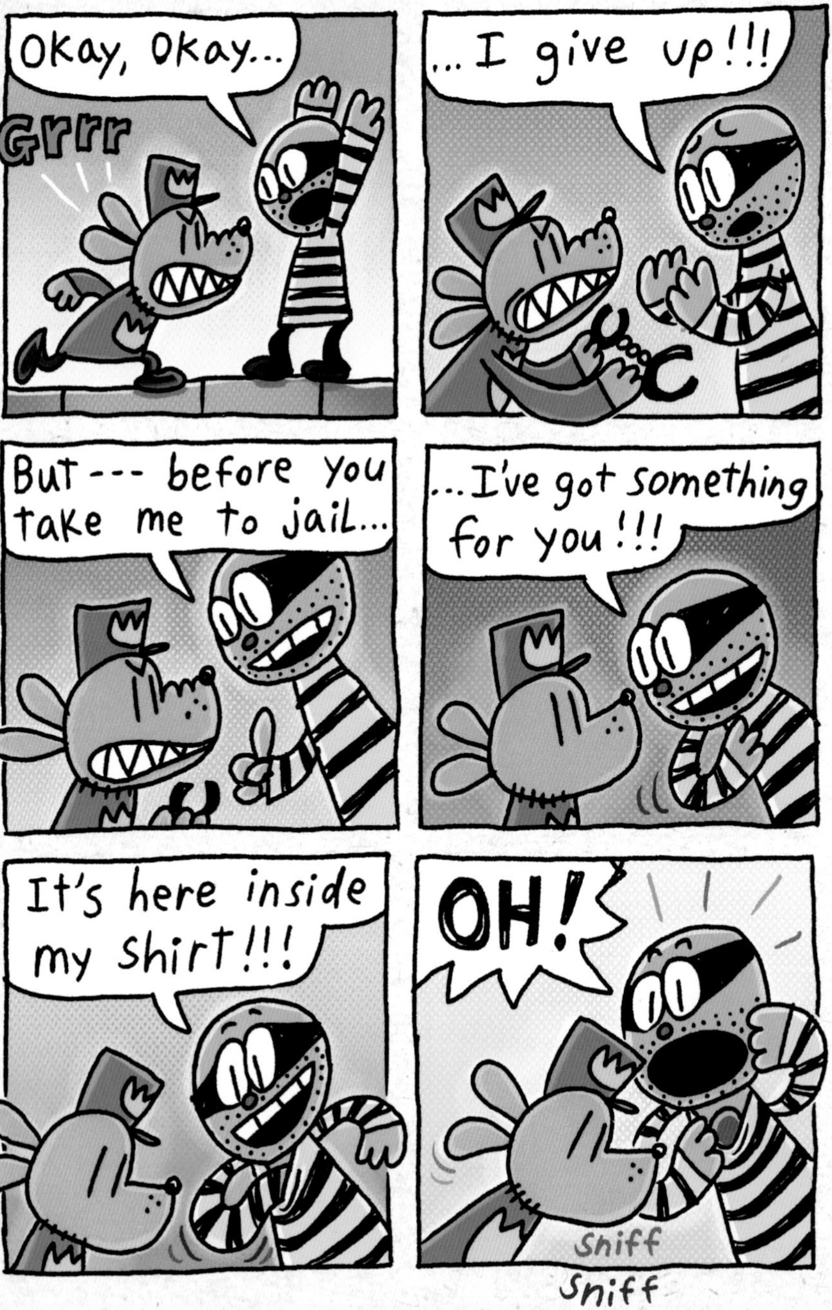
Okay, Okay...
Grrr
...I give up!!!
But --- before you take me to jaiL...
...I've got something for you!!!
It's here inside my shirT!!!
OH!
Sniff
Sniff

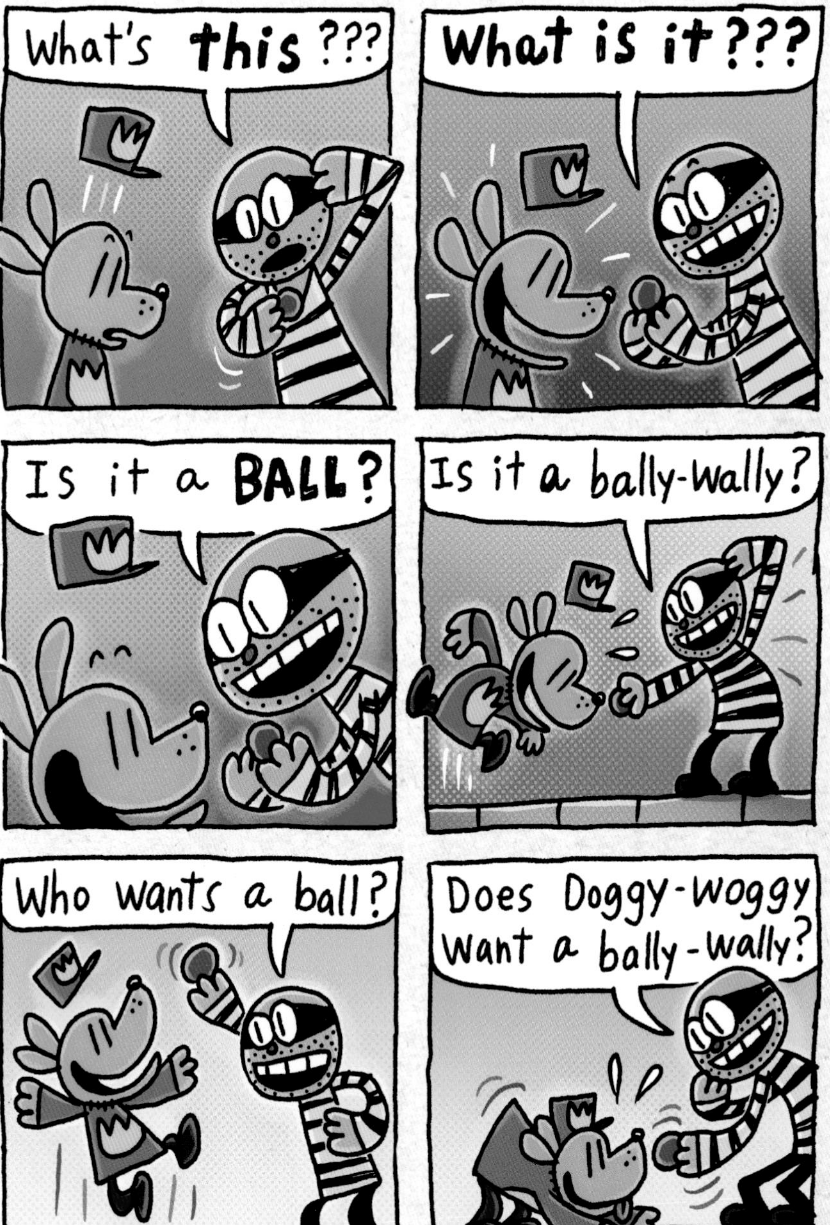
What's this???
What is it???
Is it a BALL?
Is it a bally-wally?
Who wants a ball?
Does Doggy-woggy want a bally-wally?

Who wazza ball?
Doggy wazza ball?
Get da ball! Get it!
Wazza Bazza ball?

INTRODUCING FLIP

STEP 1.
First, place your left hand inside the dotted lines marked "Left hand here." Hold the book open FLAT!

STEP 2:
Grasp the right-hand page with your thumb and index finger (inside the dotted lines marked "Right Thumb Here").

STEP 3:
Now quickly flip the right-hand page back and forth until the picture appears to be Animated.

(For extra fun, try adding your own sound-effects!)

O-RAMA

Remember,

while you are flipping,
be sure you can see
the image on page **29**
AND the image on page **31**.

If you flip quickly,
the two pictures will
start to look like
one **ANIMATED** cartoon!

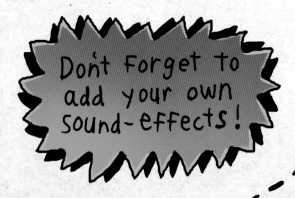

Don't forget to
add your own
sound-effects!

Left
hand here.

Who
wazza
bally
wally?

Bazza
wazza
bally
wall?

Who's a
good
doggy
wazza
bally
wally?

Right
Thumb
here.

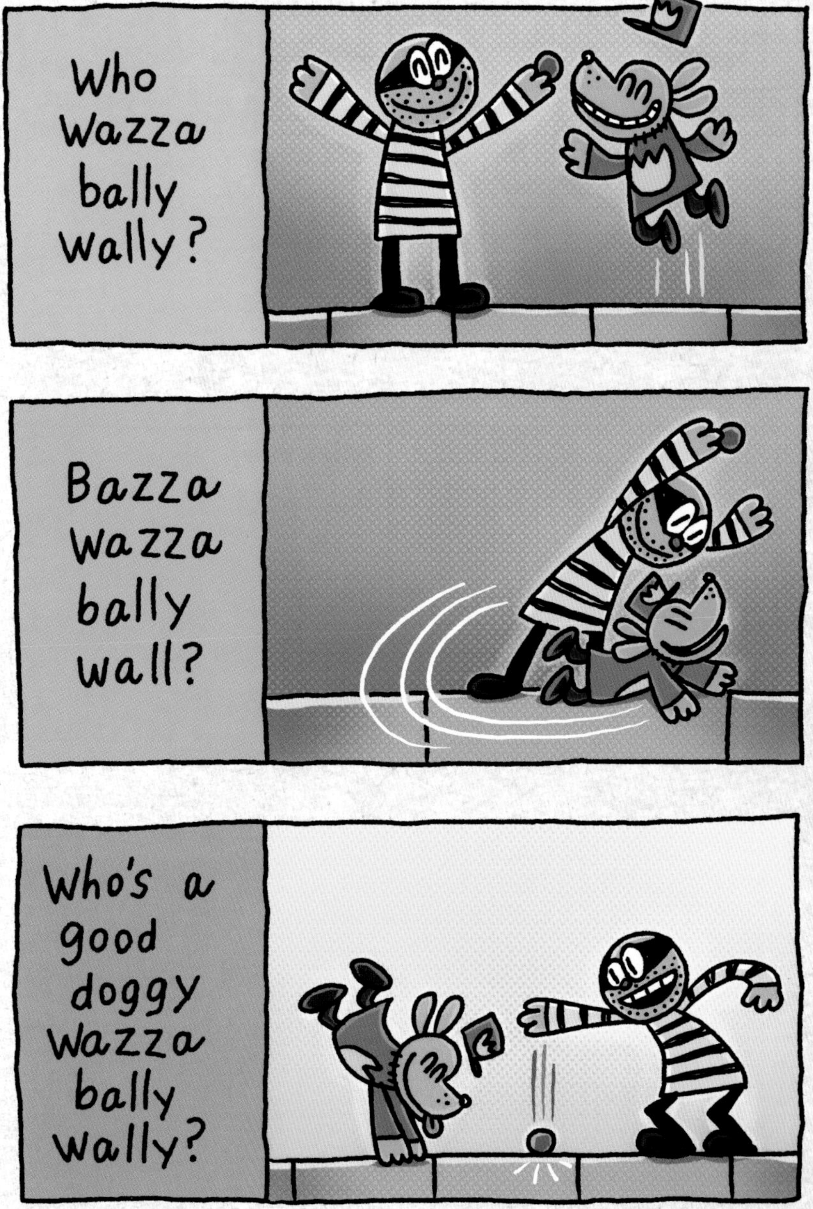
Who wazza bally wally?
Bazza wazza bally wall?
Who's a good doggy wazza bally wally?

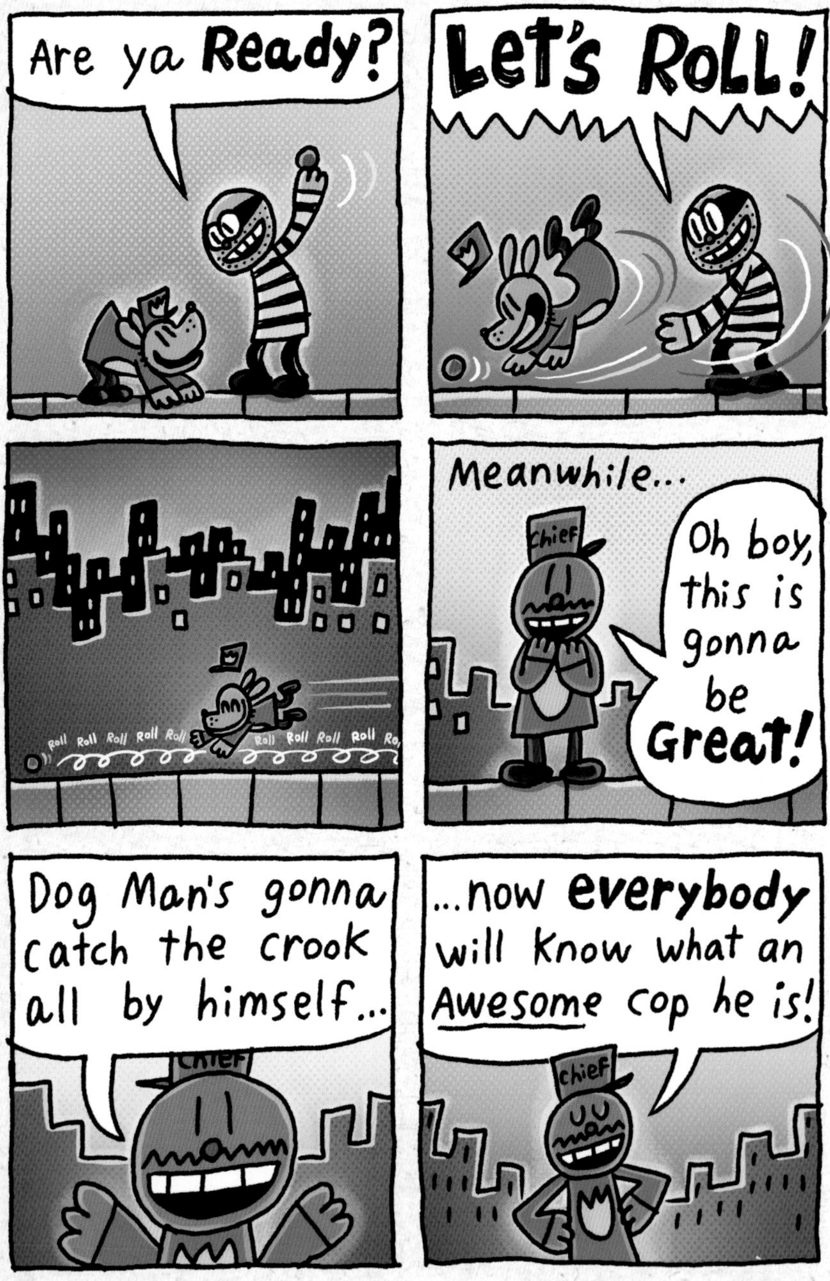

Are ya Ready?
Let's ROLL!
Roll Roll Roll Roll Roll
Roll Roll Roll Roll Ro
Meanwhile...
Chief
Oh boy, this is gonna be Great!
Dog Man's gonna catch the crook all by himself...
...now everybody will know what an Awesome cop he is!
Chief

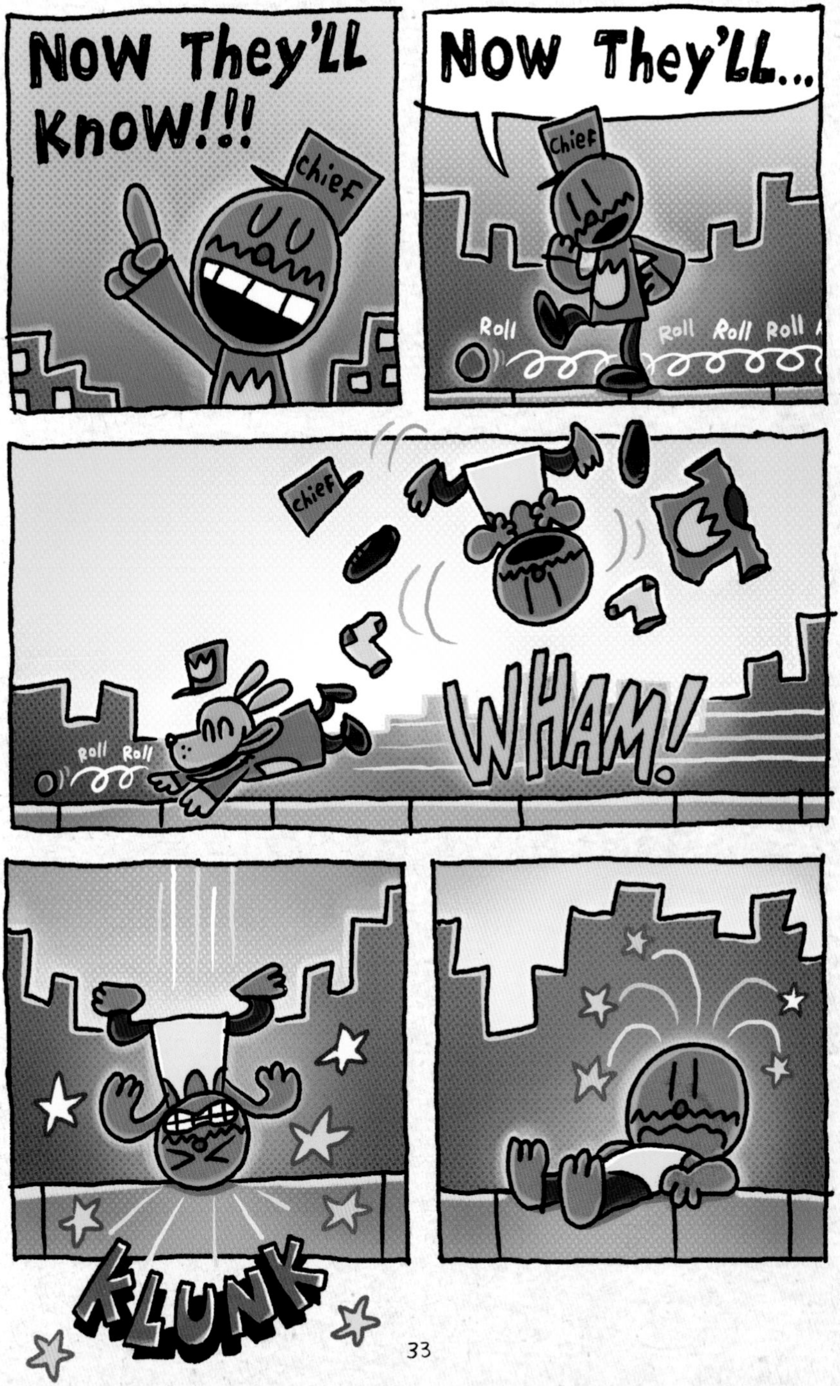
NOW They'LL KNOW!!!
chief
NOW They'LL...
Chief
Roll
Roll Roll Roll
chief
Roll Roll
WHAM!
KLUNK

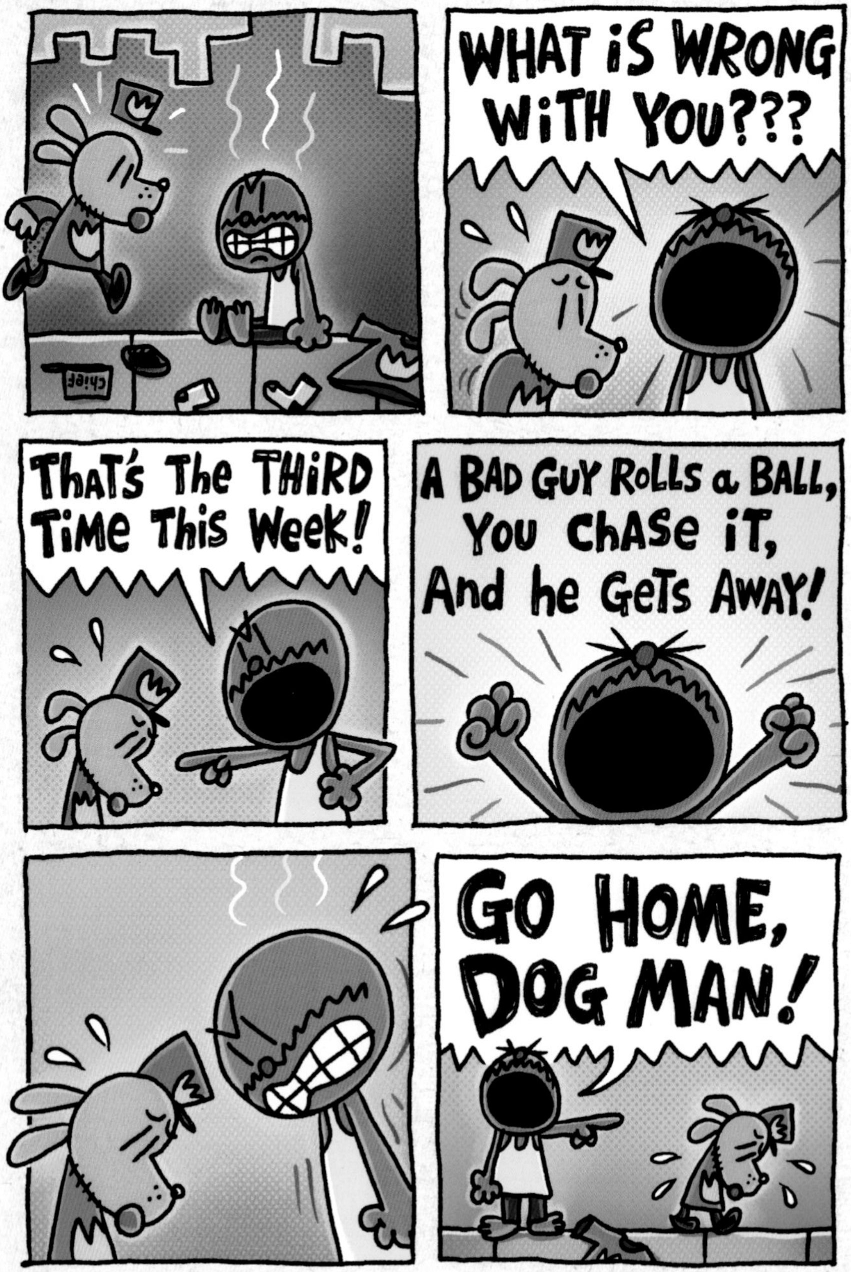
chief
WHAT iS WRONG WiTH YOU???
ThaT'S The THiRD TiMe This Week!
A BAD GUY ROLLS a BALL, You ChASe iT, And he GeTS AWAY!
GO HOME, DOG MAN!

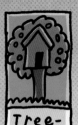

Tree-HOUSE Comix Proudly Presents

Chapter 2

Behavioral Modification Therapy

Me
CHief
CHief
YOlay
BO-HD
ball
Sarah

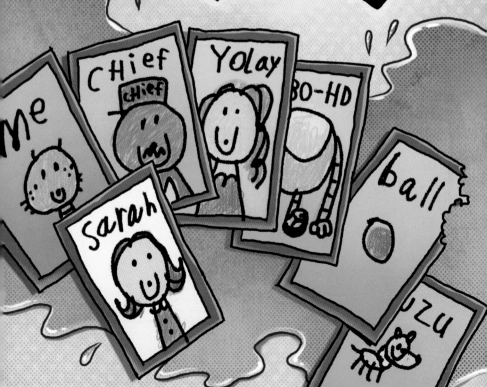

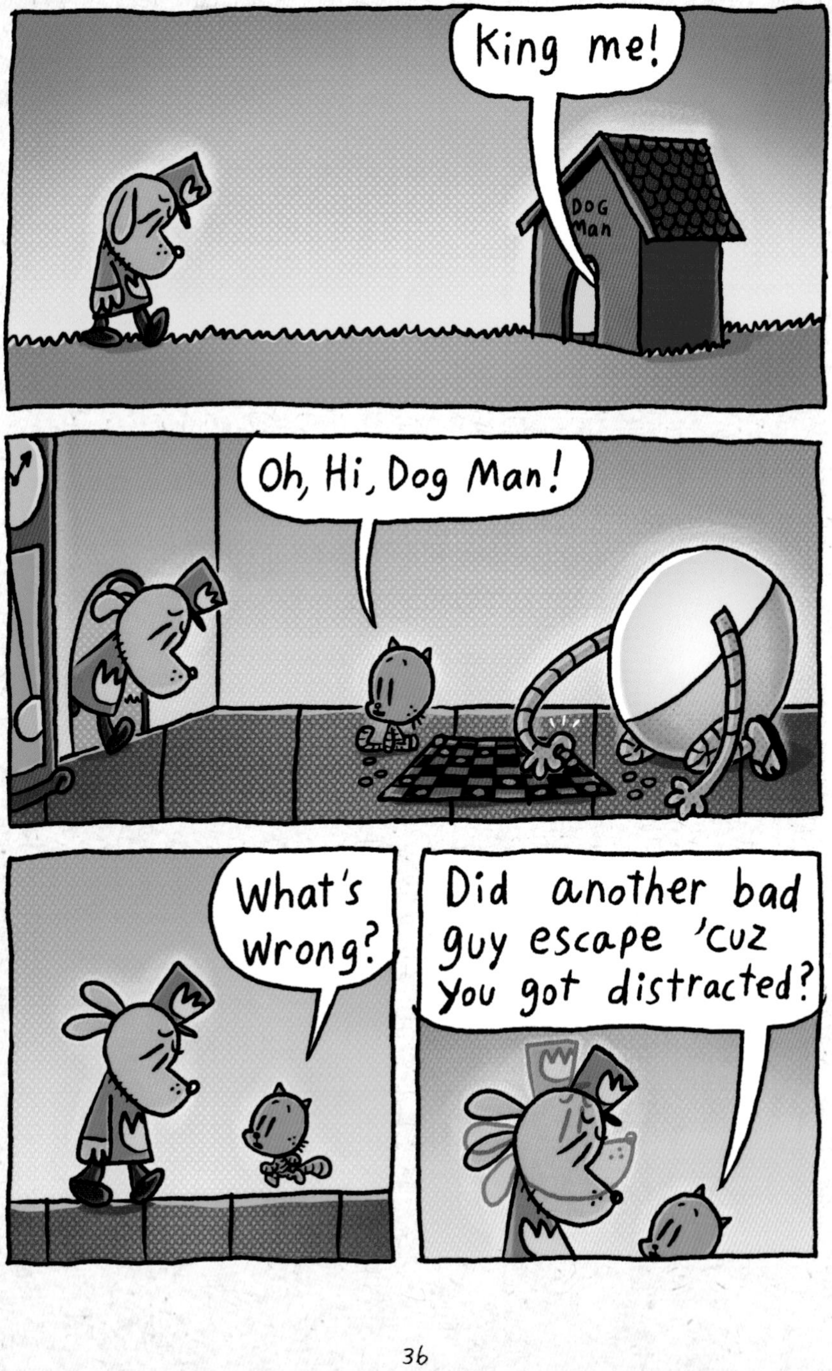
King me!
DOG Man
Oh, Hi, Dog Man!
What's wrong?
Did another bad guy escape 'cuz you got distracted?

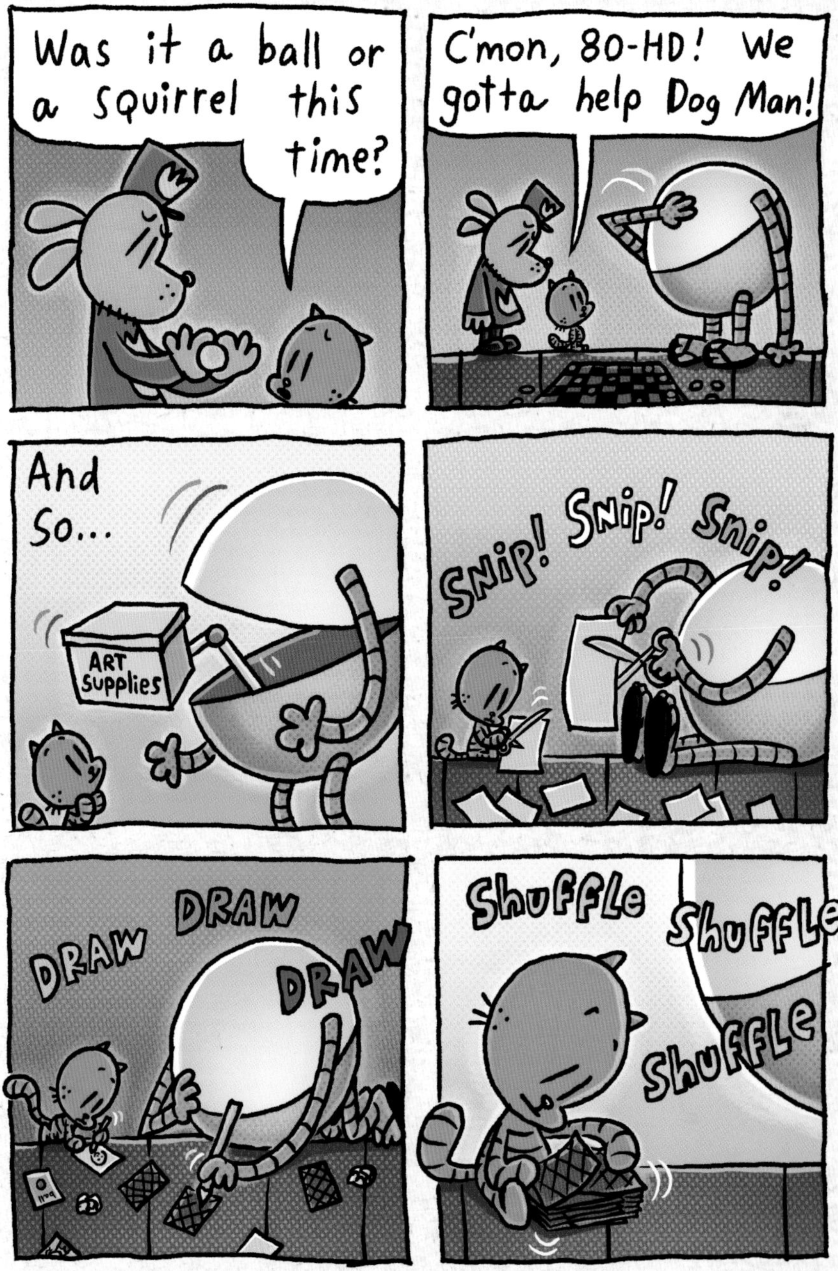
Was it a ball or a squirrel this time?
C'mon, 80-HD! We gotta help Dog Man!
And so...
ART supplies
SNIP! SNIP! SNIP!
DRAW
DRAW
DRAW
DRAW
Shuffle
Shuffle
Shuffle

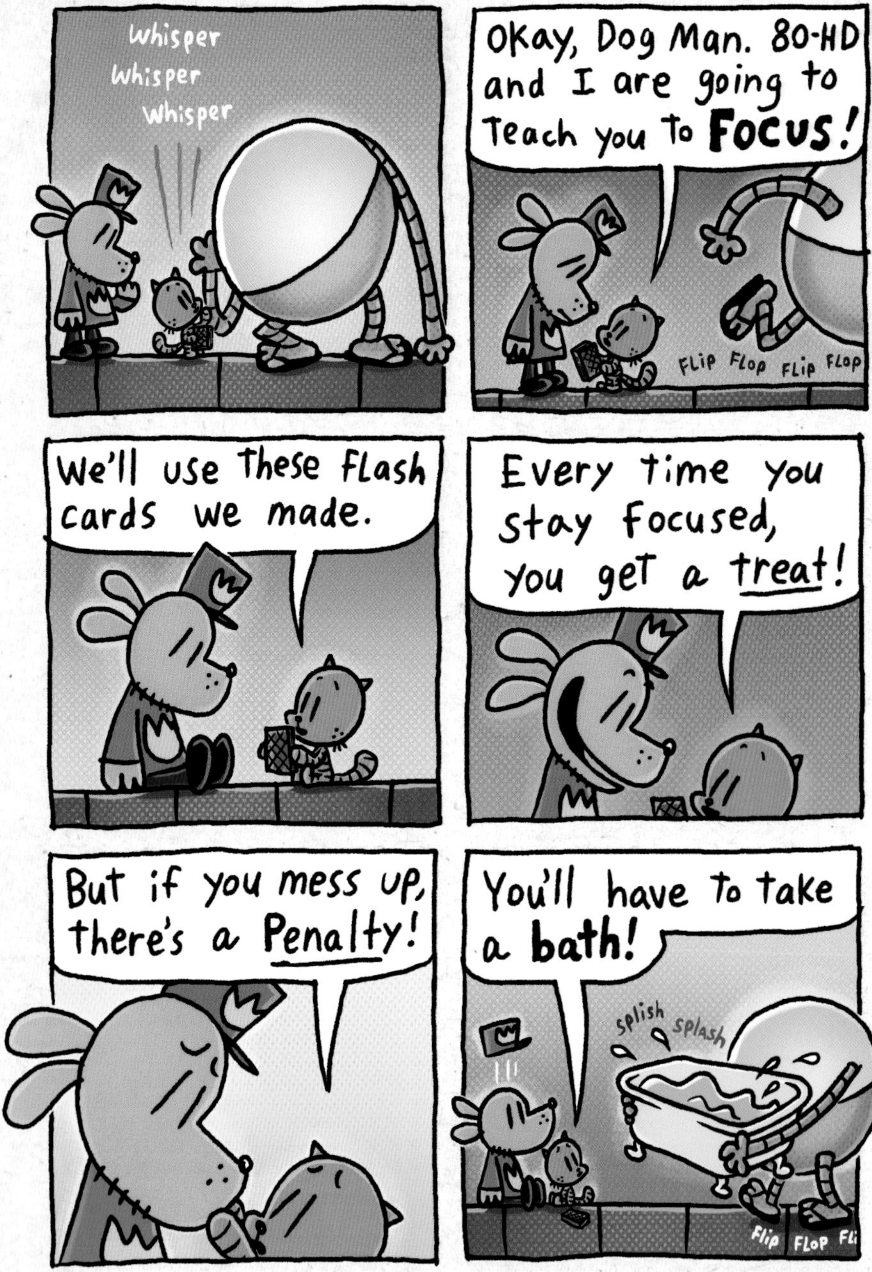

Whisper
Whisper
Whisper
Okay, Dog Man. 80-HD and I are going to Teach you to FOCUS!
FLIP FLOP FLIP FLOP
We'll use these flash cards we made.
Every time you stay focused, you get a treat!
But if you mess up, there's a Penalty!
You'll have to take a bath!
splish splash
Flip FLOP

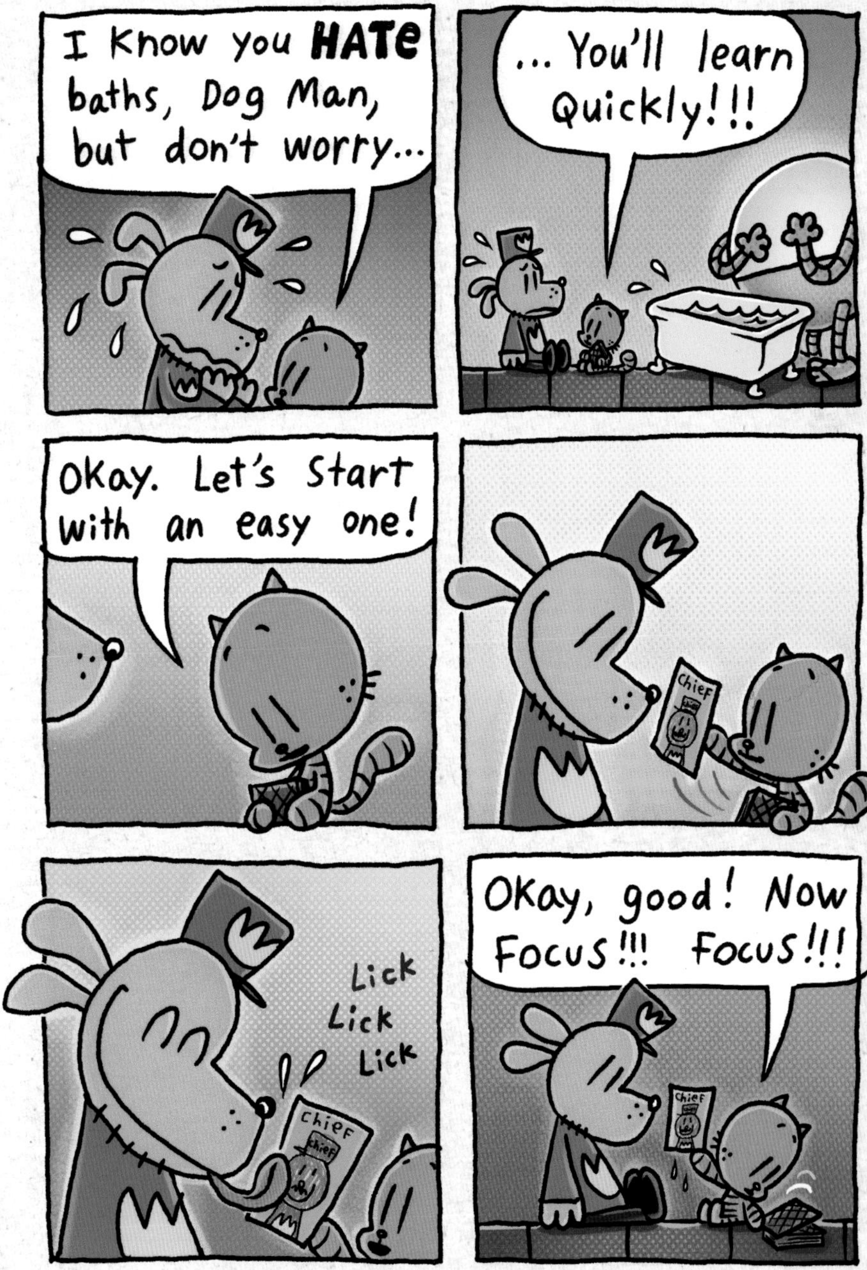
I Know you HATE baths, Dog Man, but don't worry...
... You'll learn Quickly!!!
OKay. Let's Start with an easy one!
Chief
Lick Lick Lick
Chief
OKay, good! Now Focus!!! Focus!!!
Chief

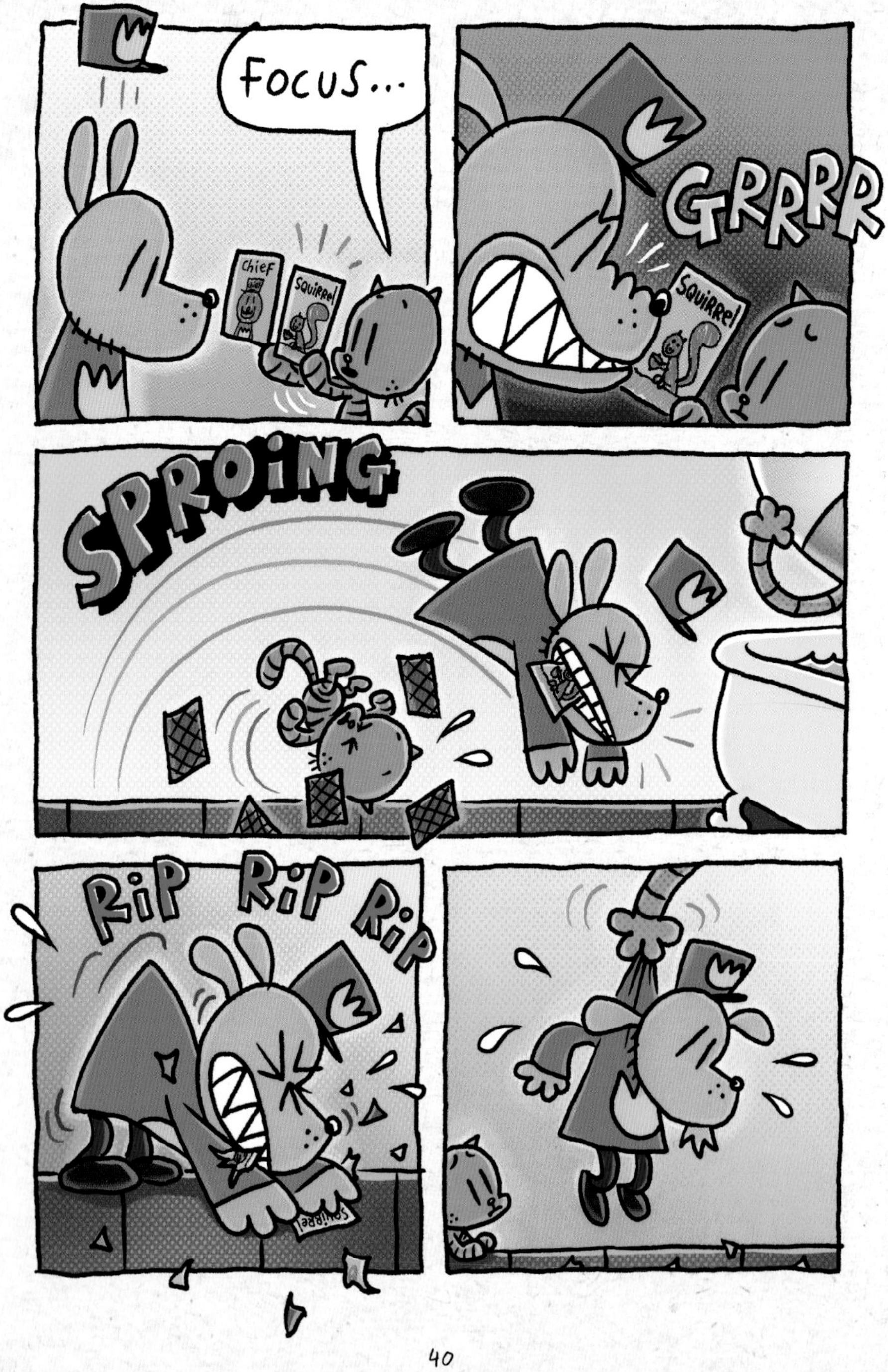
FOCUS...
CHIEF
SQUIRREL
GRRRR
SQUIRREL
SPROING
RIP RIP RIP
SQUIRREL

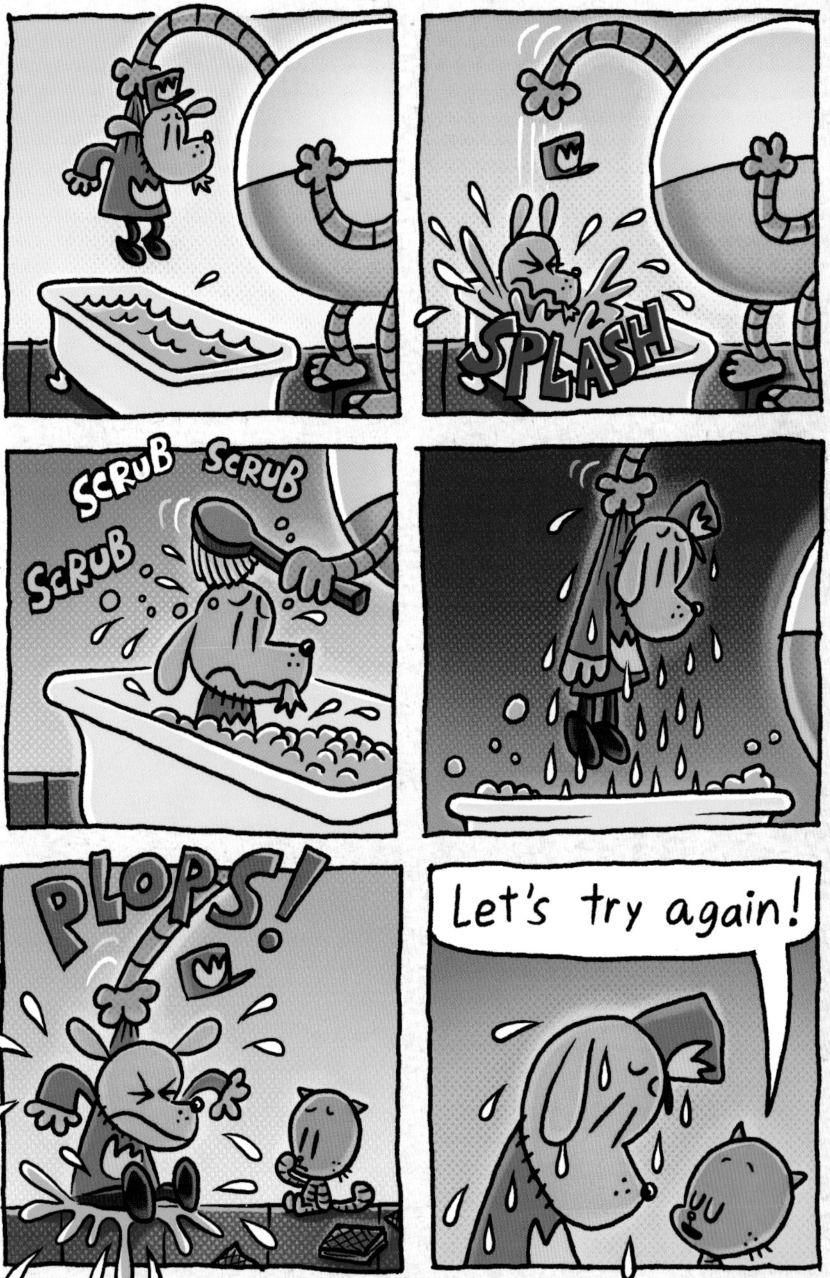
SPLASH
SCRUB
SCRUB
SCRUB
PLOPS!
Let's try again!

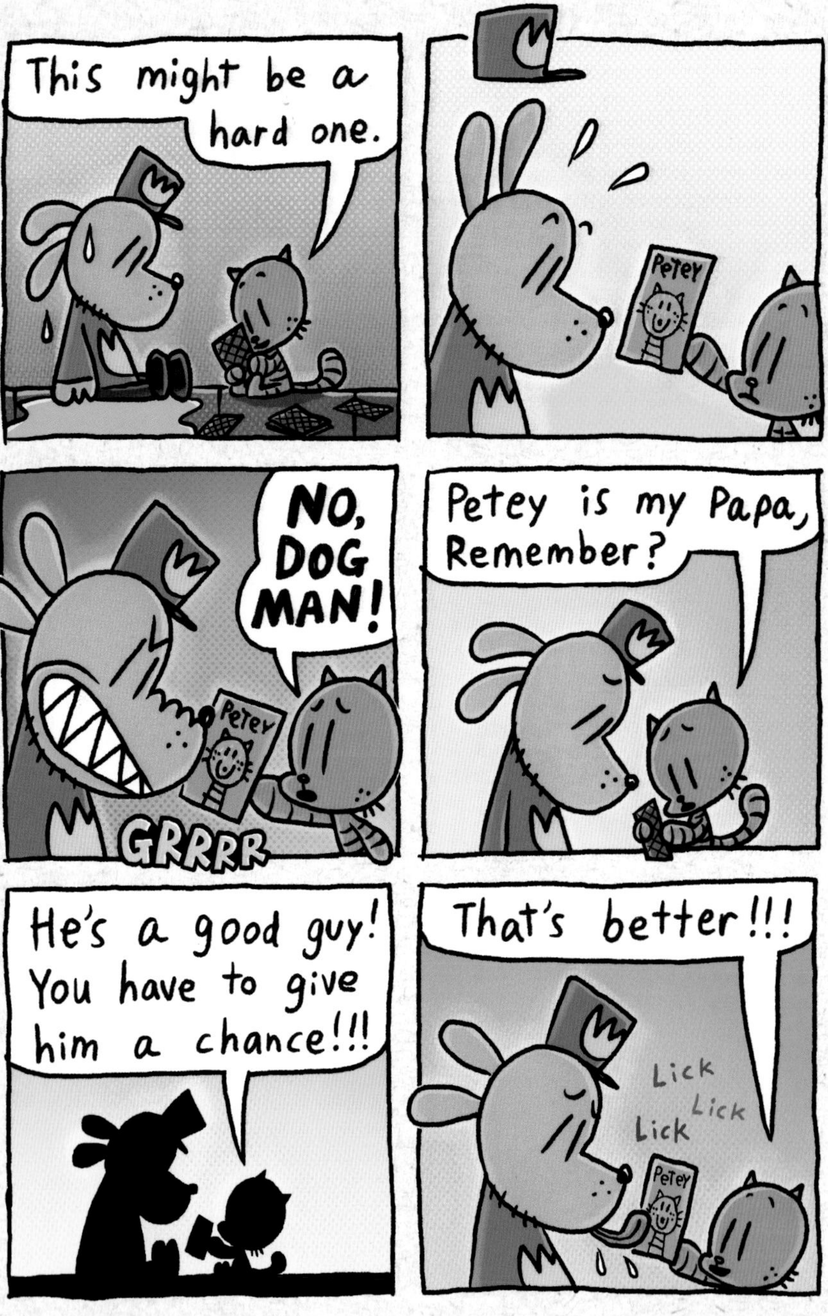

This might be a hard one.
PETEY
NO, DOG MAN!
PETEY
GRRRR
Petey is my Papa, Remember?
He's a good guy! You have to give him a chance!!!
That's better!!!
Lick
Lick
Lick
PETEY

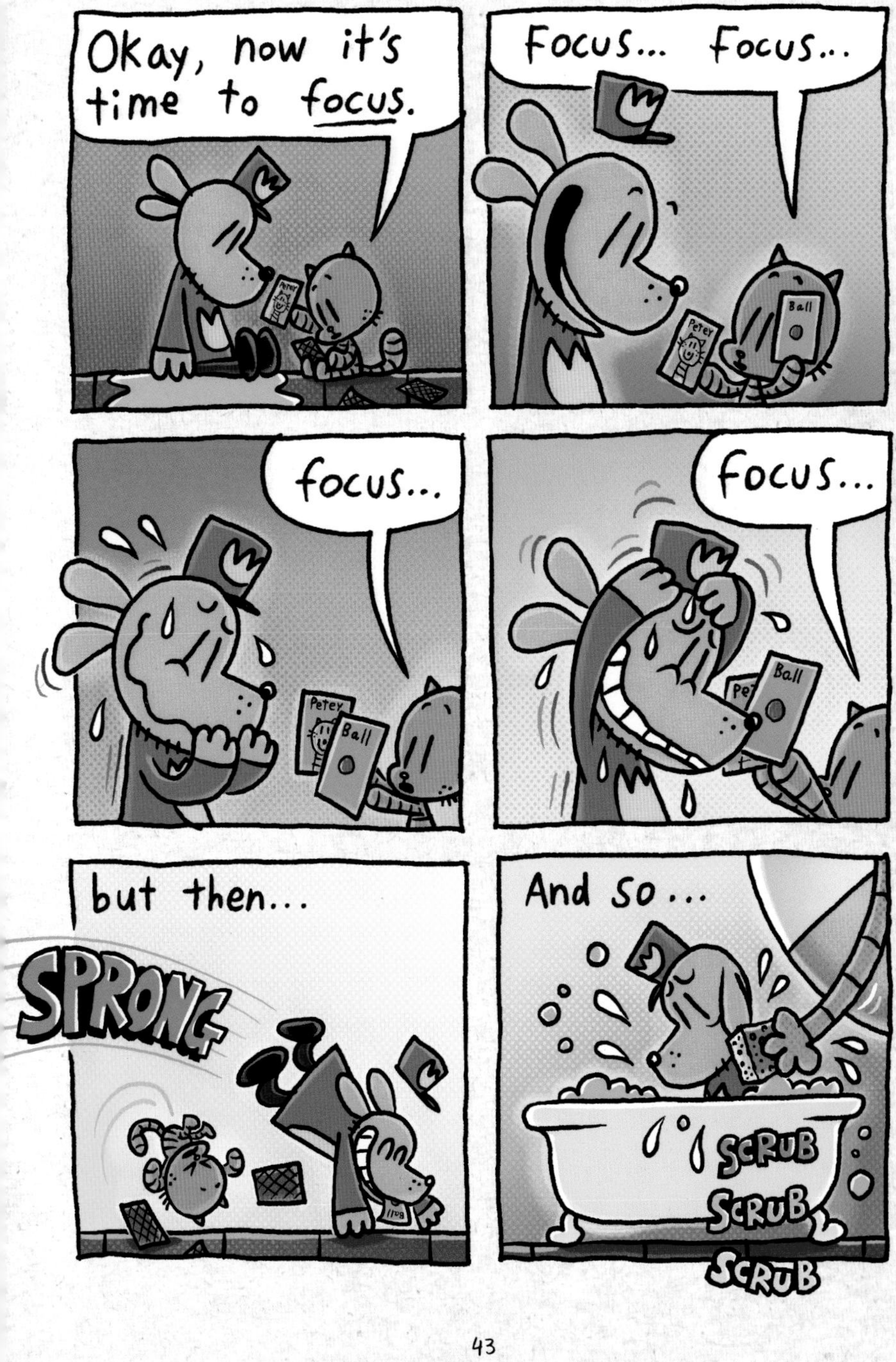

Okay, now it's time to focus.
Focus... Focus...
Petey
Ball
focus...
Petey
Ball
Focus...
Ball
but then...
SPRONG
And so...
SCRUB
SCRUB
SCRUB

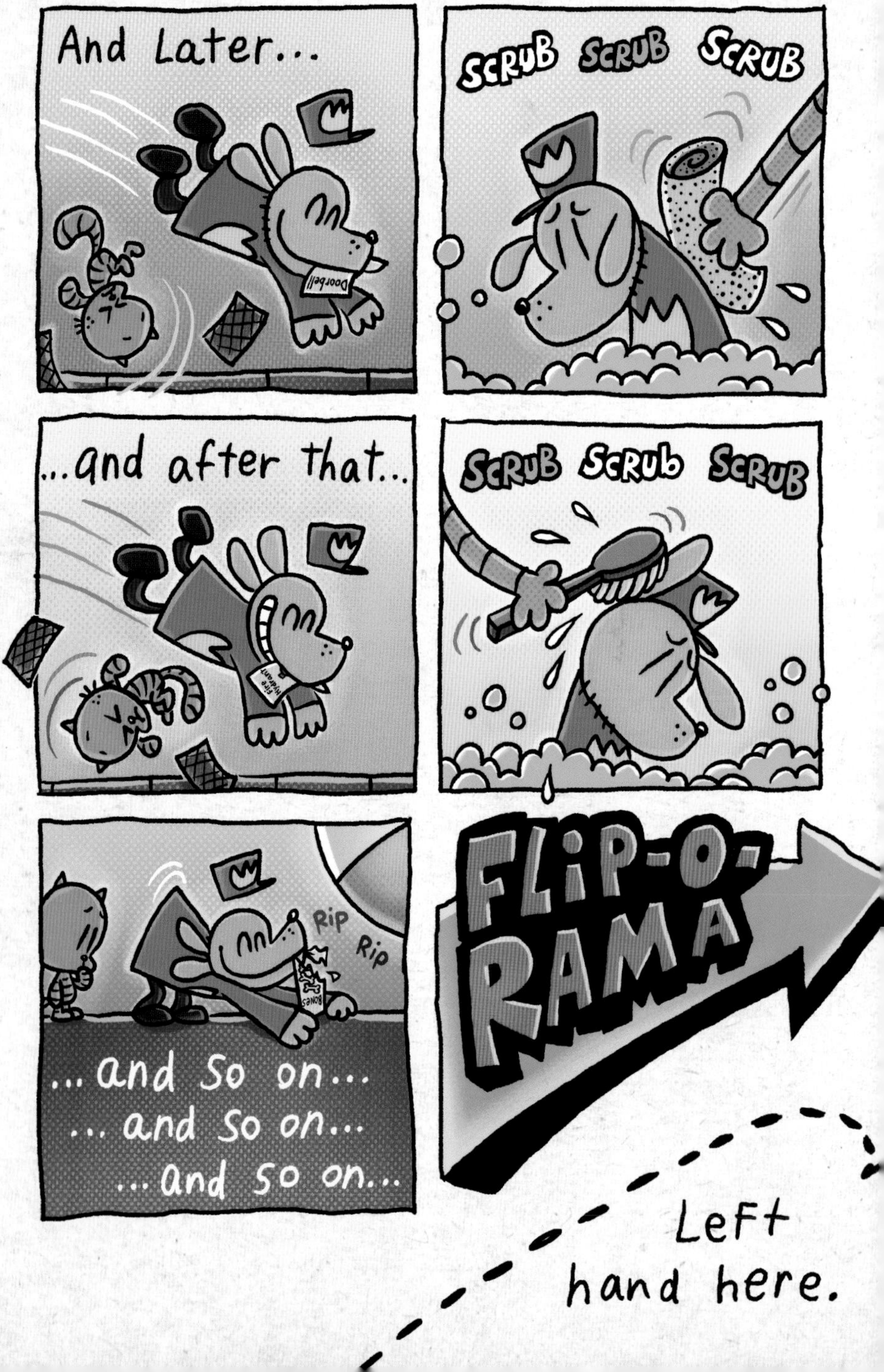
And Later...
Doorbell
SCRUB SCRUB SCRUB
...and after that...
SCRUB SCRUB SCRUB
Rip
Rip
...and so on...
...and so on...
...and so on...
FLIP-O-RAMA
Left hand here.

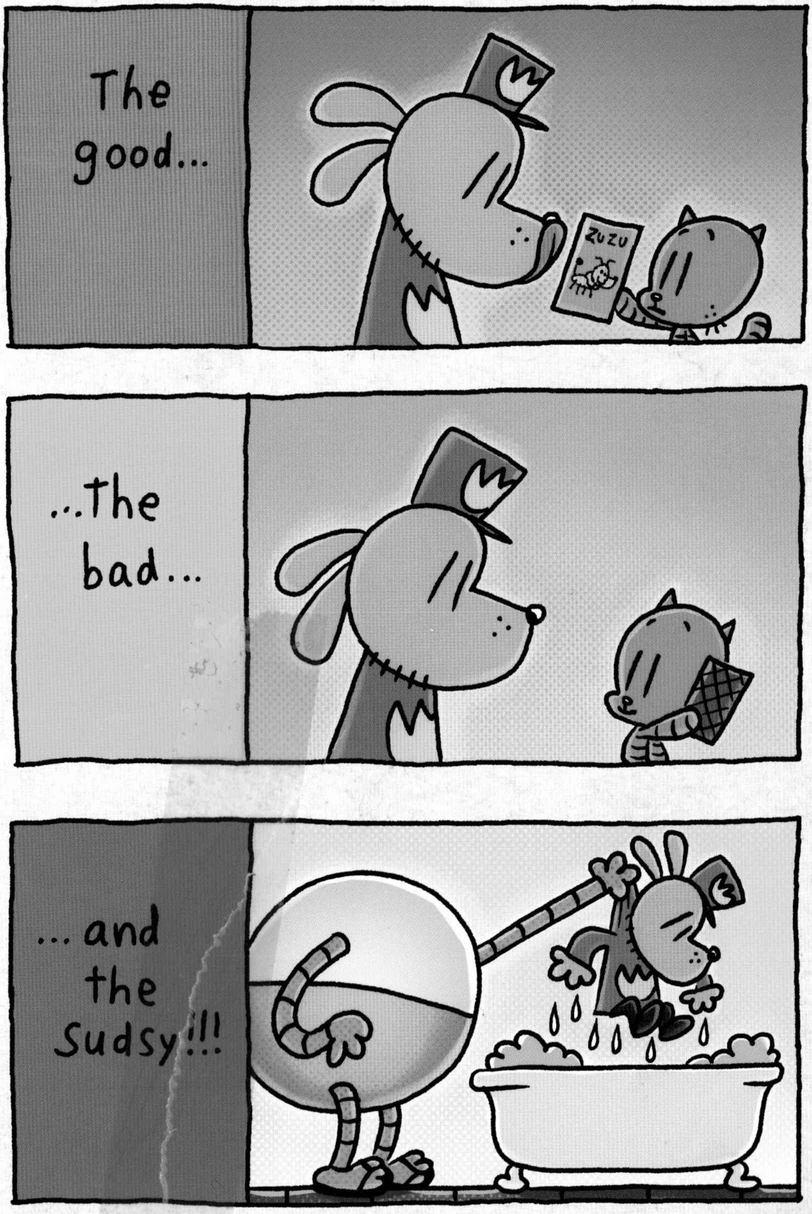
The good...
ZUZU
...the bad...
...and the sudsy!!!

Right Thumb here.

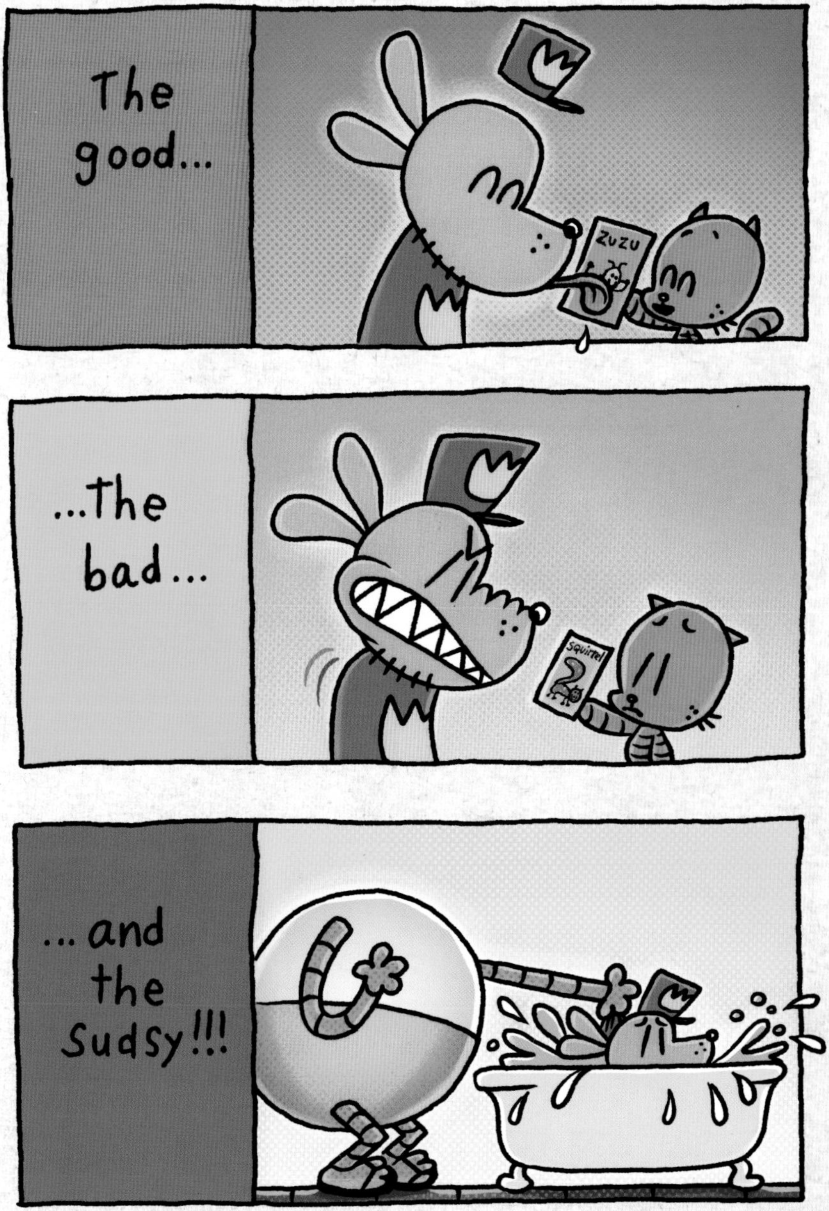
The good...
ZUZU
...the bad...
squirrel
...and the sudsy!!!

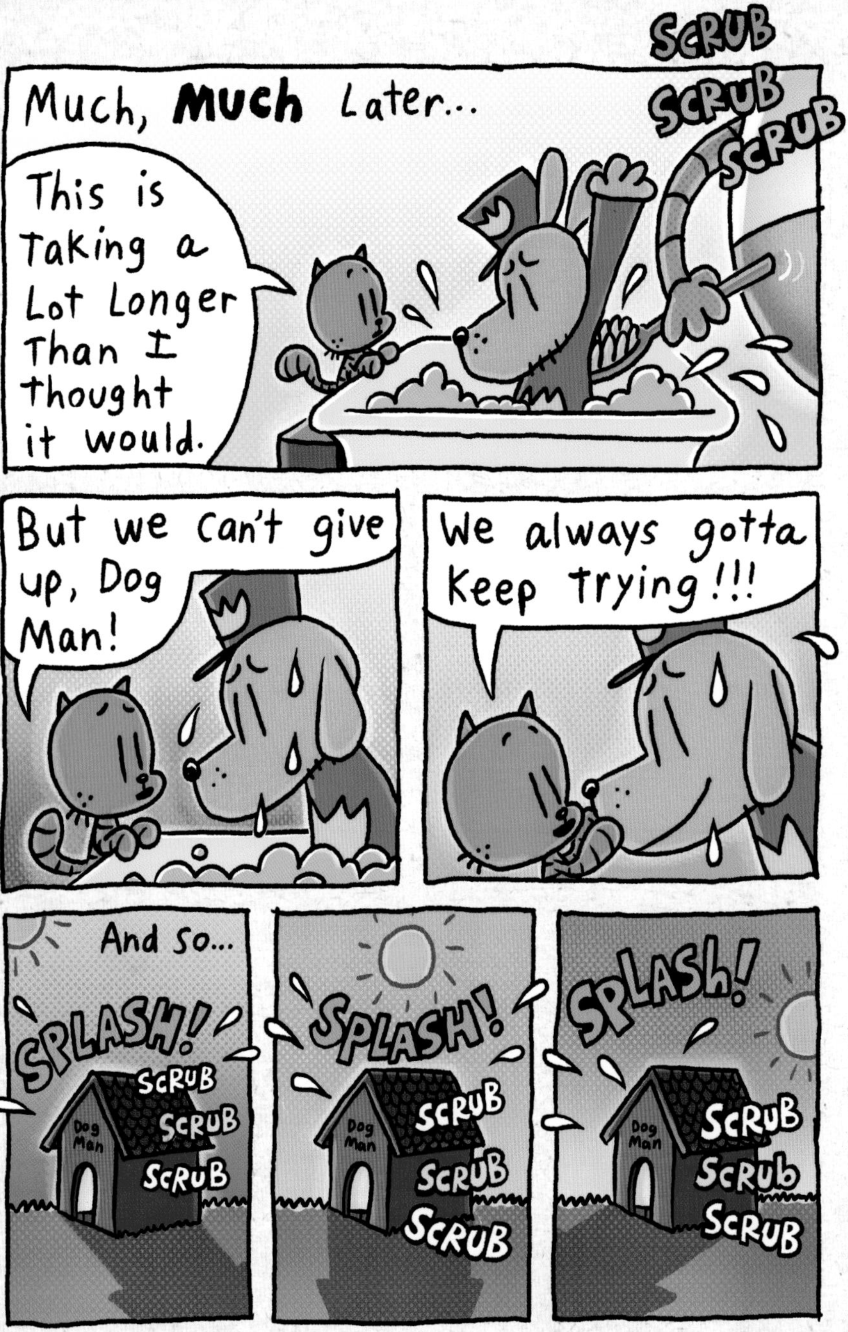

Much, MUCH Later...
SCRUB
SCRUB
SCRUB
This is Taking a Lot Longer Than I thought it would.
But we can't give up, Dog Man!
We always gotta Keep trying!!!
And so...
SPLASH!
SCRUB
SCRUB
SCRUB
Dog Man
SPLASH!
SCRUB
SCRUB
SCRUB
Dog Man
SPLASH!
SCRUB
Scrub
SCRUB
Dog Man

Tree-House Comix Proudly Presents

Chapter 3

To Heck with the Planet of the Cats

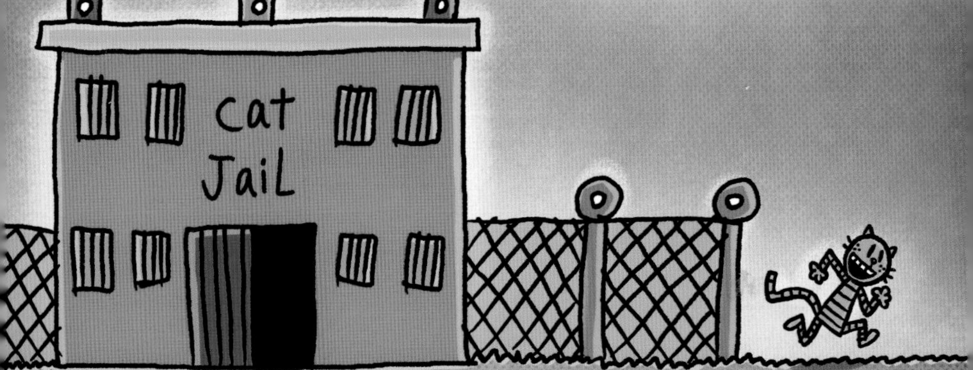
Cat Jail

by the award-winning Award winners,

George Beard & Harold Hutchins

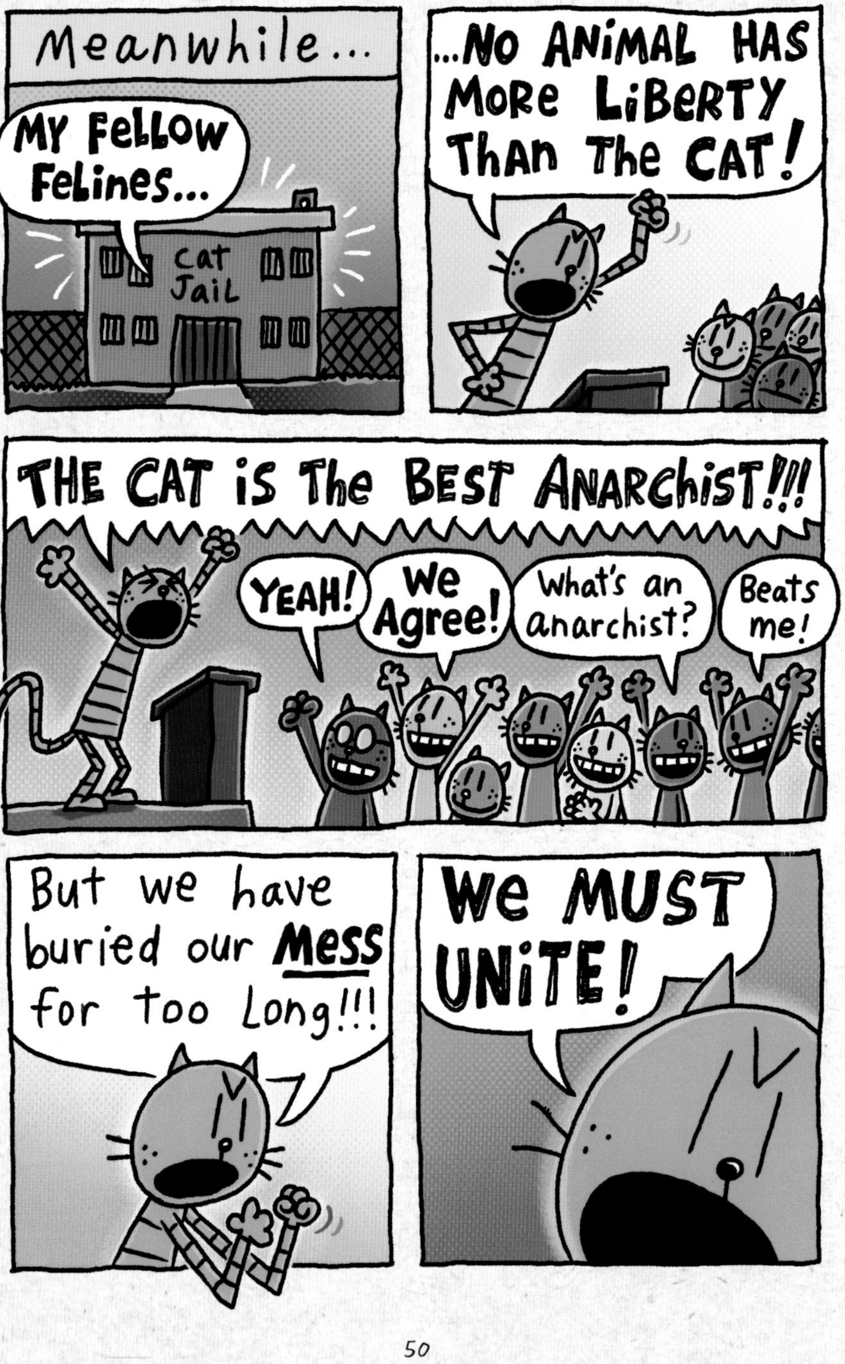
Meanwhile...
MY FELLOW FELINES...
CAT JAIL
...NO ANIMAL HAS MORE LIBERTY THAN THE CAT!
THE CAT IS THE BEST ANARCHIST!!!
YEAH!
We Agree!
What's an anarchist?
Beats me!
But we have buried our MESS for too Long!!!
We MUST UNITE!

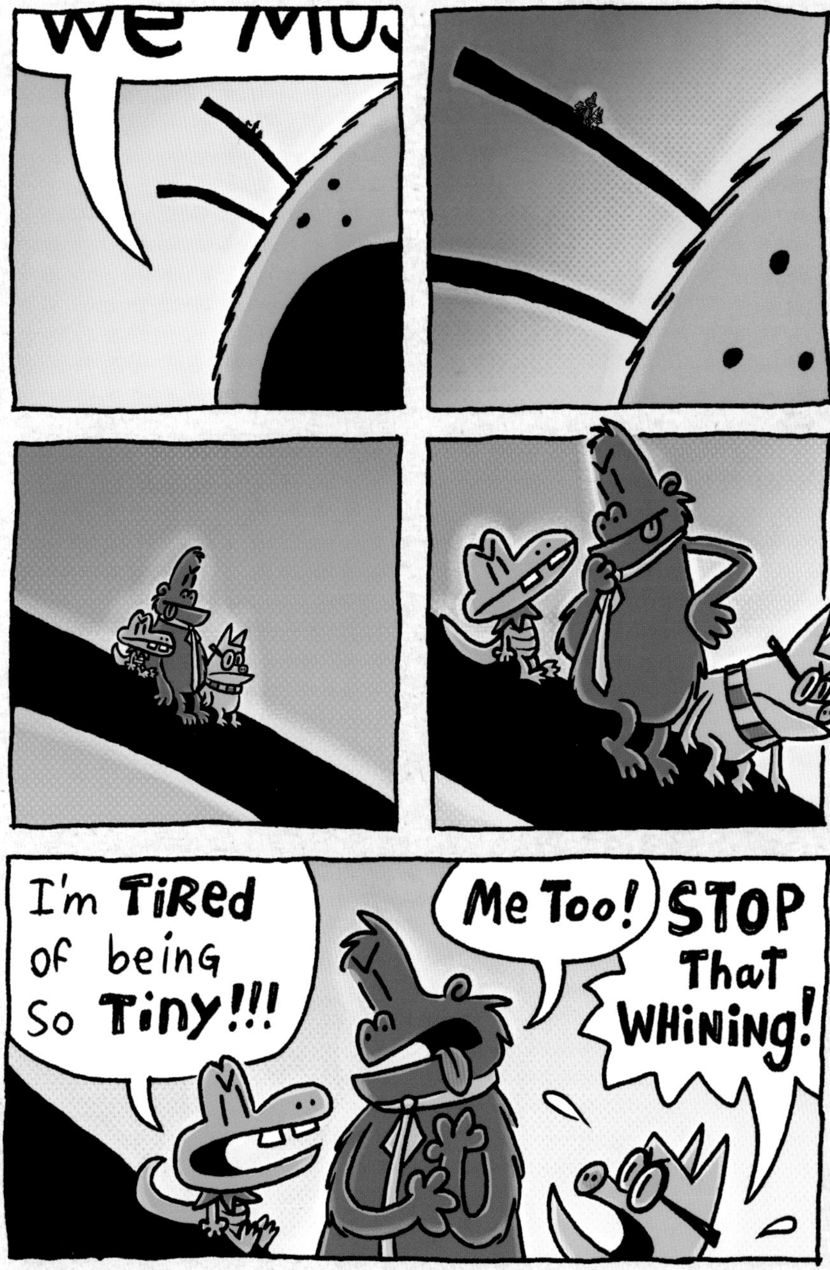
I'm TIRED of being so TINY!!!
Me Too!
STOP That WHINING!

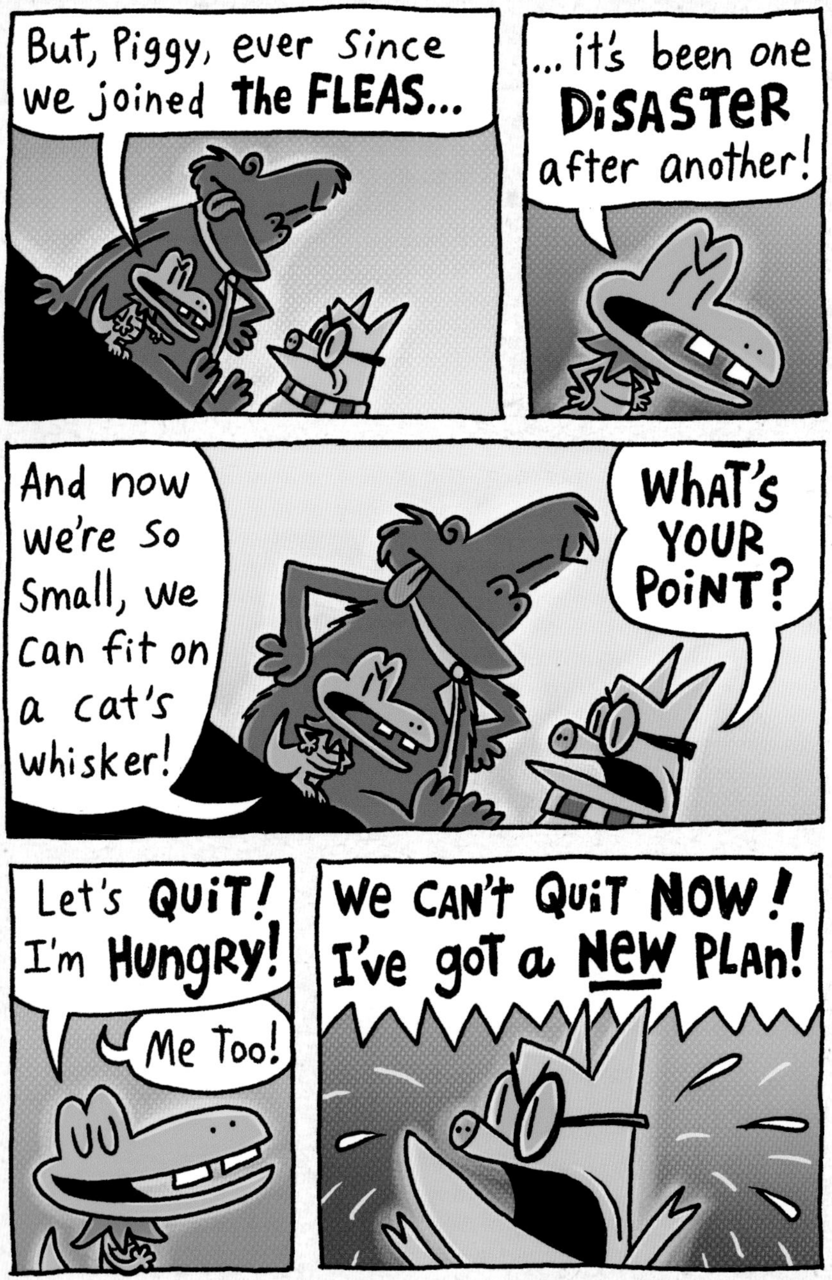
But, Piggy, ever since we joined the FLEAS...
...it's been one DISASTER after another!
And now we're so small, we can fit on a cat's whisker!
WHAT'S YOUR POINT?
Let's QUIT! I'm HUNGRY!
Me Too!
WE CAN'T QUIT NOW! I've got a NEW PLAN!

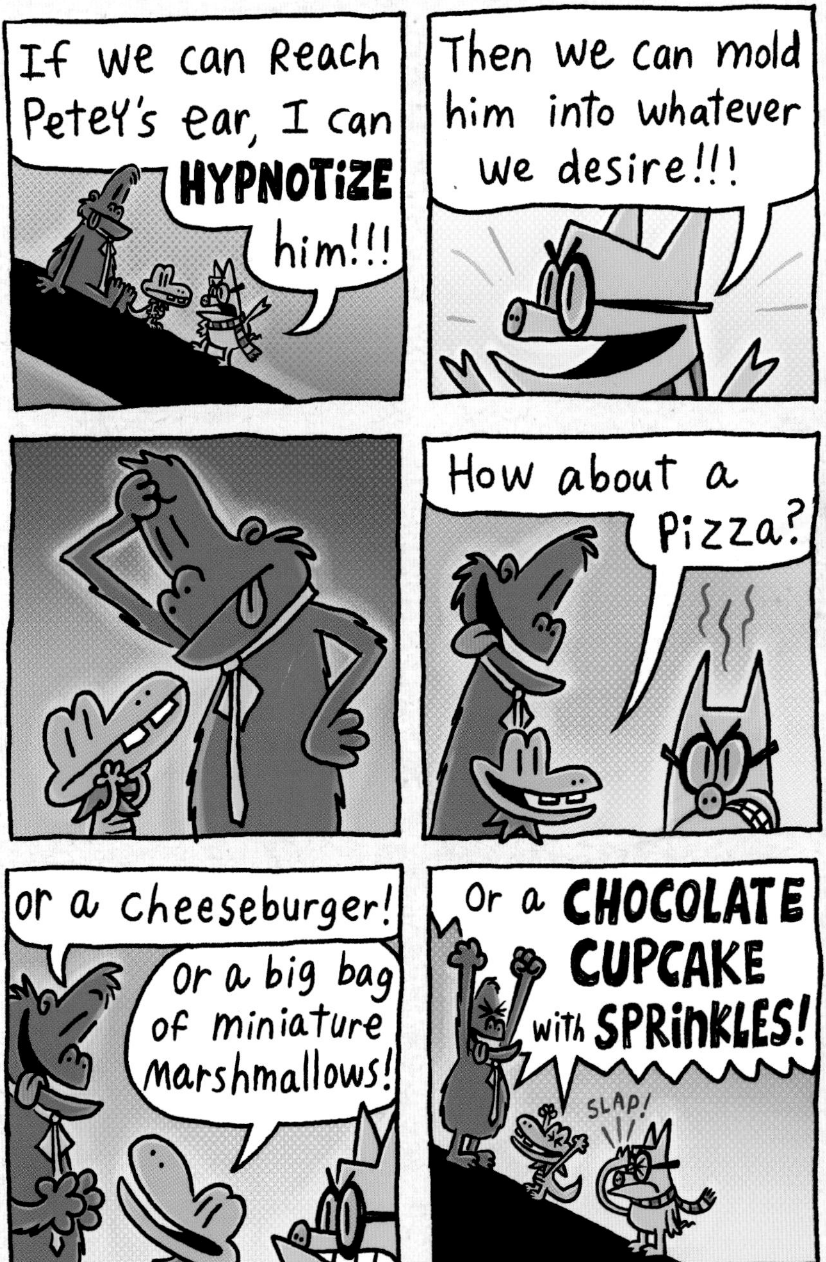
If we can Reach Petey's ear, I can HYPNOTIZE him!!!
Then we can mold him into whatever we desire!!!
How about a Pizza?
Or a cheeseburger!
Or a big bag of miniature marshmallows!
Or a CHOCOLATE CUPCAKE with SPRINKLES!
SLAP!

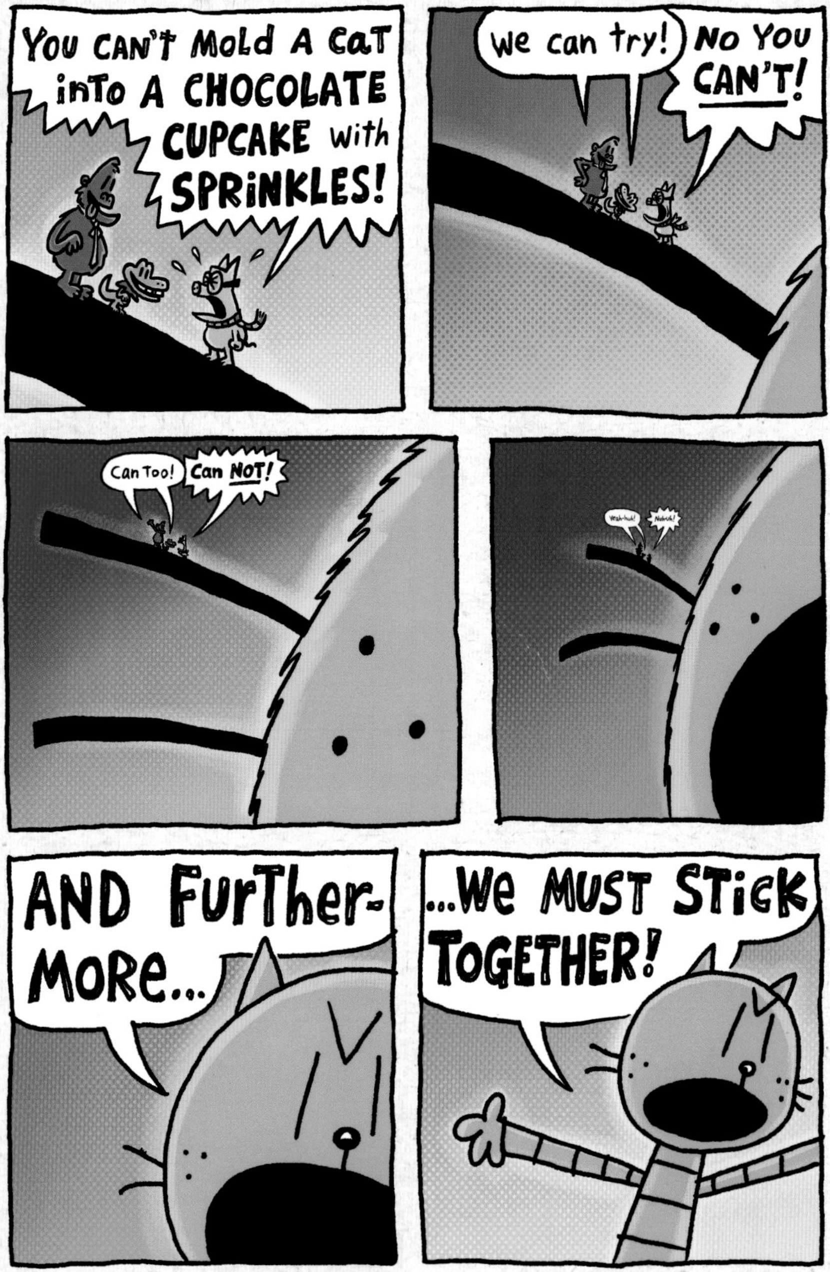
YOU CAN'T MOLD A CAT into A CHOCOLATE CUPCAKE with SPRINKLES!
We can try!
No You CAN'T!
Can Too!
Can NOT!
Yeah-huh!
Nuh-uh!
AND FurTher-MORE...
...We MUST STick TOGETHER!

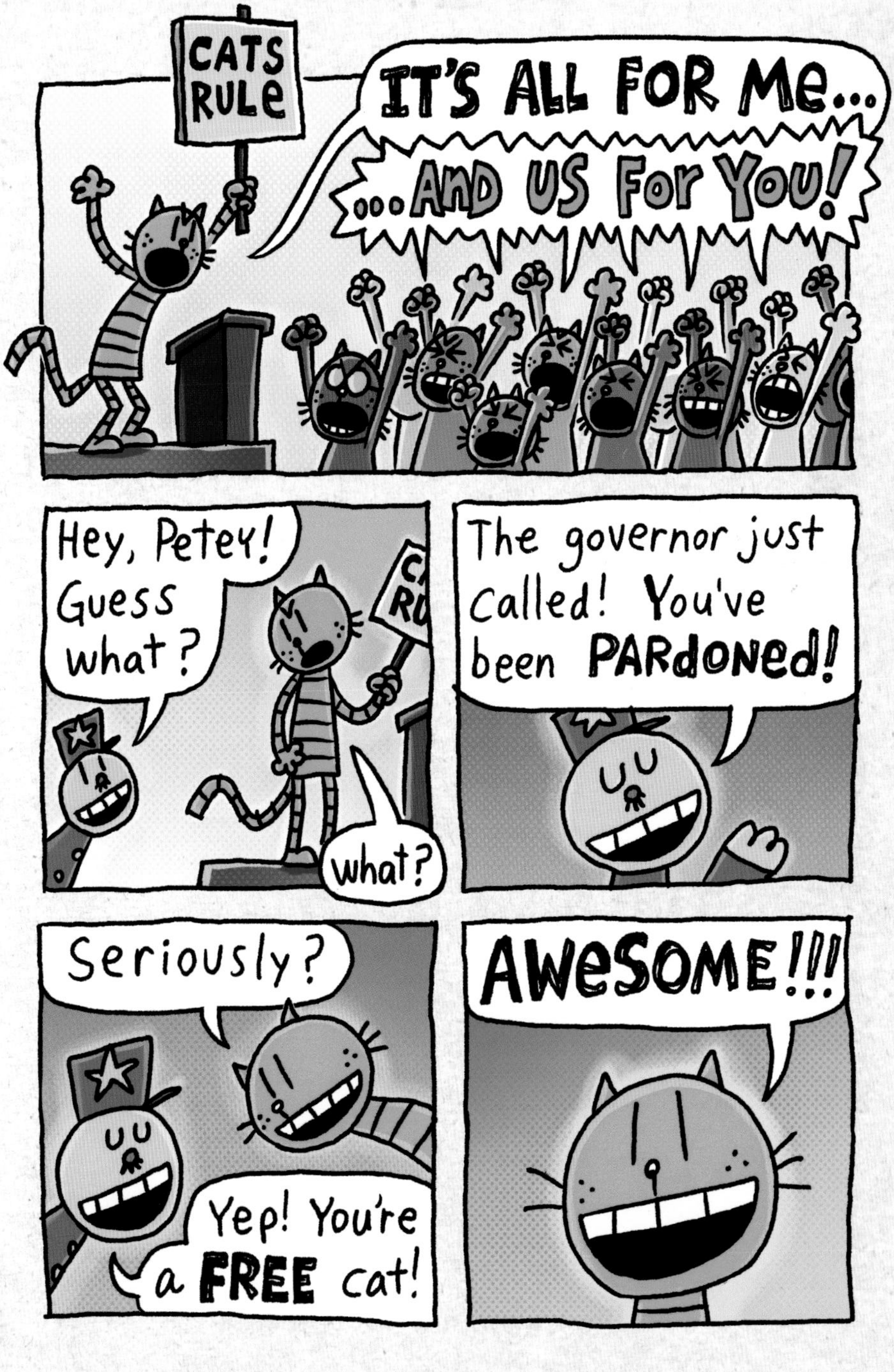
CATS RULE
IT'S ALL FOR ME...
...AND US For You!
Hey, Petey! Guess what?
what?
The governor just called! You've been PARDONED!
Seriously?
Yep! You're a FREE cat!
AWESOME!!!

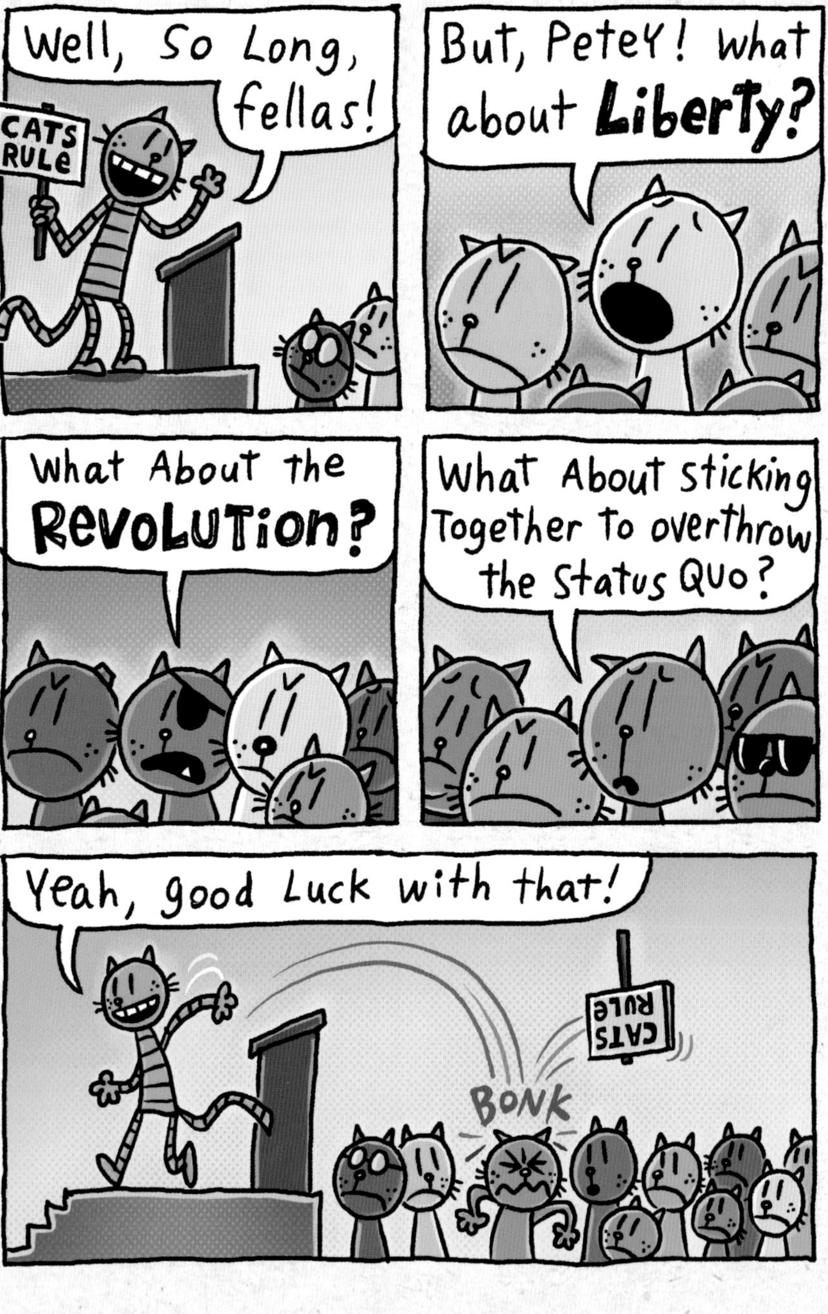
Well, So Long, fellas!
CATS RULE
But, Petey! What about Liberty?
What About the REVOLUTION?
What About Sticking Together to overthrow the Status Quo?
Yeah, good Luck with that!
CATS RULE
BONK

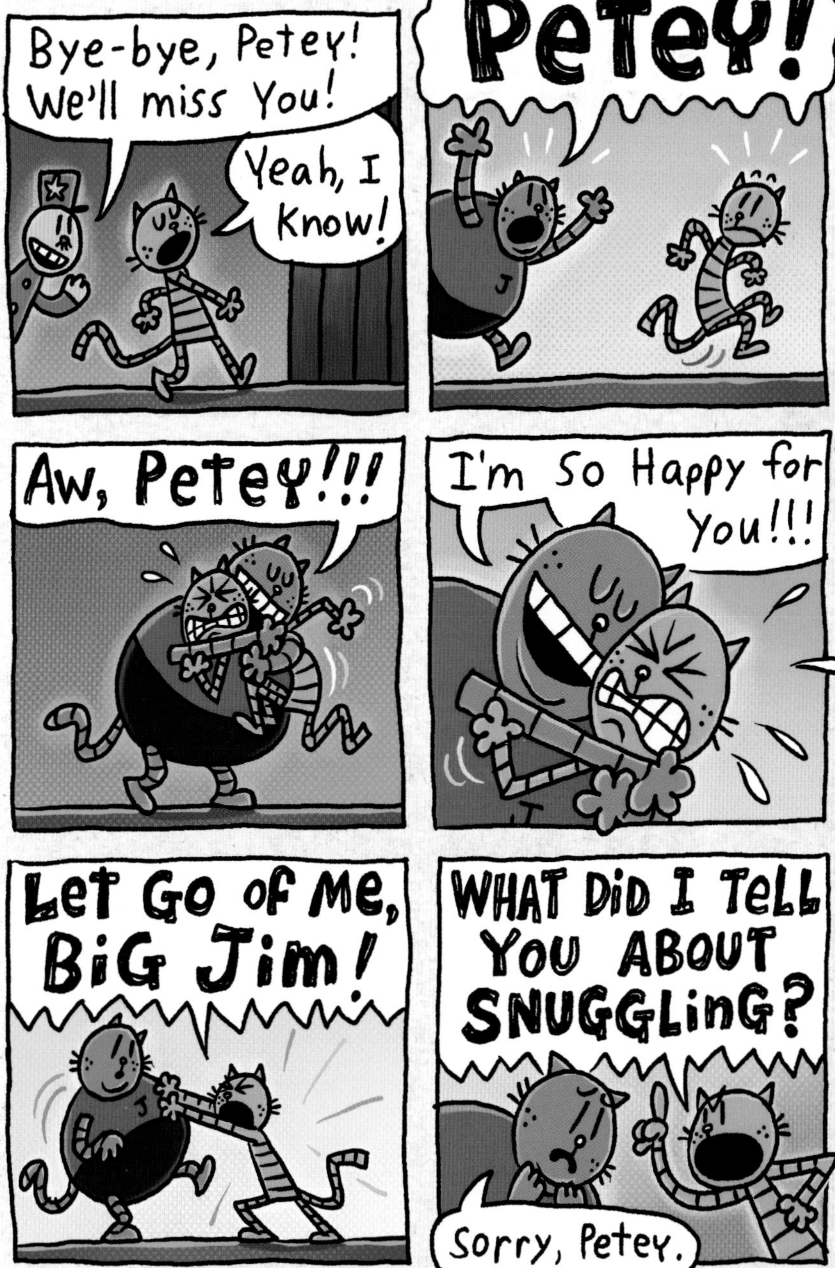
Bye-bye, Petey! We'll miss You!
Yeah, I Know!
Petey!
Aw, Petey!!!
I'm So Happy for You!!!
Let Go of Me, BiG Jim!
WHAT DiD I TeLL YOU ABOUT SNUGGLinG?
Sorry, Petey.

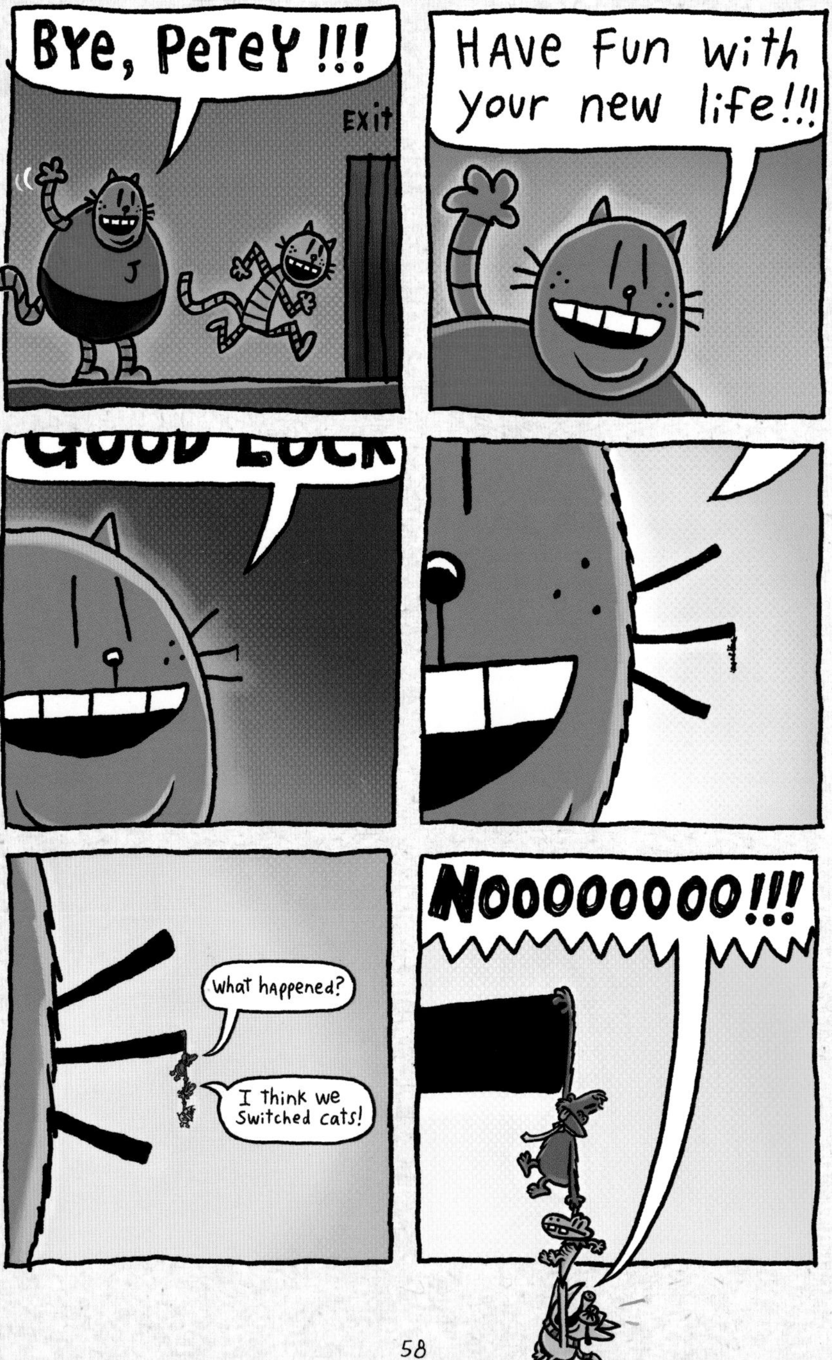
BYE, PETEY!!!
EXIT
HAVE FUN with your new life!!!
GOOD LUCK
What happened?
I think we switched cats!
NOOOOOOOOO!!!

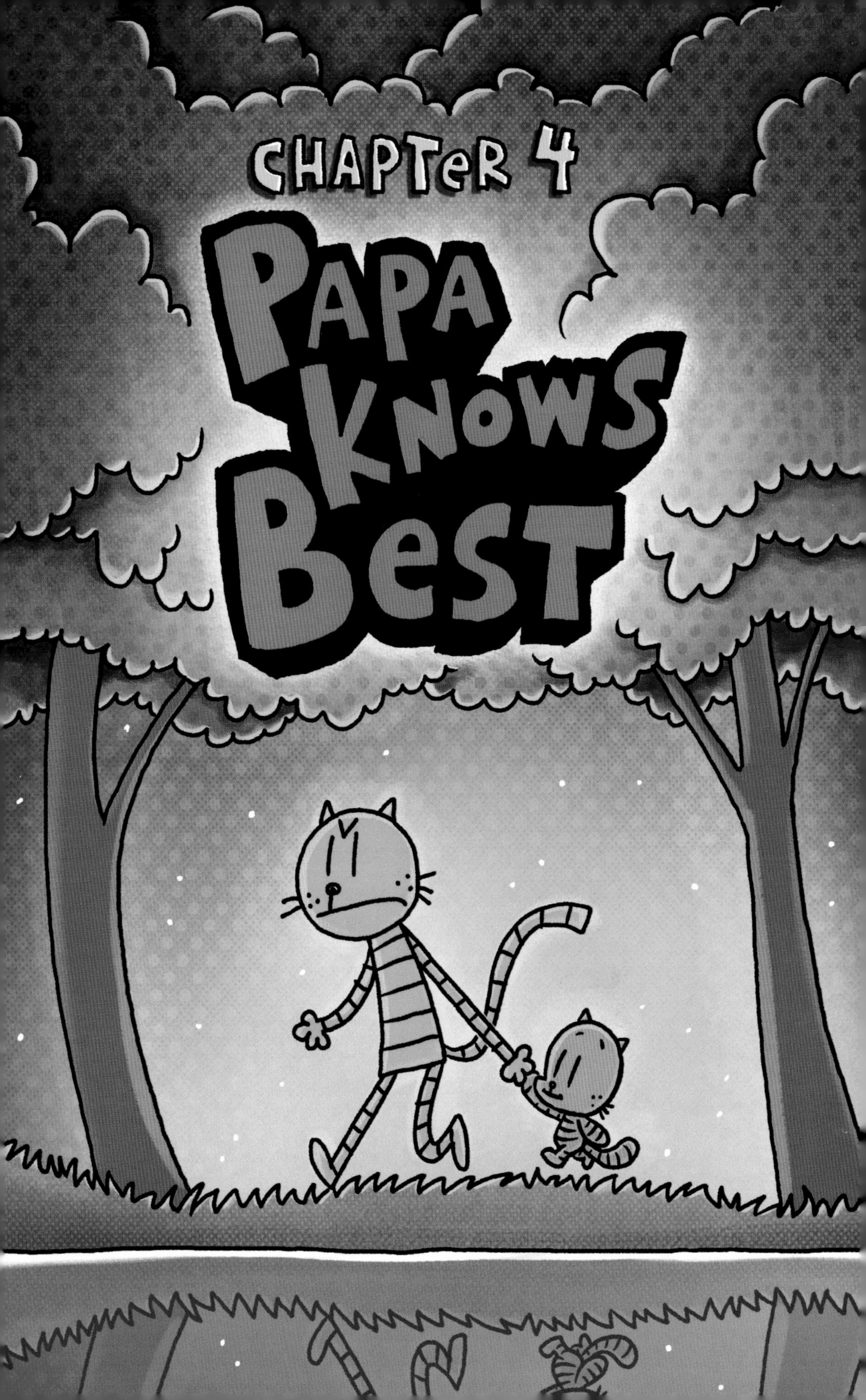
CHAPTER 4
PAPA KNOWS BEST

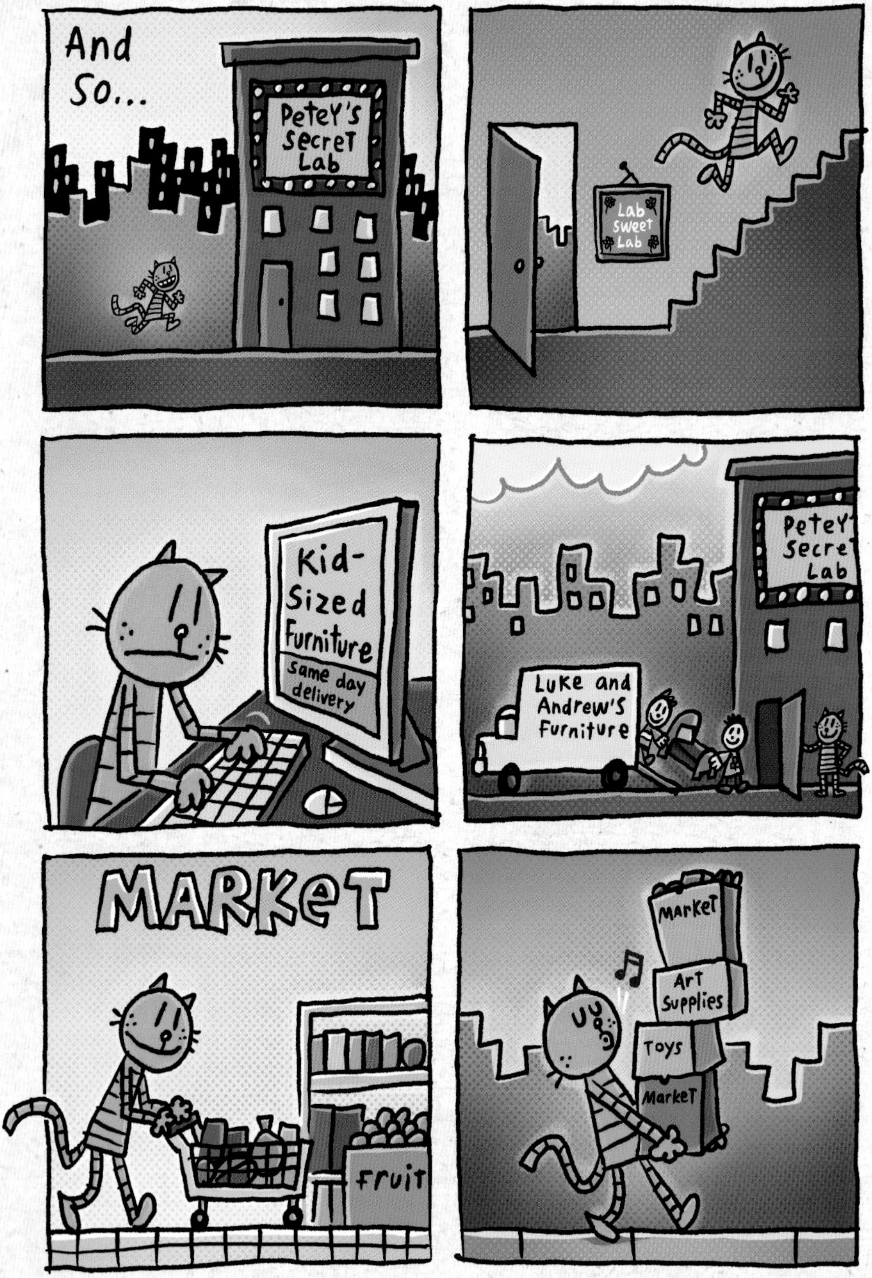

And so...
Petey's Secret Lab
Lab Sweet Lab
Kid-Sized Furniture
same day delivery
Luke and Andrew's Furniture
Petey' Secre Lab
MARKET
fruit
Market
Art Supplies
Toys
Market

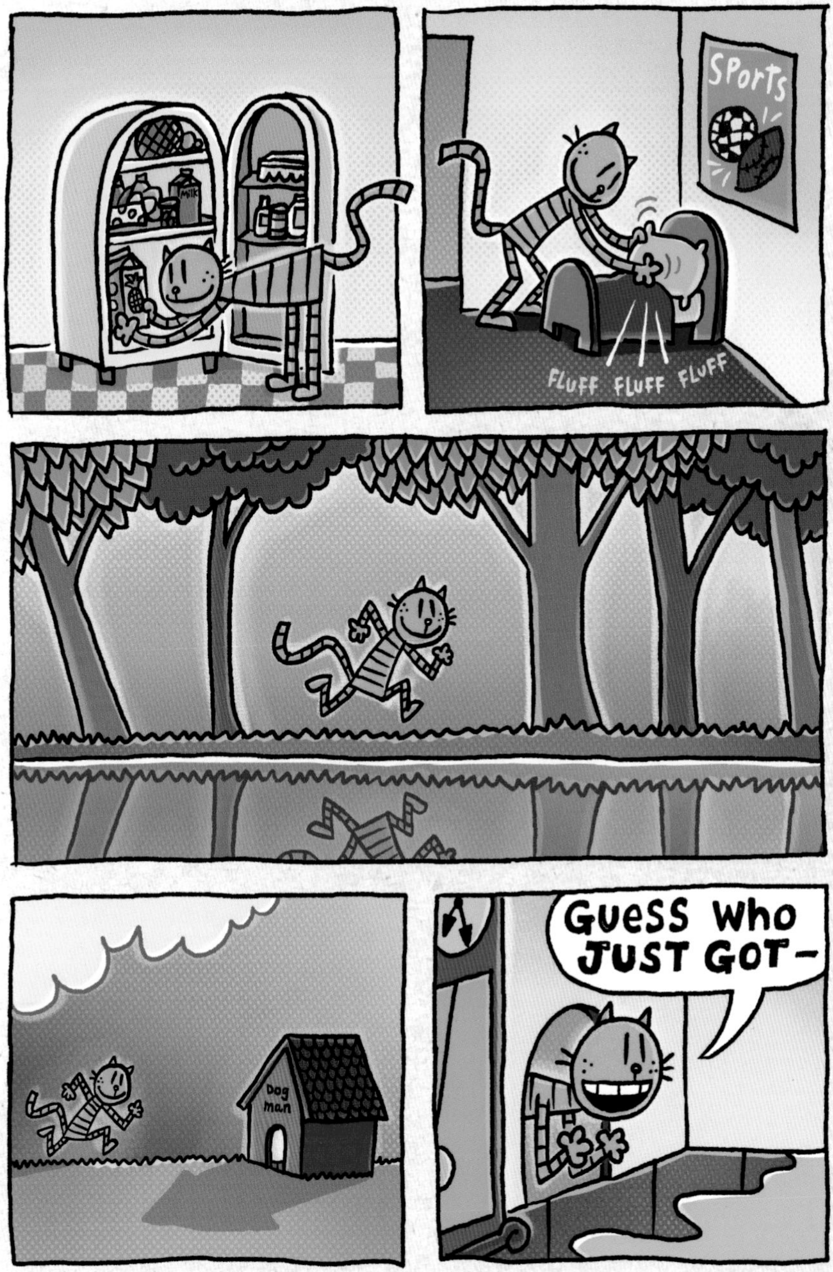
MILK
SPORTS
FLUFF FLUFF FLUFF
DOG MAN
GUESS WHO JUST GOT—

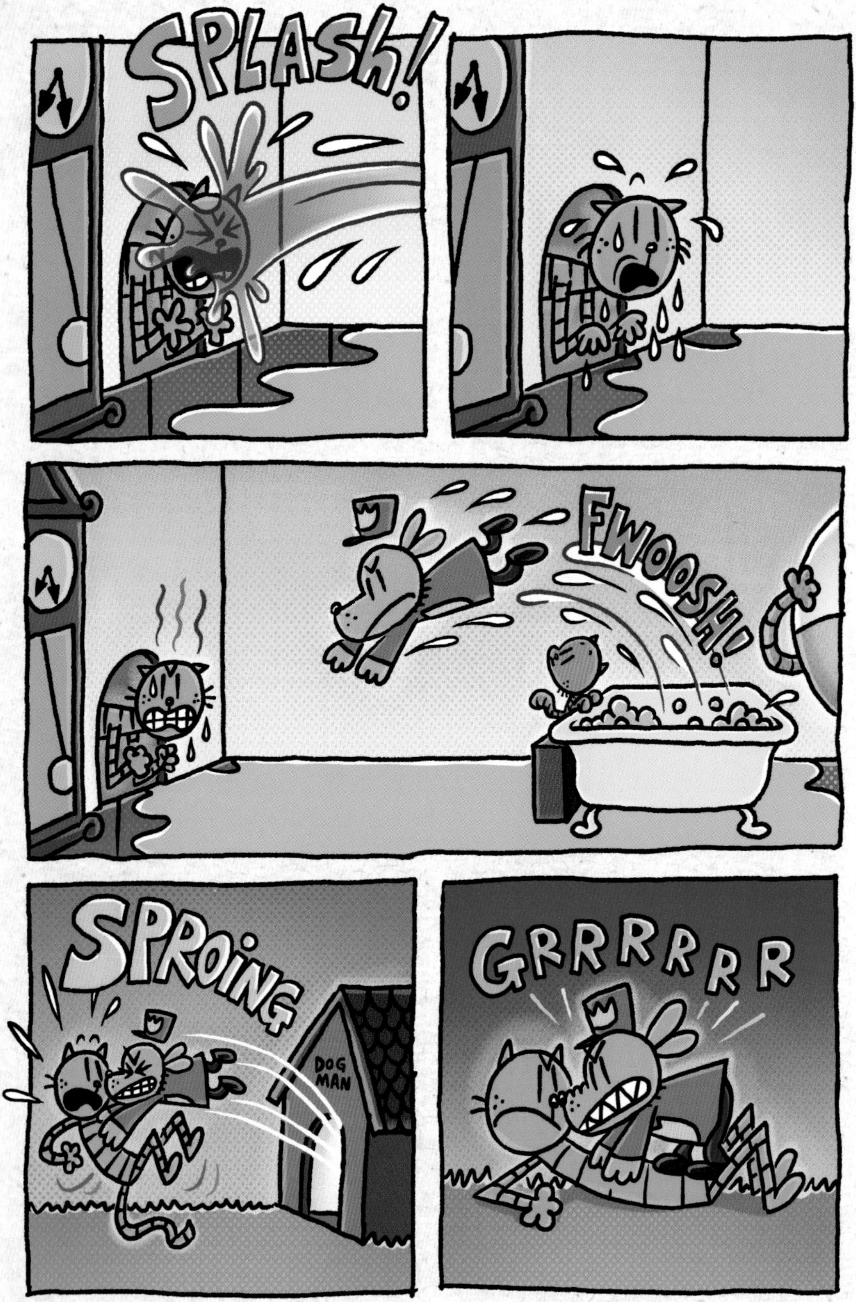
SPLASH!
FWOOSH!
SPROING
DOG MAN
GRRRRRRR

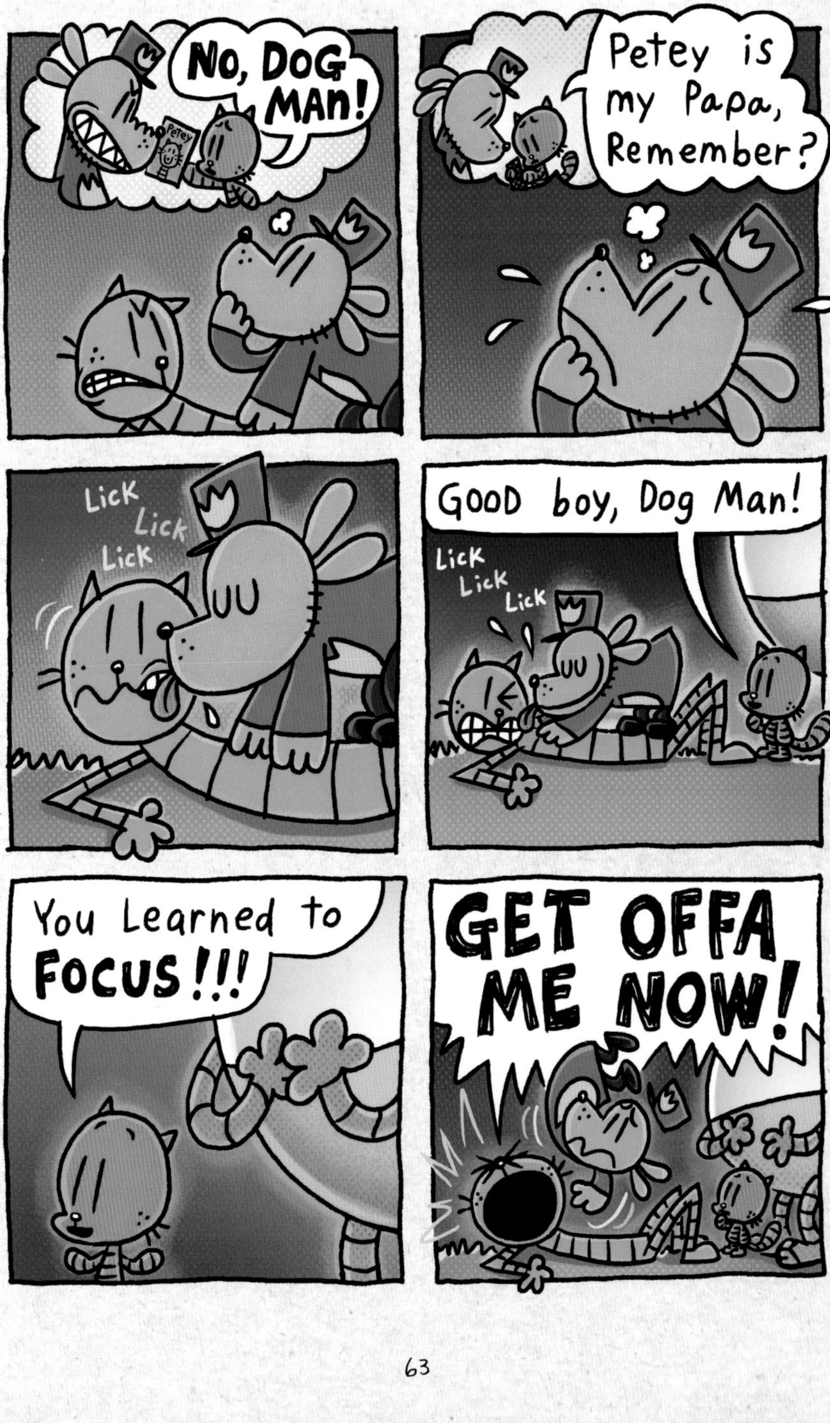

Petey
NO, DOG MAN!
Petey is my Papa, Remember?
Lick
Lick
Lick
GOOD boy, Dog Man!
Lick
Lick
Lick
You Learned to FOCUS!!!
GET OFFA ME NOW!

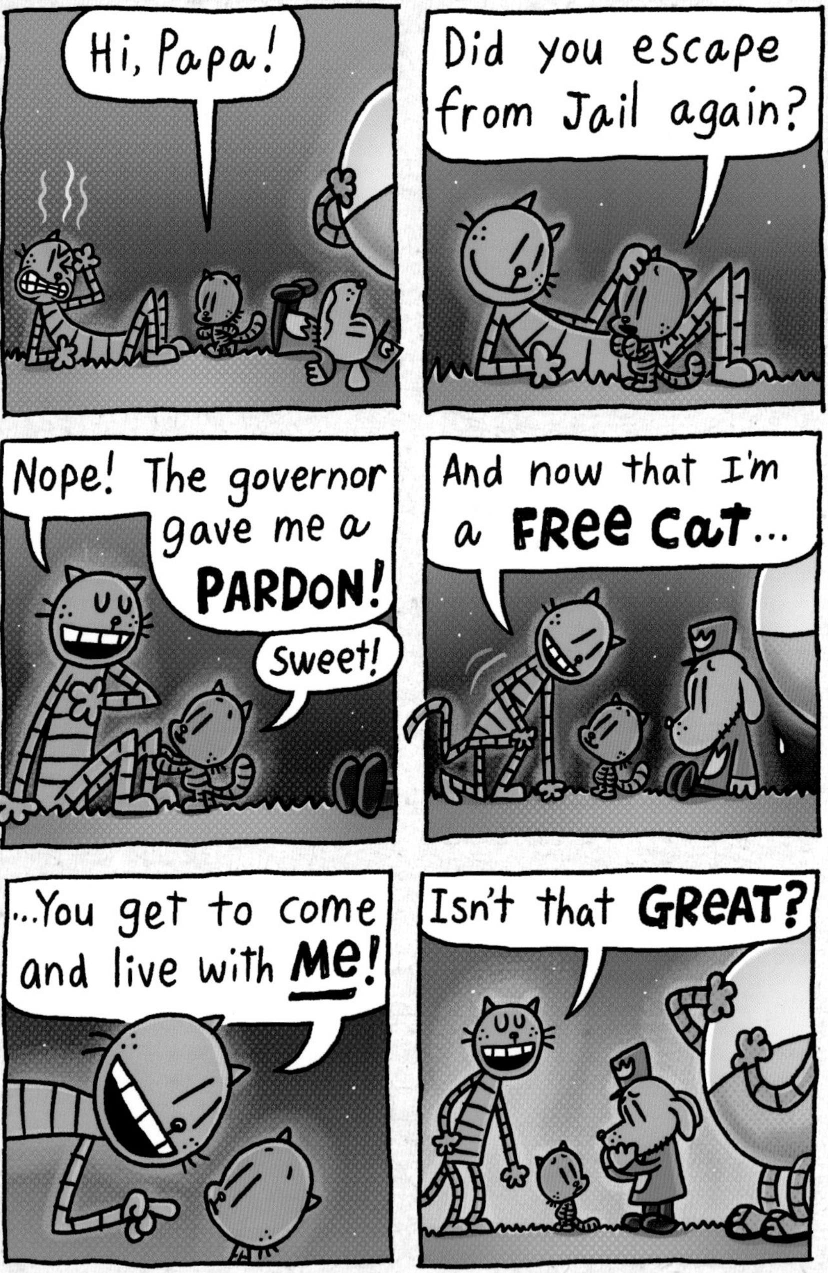
Hi, Papa!
Did you escape from Jail again?
Nope! The governor gave me a PARDON!
Sweet!
And now that I'm a FREE CaT...
...You get to come and live with ME!
Isn't that GREAT?

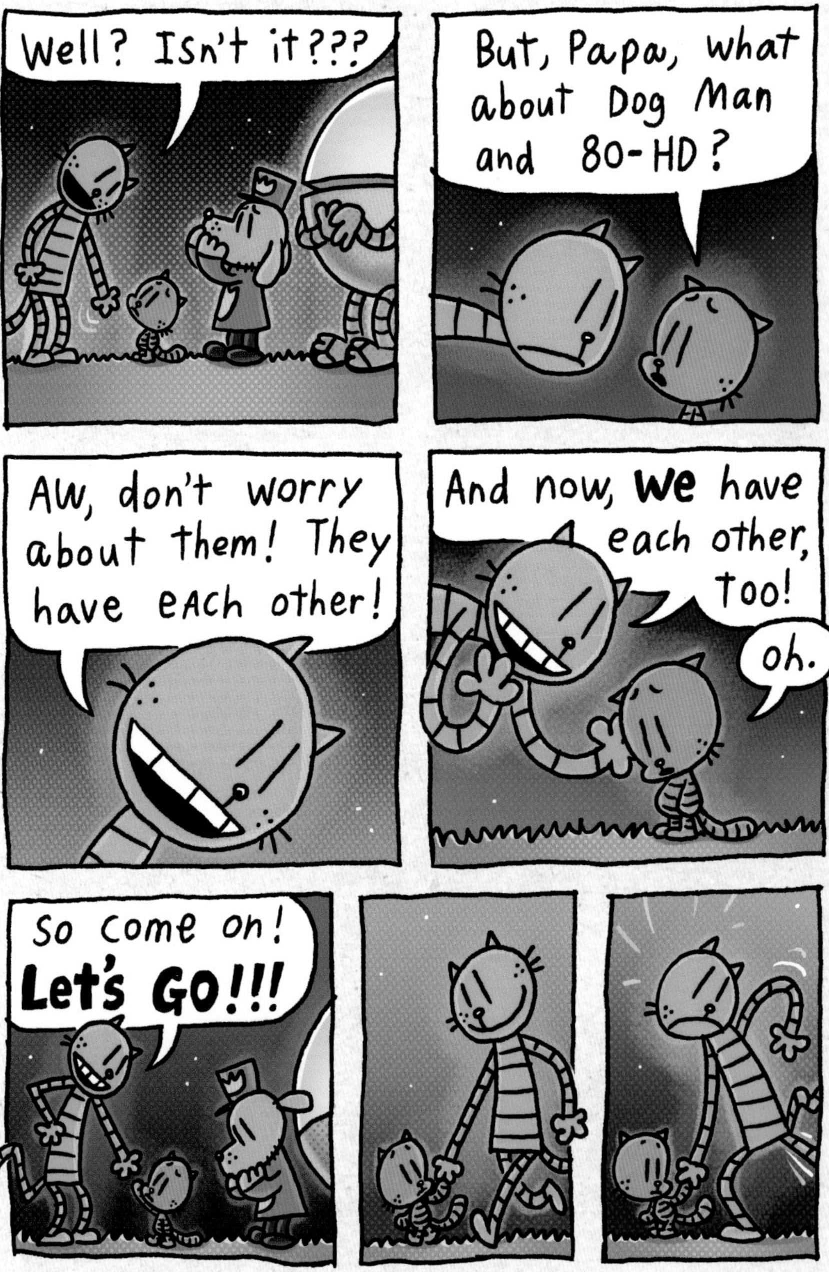
Well? Isn't it???
But, Papa, what about Dog Man and 80-HD?
Aw, don't worry about them! They have each other!
And now, **we** have each other, too!
oh.
So come on! **Let's GO!!!**

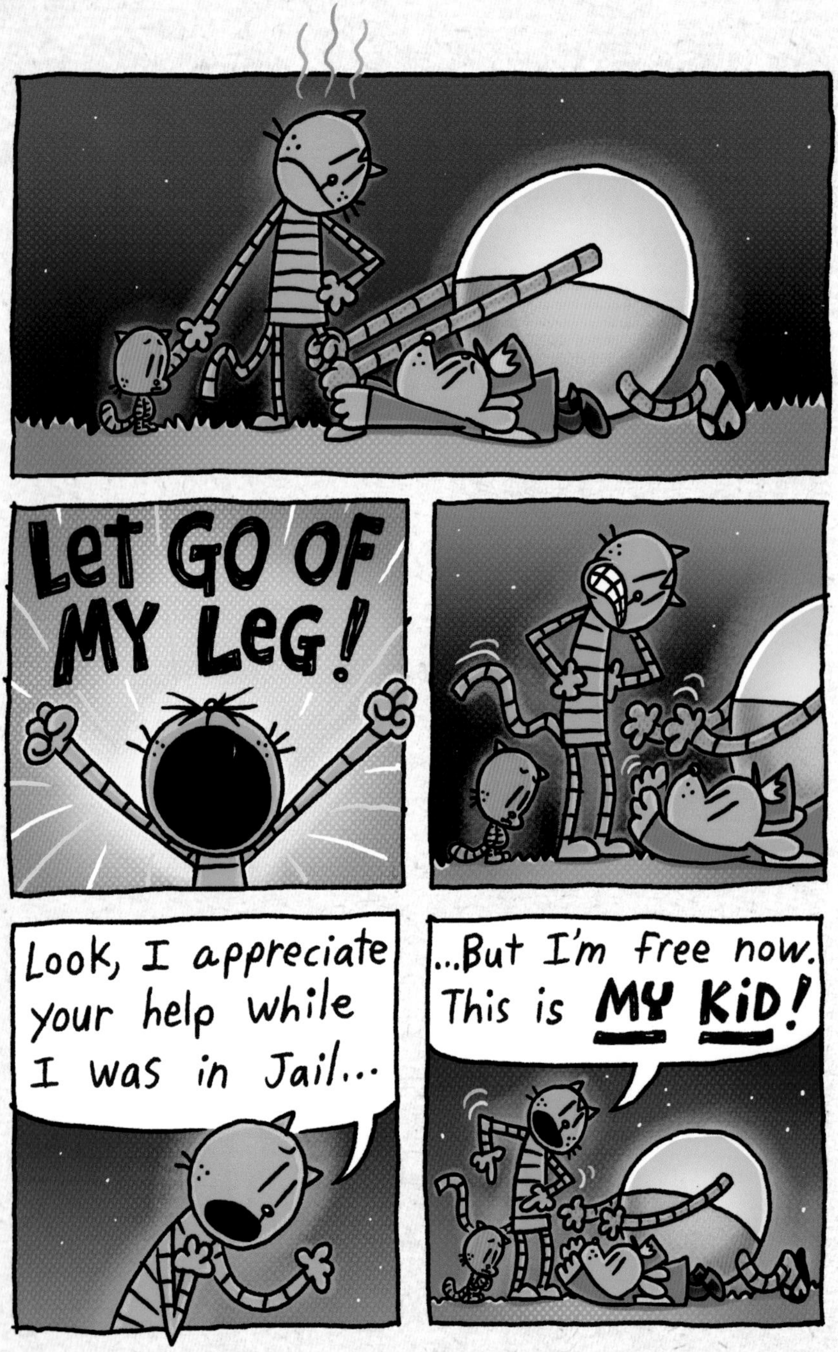
LET GO OF MY LEG!
Look, I appreciate your help while I was in Jail...
...But I'm free now. This is MY KID!

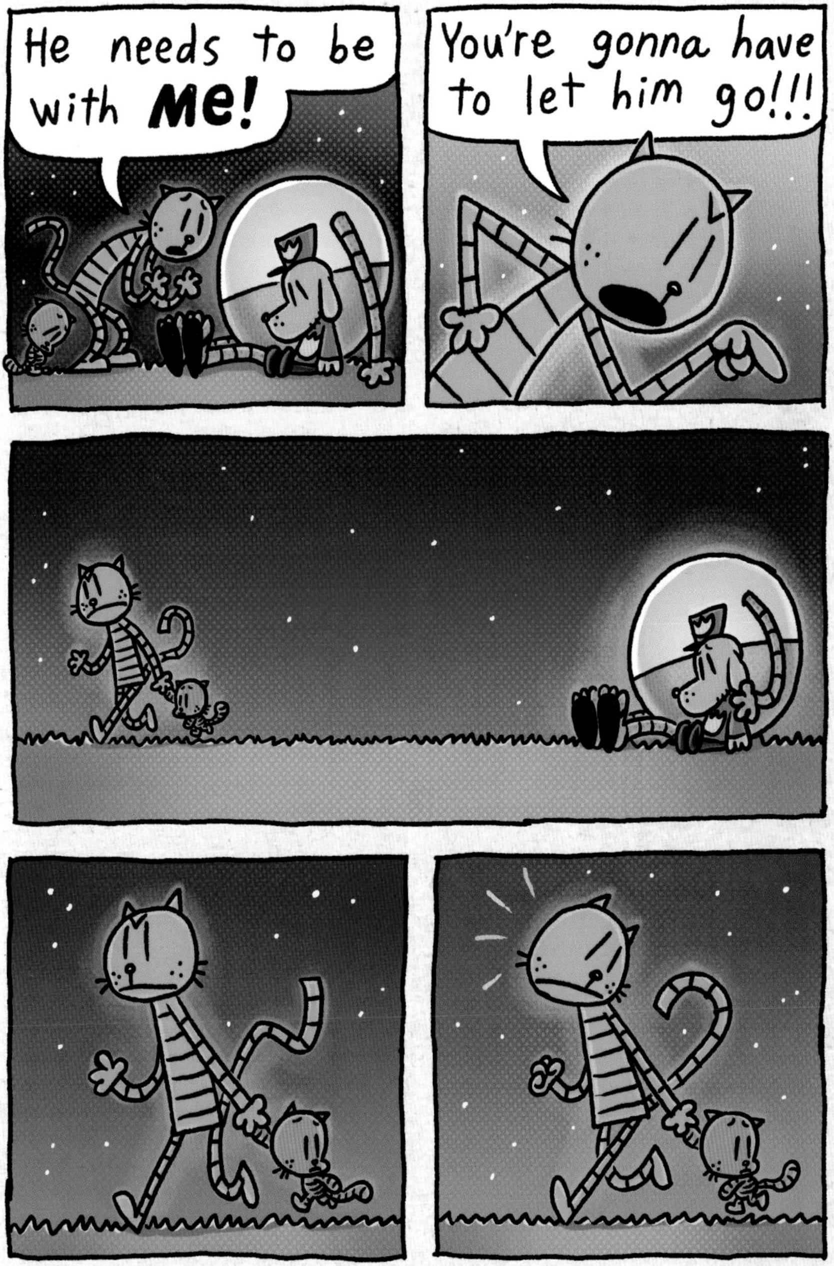
He needs to be with ME!
You're gonna have to let him go!!!

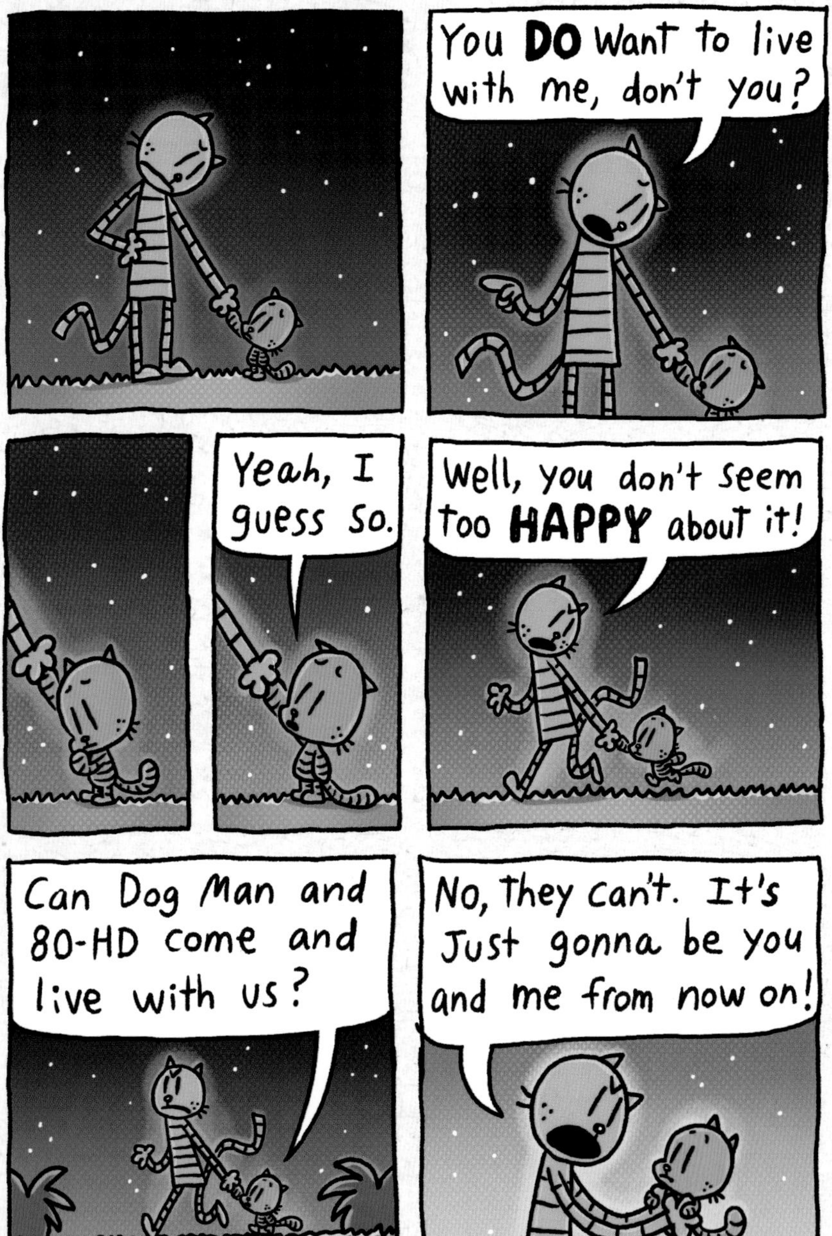
You DO want to live with me, don't you?
Yeah, I guess so.
Well, you don't seem too HAPPY about it!
Can Dog Man and 80-HD come and live with us?
No, they can't. It's just gonna be you and me from now on!

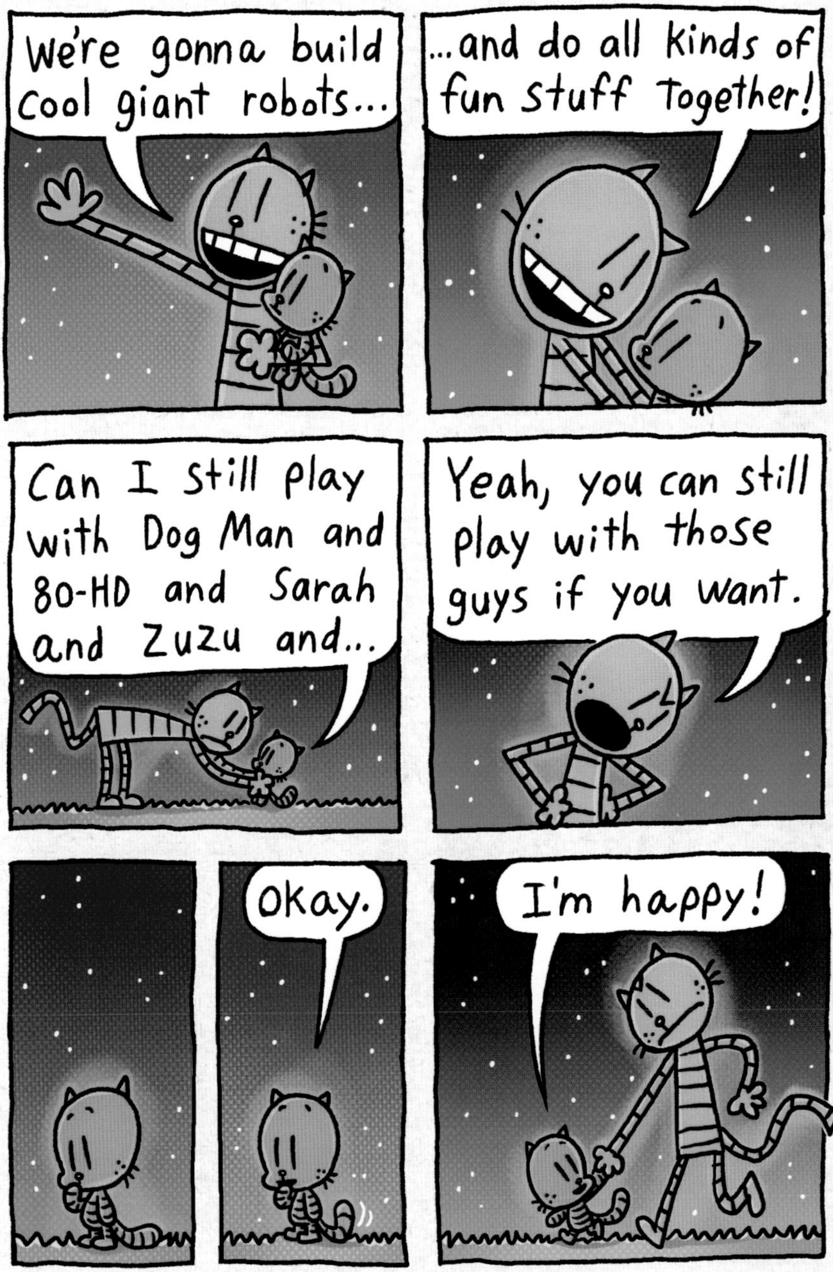
We're gonna build cool giant robots...
...and do all kinds of fun stuff together!
Can I still play with Dog Man and 80-HD and Sarah and Zuzu and...
Yeah, you can still play with those guys if you want.
Okay.
I'm happy!

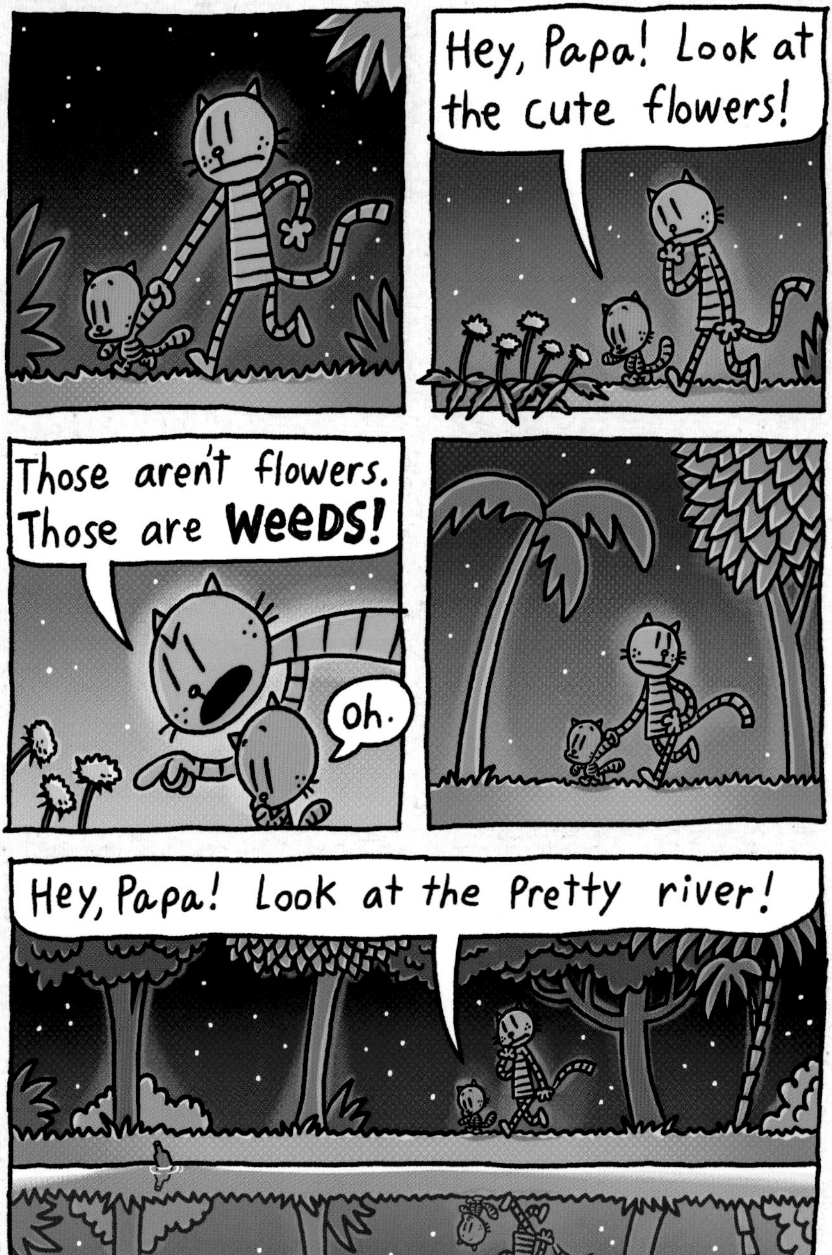
Hey, Papa! Look at the cute flowers!
Those aren't flowers. Those are WEEDS!
Oh.
Hey, Papa! Look at the pretty river!

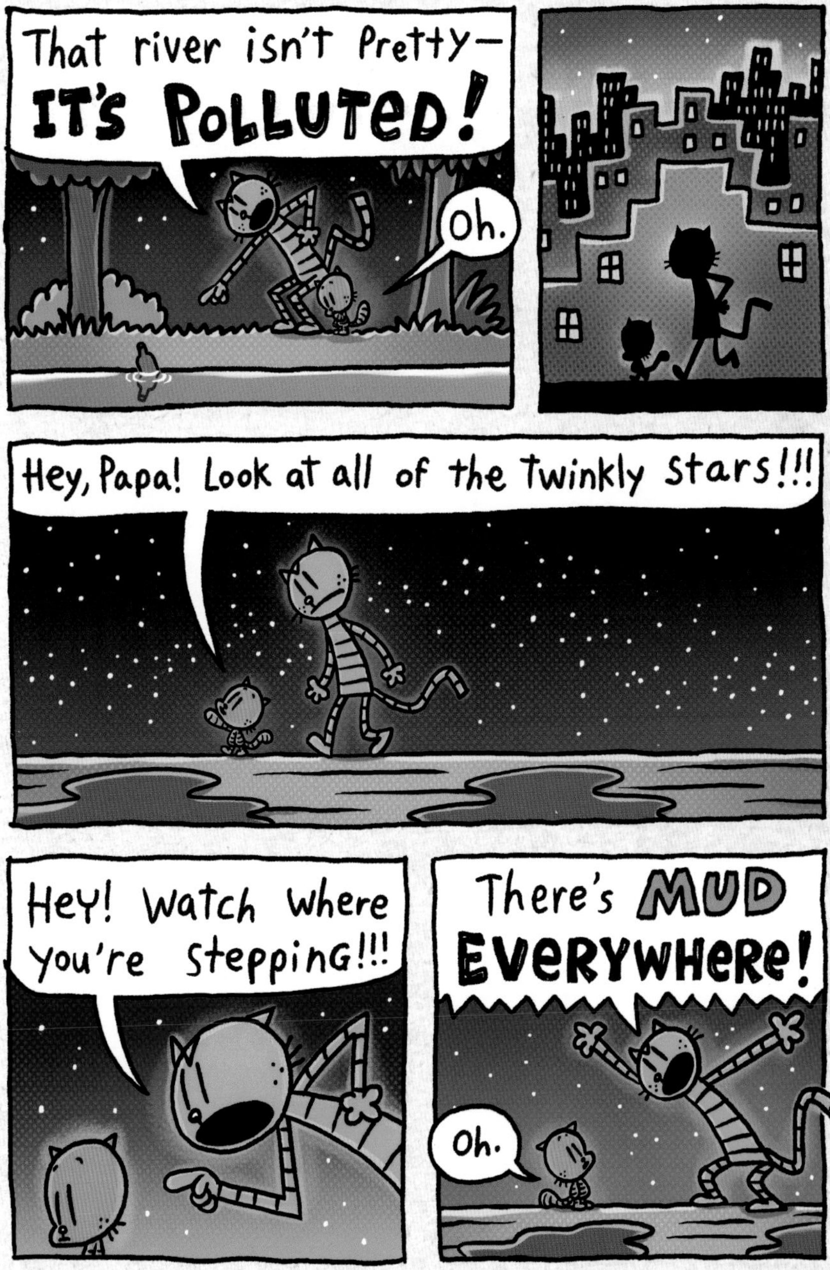
That river isn't pretty—
IT'S POLLUTED!
Oh.
Hey, Papa! Look at all of the twinkly stars!!!
Hey! Watch where you're stepping!!!
There's MUD EVERYWHERE!
Oh.

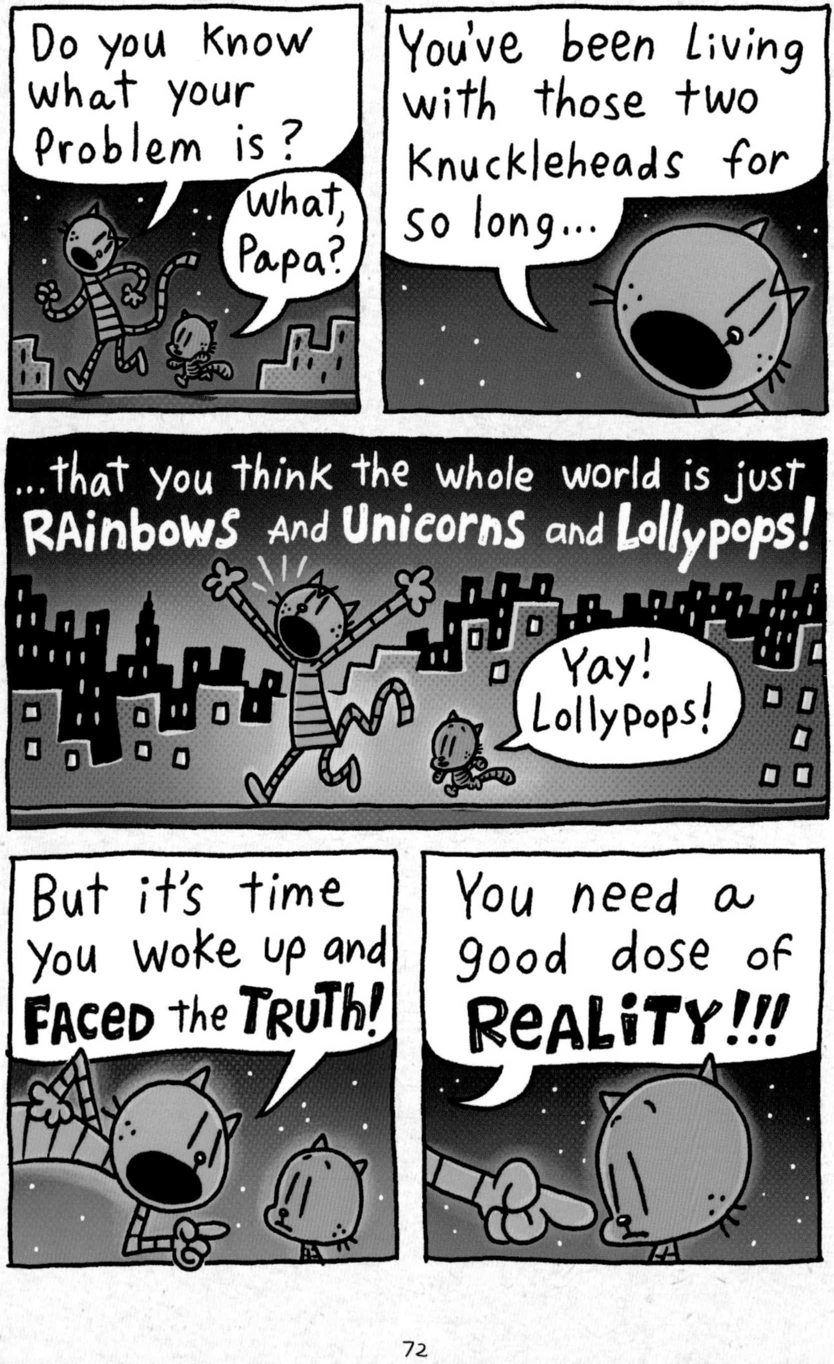
Do you know what your problem is?
What, Papa?
You've been living with those two knuckleheads for so long...
...that you think the whole world is just RAINBOWS And Unicorns and Lollypops!
Yay! Lollypops!
But it's time you woke up and FACED the TRUTh!
You need a good dose of REALiTY!!!

CHAPTER 5

A good Dose of Reality

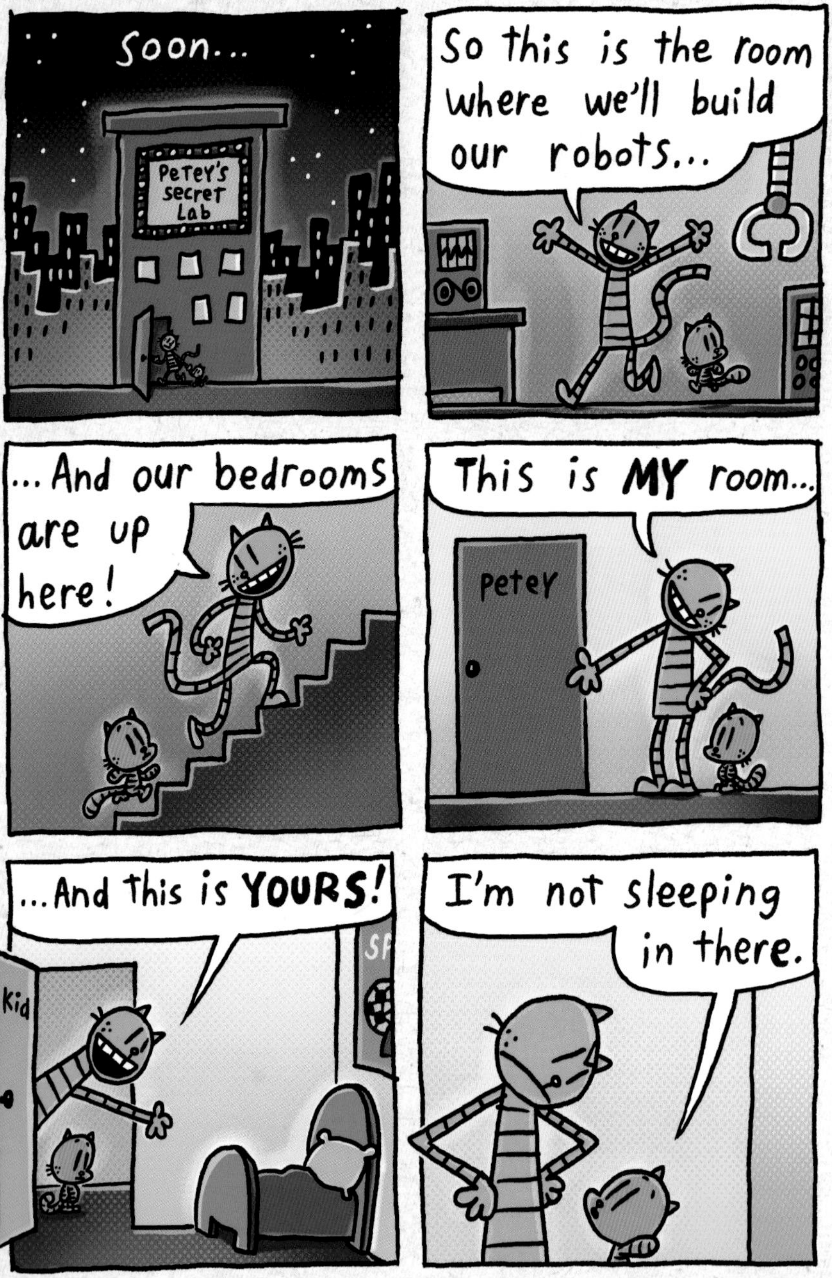
Soon...
Petey's Secret Lab
So this is the room where we'll build our robots...
...And our bedrooms are up here!
This is MY room...
Petey
...And this is YOURS!
Kid
I'm not sleeping in there.

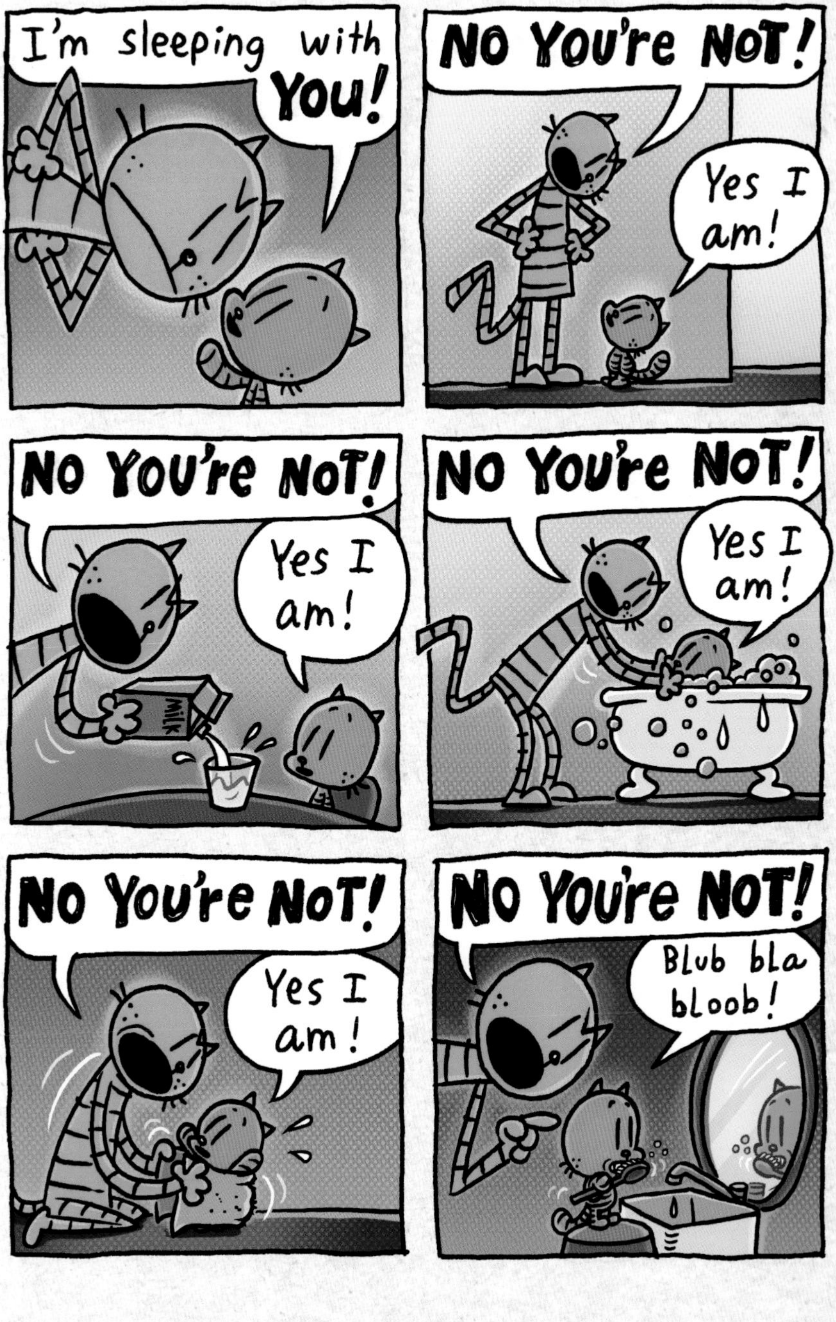
I'm sleeping with YOU!
NO YOU're NOT!
Yes I am!
NO YOU're NOT!
Yes I am!
NO YOU're NOT!
Yes I am!
NO YOU're NOT!
Yes I am!
NO YOU're NOT!
Blub bla bloob!

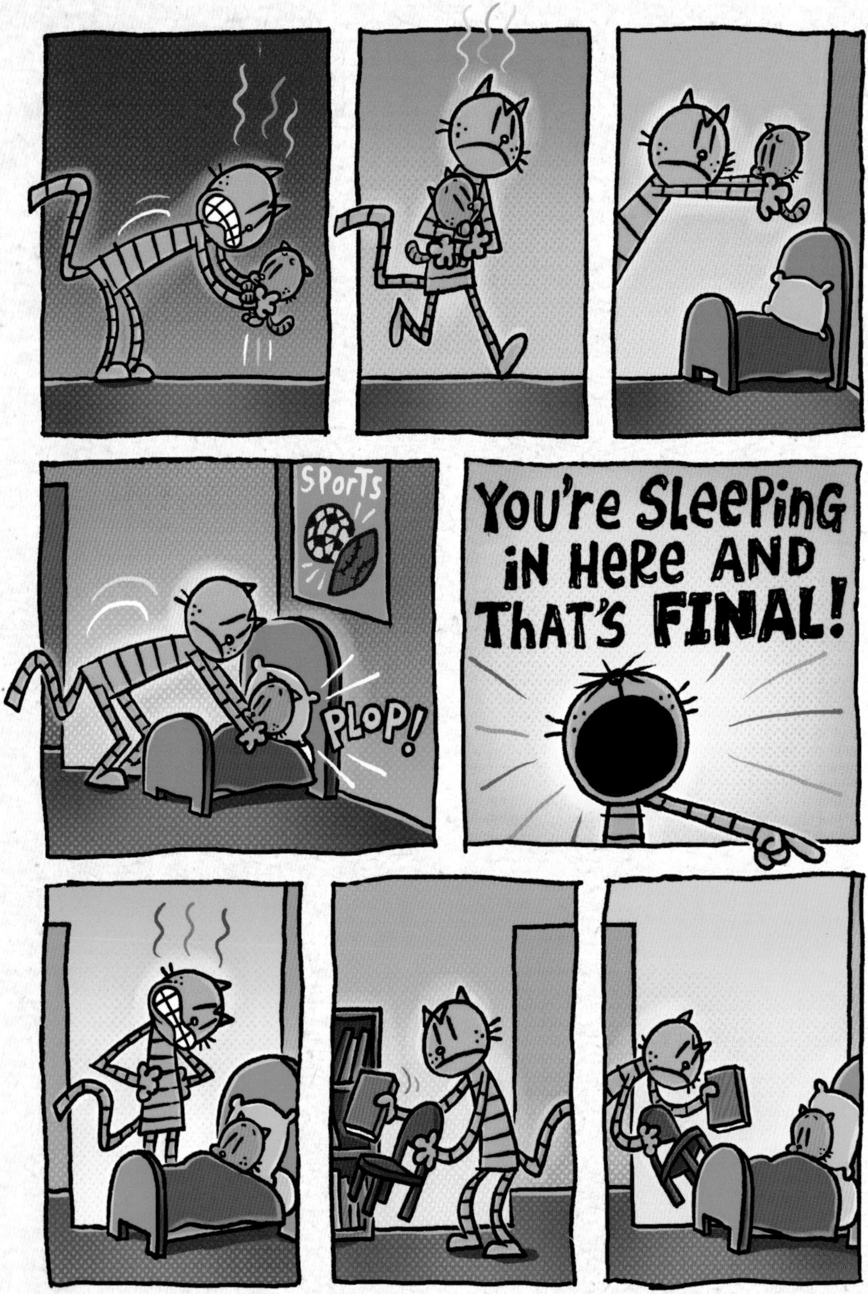
SPORTS
PLOP!
YOU'RE SLEEPING IN HERE AND THAT'S FINAL!

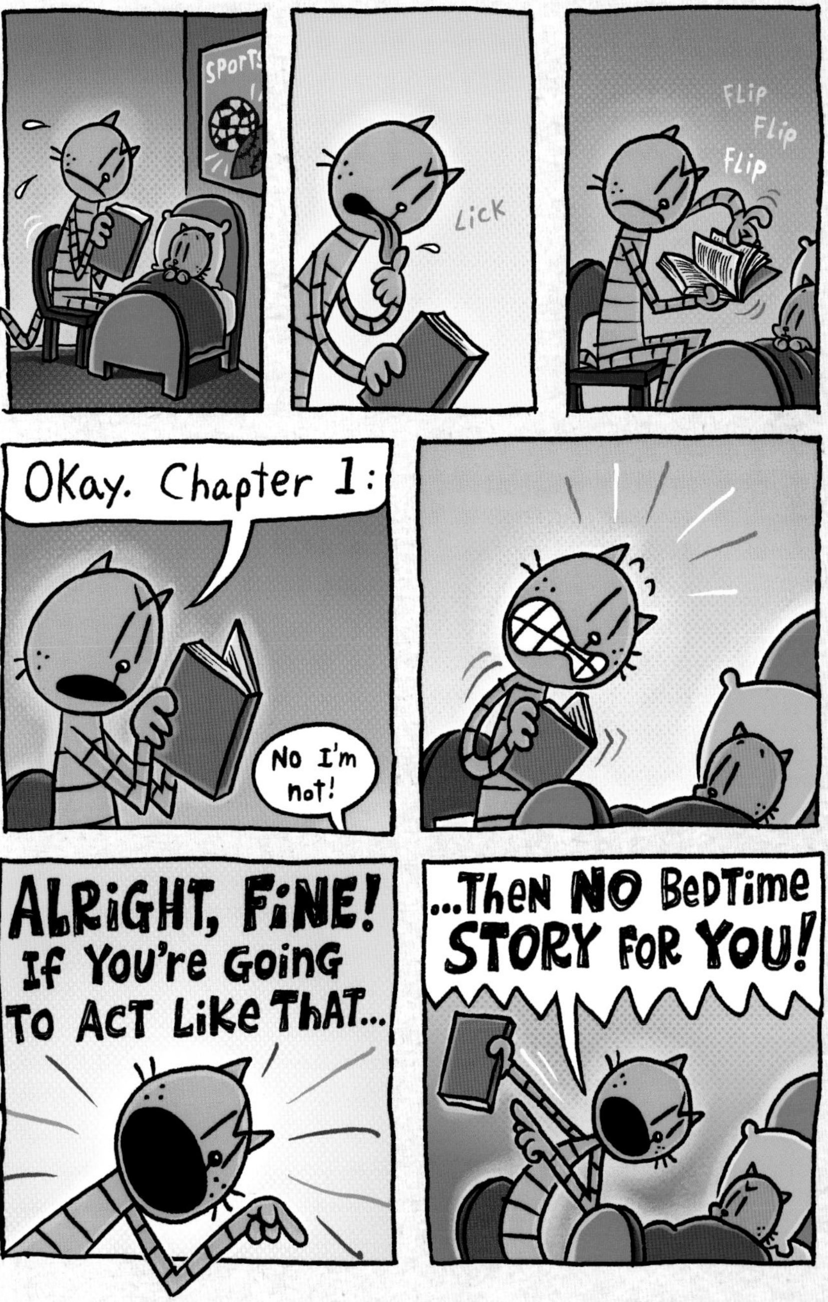
SPORTS
LICK
FLIP
FLIP
FLIP
OKay. Chapter 1:
No I'm not!
ALRIGHT, FINE! If YOU're GOING TO ACT LIKE THAT...
...THEN NO BEDTIME STORY FOR YOU!

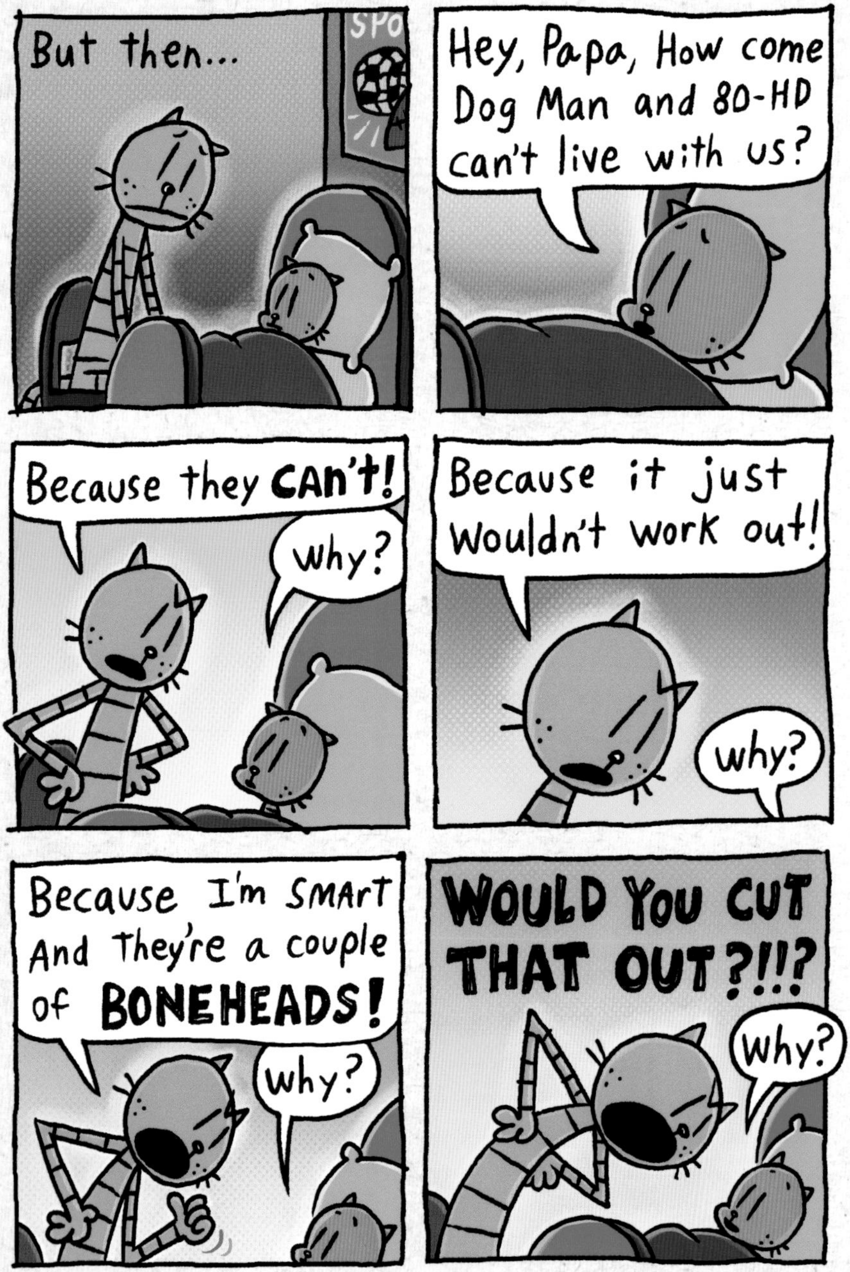
But then...
SPO
Hey, Papa, How come Dog Man and 80-HD can't live with us?
Because they CAN'T!
Why?
Because it just wouldn't work out!
Why?
Because I'm SMART And They're a couple of BONEHEADS!
Why?
WOULD YOU CUT THAT OUT?!!?
Why?

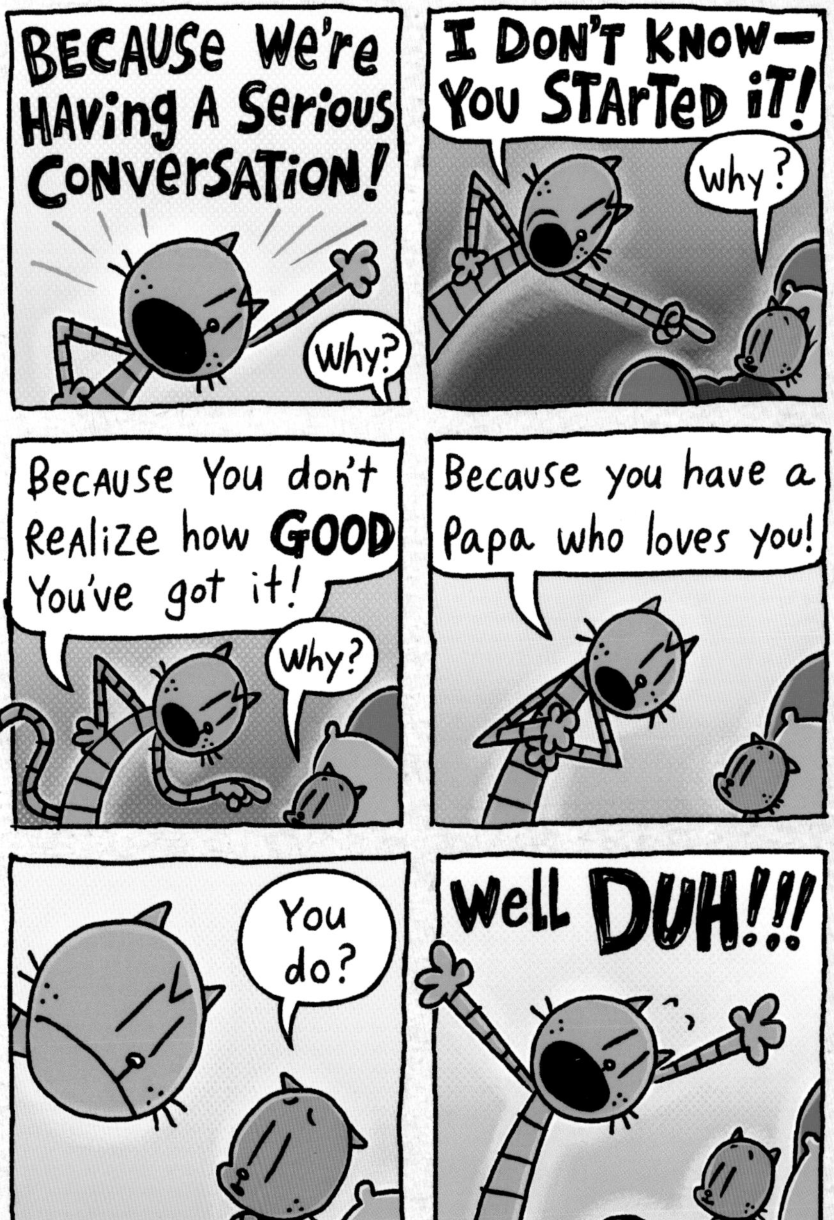
BECAUSE We're HAVing A Serious CONVerSATION!
Why?
I DON'T KNOW— YOU STArTED iT!
Why?
BECAUSE You don't Realize how GOOD You've got it!
Why?
Because you have a Papa who loves you!
You do?
Well DUH!!!

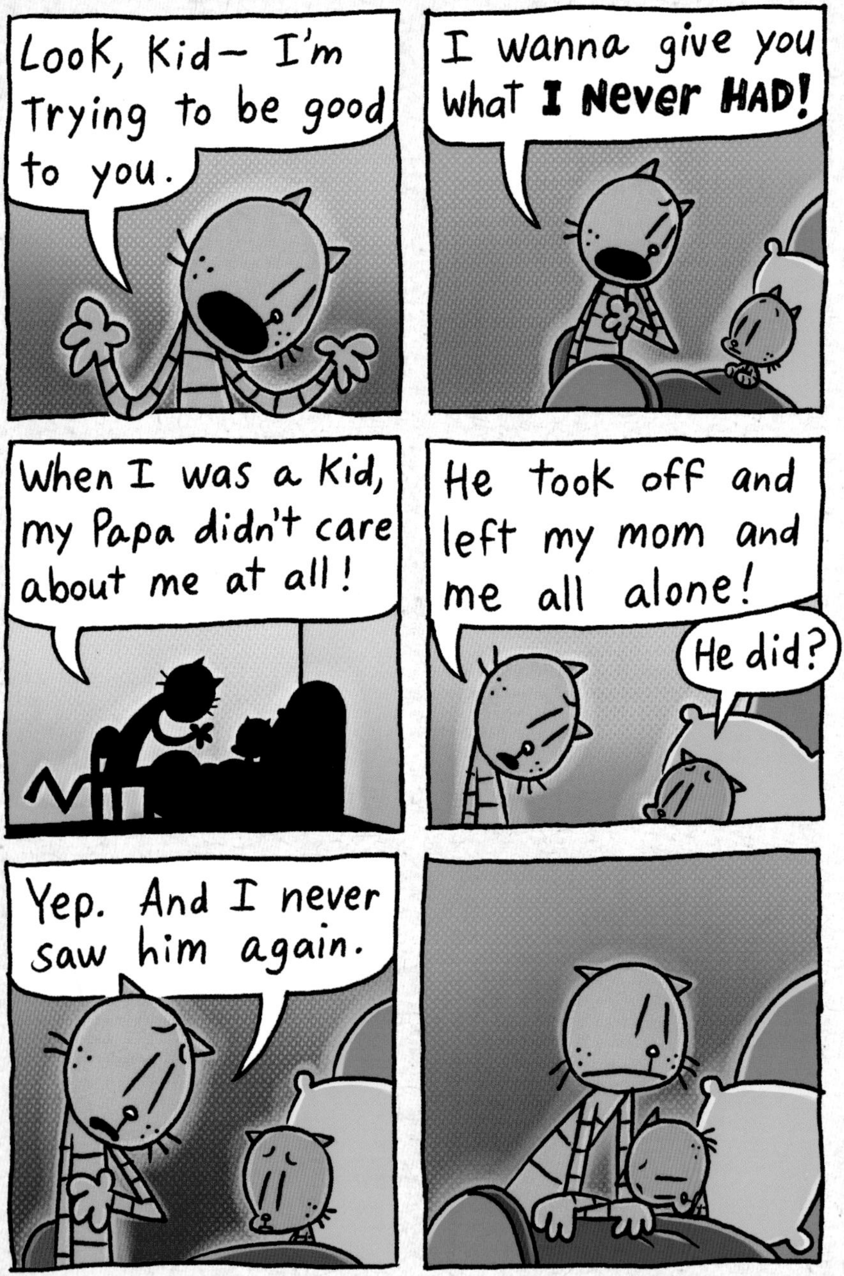
Look, Kid— I'm Trying to be good to you.
I wanna give you what I NEVER HAD!
When I was a Kid, my Papa didn't care about me at all!
He took off and left my mom and me all alone!
He did?
Yep. And I never saw him again.

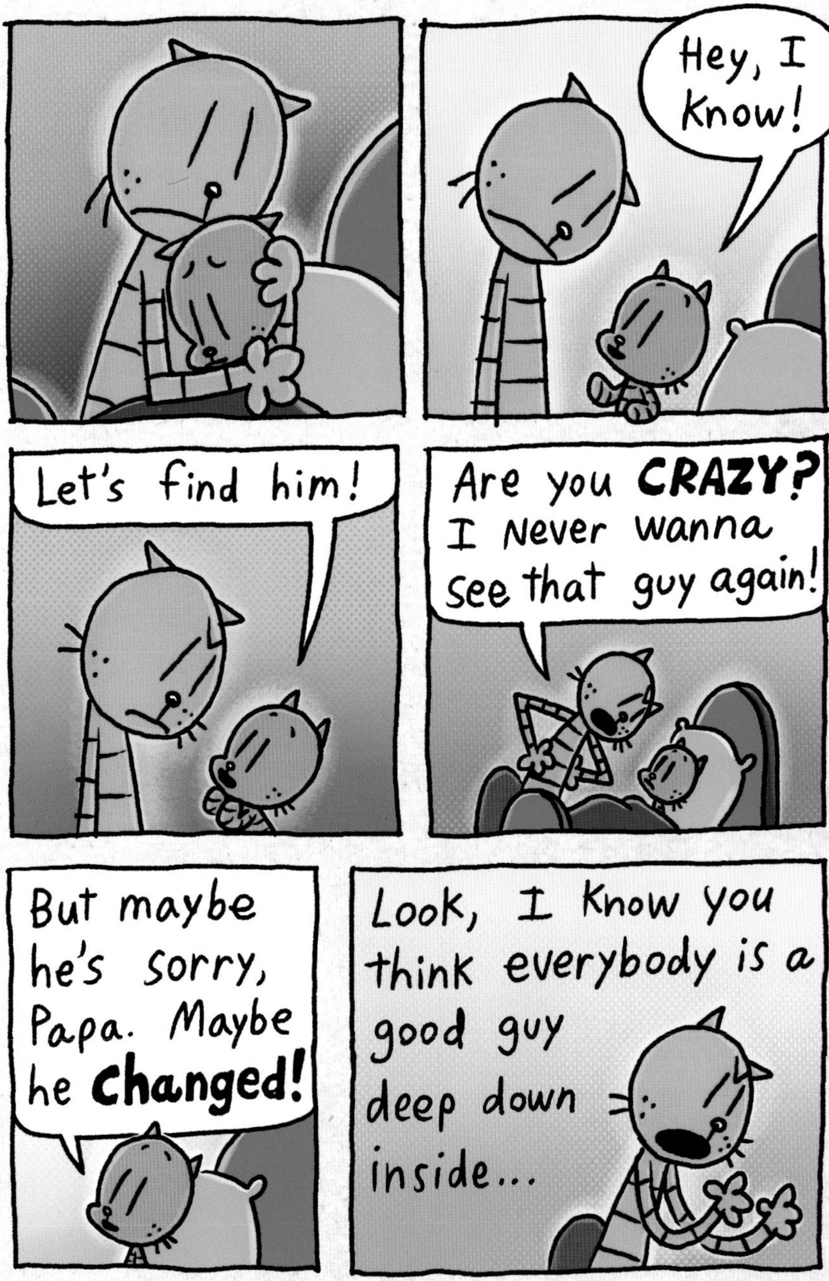
Hey, I Know!
Let's find him!
Are you **CRAZY?** I Never wanna see that guy again!
But maybe he's sorry, Papa. Maybe he **Changed!**
Look, I Know you think everybody is a good guy deep down inside...

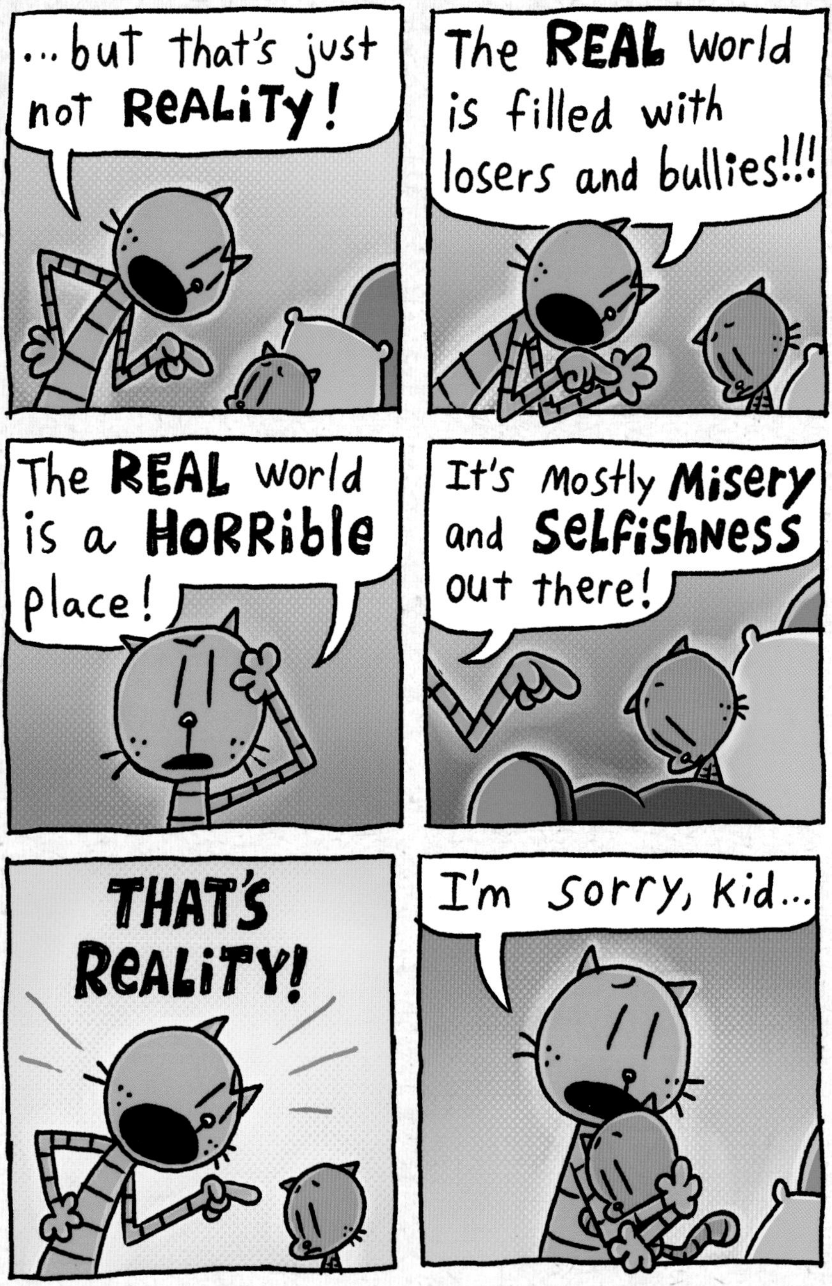
...but that's just not REALITY!
The REAL world is filled with losers and bullies!!!
The REAL world is a HORRIBLE place!
It's mostly MISERY and SELFISHNESS out there!
THAT'S REALITY!
I'm sorry, kid...

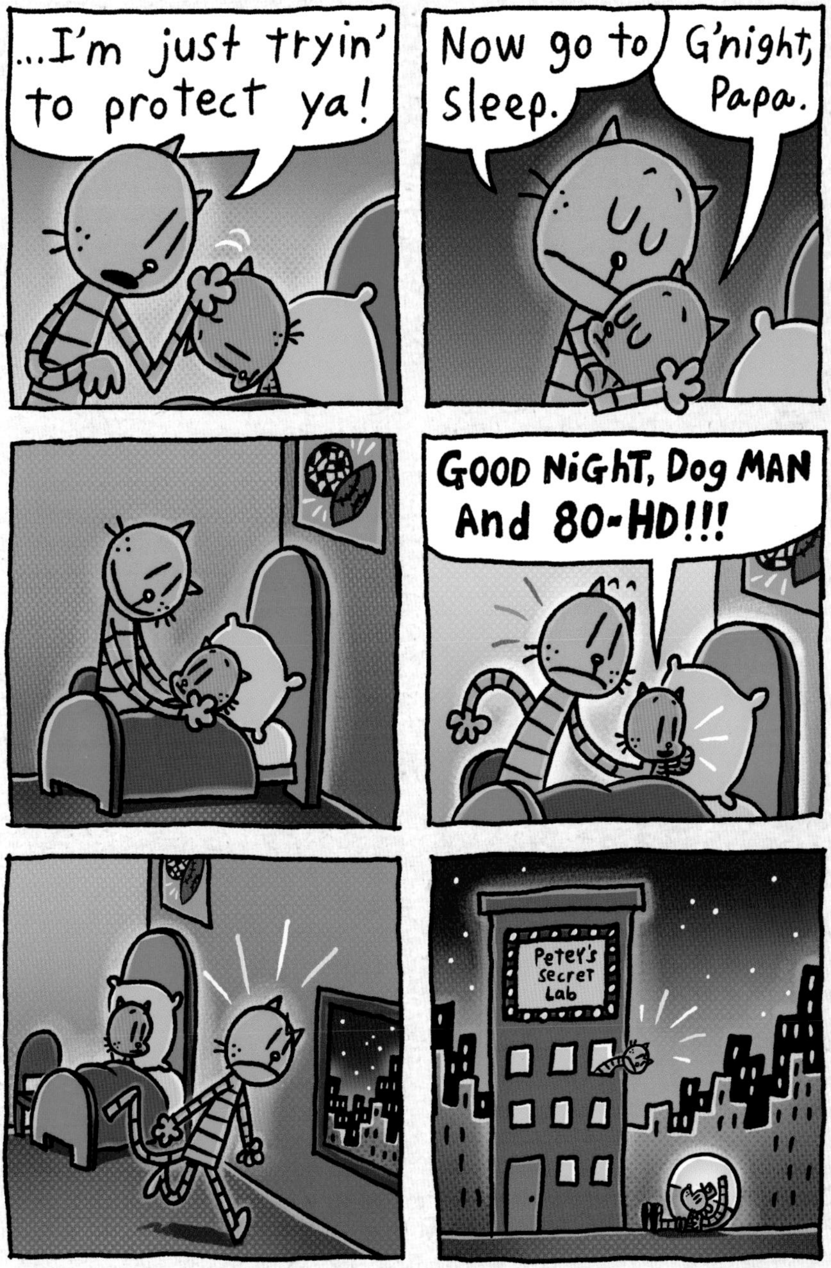
...I'm just tryin' to protect ya!
Now go to sleep.
G'night, Papa.
GOOD NIGHT, Dog MAN And 80-HD!!!
Petey's Secret Lab

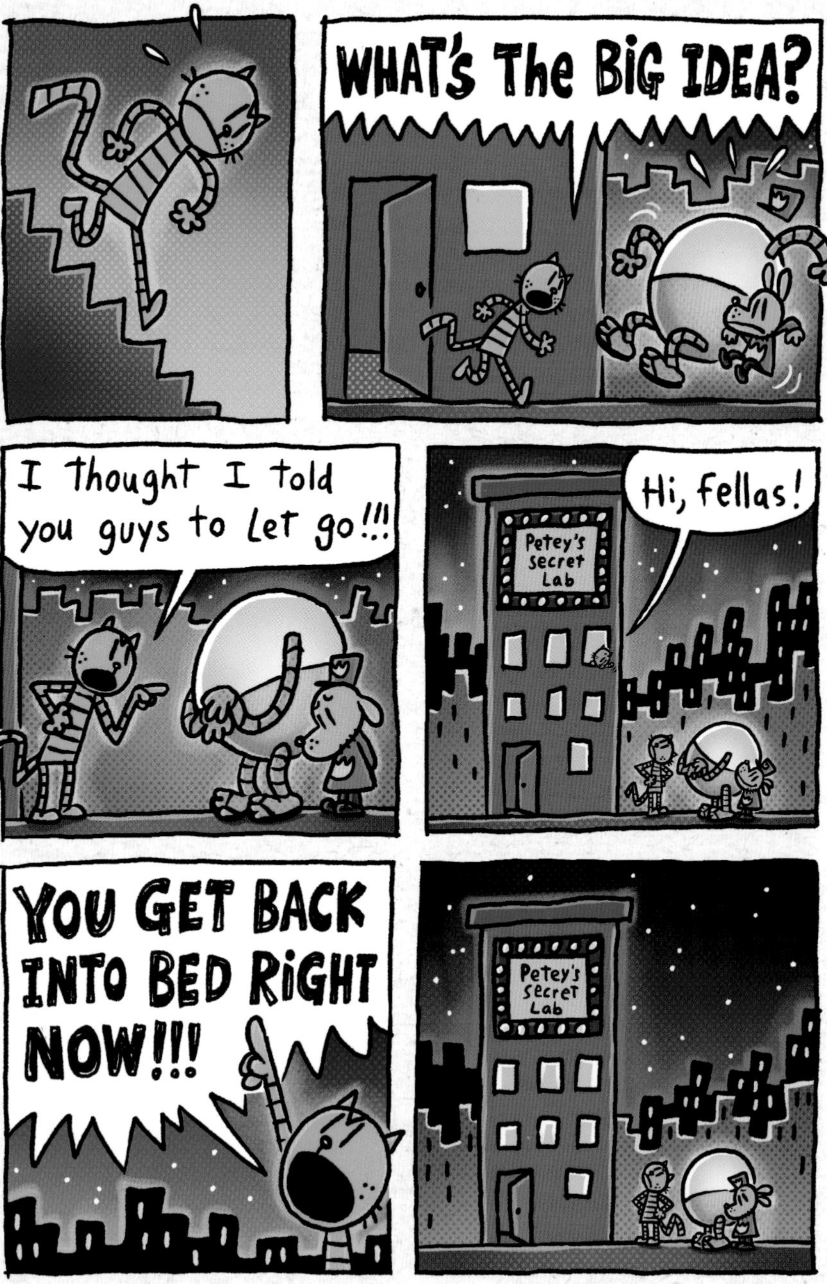
WHAT'S The BIG IDEA?
I thought I told you guys to let go!!!
Hi, Fellas!
Petey's secret Lab
YOU GET BACK INTO BED RIGHT NOW!!!
Petey's secret Lab

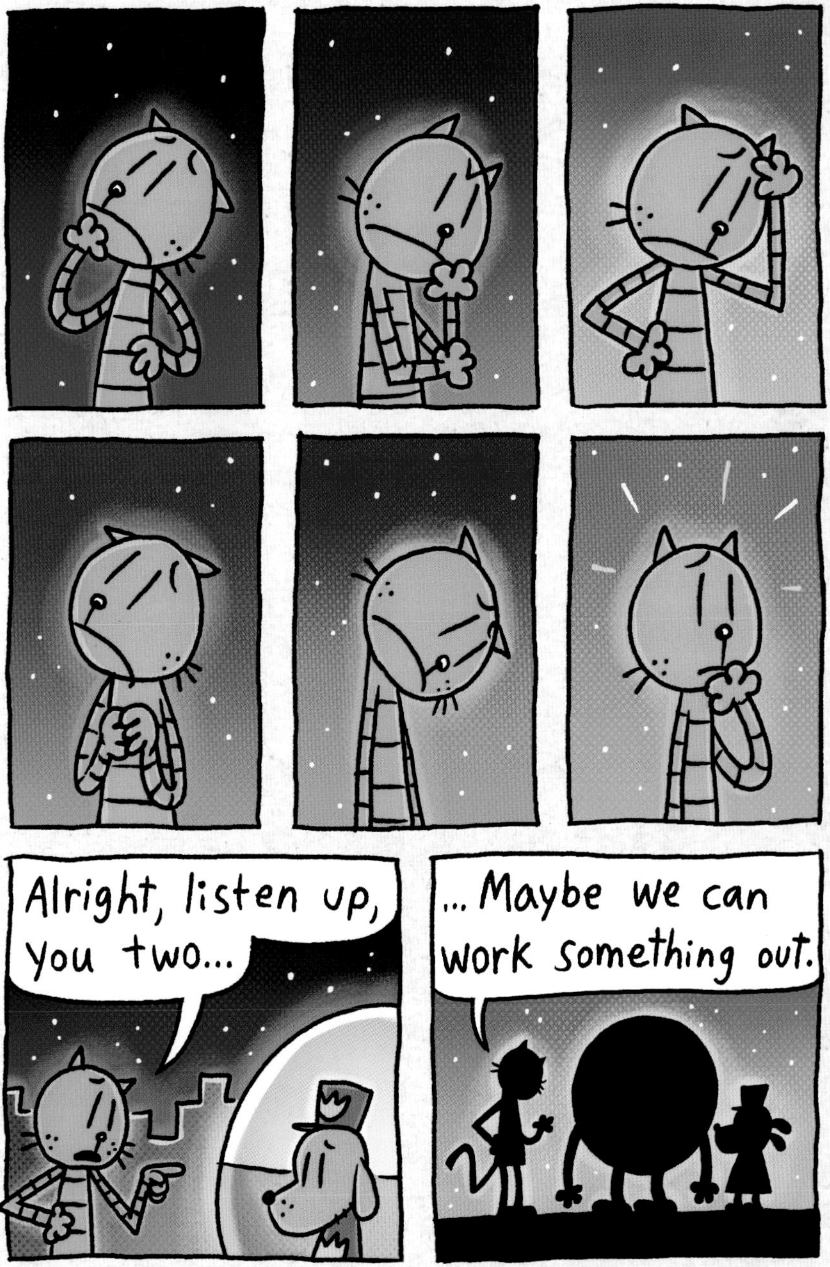
Alright, listen up, you two...
...Maybe we can work something out.

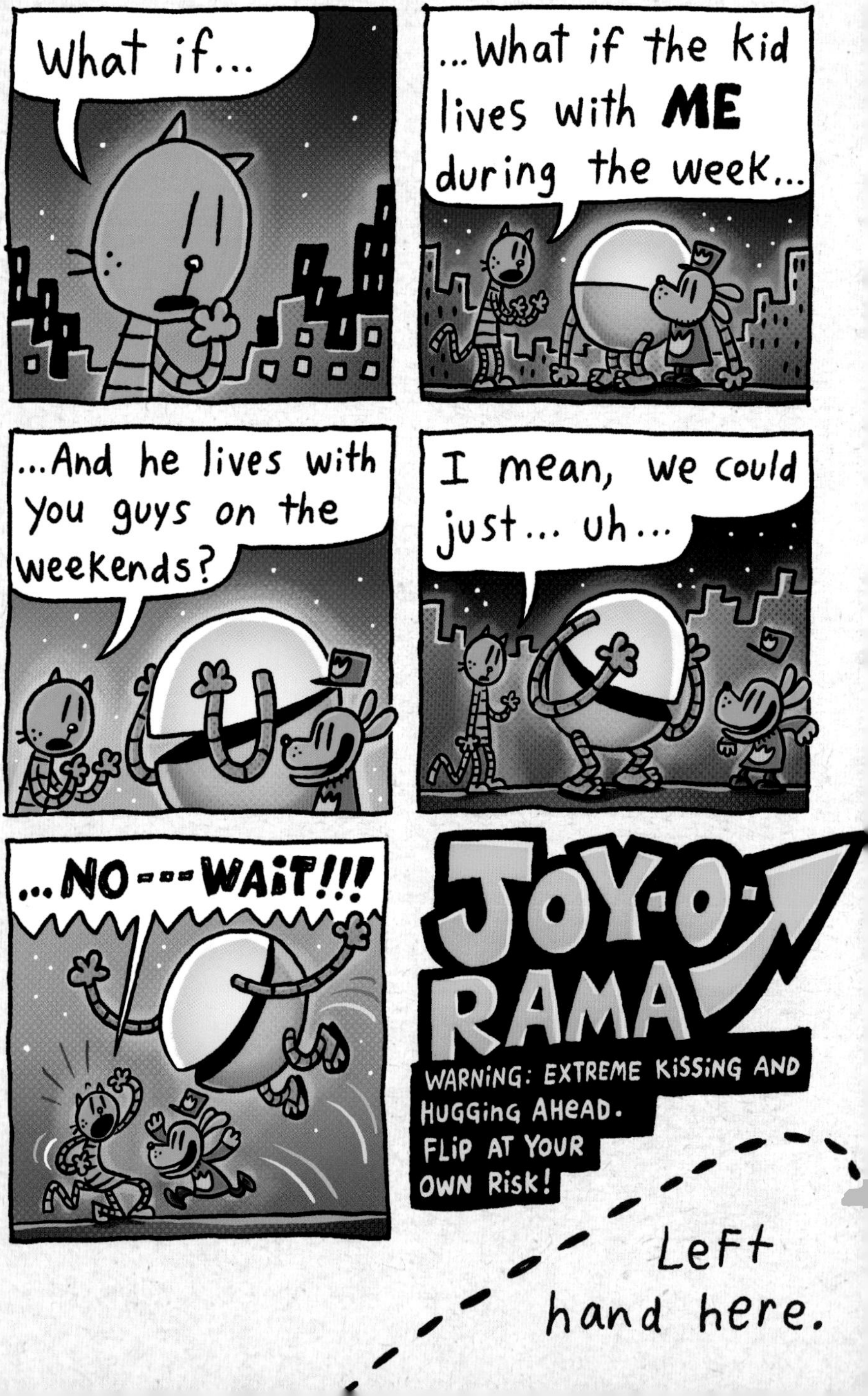
What if...
...What if the kid lives with **ME** during the week...
...And he lives with you guys on the weekends?
I mean, we could just... uh...
...NO---WAIT!!!
JOY-O-RAMA
WARNING: EXTREME KISSING AND HUGGING AHEAD. FLIP AT YOUR OWN RISK!
Left hand here.

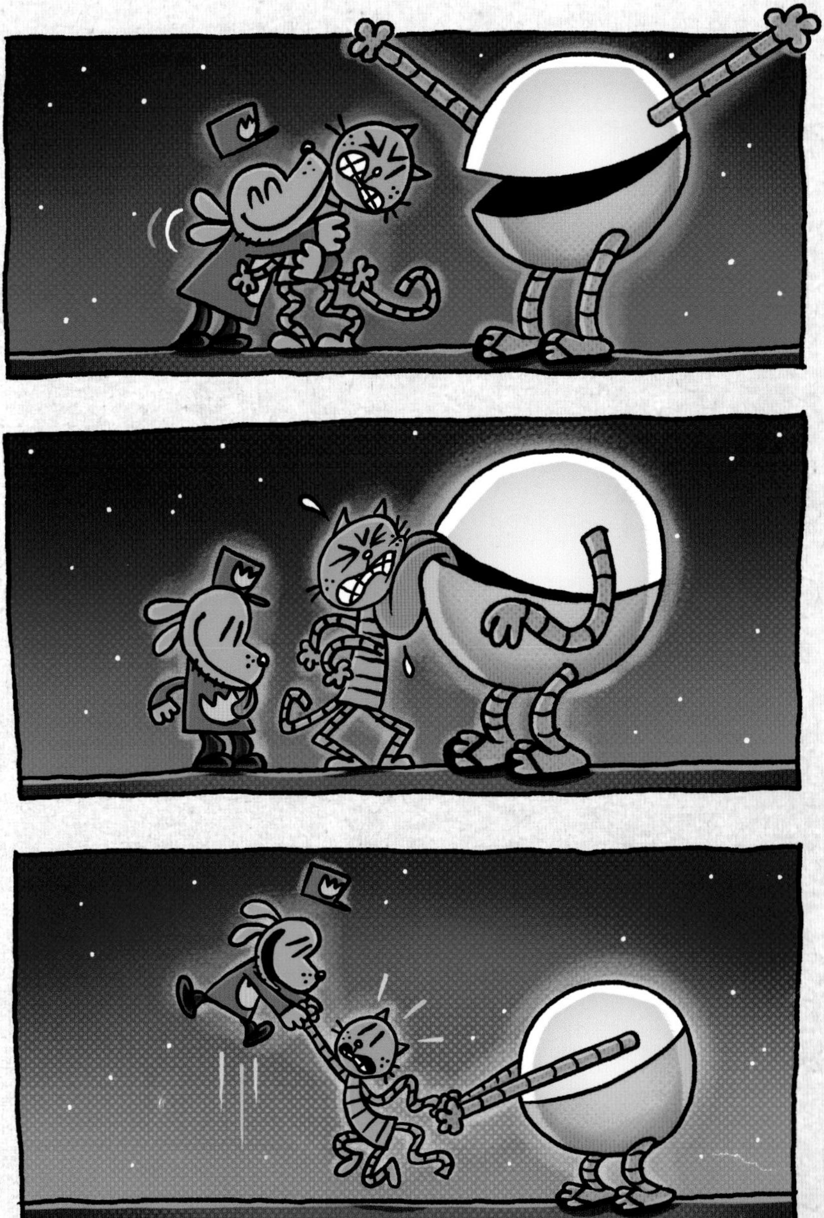

Right Thumb here.

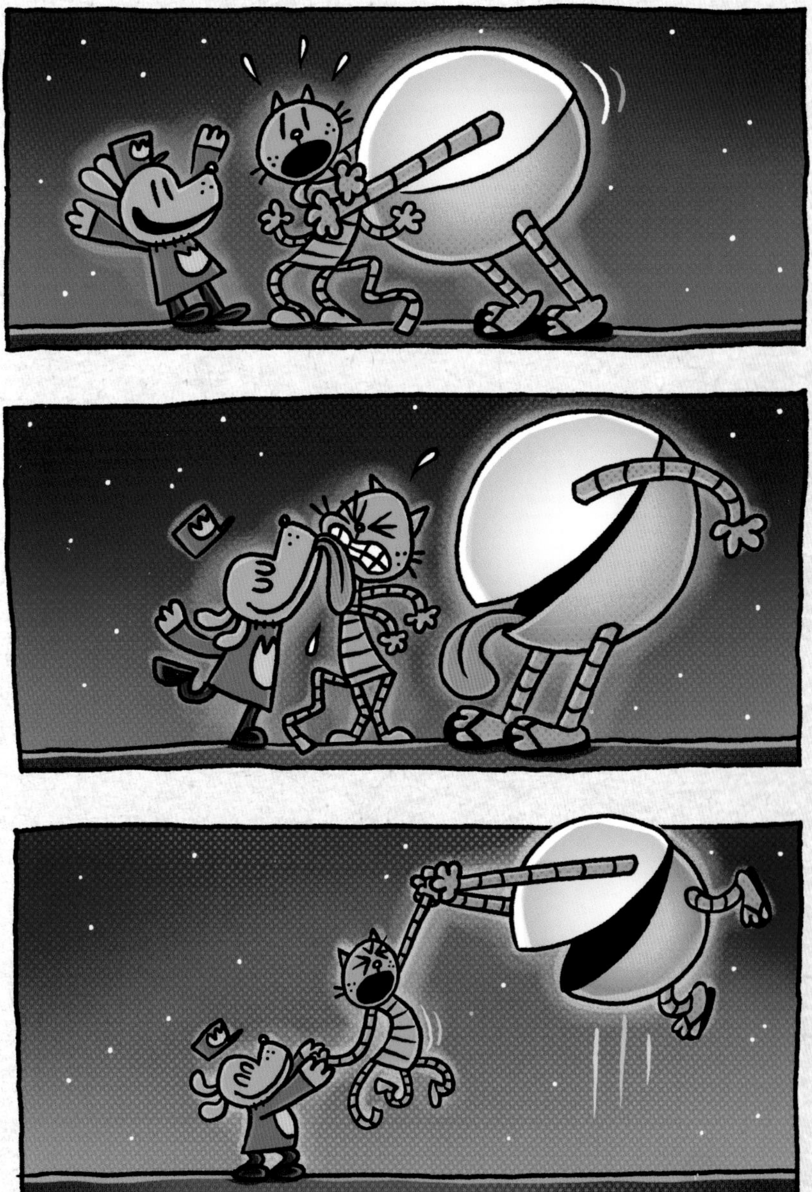

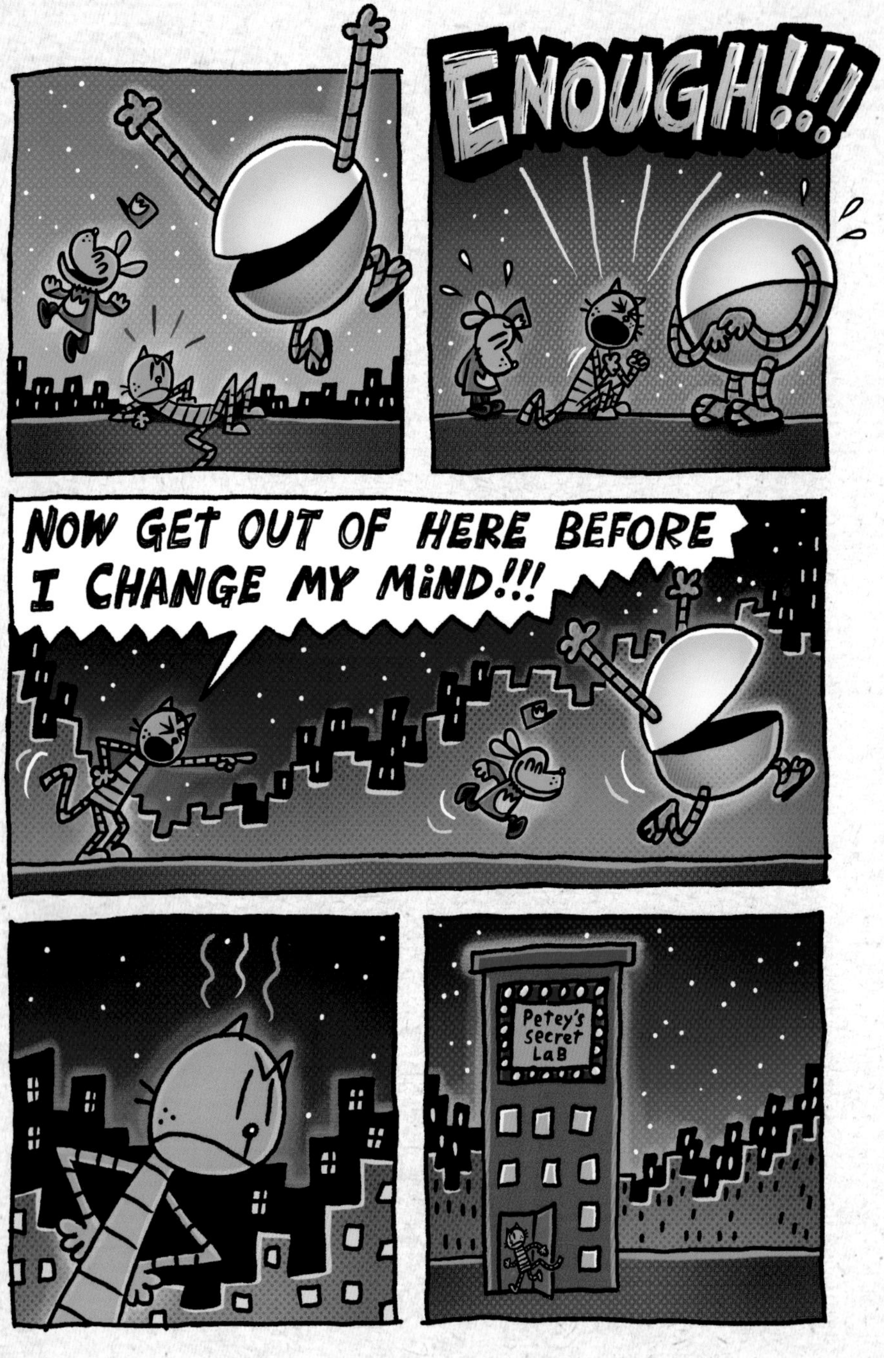
ENOUGH!!!
NOW GET OUT OF HERE BEFORE I CHANGE MY MIND!!!
Petey's Secret LaB

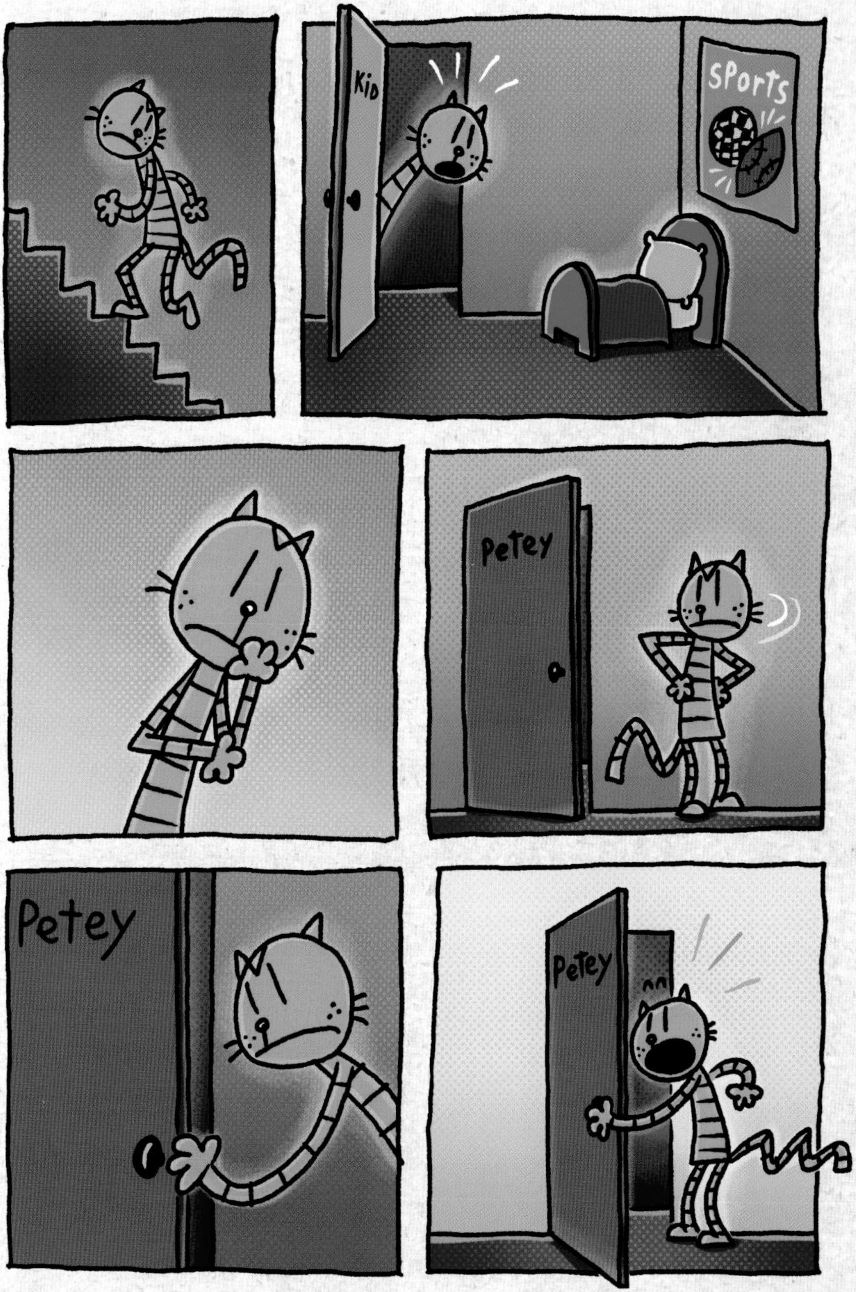
Kid
SPorts
Petey
Petey
Petey

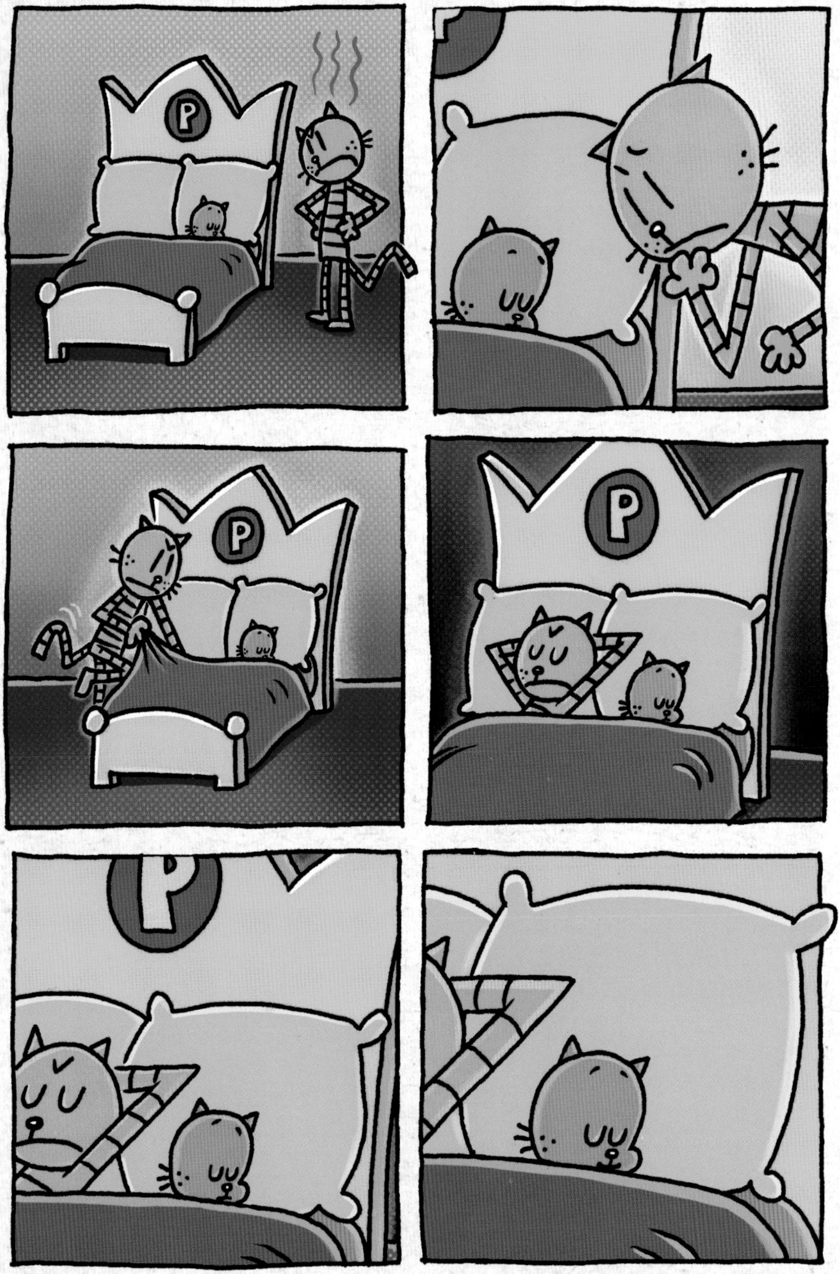

CHAPTER 6

A Buncha Stuff That Happened Next

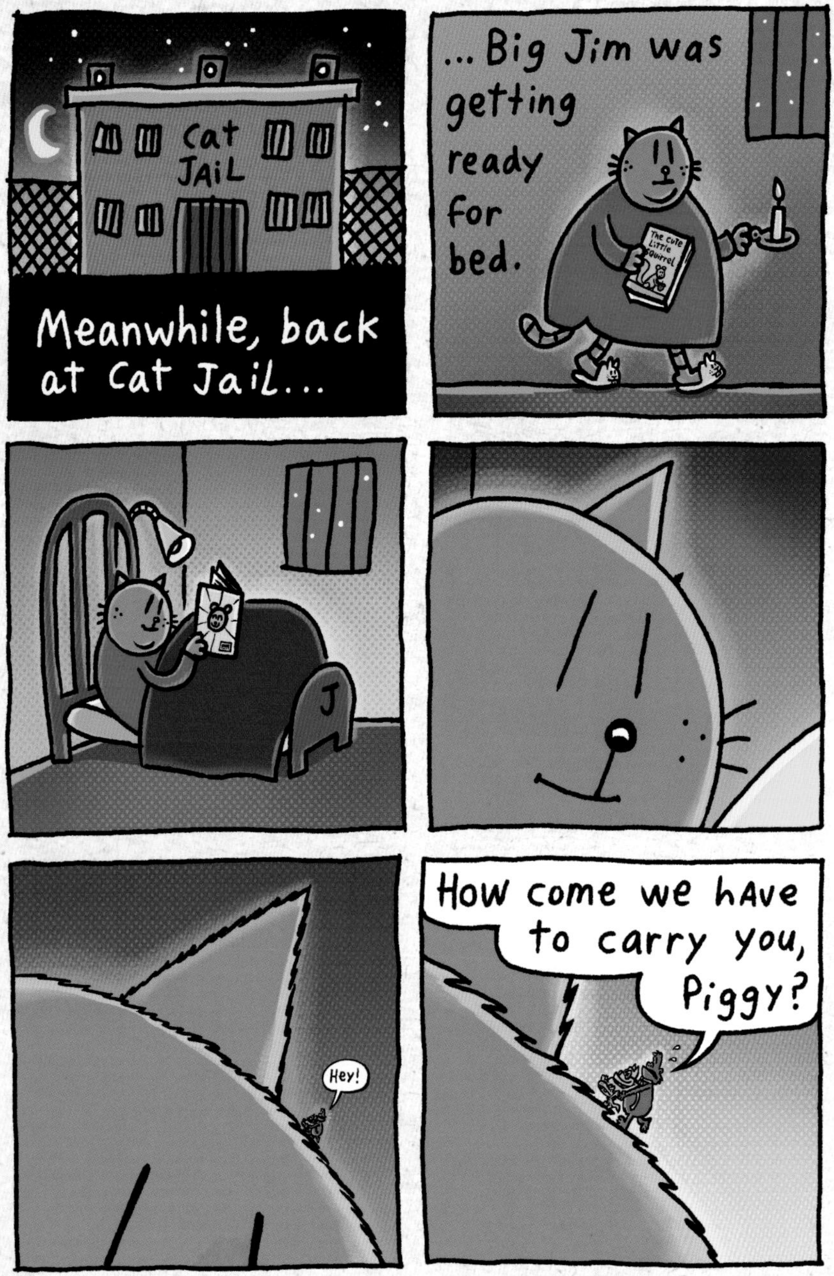
CAT JAIL
Meanwhile, back at Cat Jail...
...Big Jim was getting ready for bed.
The Cute Little Squirrel
Hey!
How come we have to carry you, Piggy?

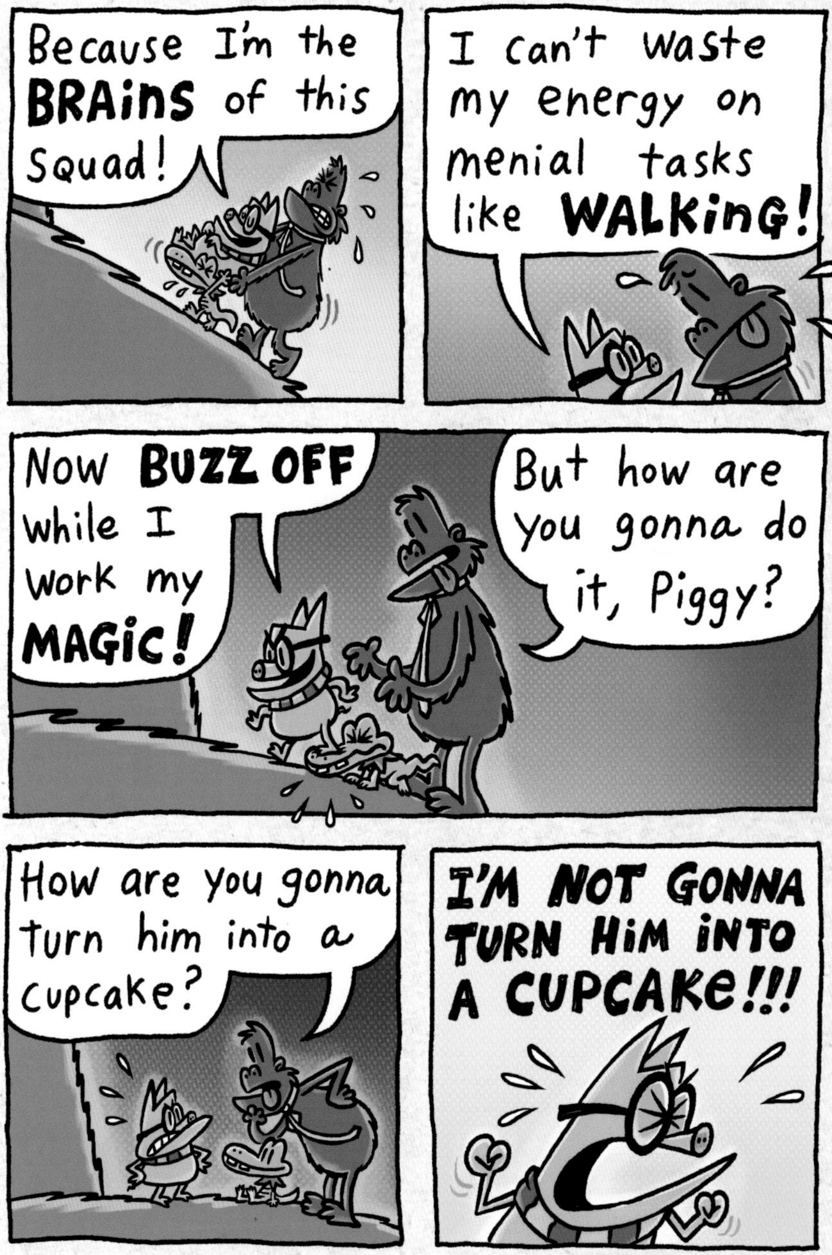
Because I'm the BRAINS of this Squad!
I can't waste my energy on menial tasks like WALKING!
Now BUZZ OFF while I work my MAGIC!
But how are you gonna do it, Piggy?
How are you gonna turn him into a cupcake?
I'M NOT GONNA TURN HIM INTO A CUPCAKE!!!

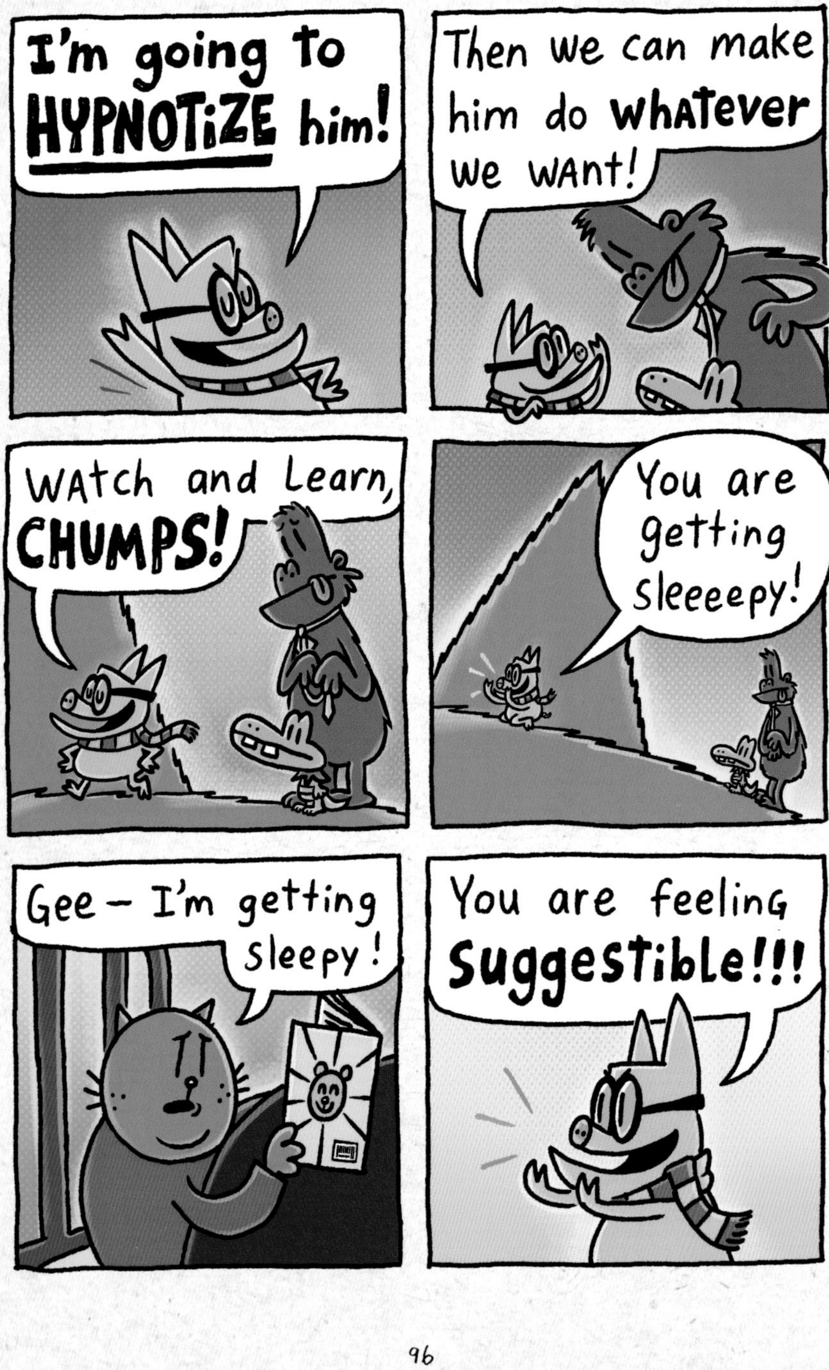
I'm going to HYPNOTIZE him!
Then we can make him do WHATEVER we WANT!
WATCH and Learn, CHUMPS!
You are getting sleeeepy!
Gee — I'm getting sleepy!
You are feeling SUGGESTIBLE!!!

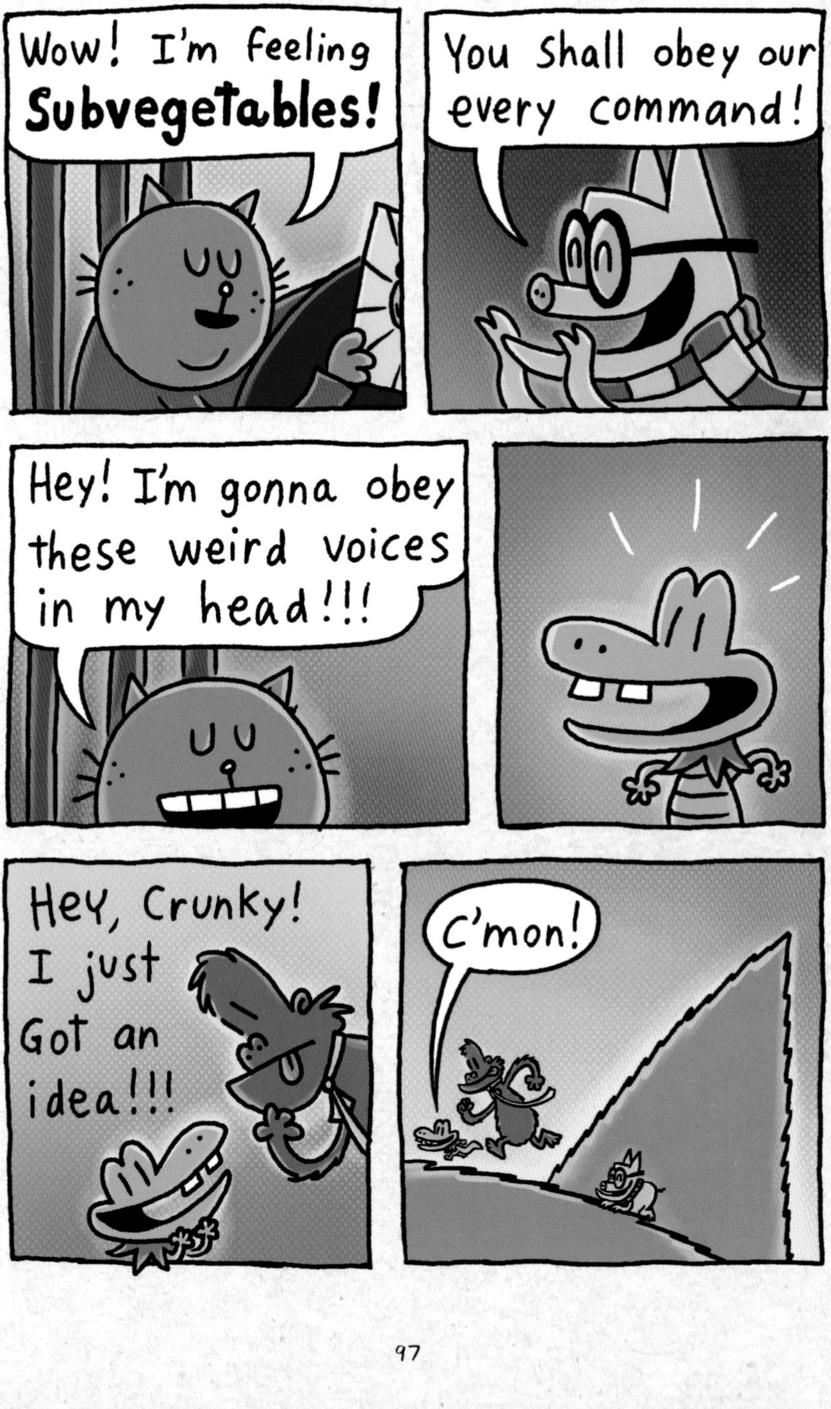
Wow! I'm feeling **Subvegetables!**
You Shall obey our every command!
Hey! I'm gonna obey these weird voices in my head!!!
Hey, Crunky! I just Got an idea!!!
C'mon!

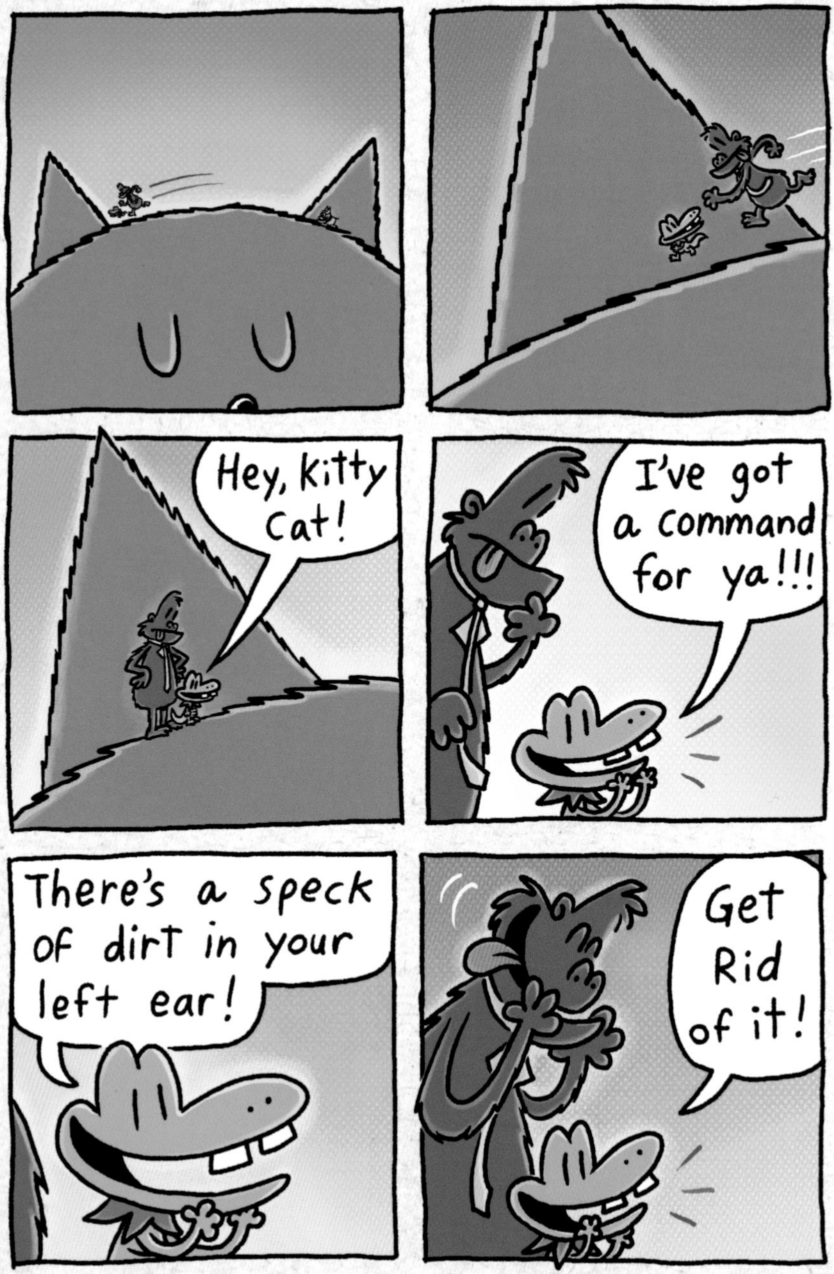
Hey, kitty cat!
I've got a command for ya!!!
There's a speck of dirt in your left ear!
Get Rid of it!

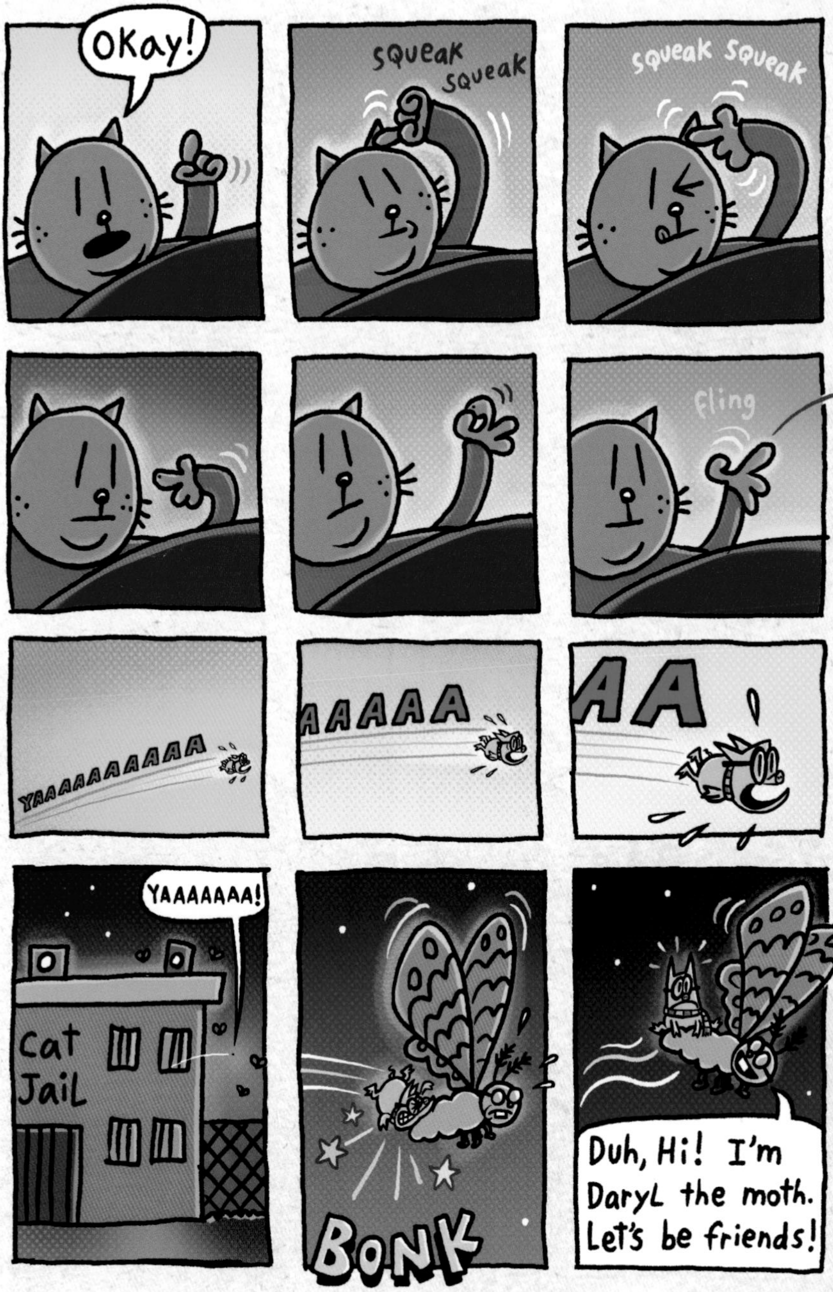
OKay!
SQueak SQueak
SQueak SQueak
fling
YAAAAAAAAAAA
AAAAA
AA
YAAAAAAA!
Cat Jail
BONK
Duh, Hi! I'm DaryL the moth. Let's be friends!

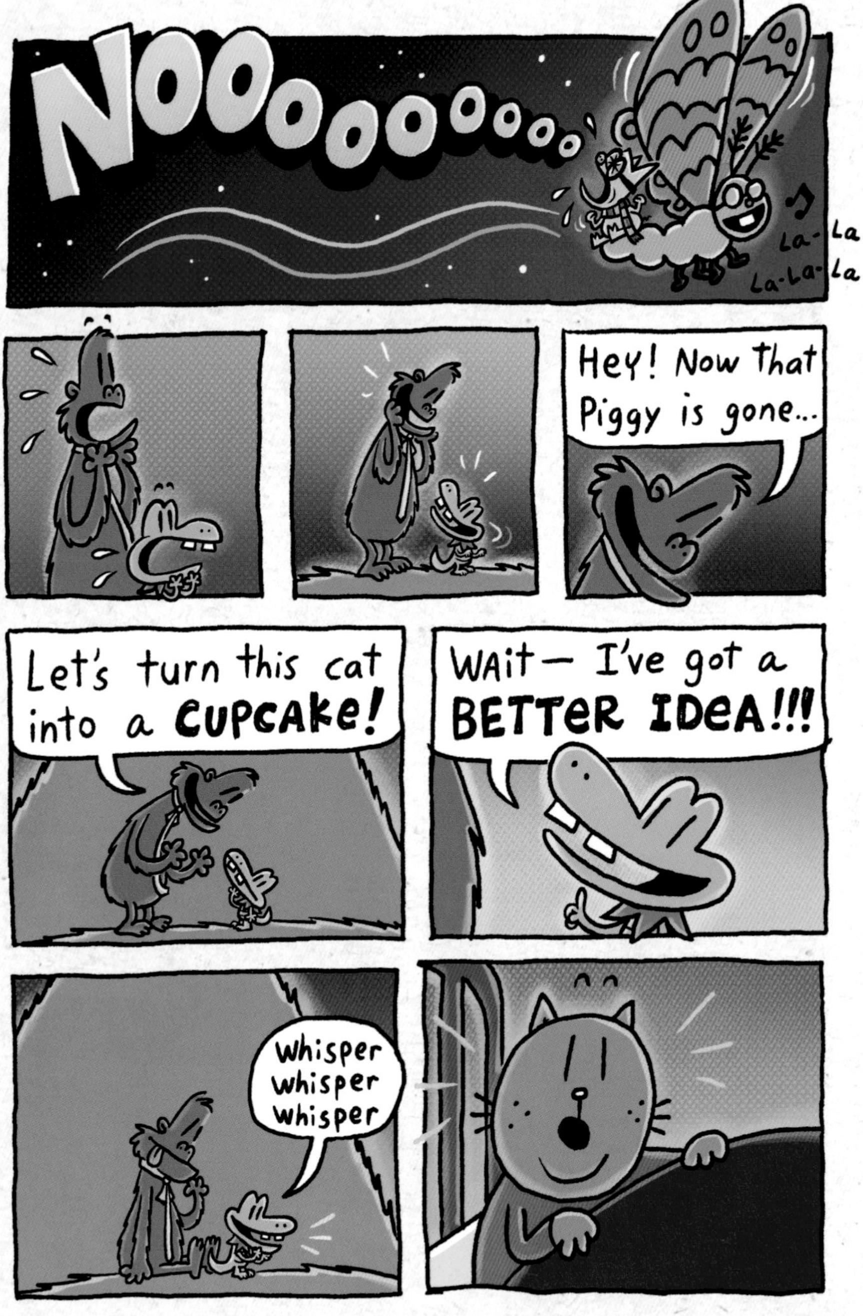
NOOOOOOOOOO
La-La
La-La-La
Hey! Now that Piggy is gone...
Let's turn this cat into a CUPCAKE!
WAIT— I've got a BETTER IDEA!!!
whisper whisper whisper

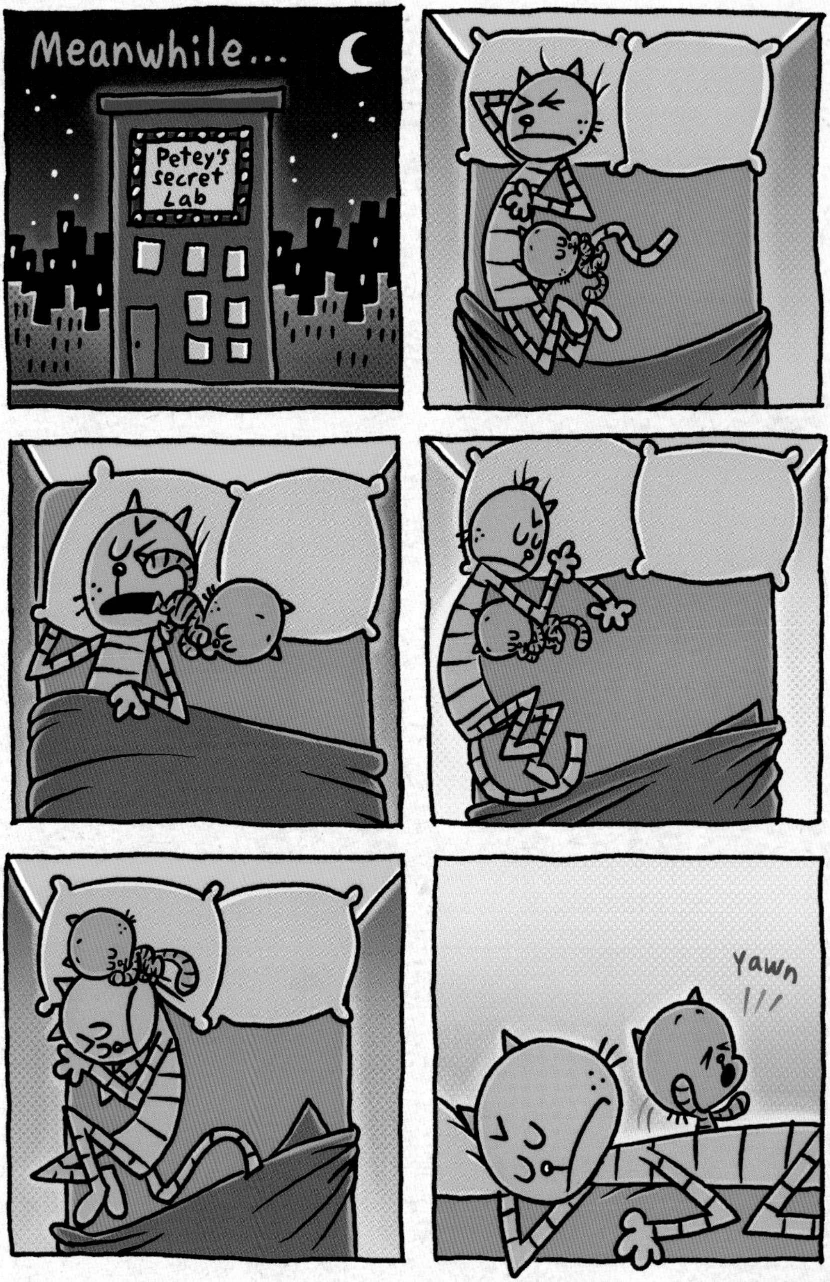
Meanwhile...
Petey's secret Lab
Yawn

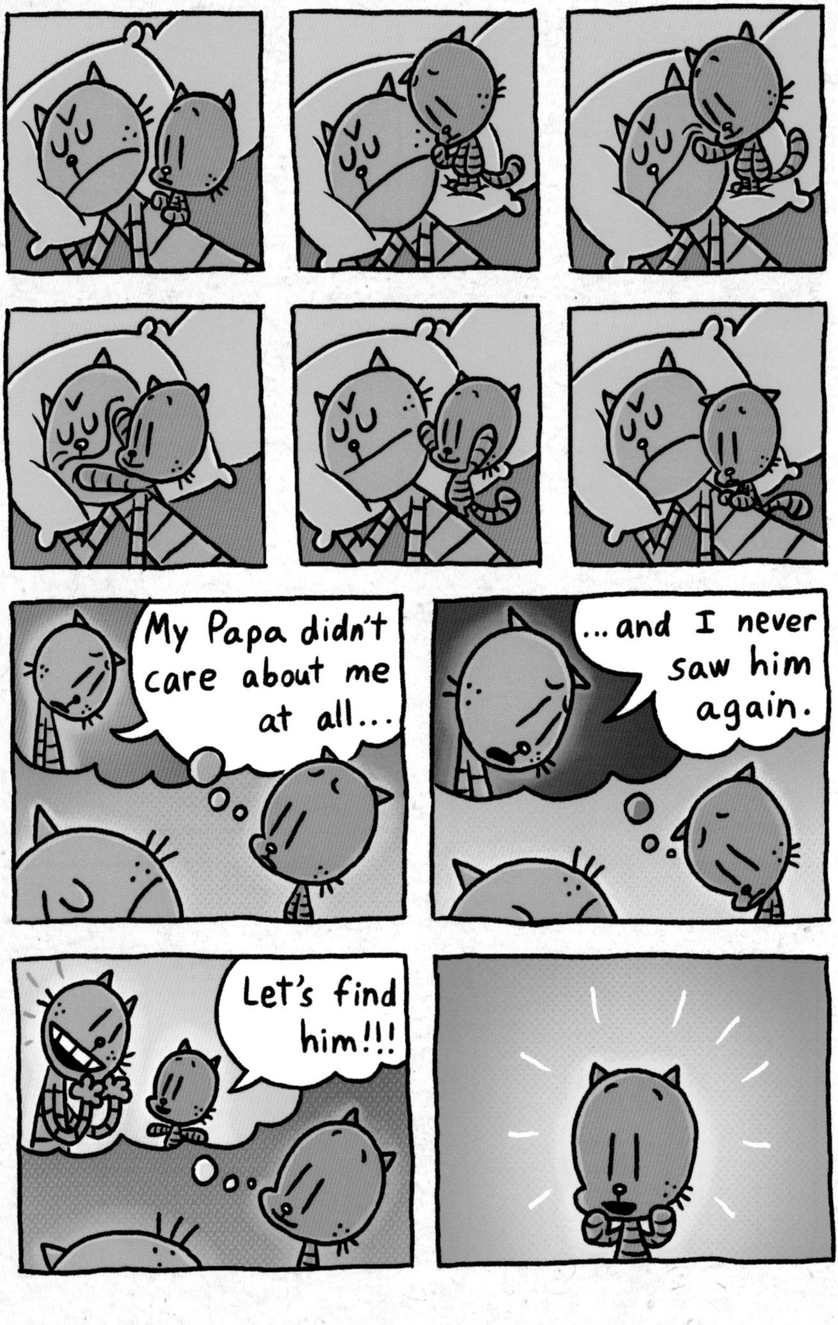
My Papa didn't care about me at all...
...and I never saw him again.
Let's find him!!!

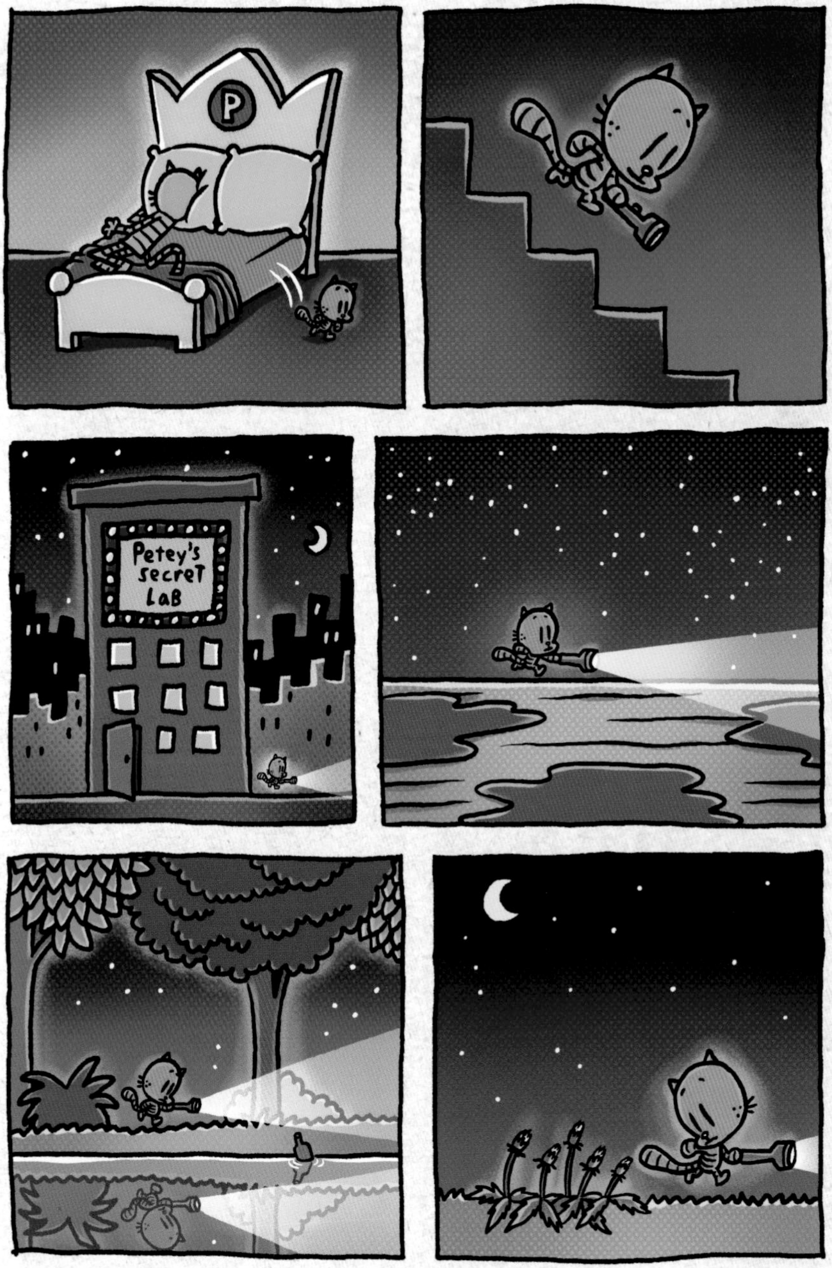
P
Petey's
secret
Lab

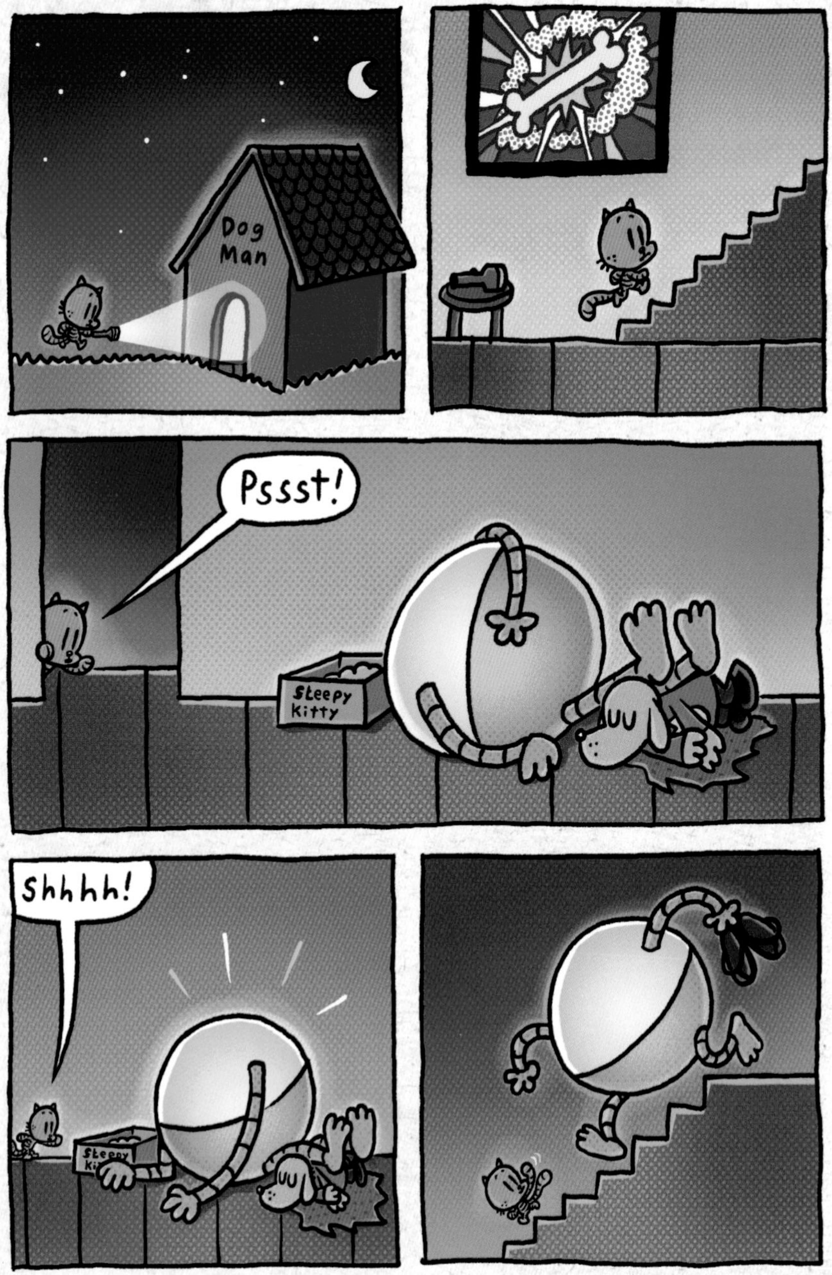
Dog Man
Pssst!
Sleepy Kitty
Shhhh!

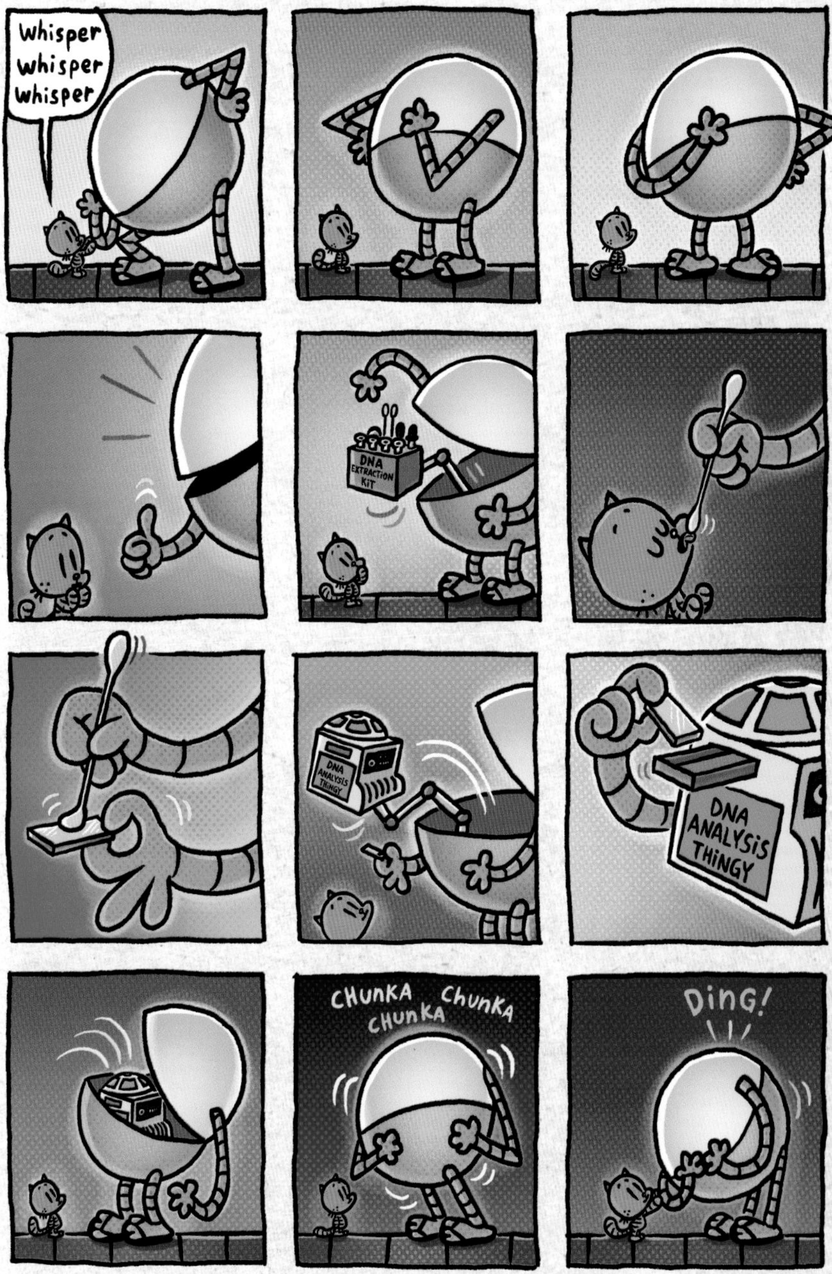

whisper whisper whisper
DNA EXTRACTION KIT
DNA ANALYSIS THINGY
DNA ANALYSIS THINGY
CHUNKA CHUNKA CHUNKA
DING!

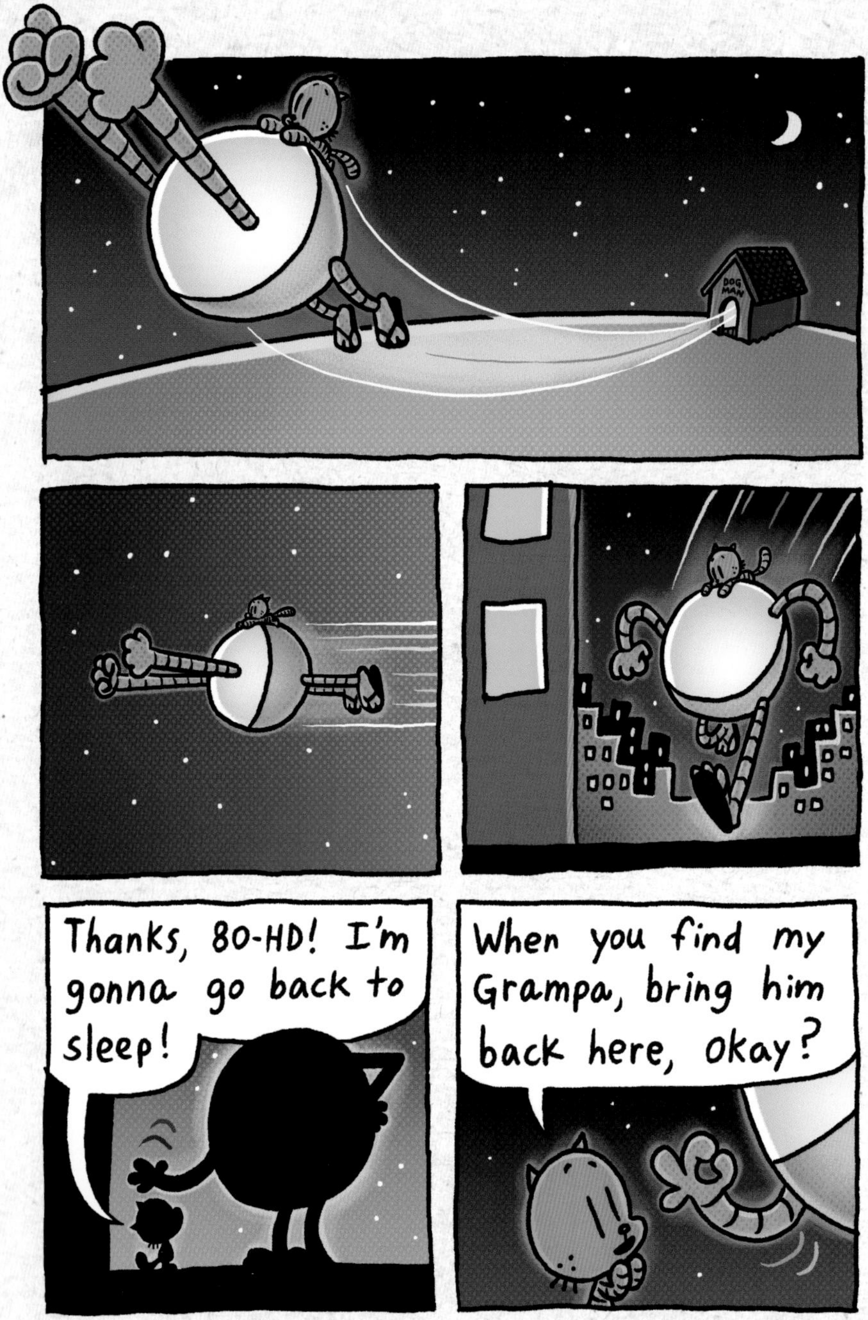
DOG MAN
Thanks, 80-HD! I'm gonna go back to sleep!
When you find my Grampa, bring him back here, okay?

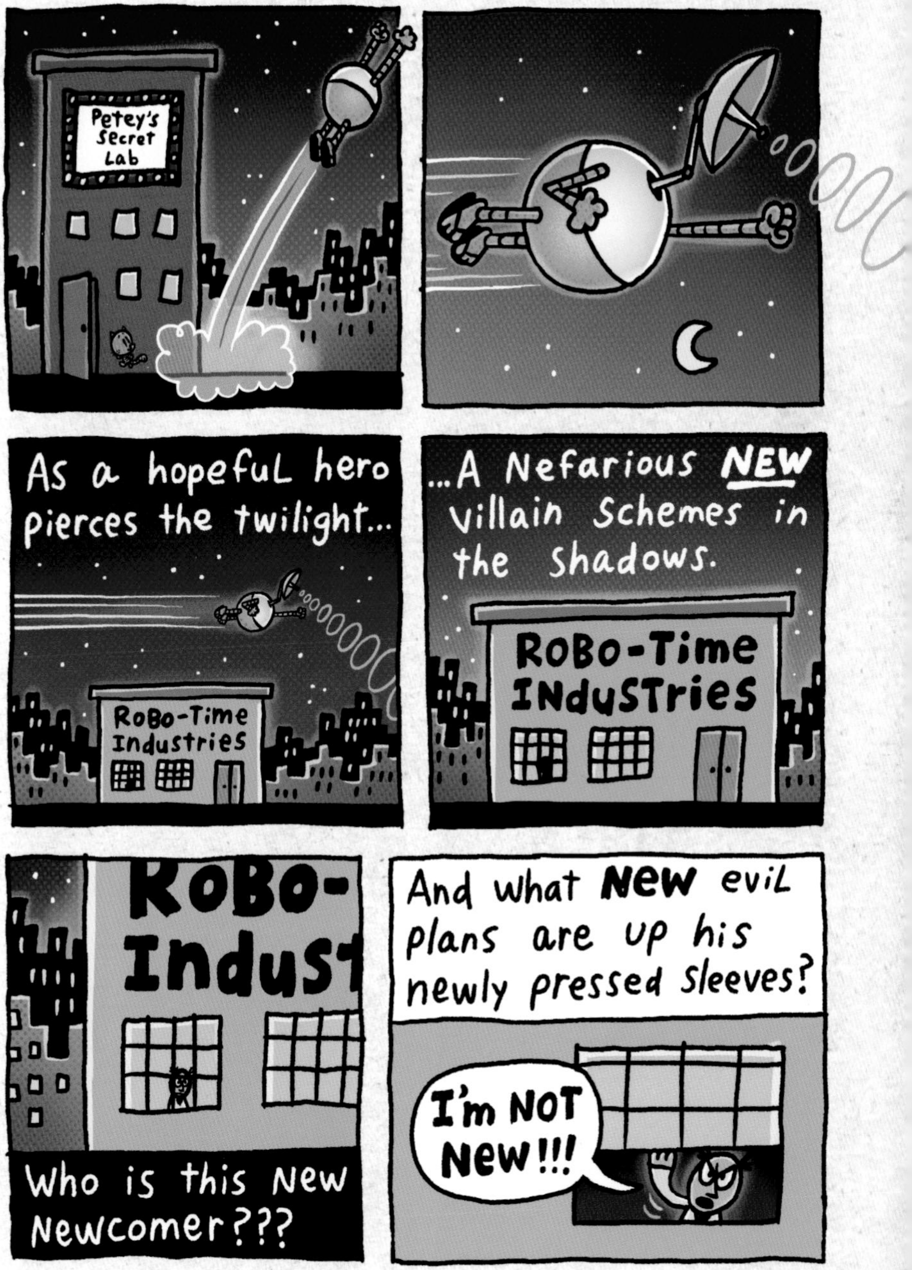

Petey's Secret Lab
As a hopeful hero pierces the twilight...
RoBo-Time Industries
...A Nefarious NEW villain Schemes in the Shadows.
RoBo-Time INduSTries
RoBo-
Indust
Who is this New Newcomer???
And what New eviL plans are up his newly pressed sleeves?
I'm NOT NEW!!!

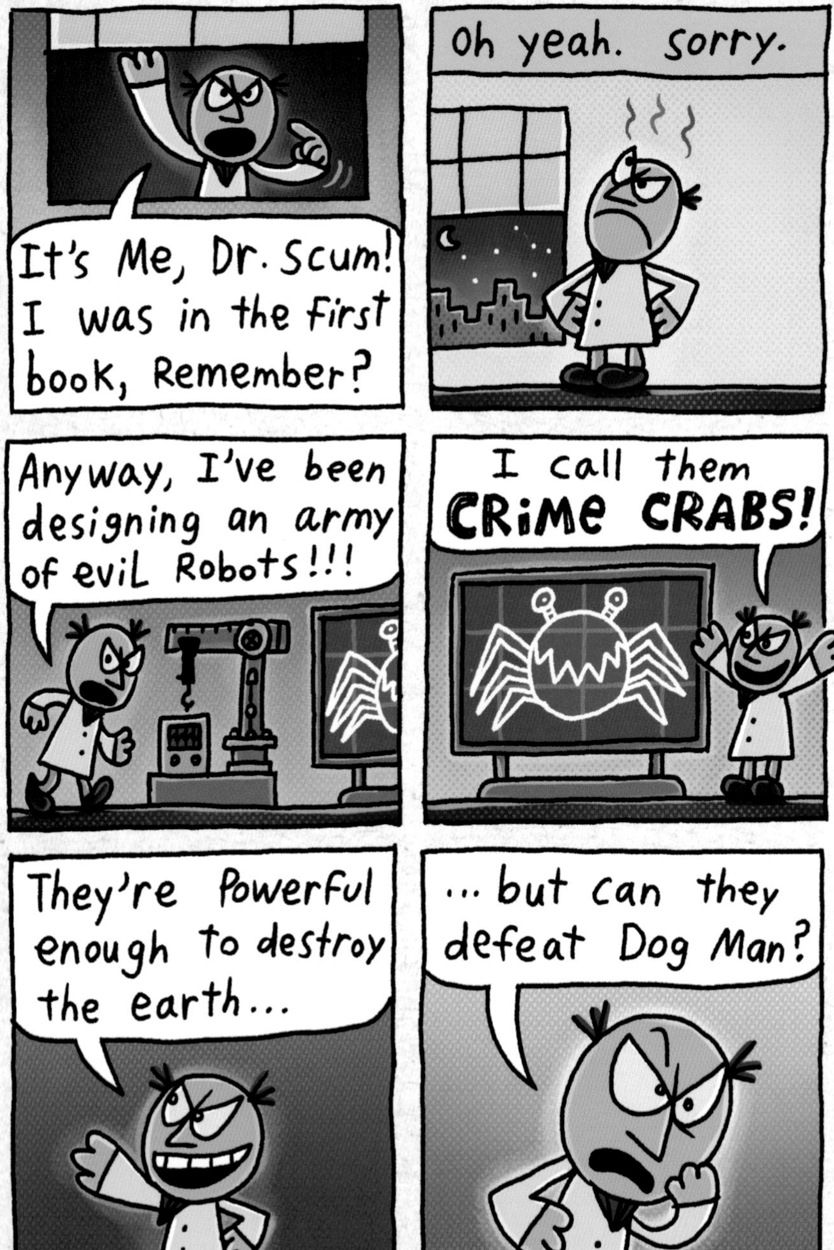
It's Me, Dr. Scum! I was in the first book, Remember?
Oh yeah. sorry.
Anyway, I've been designing an army of evil Robots!!!
I call them CRIME CRABS!
They're Powerful enough to destroy the earth...
... but can they defeat Dog Man?

CHAPTER 7

Guess Who's Coming to Breakfast!

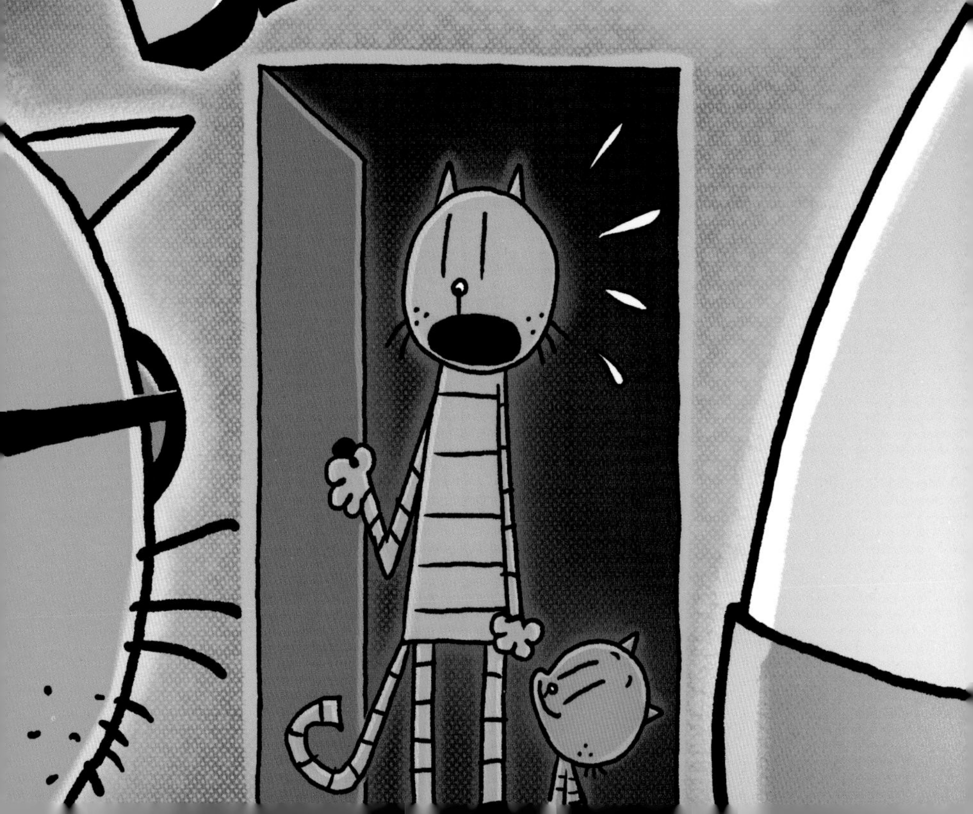

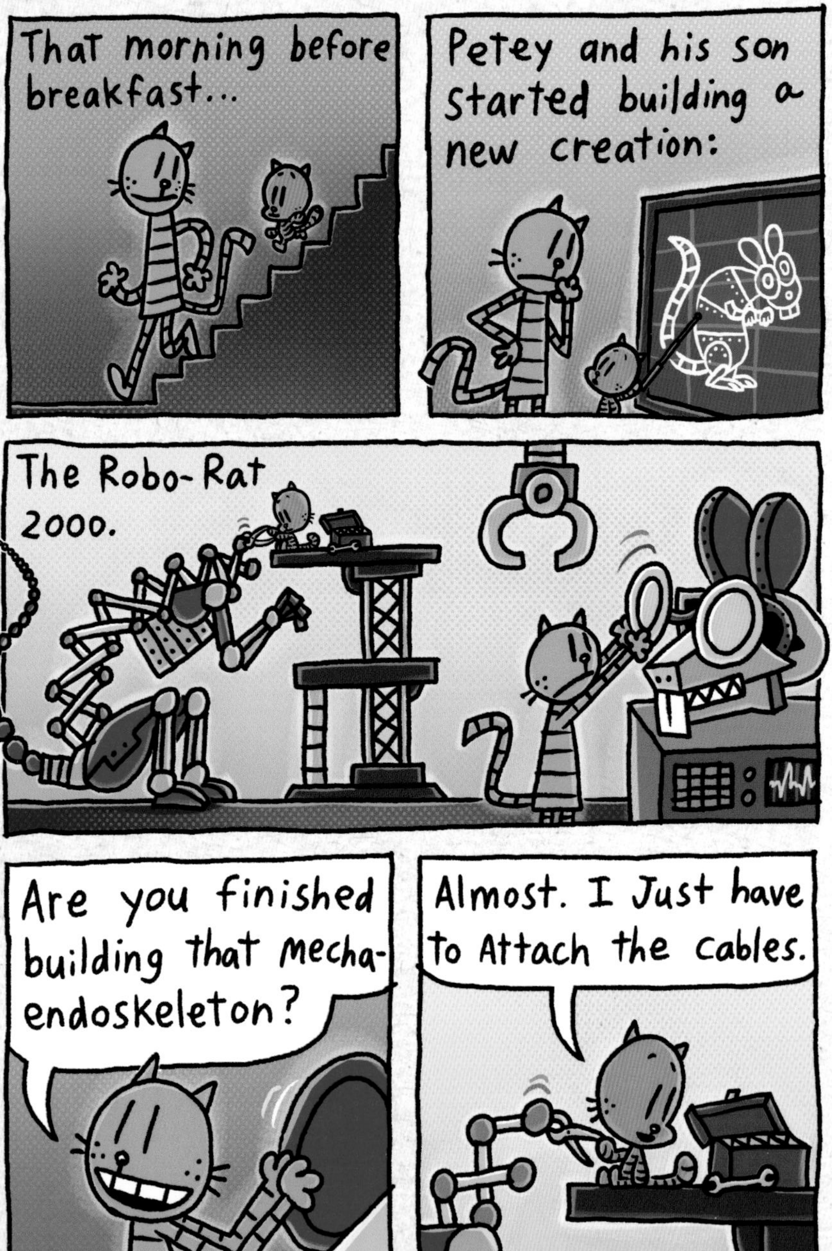
That morning before breakfast...
Petey and his son started building a new creation:
The Robo-Rat 2000.
Are you finished building that mecha-endoskeleton?
Almost. I just have to attach the cables.

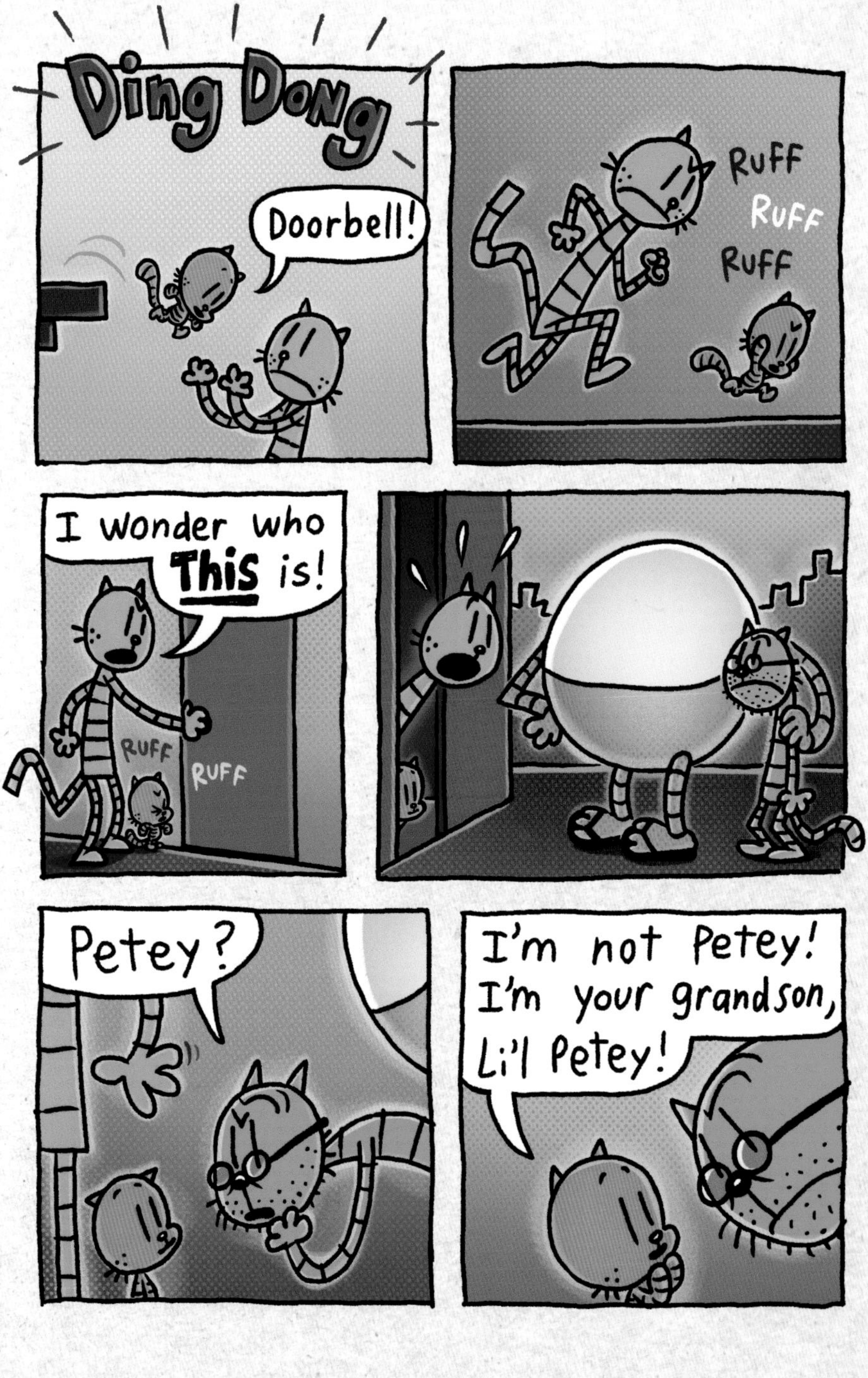
Ding Dong
Doorbell!
RUFF
RUFF
RUFF
I wonder who THIS is!
RUFF
RUFF
Petey?
I'm not Petey! I'm your grandson, Li'l Petey!

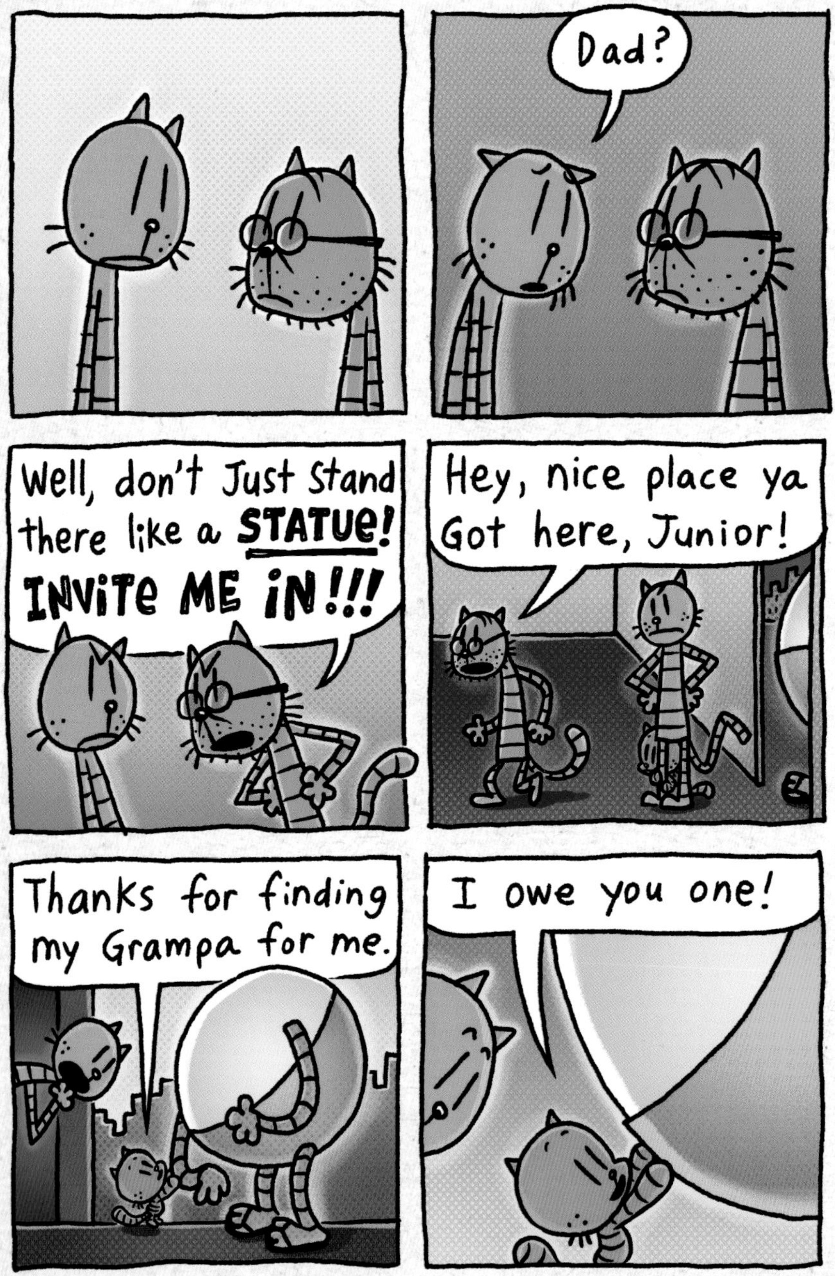
Dad?
Well, don't Just Stand there like a STATUE! INVITE ME IN!!!
Hey, nice place ya Got here, Junior!
Thanks for finding my Grampa for me.
I owe you one!

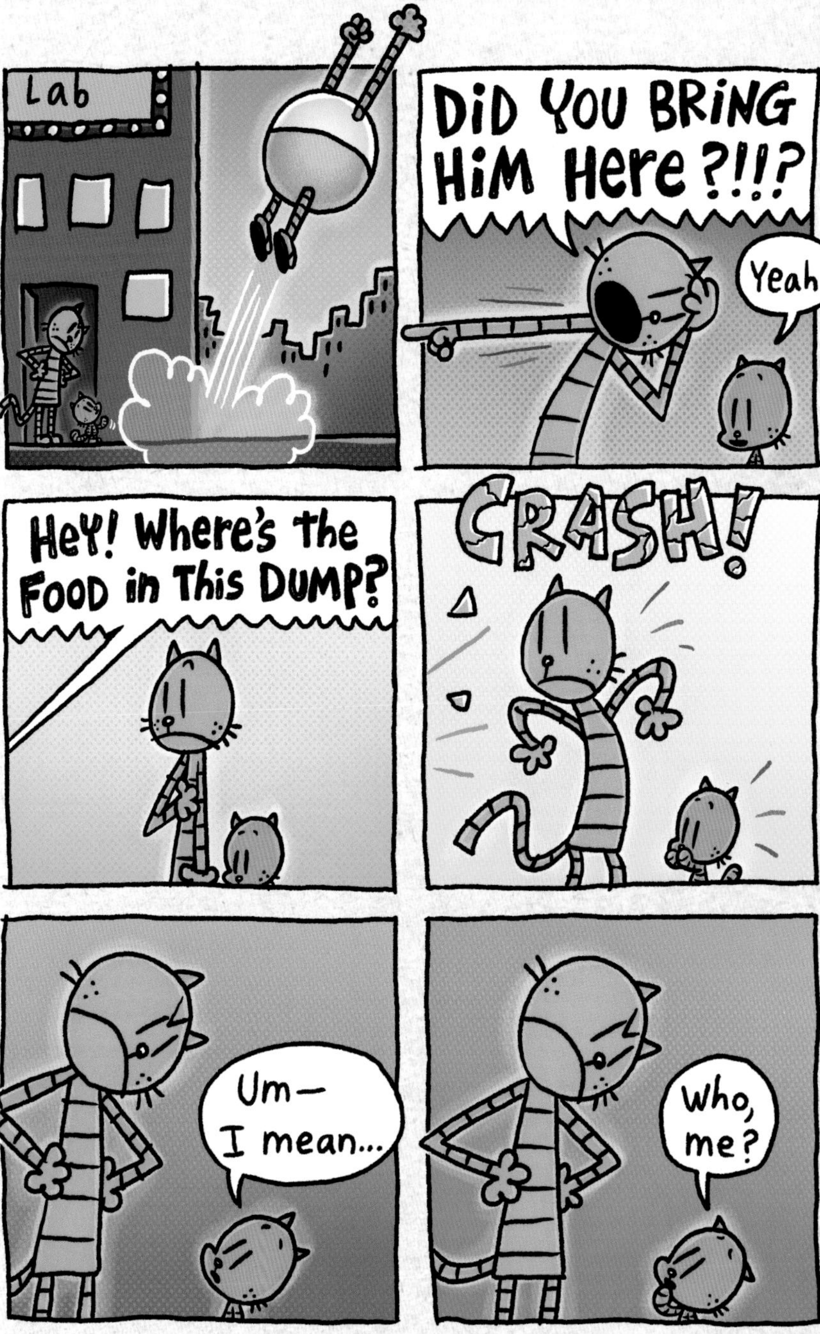
Lab
DID YOU BRING HIM Here?!!?
Yeah.
Hey! Where's the Food in This DUMP?
CRASH!
Um— I mean...
Who, me?

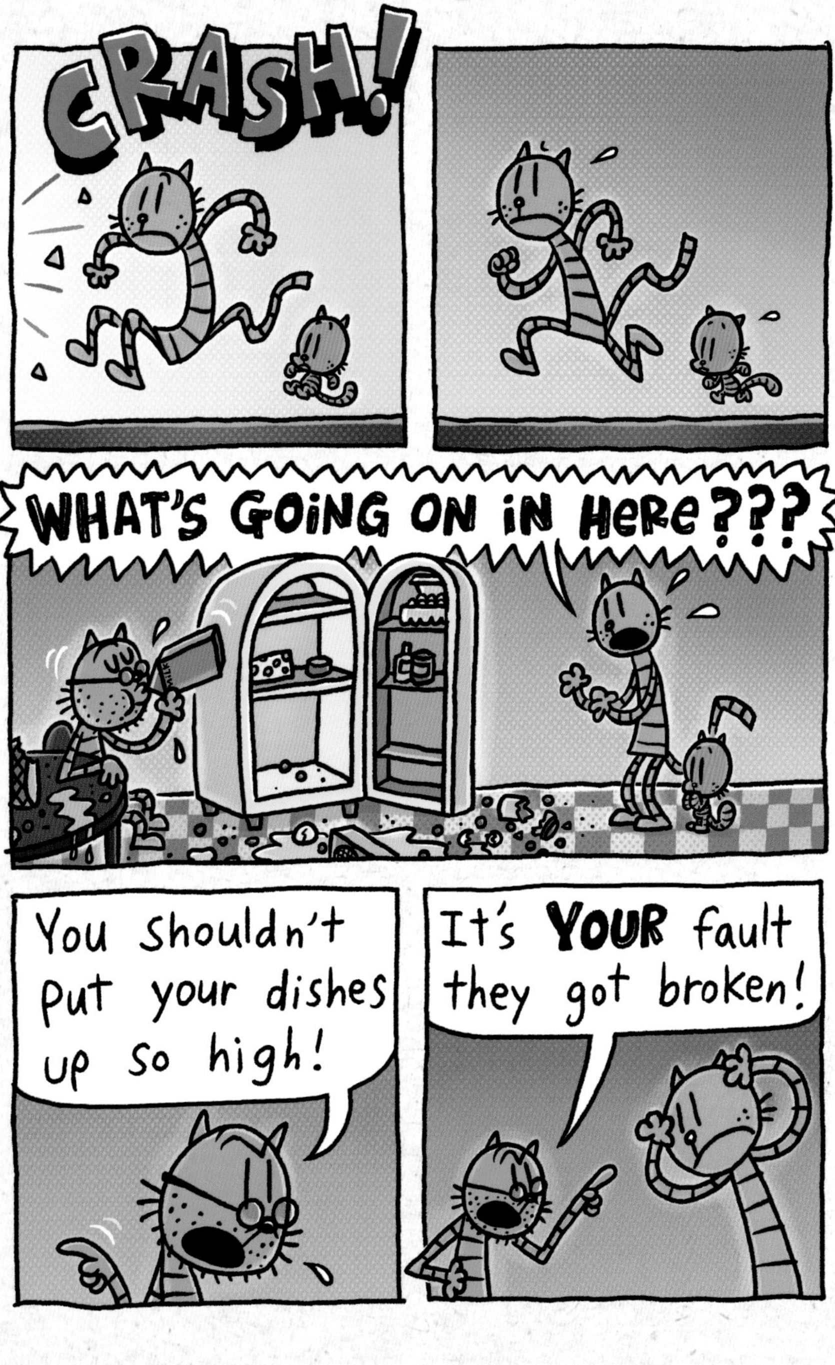
CRASH!
WHAT'S GOING ON IN HERE???
MILK
You shouldn't put your dishes up so high!
It's YOUR fault they got broken!

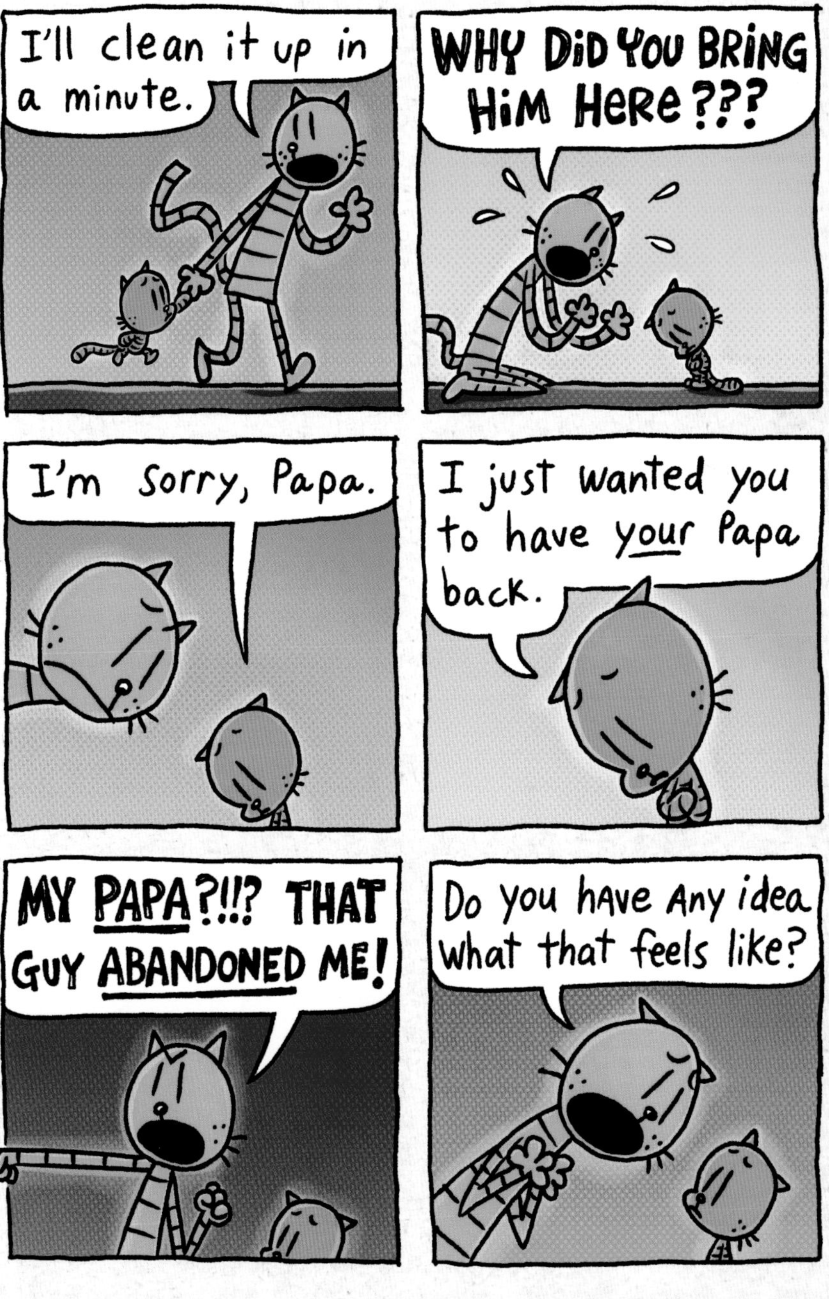
I'll clean it up in a minute.
WHY DID YOU BRING HIM HERE???
I'm sorry, Papa.
I just wanted you to have your Papa back.
MY PAPA?!!? THAT GUY ABANDONED ME!
Do you have any idea what that feels like?

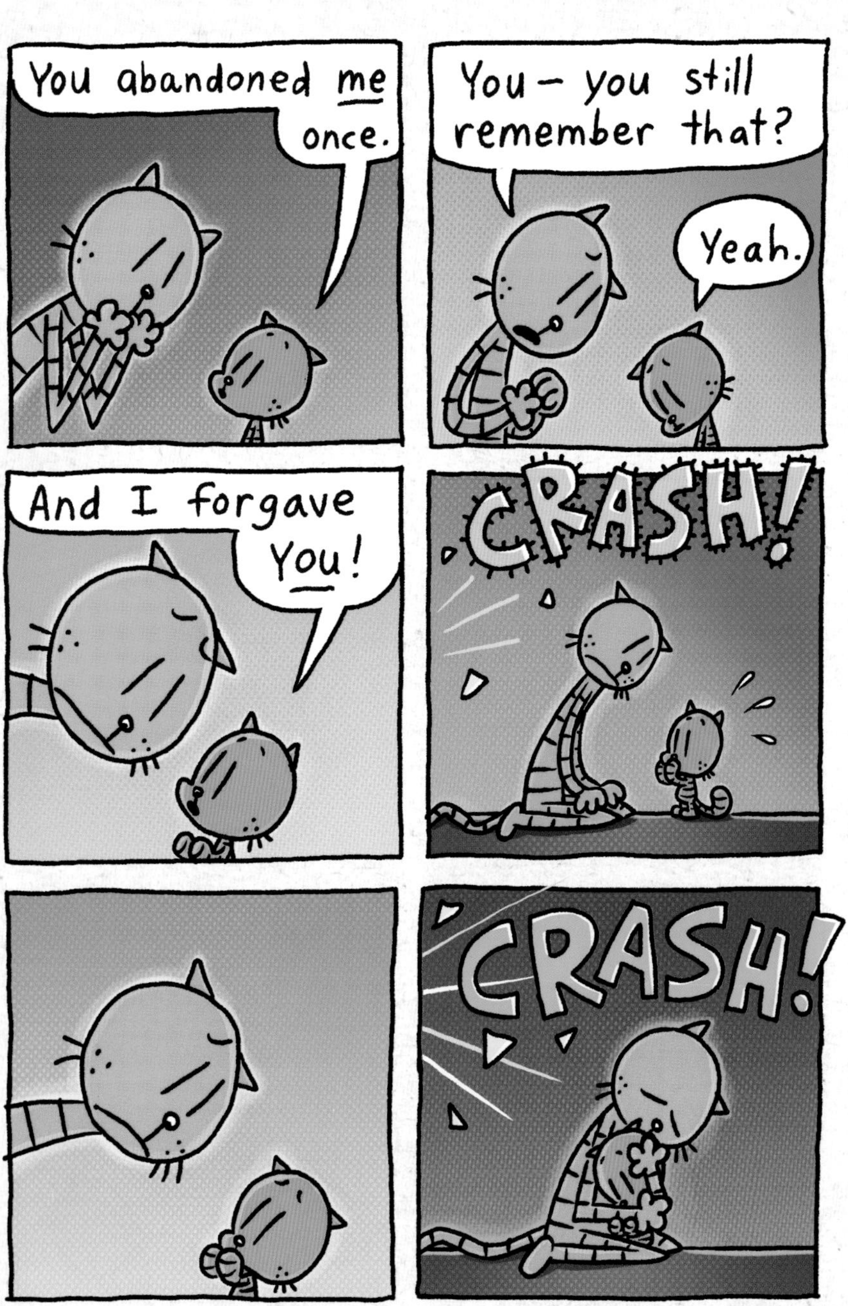
You abandoned me once.
You – you still remember that?
Yeah.
And I forgave You!
CRASH!
CRASH!

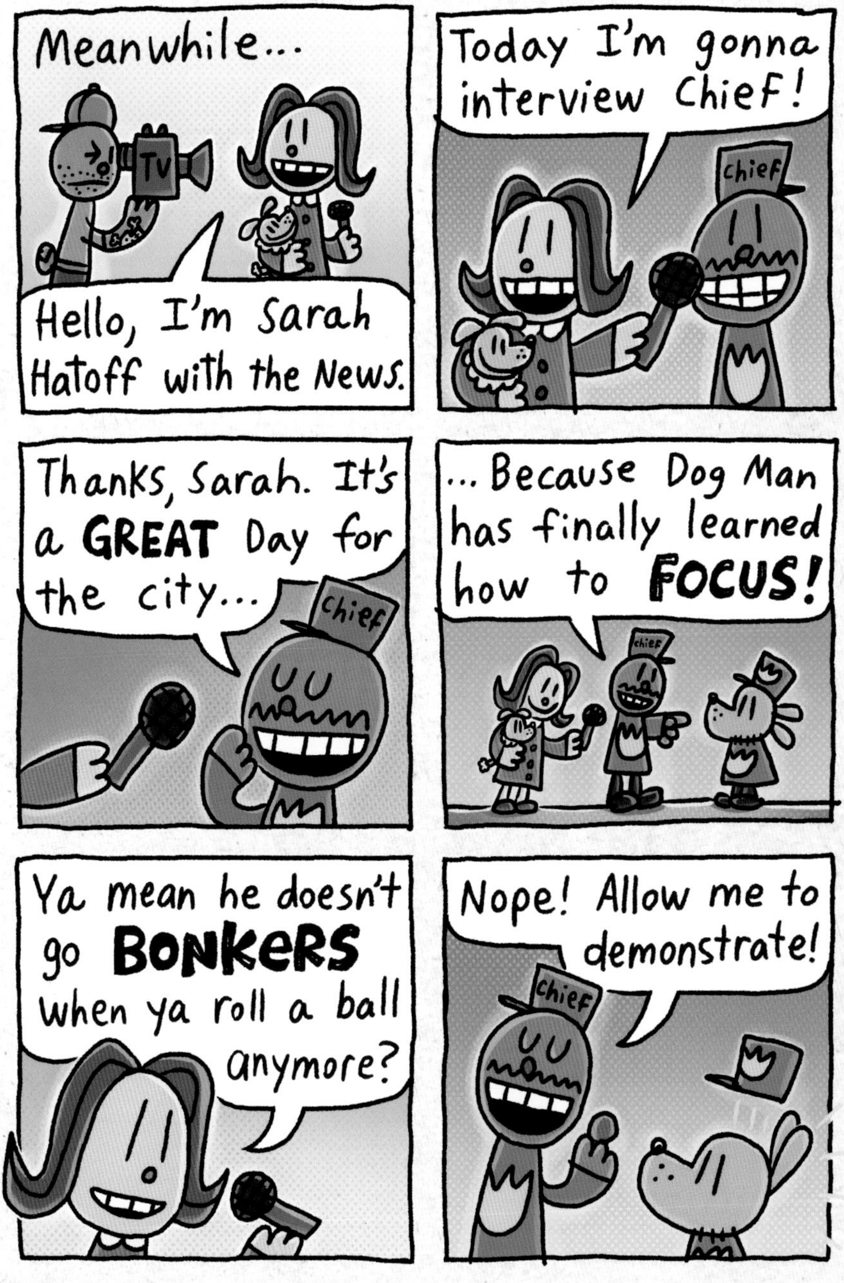
Meanwhile...
TV
Hello, I'm Sarah Hatoff with the News.
Today I'm gonna interview Chief!
Chief
Thanks, Sarah. It's a GREAT Day for the city...
Chief
...Because Dog Man has finally learned how to FOCUS!
Chief
Ya mean he doesn't go BONKERS when ya roll a ball anymore?
Nope! Allow me to demonstrate!
Chief

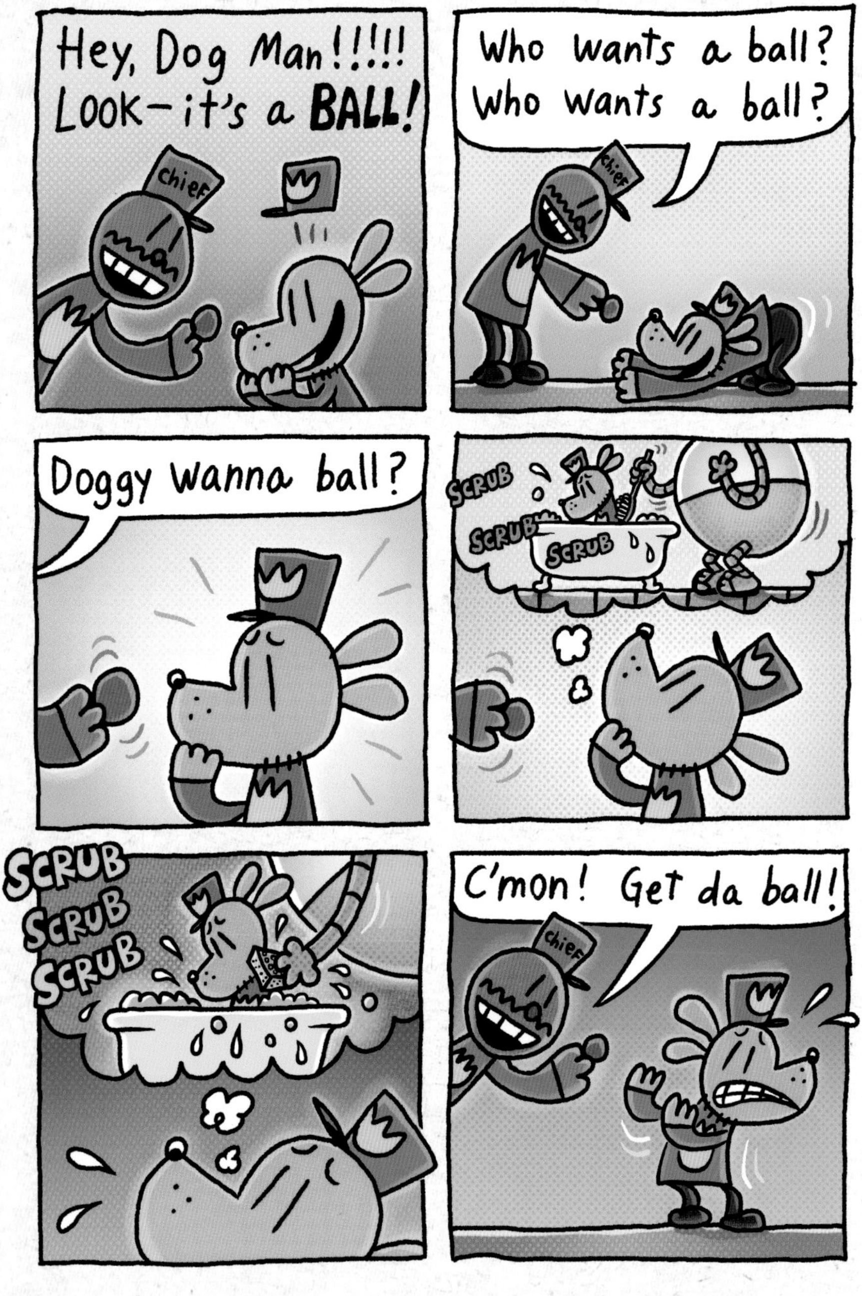
Hey, Dog Man!!!!! LOOK—it's a BALL!
chief
Who wants a ball? Who wants a ball?
chief
Doggy wanna ball?
SCRUB
SCRUB
SCRUB
SCRUB
SCRUB
SCRUB
C'mon! Get da ball!
chief

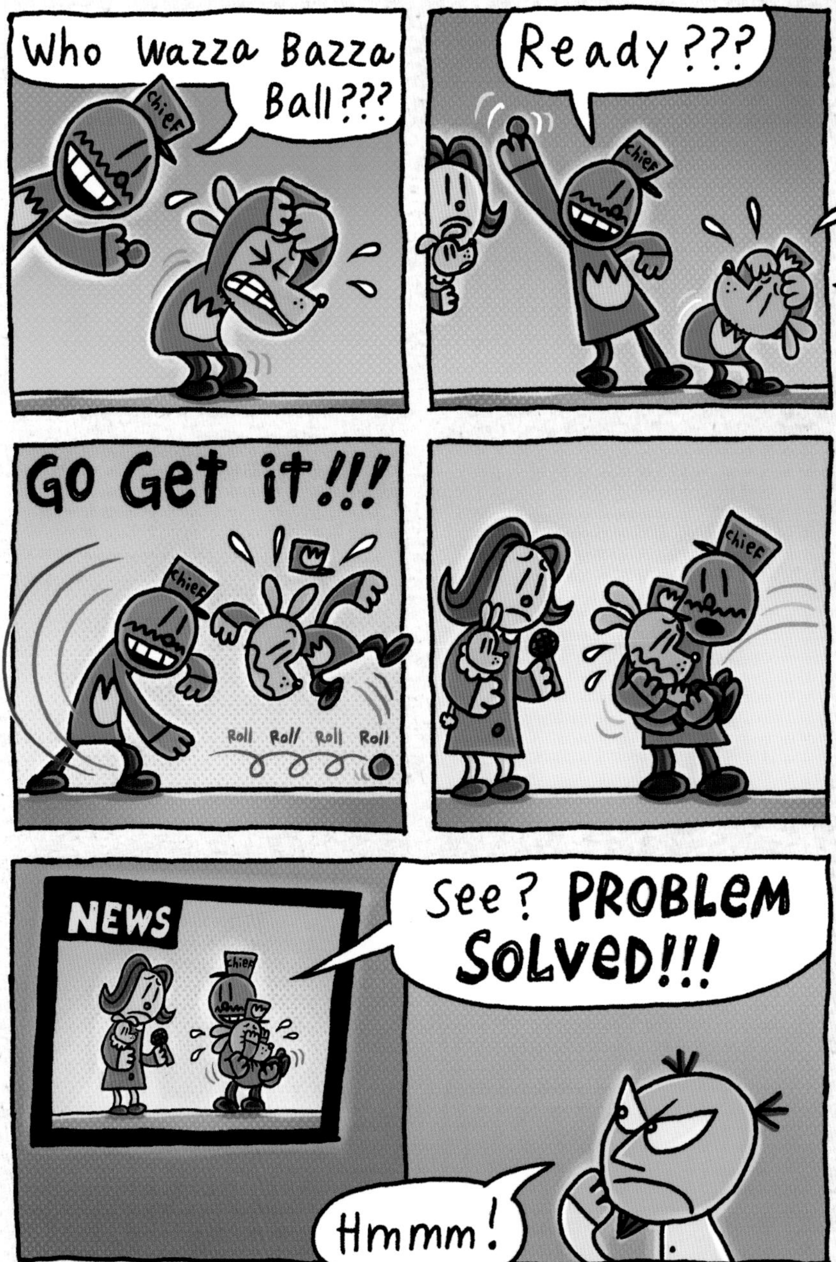
Who Wazza Bazza Ball???
Ready???
chief
Go Get it!!!
Roll Roll Roll Roll
chief
NEWS
See? PROBLEM SOLVED!!!
Hmmm!

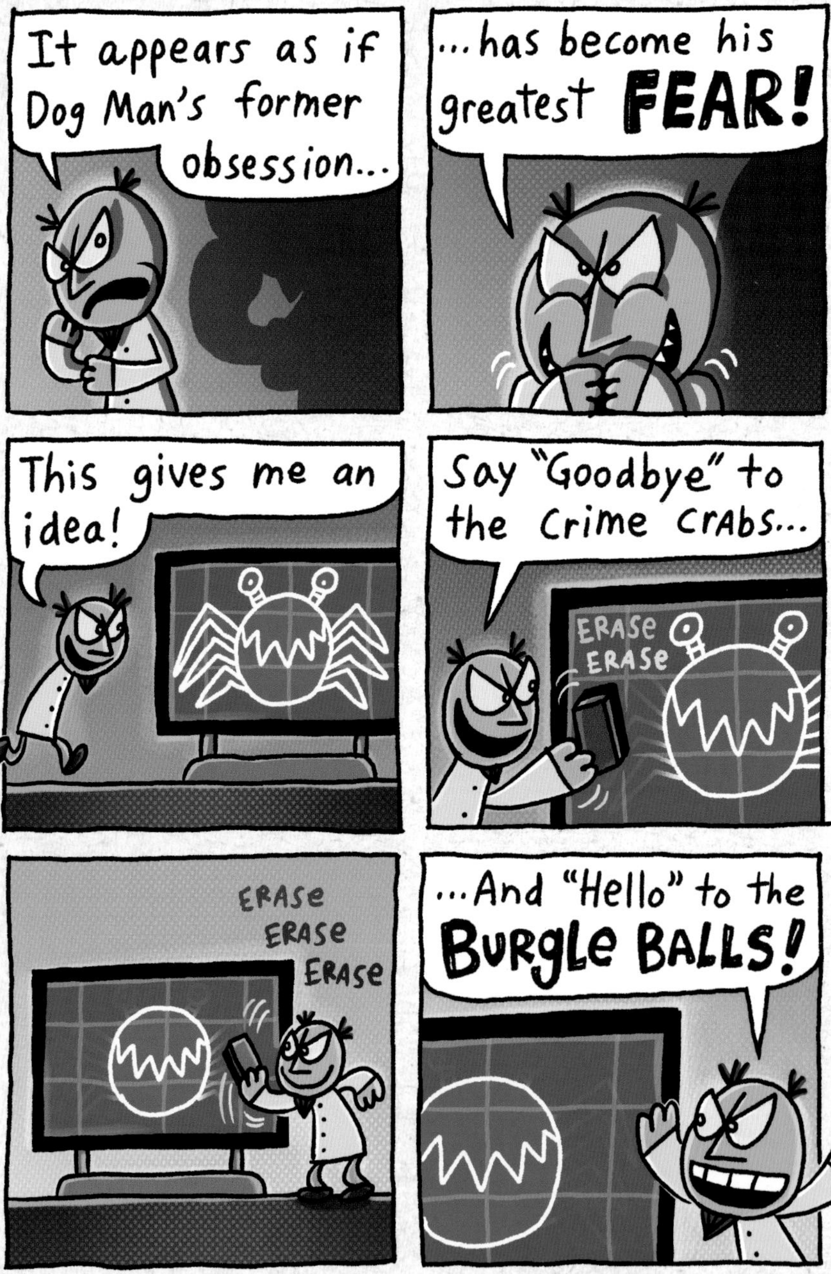
It appears as if Dog Man's former obsession...
...has become his greatest FEAR!
This gives me an idea!
Say "Goodbye" to the Crime Crabs...
ERASE
ERASE
ERASE
ERASE
ERASE
...And "Hello" to the BURGLE BALLS!

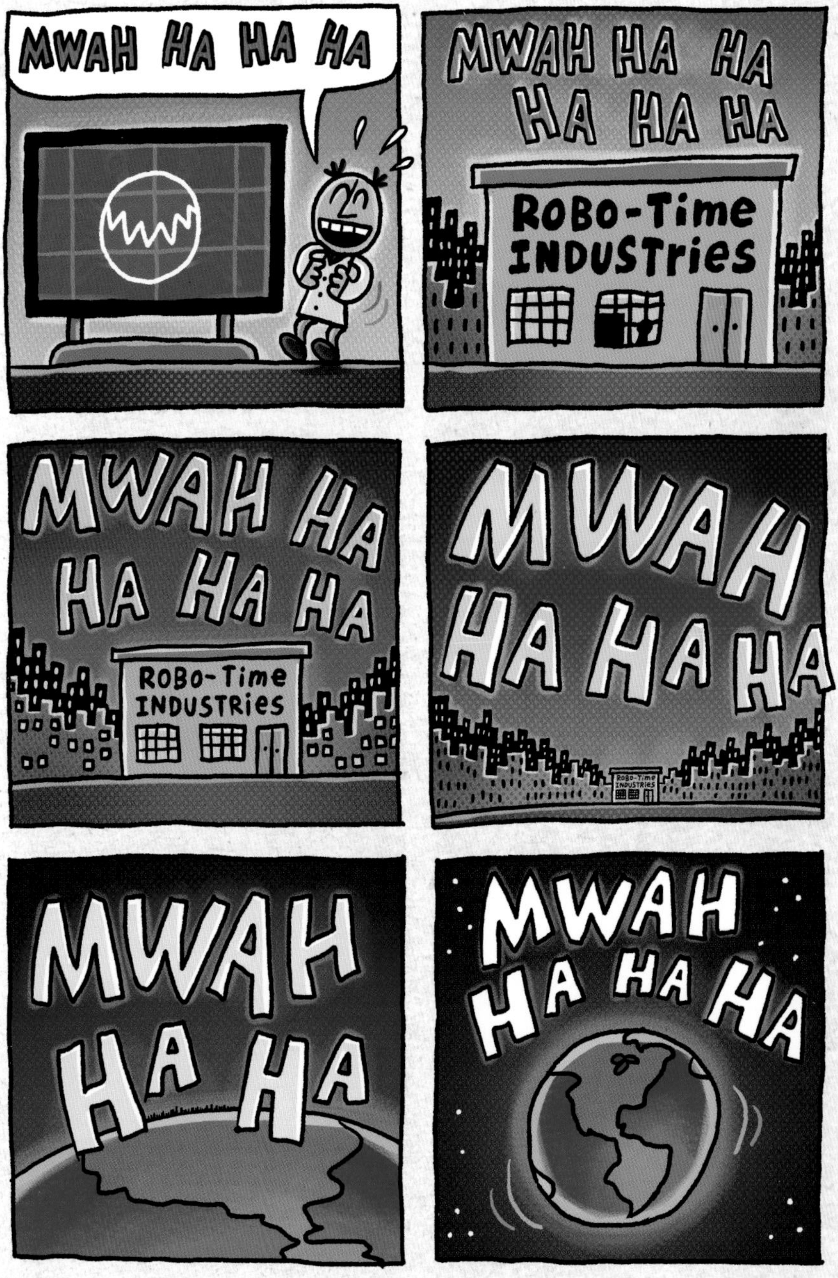
MWAH HA HA HA
MWAH HA HA
HA HA HA
ROBO-Time INDUSTRIES
MWAH HA
HA HA HA
ROBO-Time INDUSTRIES
MWAH
HA HA HA HA
MWAH
HA HA
MWAH
HA HA HA HA

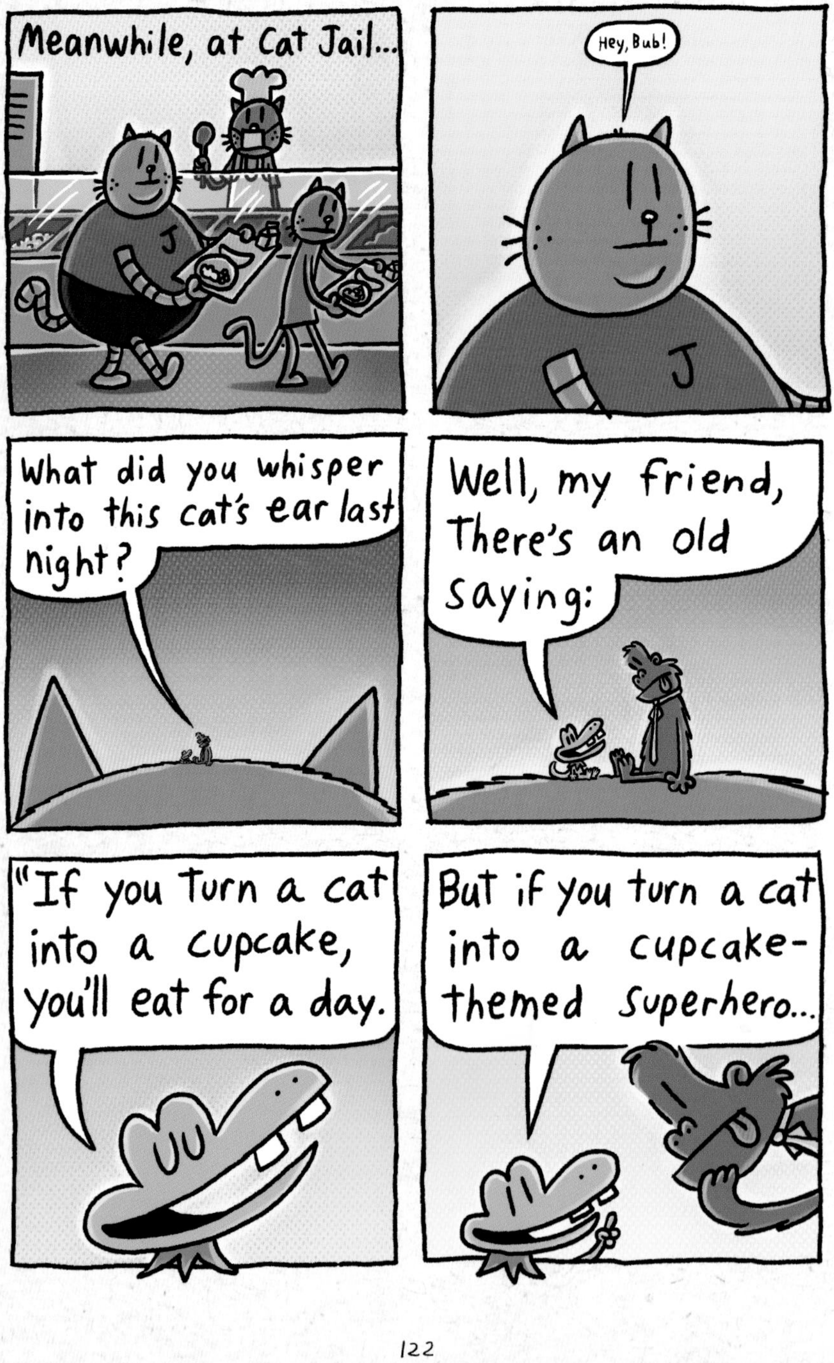
Meanwhile, at Cat Jail...
Hey, Bub!
What did you whisper into this cat's ear last night?
Well, my friend, There's an old saying:
"If you turn a cat into a cupcake, you'll eat for a day.
But if you turn a cat into a cupcake-themed superhero...

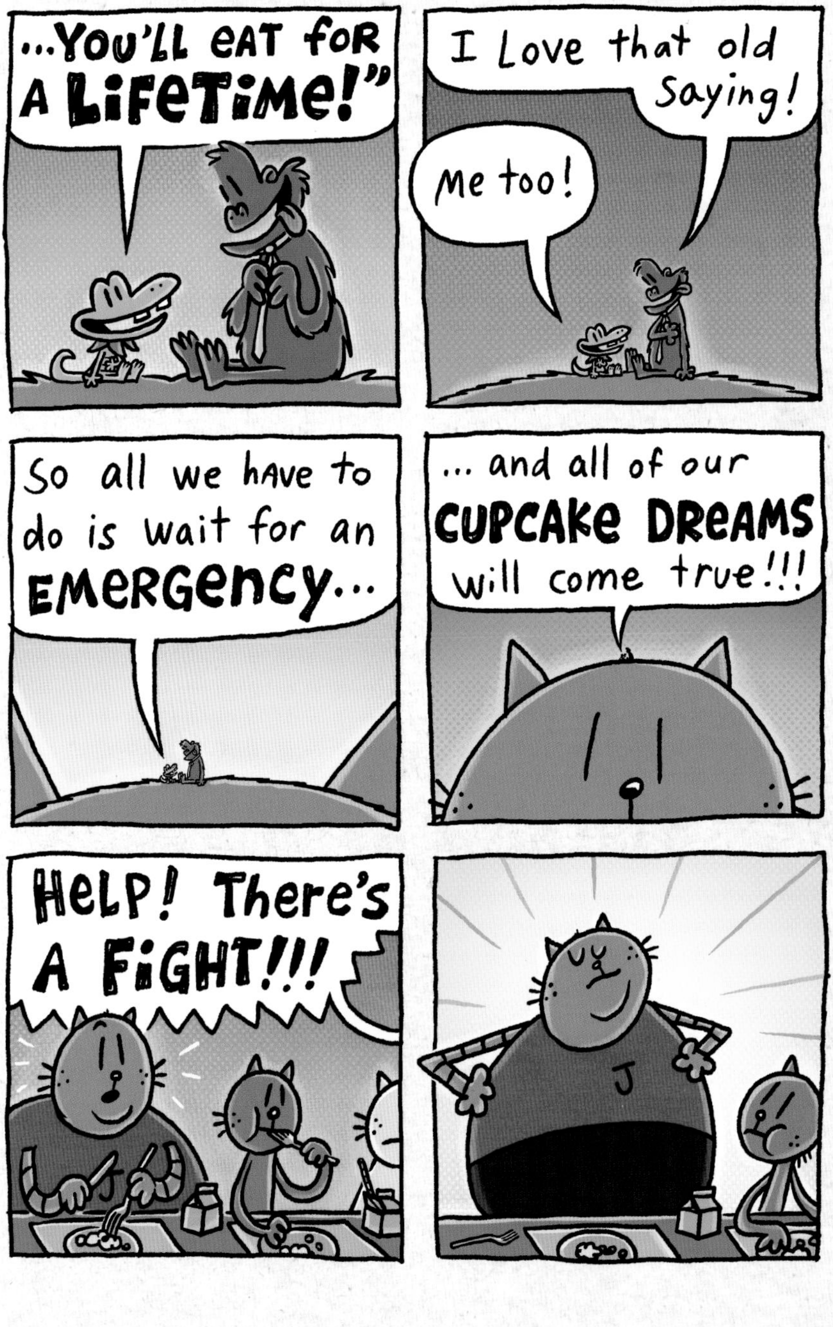
...YOU'LL EAT FOR A LIFETIME!"
I Love that old Saying!
Me too!
So all we have to do is wait for an EMERGENCY...
... and all of our CUPCAKE DREAMS will come true!!!
HELP! There's A FIGHT!!!
J
J

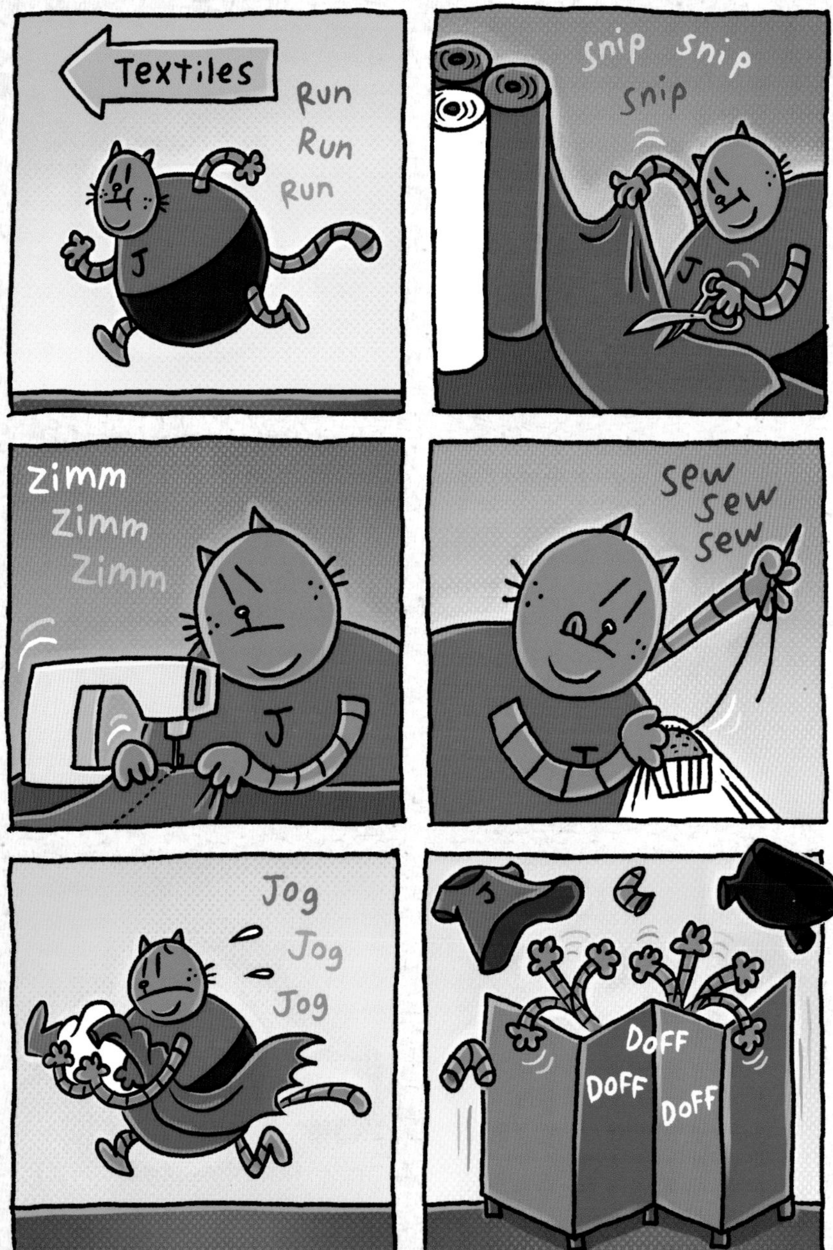
Textiles
Run
Run
Run
snip snip
snip
Zimm
Zimm
Zimm
sew
sew
sew
Jog
Jog
Jog
DOFF
DOFF
DOFF

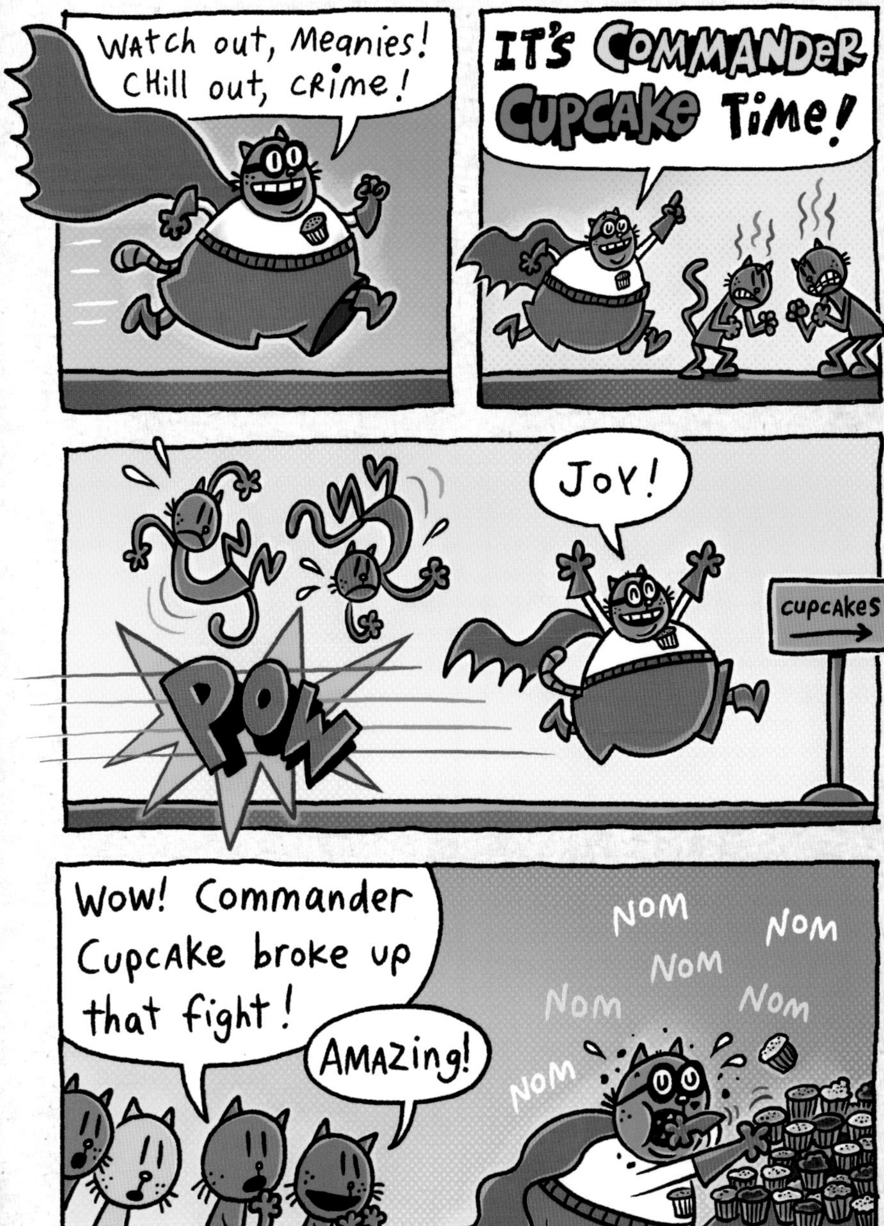
Watch out, Meanies! Chill out, crime!
IT'S COMMANDER CUPCAKE TIME!
POW
JOY!
cupcakes
Wow! Commander Cupcake broke up that fight!
AMAZING!
NOM
NOM
NOM
Nom
Nom
NOM

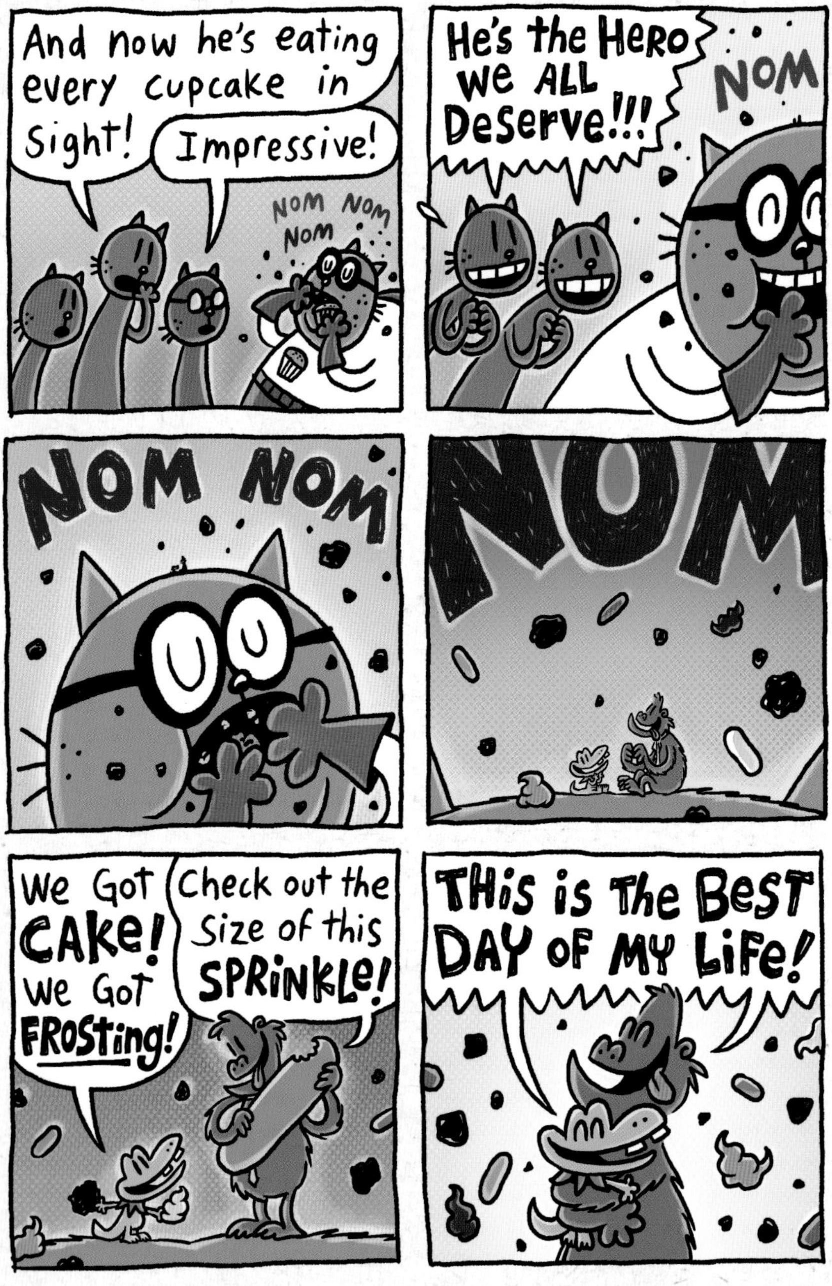
And now he's eating every cupcake in sight!
Impressive!
NOM NOM NOM
He's the HERO we ALL Deserve!!!
NOM
NOM NOM
NOM
We Got CAKE! We Got FROSTing!
Check out the Size of this SPRINKLE!
THIS is The BEST DAY OF MY LIFE!

CHAPTER 8

The Old Man And the Sea-Food Crackers

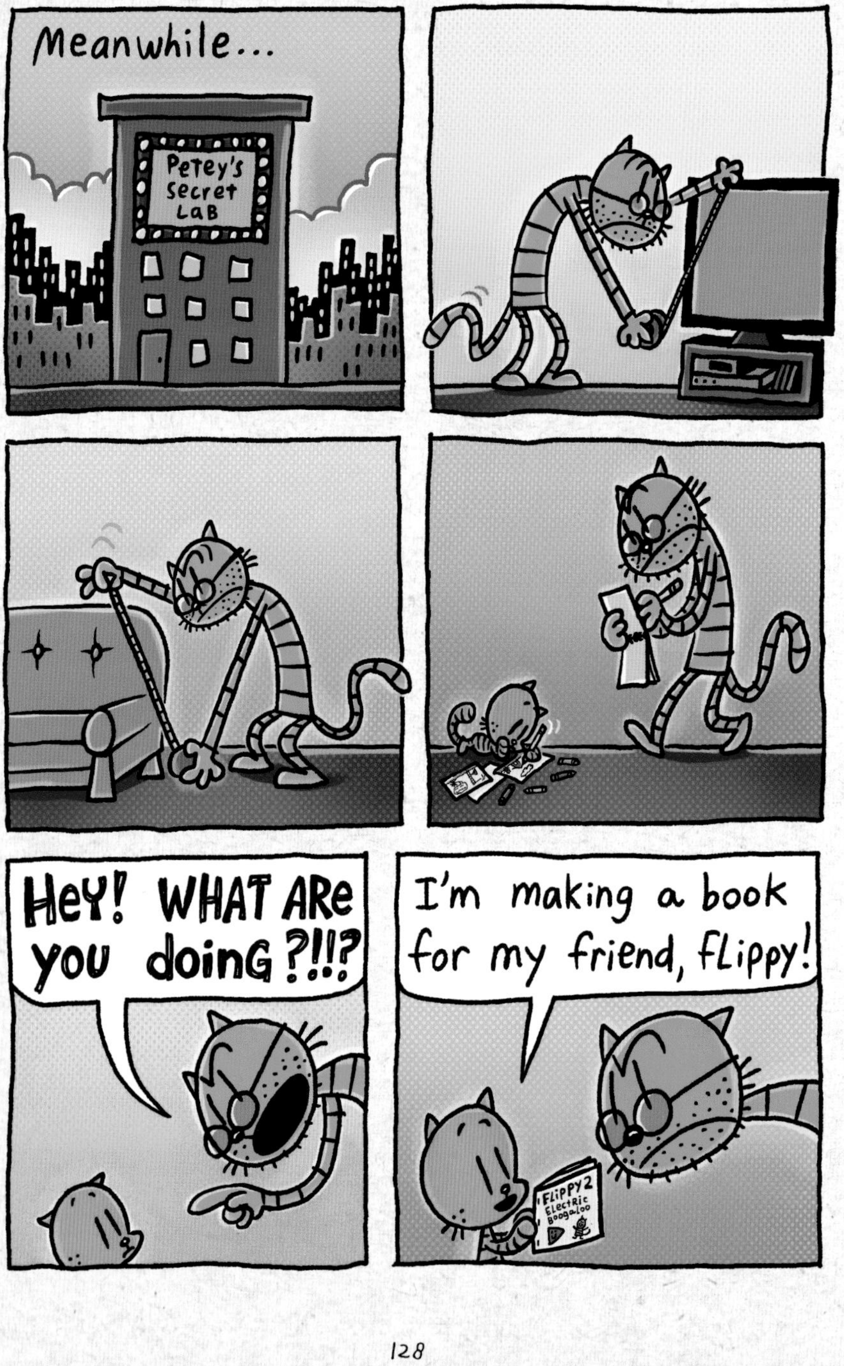
Meanwhile...
Petey's Secret Lab
HEY! WHAT ARE you doing?!!?
I'm making a book for my friend, Flippy!
Flippy 2 Electric Boogaloo

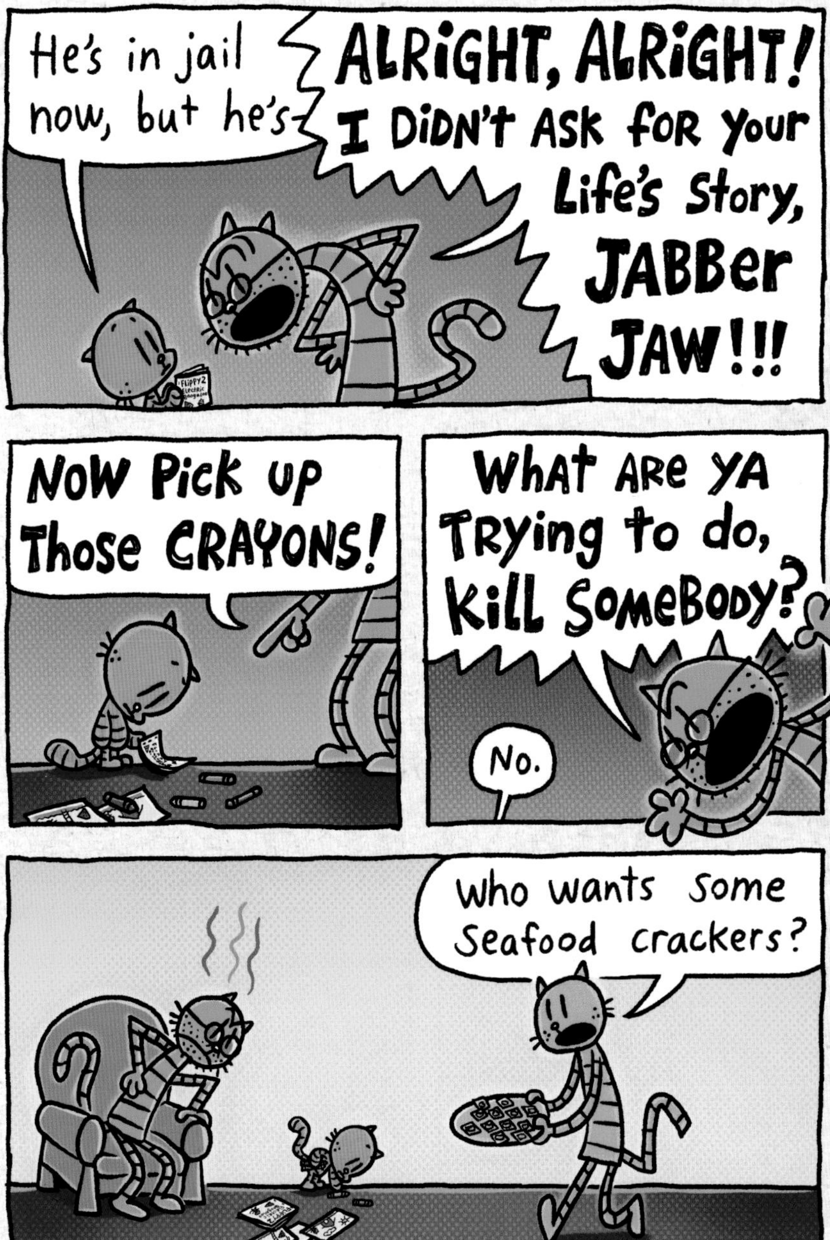
He's in jail now, but he's
ALRIGHT, ALRIGHT! I DIDN'T ASK FOR YOUR LIFE'S STORY, JABBER JAW!!!
FLIPPY'Z ELECTRIC
NOW PICK UP THOSE CRAYONS!
WHAT ARE YA TRYING TO DO, KILL SOMEBODY?
NO.
Who wants some seafood crackers?

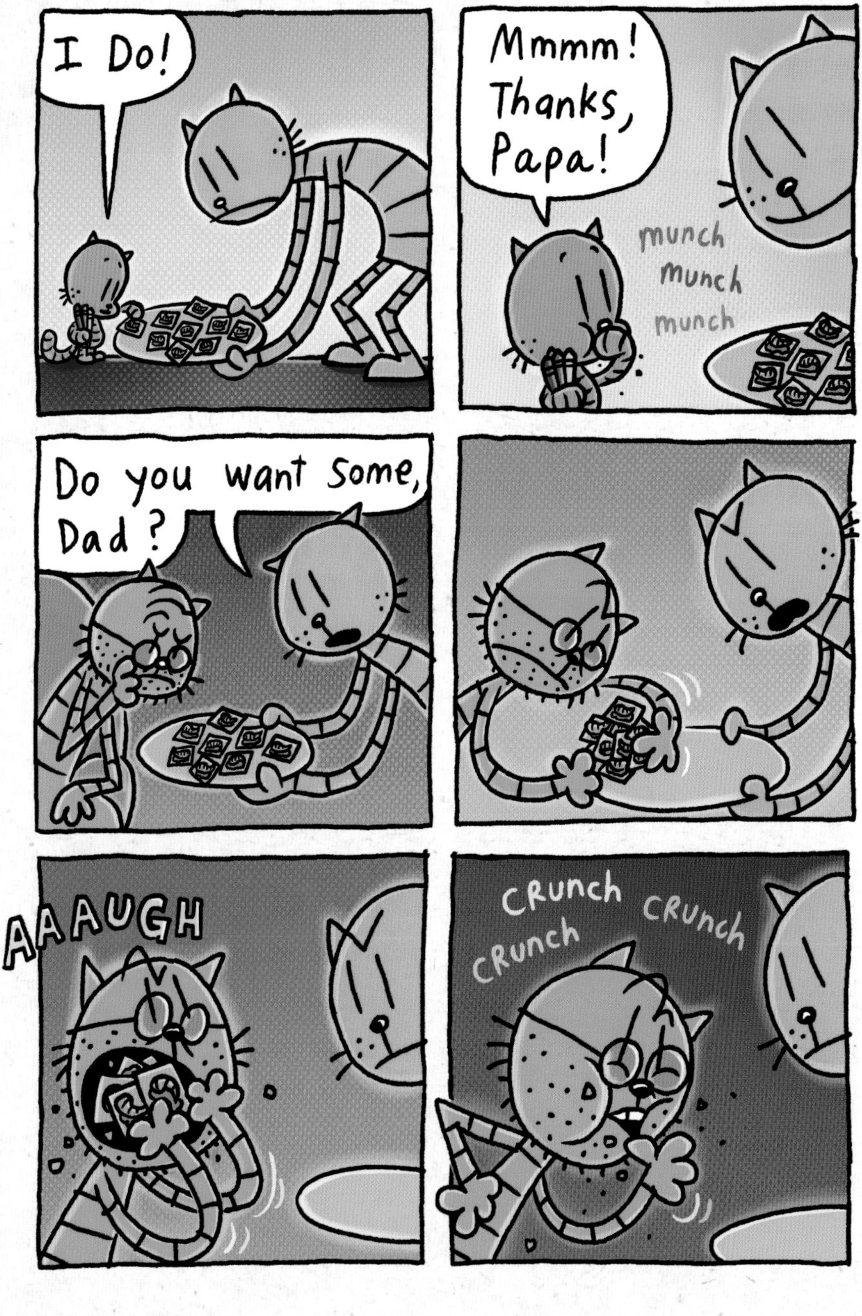
I Do!
Mmmm! Thanks, Papa!
munch munch munch
Do you want some, Dad?
AAAUGH
CRUNCH CRUNCH CRUNCH

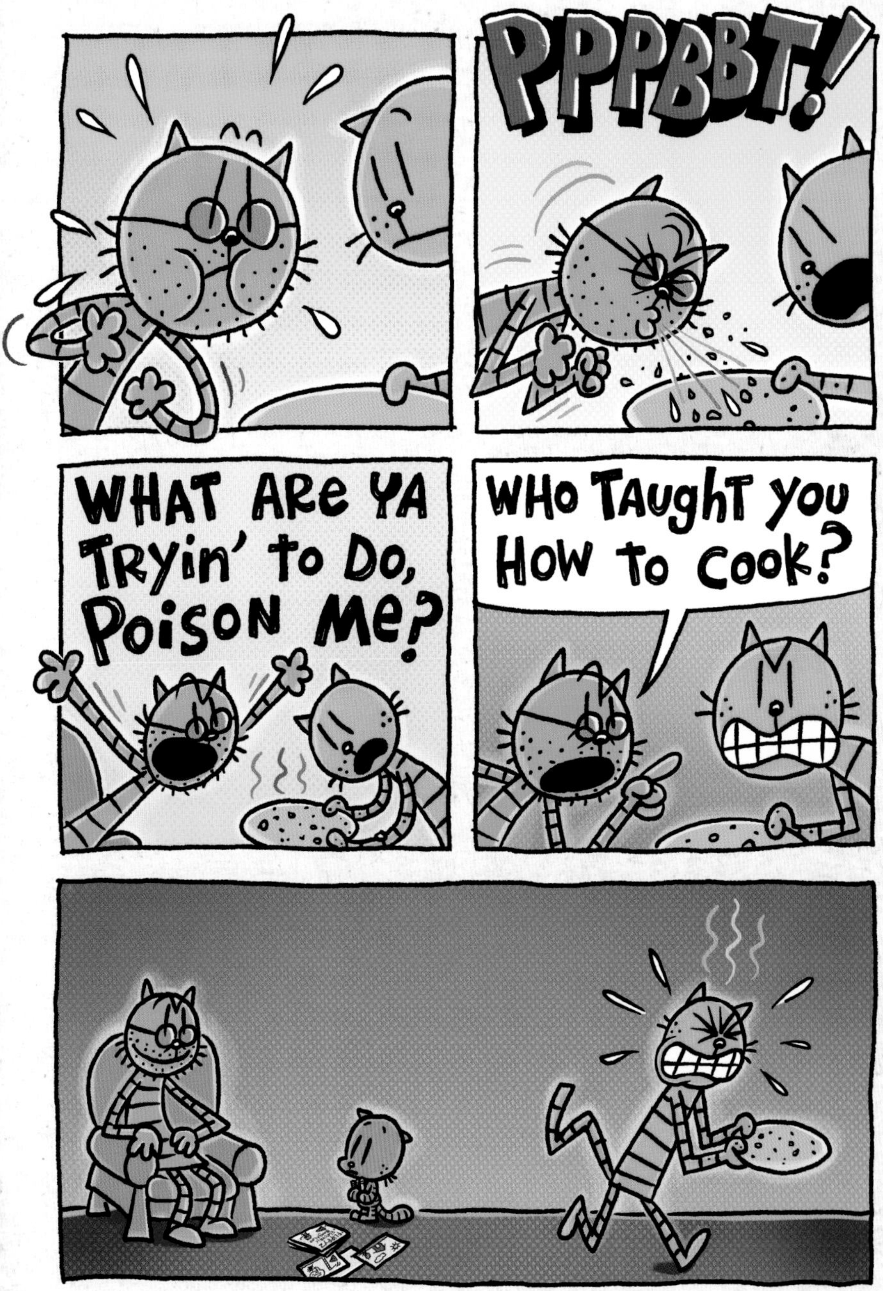
PPPBBT!
WHAT ARe YA Tryin' to Do, Poison Me?
WHO TAught you How To Cook?

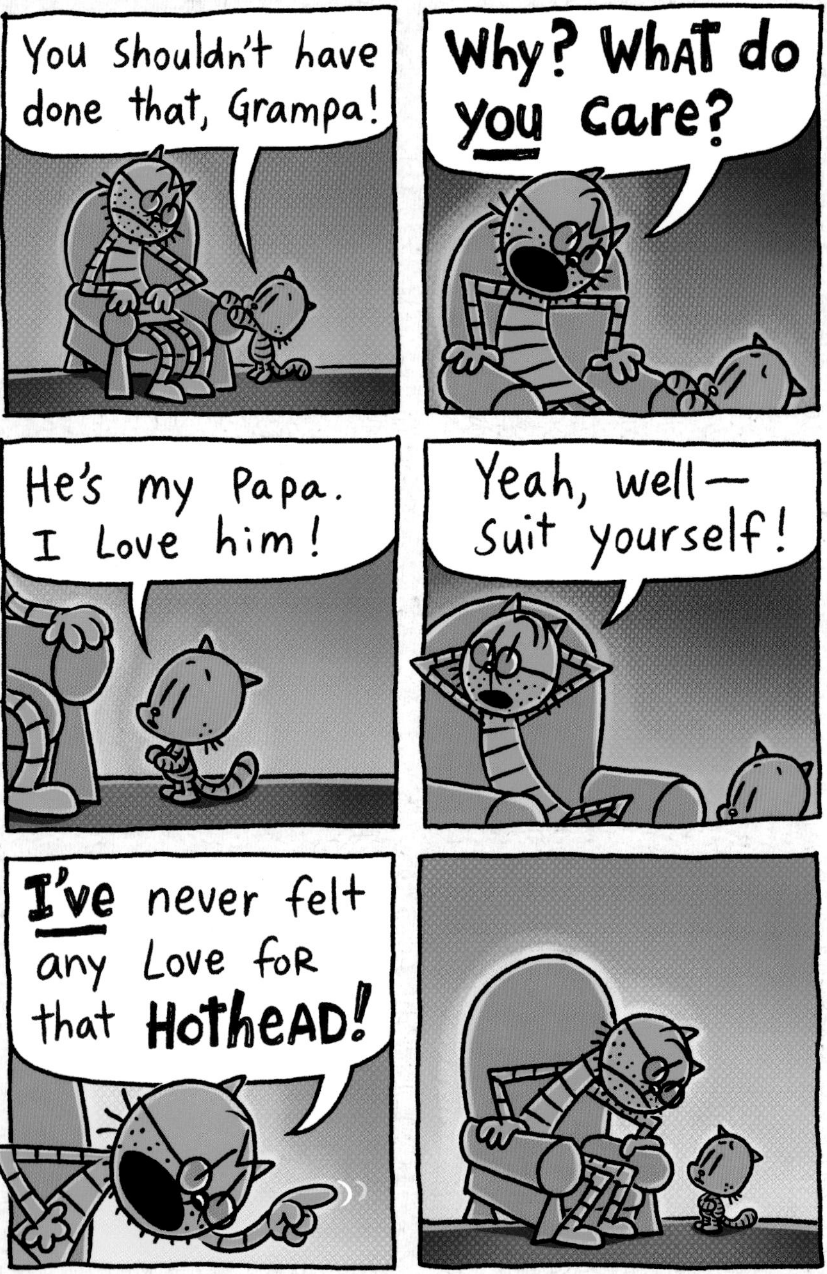
You Shouldn't have done that, Grampa!
Why? WHAT do you care?
He's my Papa. I Love him!
Yeah, well— Suit yourself!
I've never felt any Love for that HOTHEAD!

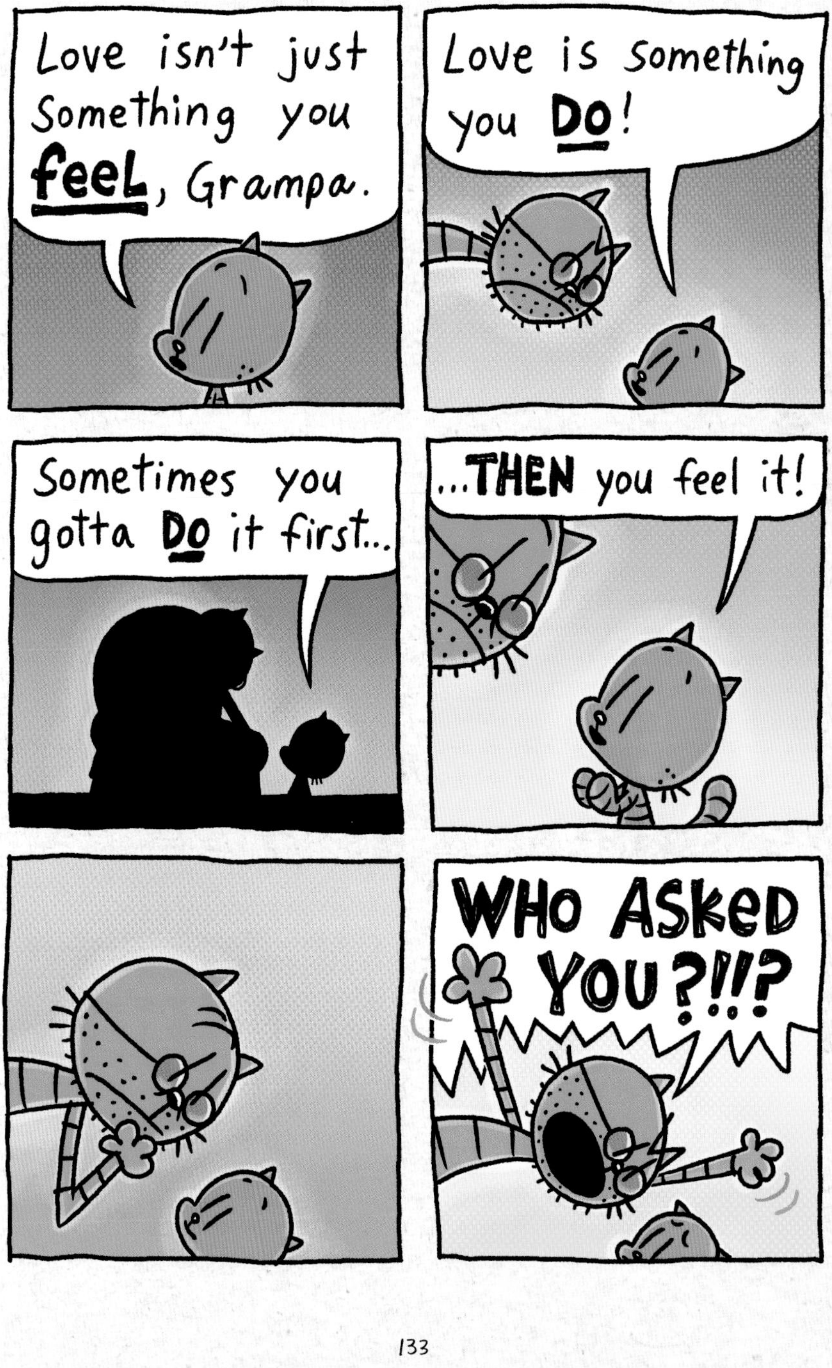
Love isn't just something you feeL, Grampa.
Love is something you DO!
Sometimes you gotta DO it first...
...THEN you feel it!
WHO ASKED YOU?!!?

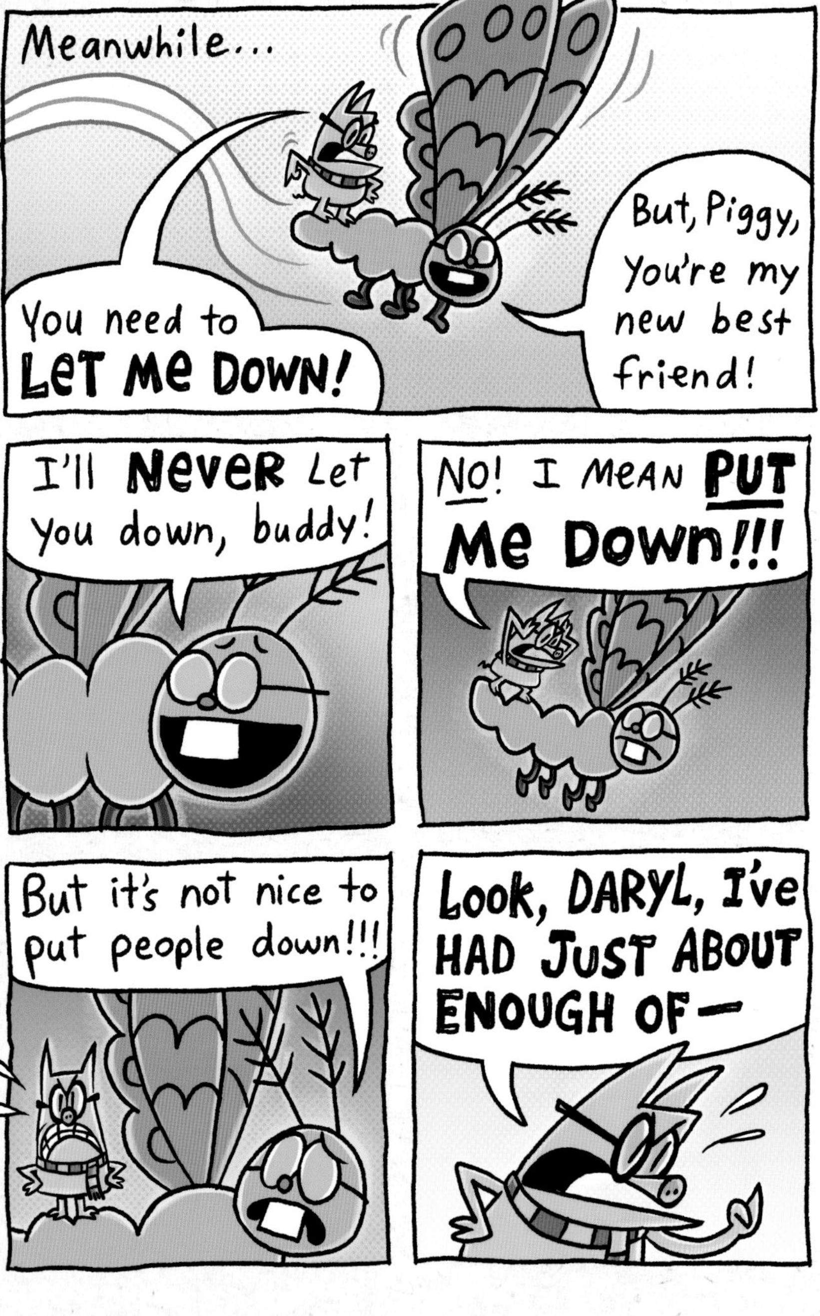
Meanwhile...
You need to LET ME DOWN!
But, Piggy, You're my new best friend!
I'll NEVER Let you down, buddy!
NO! I MEAN PUT ME DOWN!!!
But it's not nice to put people down!!!
Look, DARYL, I've HAD JUST ABOUT ENOUGH OF—

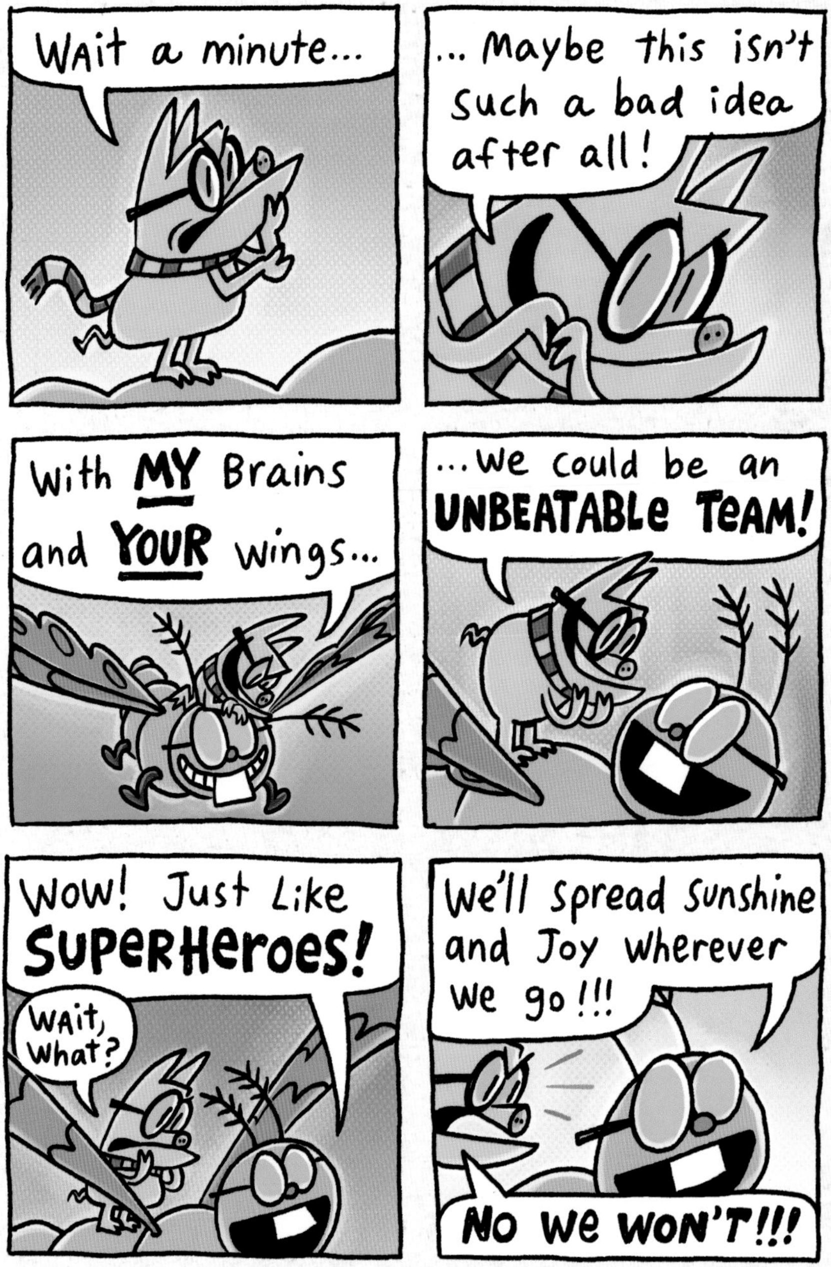
WAit a minute...
... Maybe this isn't such a bad idea after all!
With MY Brains and YOUR wings...
...we could be an UNBEATABLE TEAM!
WOW! Just Like SUPERHeroes!
WAit, what?
We'll spread Sunshine and Joy wherever we go!!!
NO We WON'T!!!

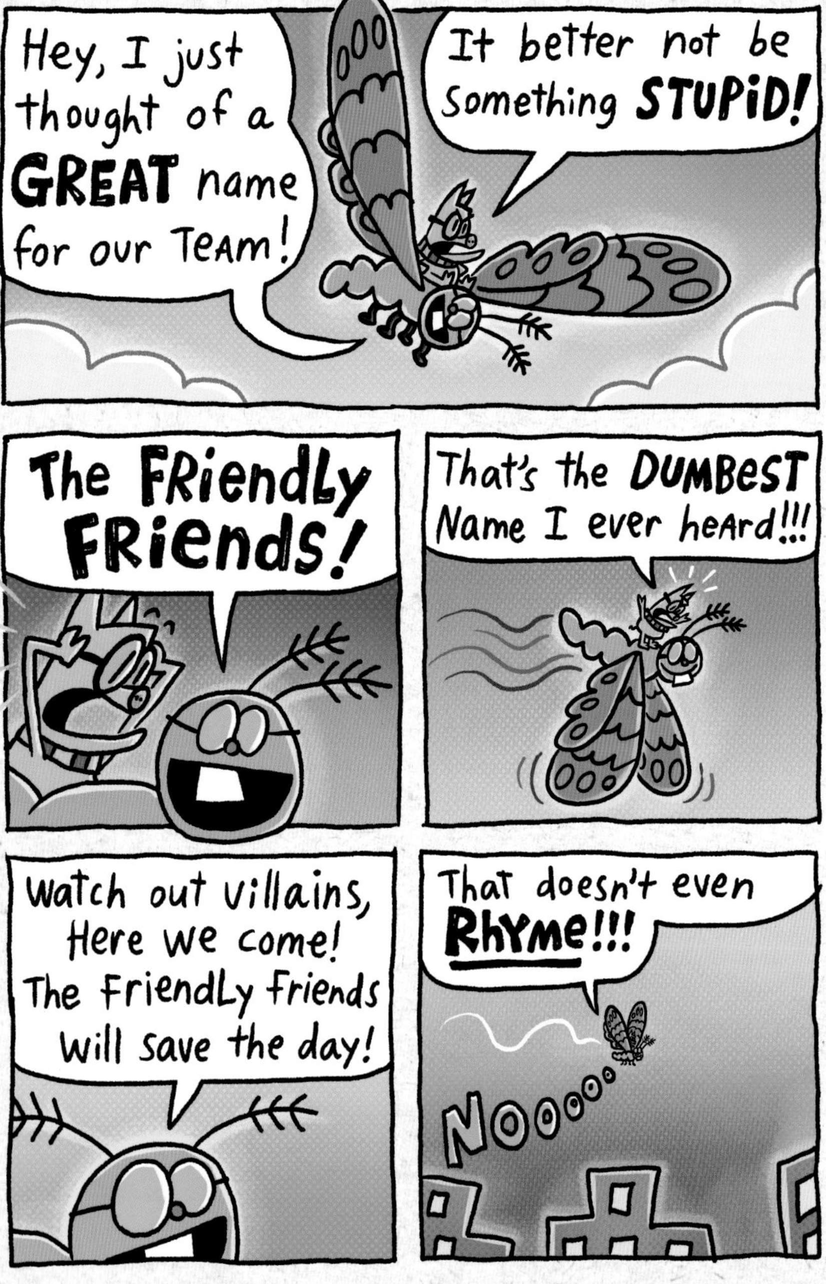
Hey, I just thought of a GREAT name for our Team!
It better not be Something STUPiD!
The FRiendLy FRiends!
That's the DUMBEST Name I ever heArd!!!
Watch out villains, Here we come! The FriendLy friends will save the day!
That doesn't even RhYMe!!!
NOoooo

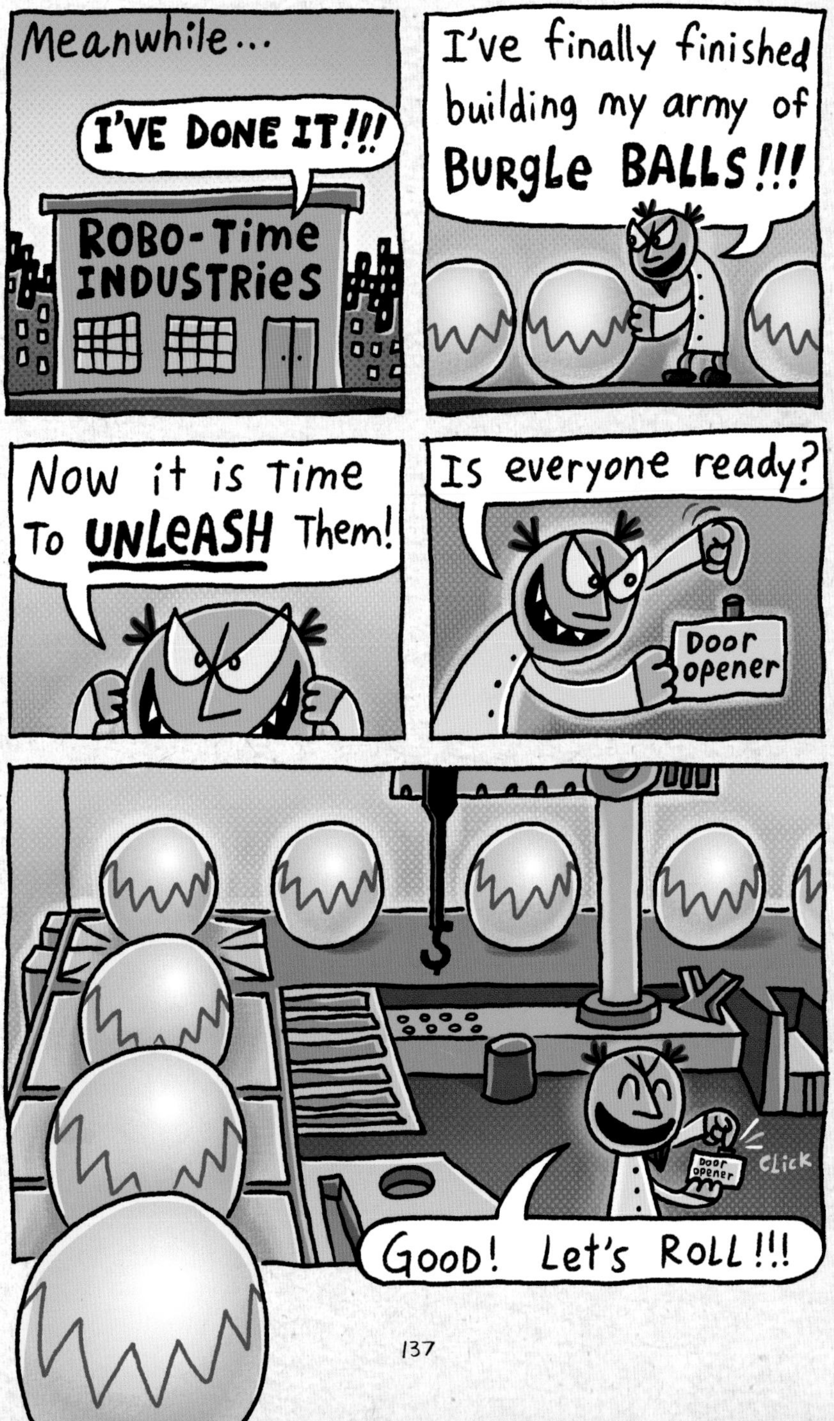
Meanwhile...
I'VE DONE IT!!!
ROBO-Time INDUSTRIES
I've finally finished building my army of BURGLE BALLS!!!
Now it is Time To UNLEASH Them!
Is everyone ready?
Door opener
Door opener
CLick
GOOD! Let's ROLL!!!

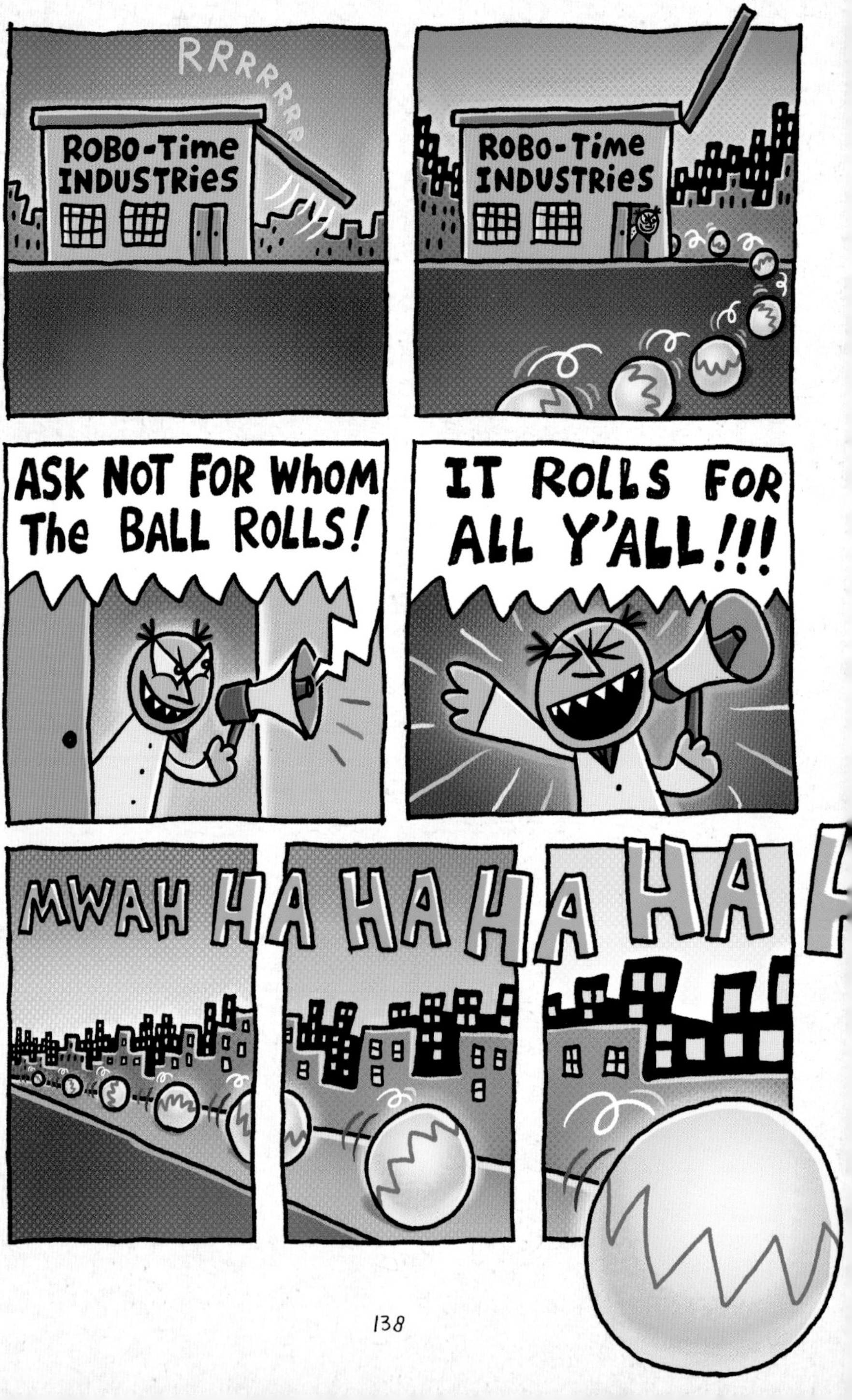
RRRRRRRR
ROBO-Time INDUSTRIES
ROBO-Time INDUSTRIES
ASK NOT FOR WhoM The BALL ROLLS!
IT ROLLS FOR ALL Y'ALL!!!
MWAH HA HA HA HA HA H

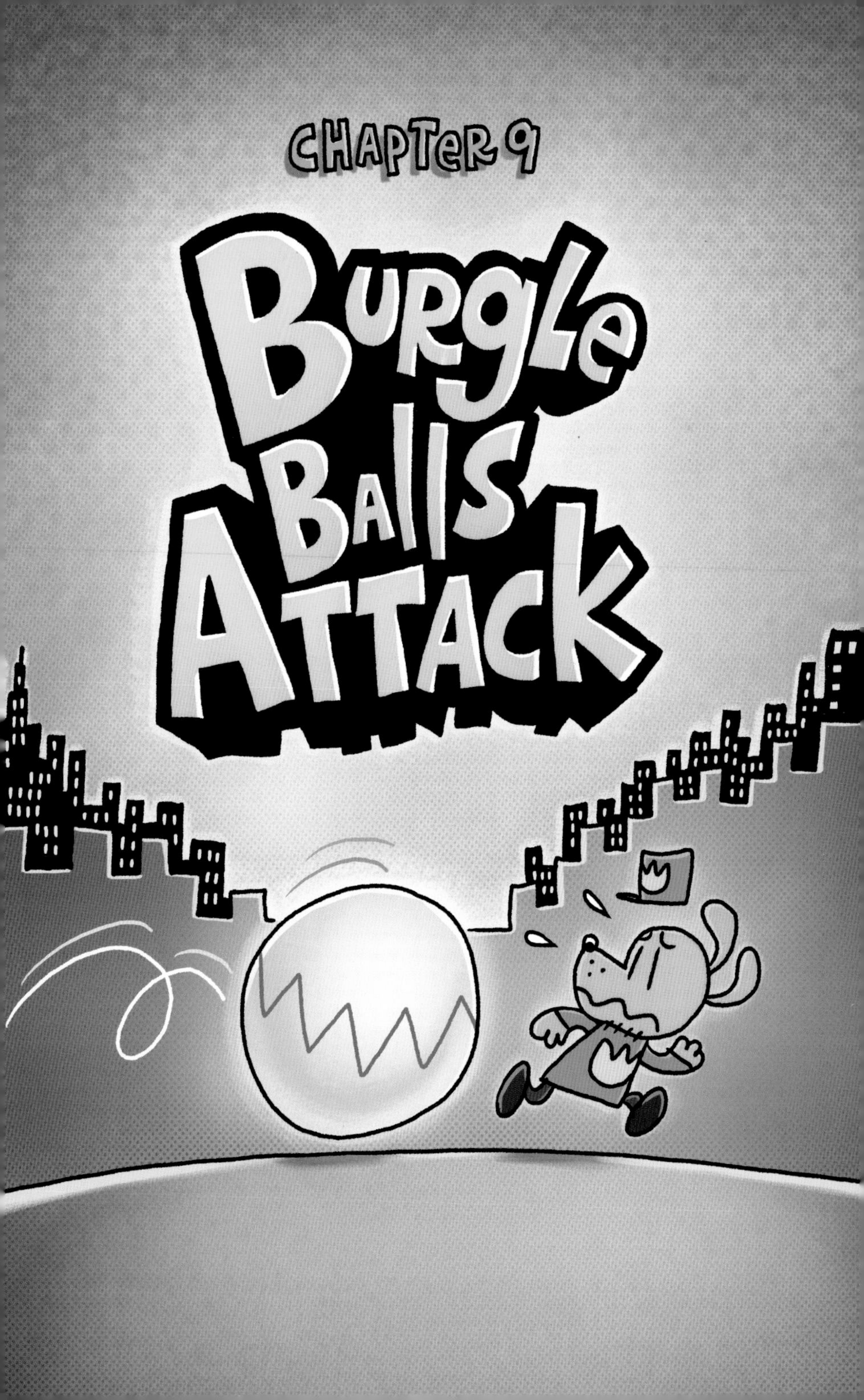
CHAPTER 9
Burgle Balls Attack

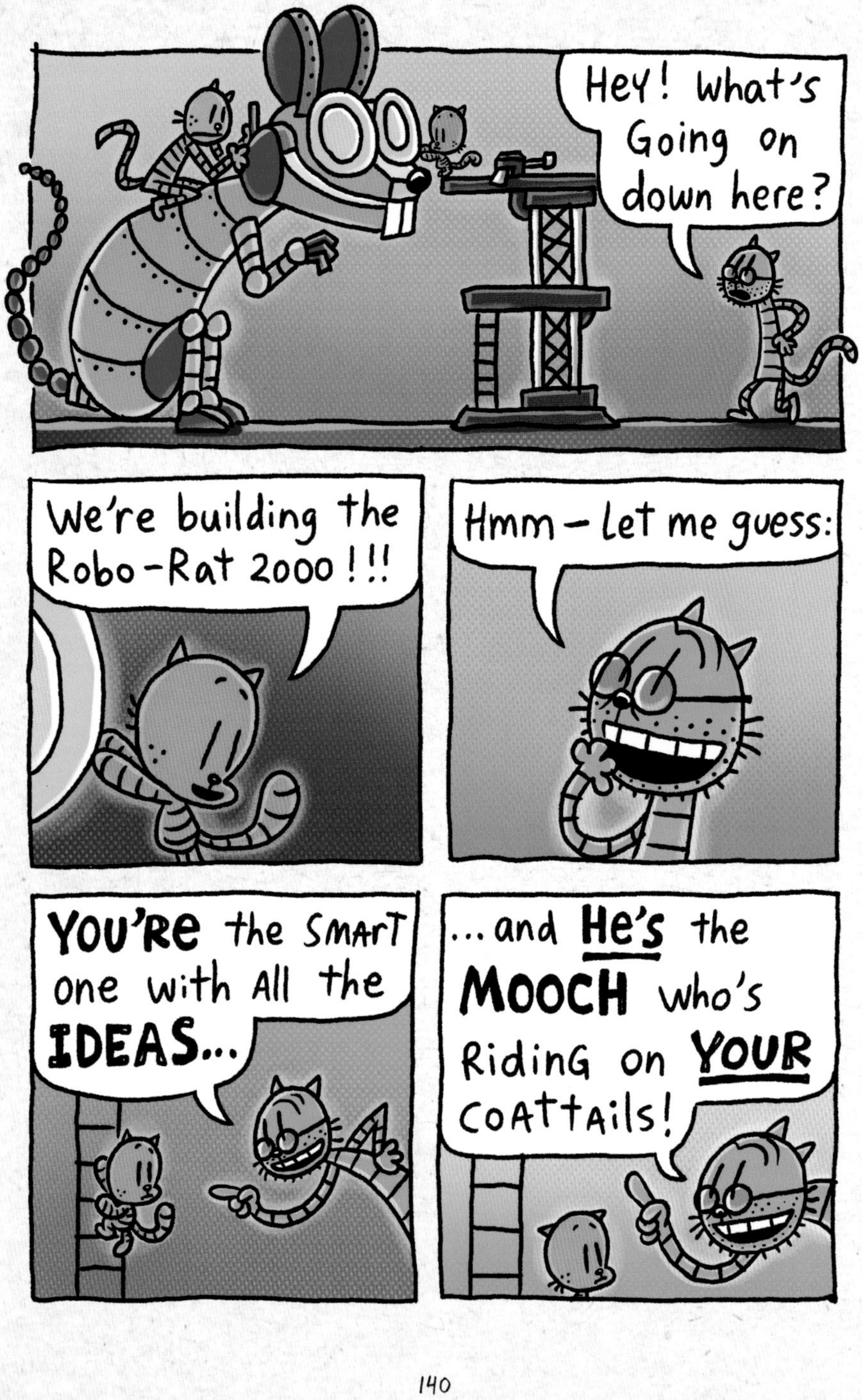
Hey! What's Going on down here?
We're building the Robo-Rat 2000!!!
Hmm—Let me guess:
YOU'RE the SMART one with All the IDEAS...
...and He's the MOOCH who's Riding on YOUR COATTAILS!

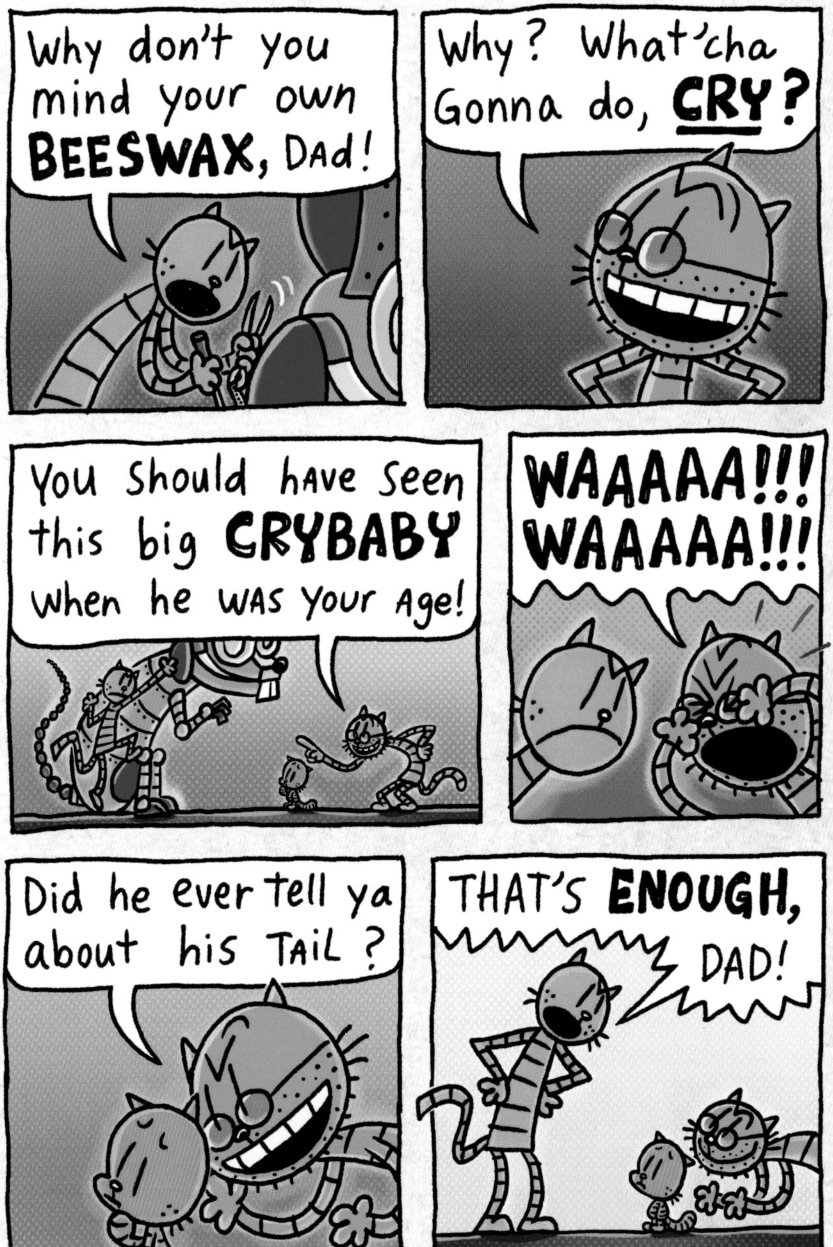
Why don't you mind your own BEESWAX, DAD!
Why? What'cha Gonna do, CRY?
You should have seen this big CRYBABY when he WAS your Age!
WAAAAA!!! WAAAAA!!!
Did he ever tell ya about his TAIL?
THAT'S ENOUGH, DAD!

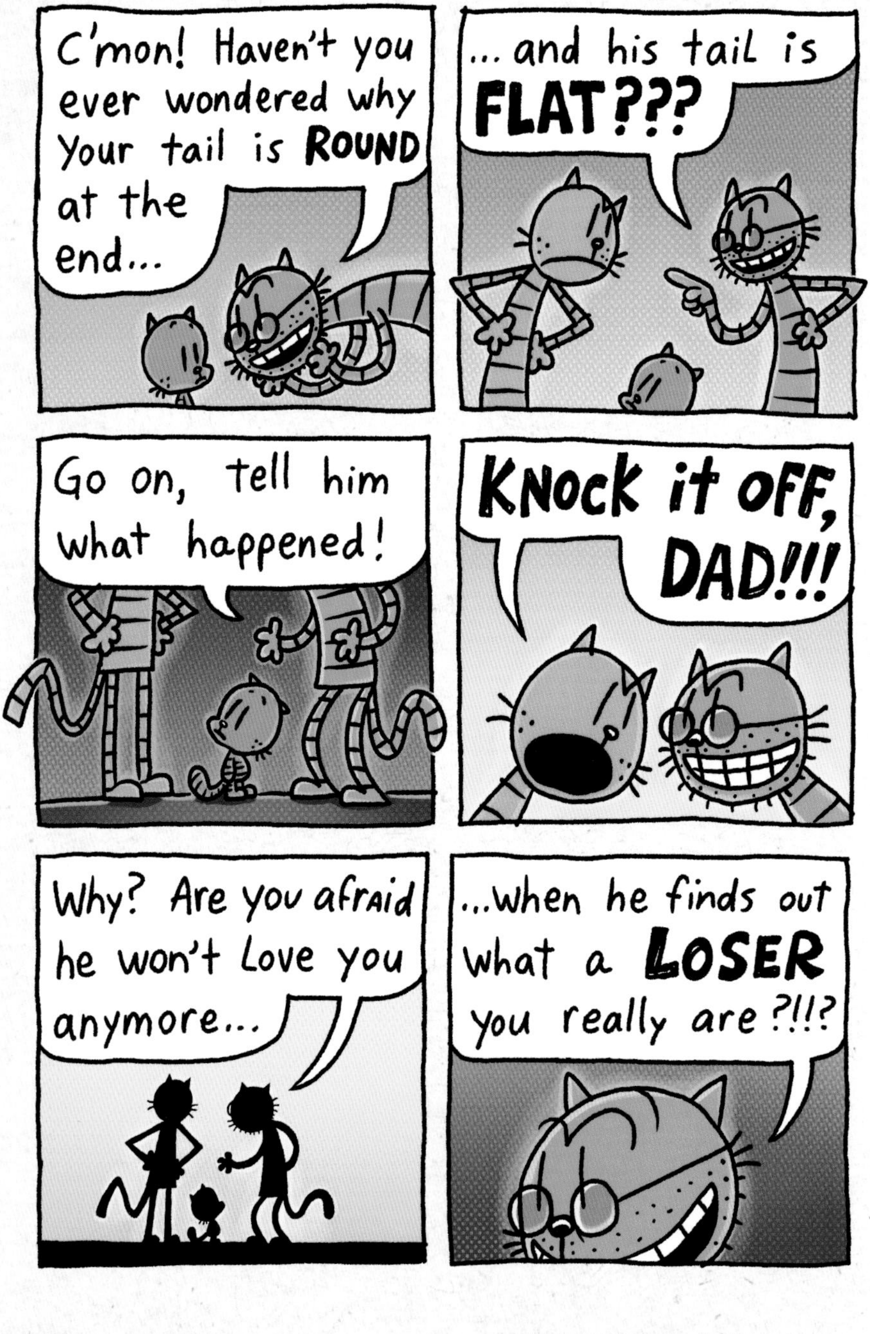
C'mon! Haven't you ever wondered why your tail is ROUND at the end...
...and his tail is FLAT???
Go on, tell him what happened!
KNOCK it OFF, DAD!!!
Why? Are you afraid he won't love you anymore...
...when he finds out what a LOSER you really are?!!?

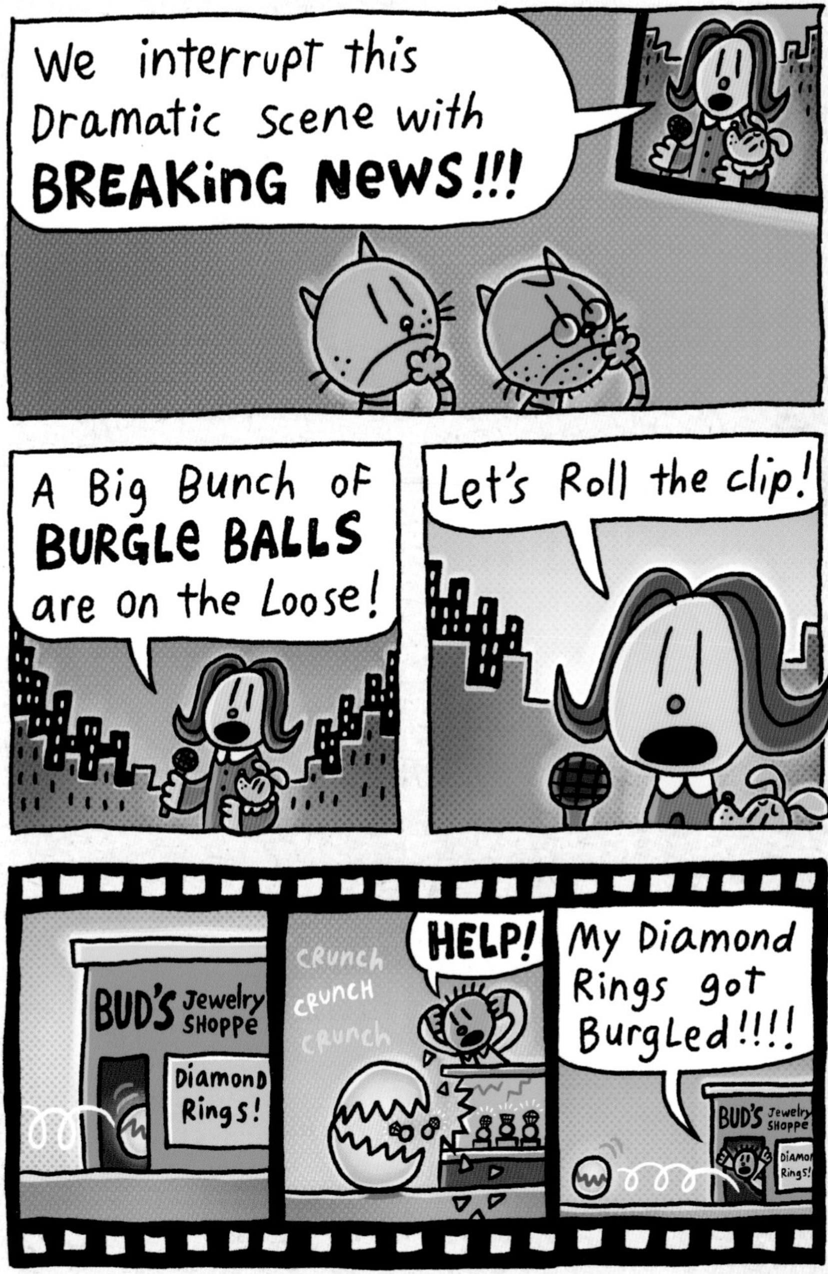

We interrupt this Dramatic Scene with BREAKinG NeWS!!!
A Big Bunch of BURGLe BALLS are on the Loose!
Let's Roll the clip!
BUD'S Jewelry SHoppe
Diamond Rings!
CRunch
CRUNCH
CRunch
HELP!
My Diamond Rings got BurgLed!!!!
BUD'S Jewelry SHoppe
Diamon Rings!

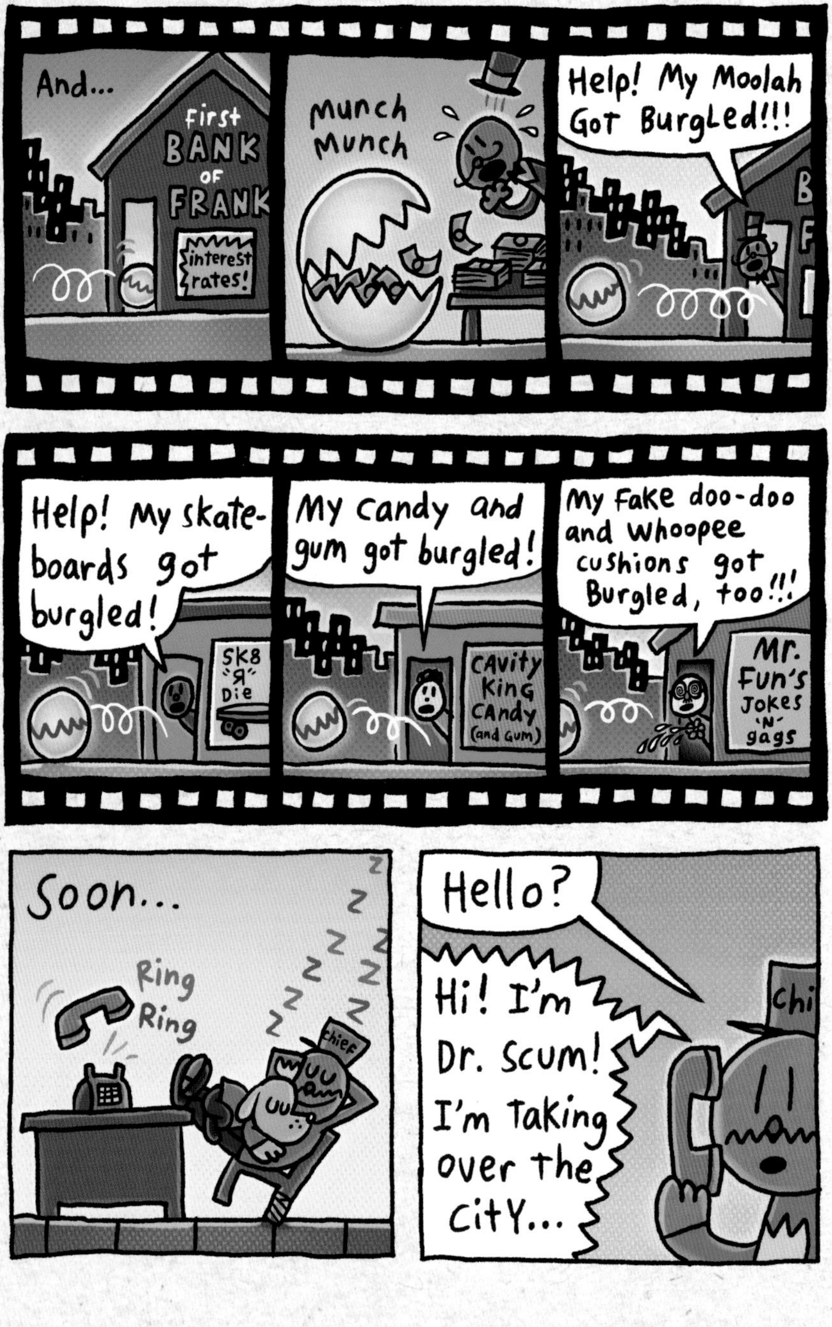
And...
First BANK OF FRANK
interest rates!
munch munch
Help! My Moolah Got Burgled!!!
Help! My skate-boards got burgled!
SK8 "Я" Die
My candy and gum got burgled!
CAvity King CAndy (and Gum)
My Fake doo-doo and whoopee cushions got Burgled, too!!!
Mr. Fun's Jokes 'N' gags
Soon...
Ring Ring
Chief
Hello?
Hi! I'm Dr. Scum! I'm Taking over the City...

...And DoG Man can't stop me! **MWAH HA HA!**

chief

DoG Man! There's a **NEW** Villain in Town!

chief

I'm Not New!

You must stop this **NEW** threat to Society!

chief

Come on! I was in the First Book!

Go catch the new bad guy!!!

chief

Seriously! I had a really big Role in Chapter 2!!!

And so...

COPS

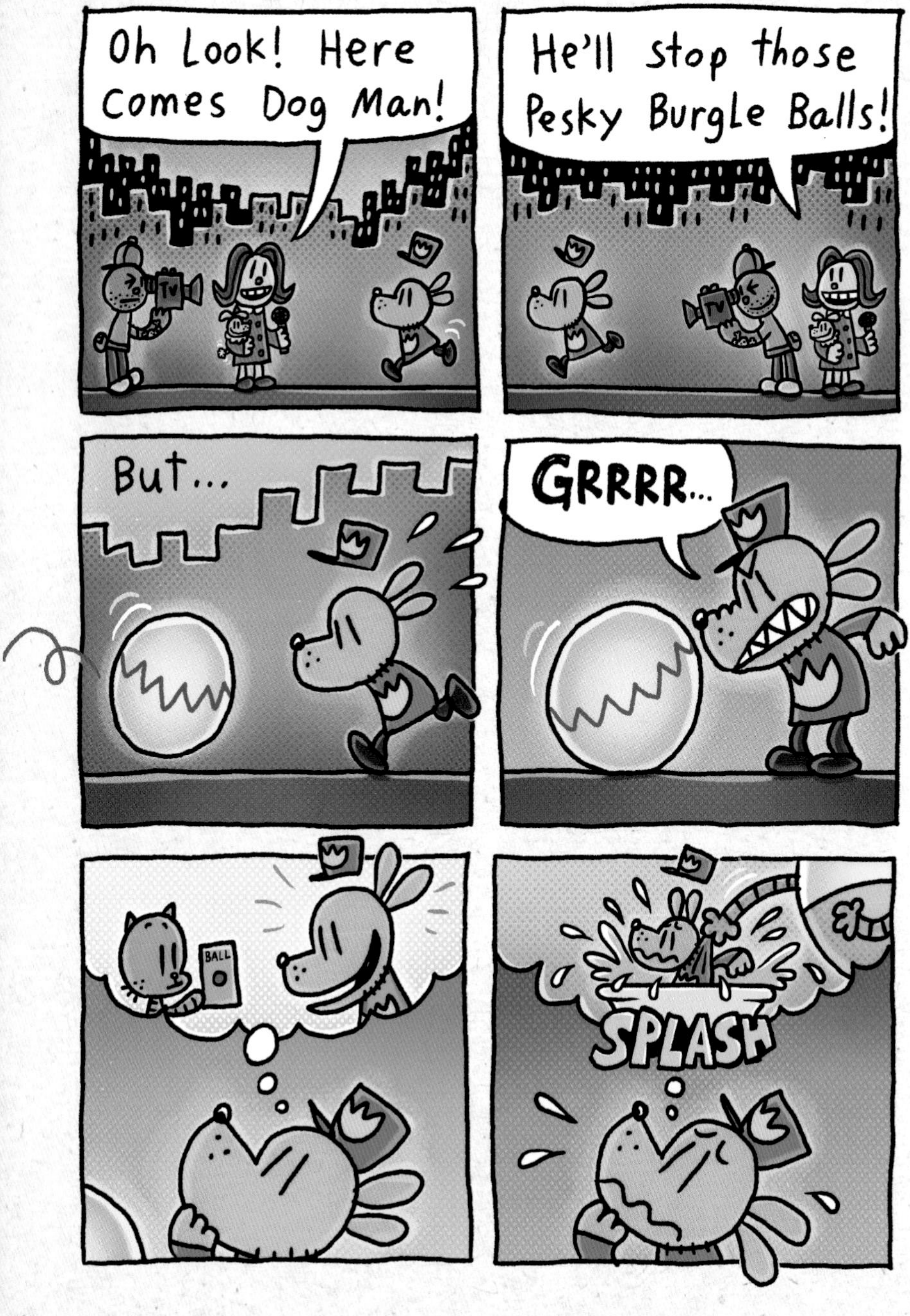
Oh Look! Here Comes Dog Man!
He'll stop those Pesky Burgle Balls!
But...
GRRRR...
BALL
SPLASH

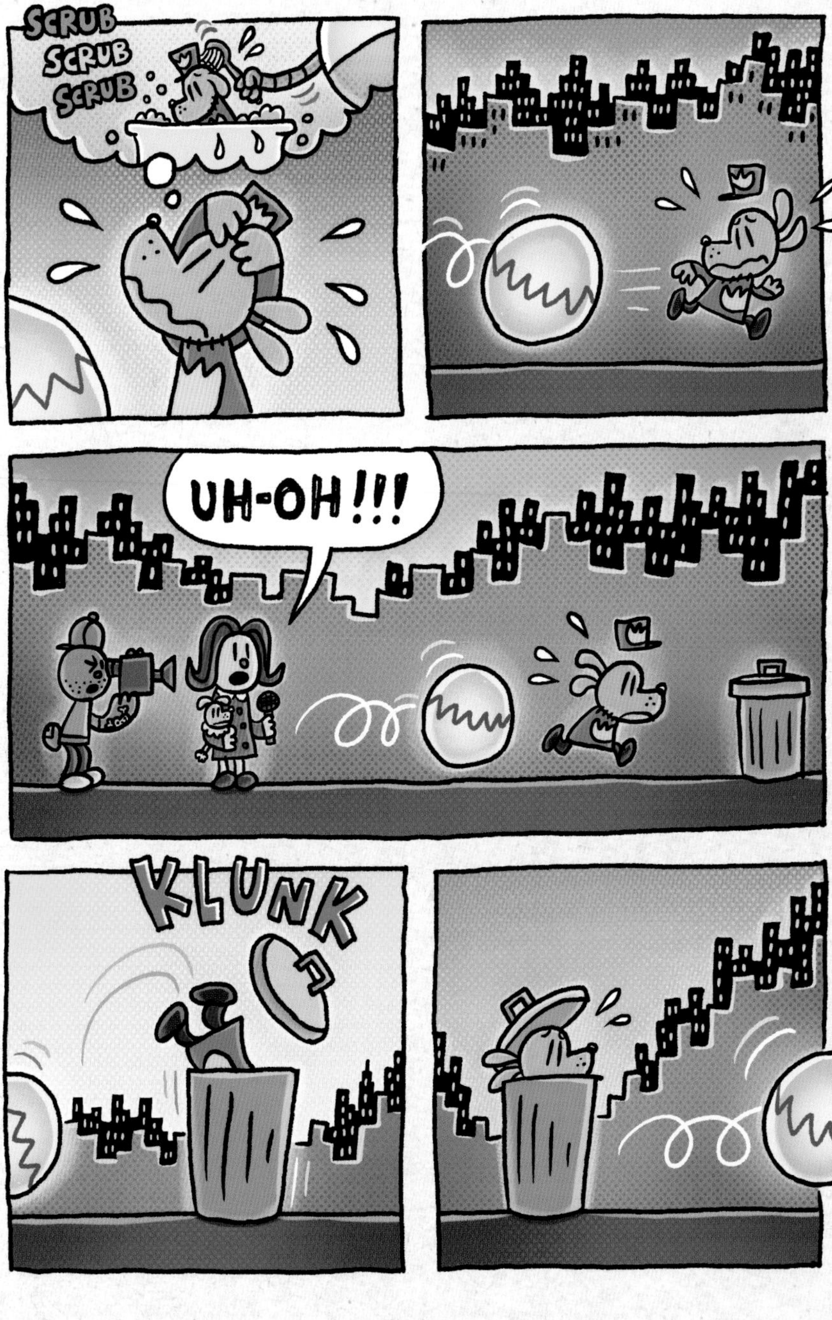
SCRUB
SCRUB
SCRUB
UH-OH!!!
KLUNK

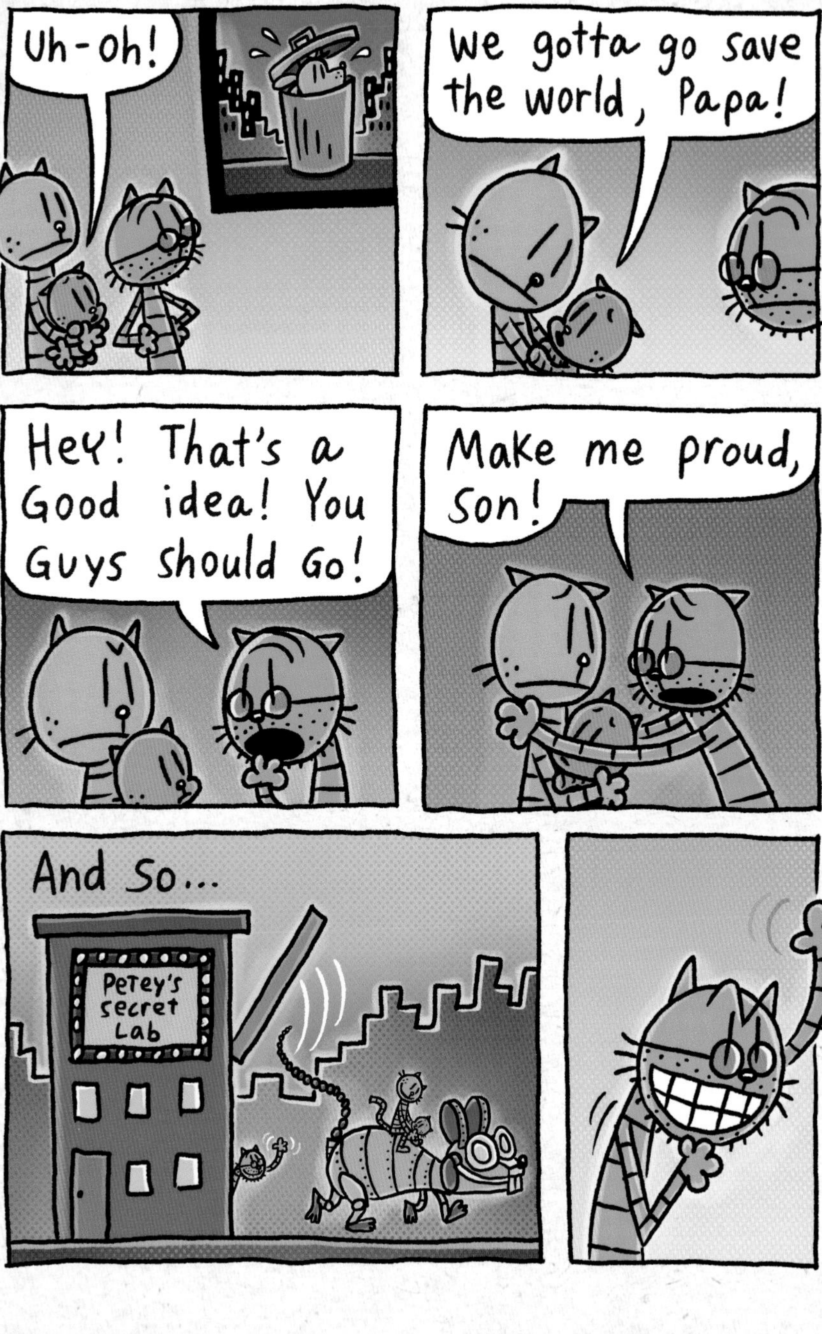

Uh-Oh!
We gotta go save the world, Papa!
Hey! That's a Good idea! You Guys should Go!
Make me proud, Son!
And So...
Petey's secret Lab

CHAPTER 10
DO GOOD

Maturity Award Winner
By George Beard   and

Maturity Award Winner
Harold Hutchins

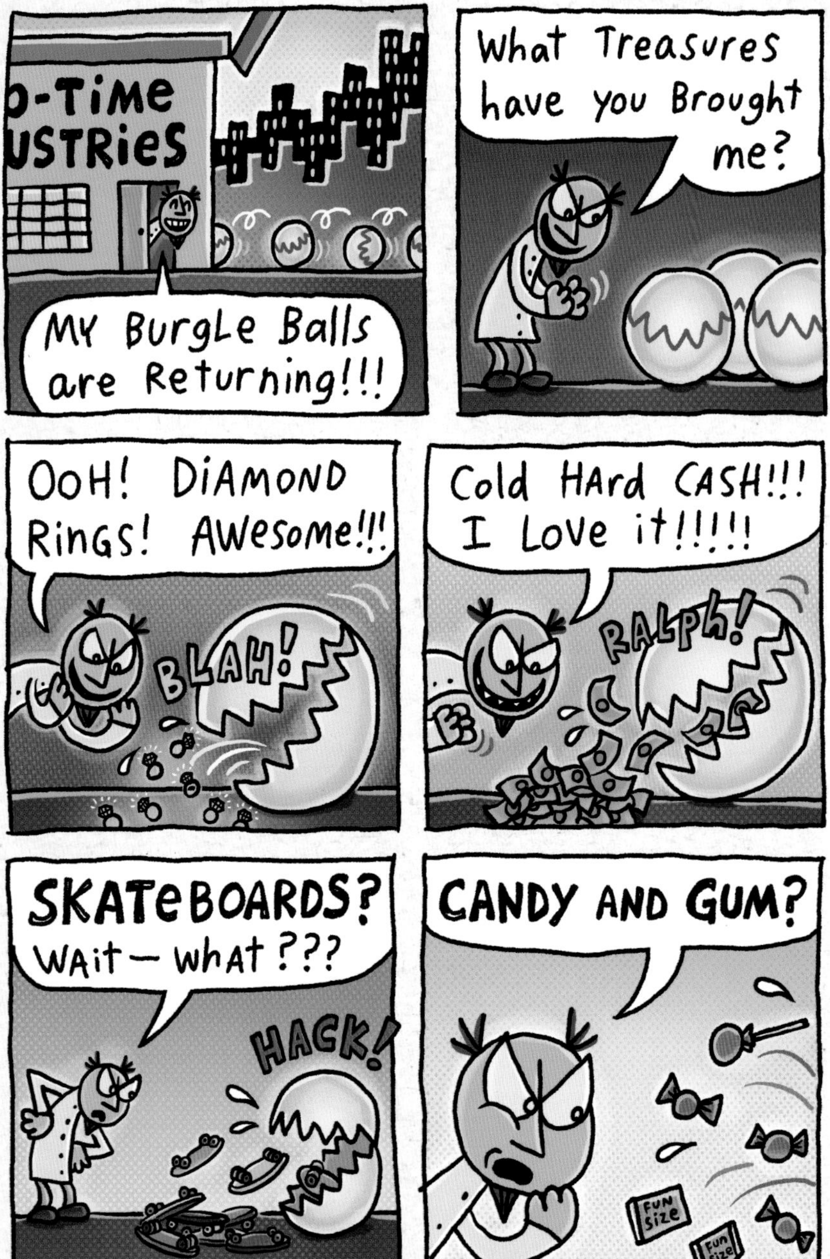

O-TIME
USTRIES
My Burgle Balls are Returning!!!
What Treasures have you Brought me?
OOH! DIAMOND RINGS! AWESOME!!!
BLAH!
Cold HARD CASH!!! I Love it!!!!!
RALPH!
SKATEBOARDS? WAIT—WHAT???
HACK!
CANDY AND GUM?
FUN SIZE
FUN SIZE

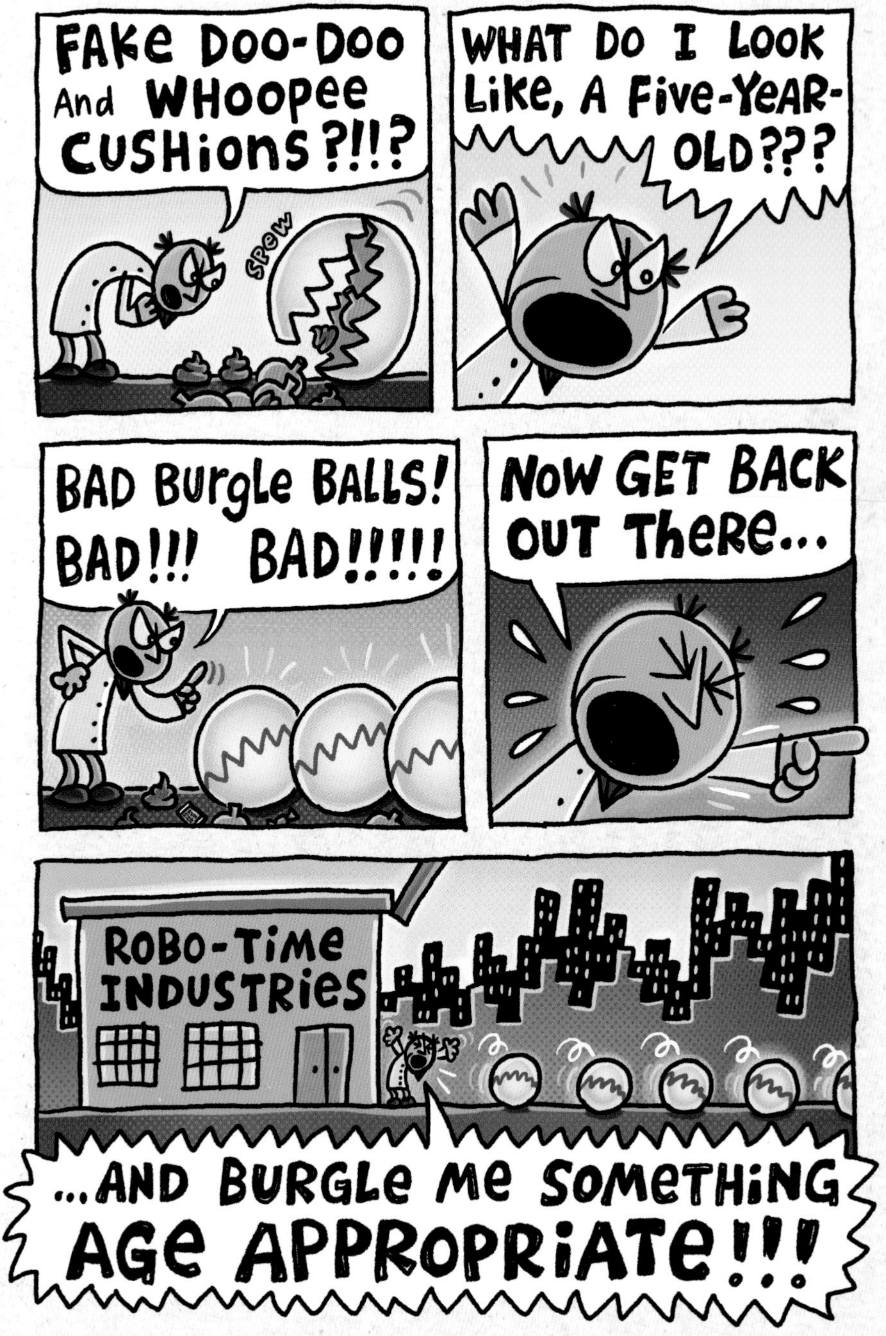
FAKE DOO-DOO And WHOOPEE CUSHIONS?!!?
SPEW
WHAT DO I LOOK LIKE, A FIVE-YEAR-OLD???
BAD BURGLE BALLS! BAD!!! BAD!!!!!
NOW GET BACK OUT THERE...
ROBO-TIME INDUSTRIES
...AND BURGLE ME SOMETHING AGE APPROPRIATE!!!

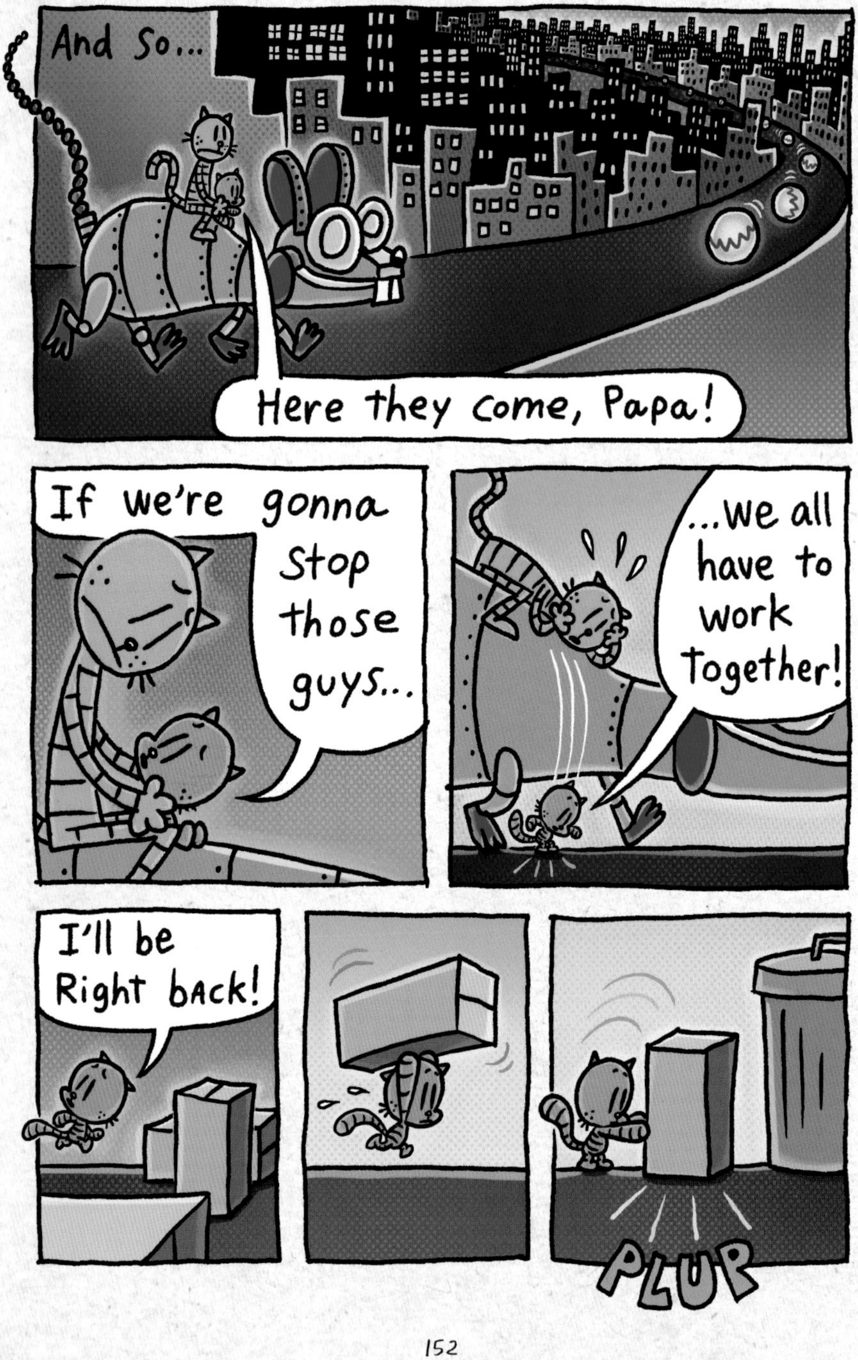
And so...
Here they come, Papa!
If we're gonna stop those guys...
...we all have to work together!
I'll be Right back!
PLUP

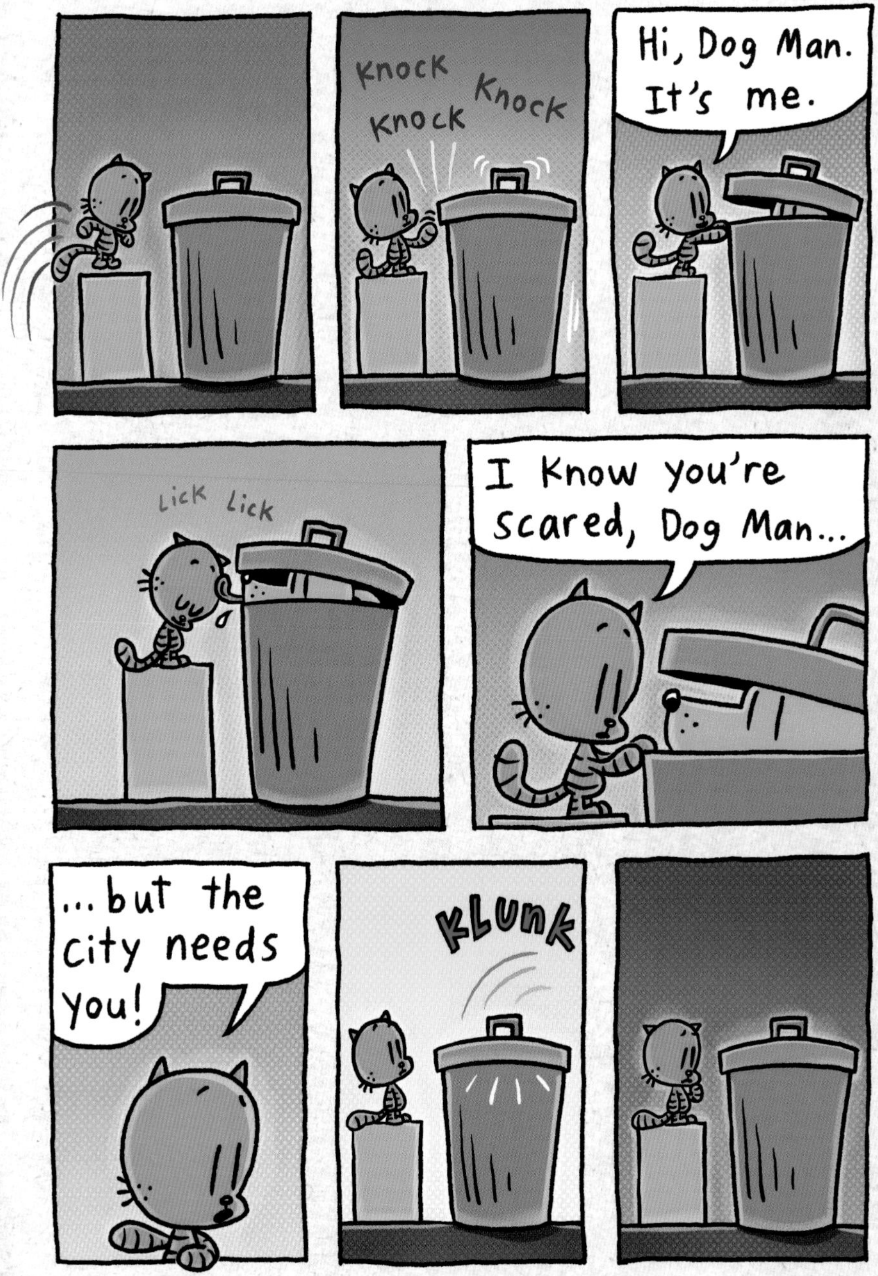
Knock
Knock
Knock
Hi, Dog Man. It's me.
Lick Lick
I Know you're scared, Dog Man...
...but the city needs you!
KLUNK

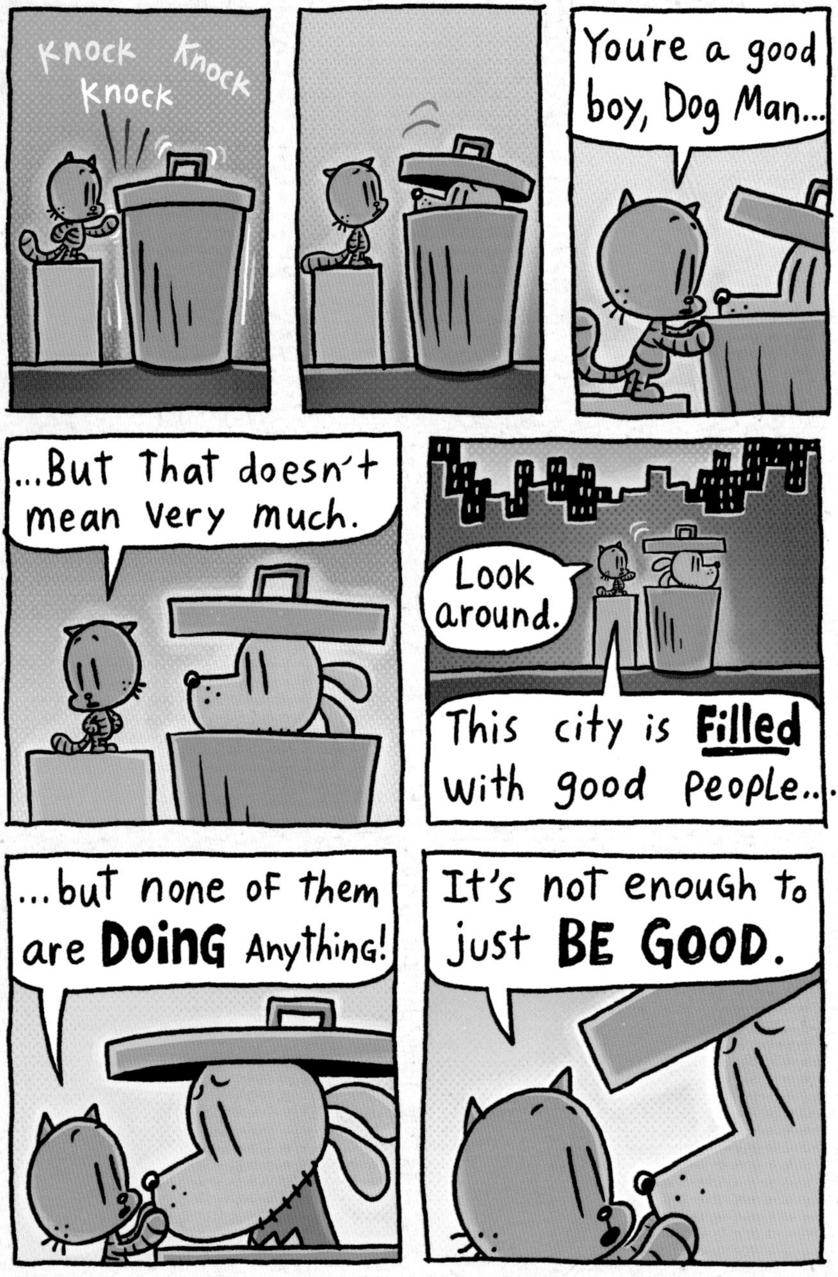
Knock Knock
Knock
You're a good boy, Dog Man...
...But That doesn't mean very much.
Look around.
This city is Filled with good people...
...but none of them are DOING Anything!
It's not enough to just BE GOOD.

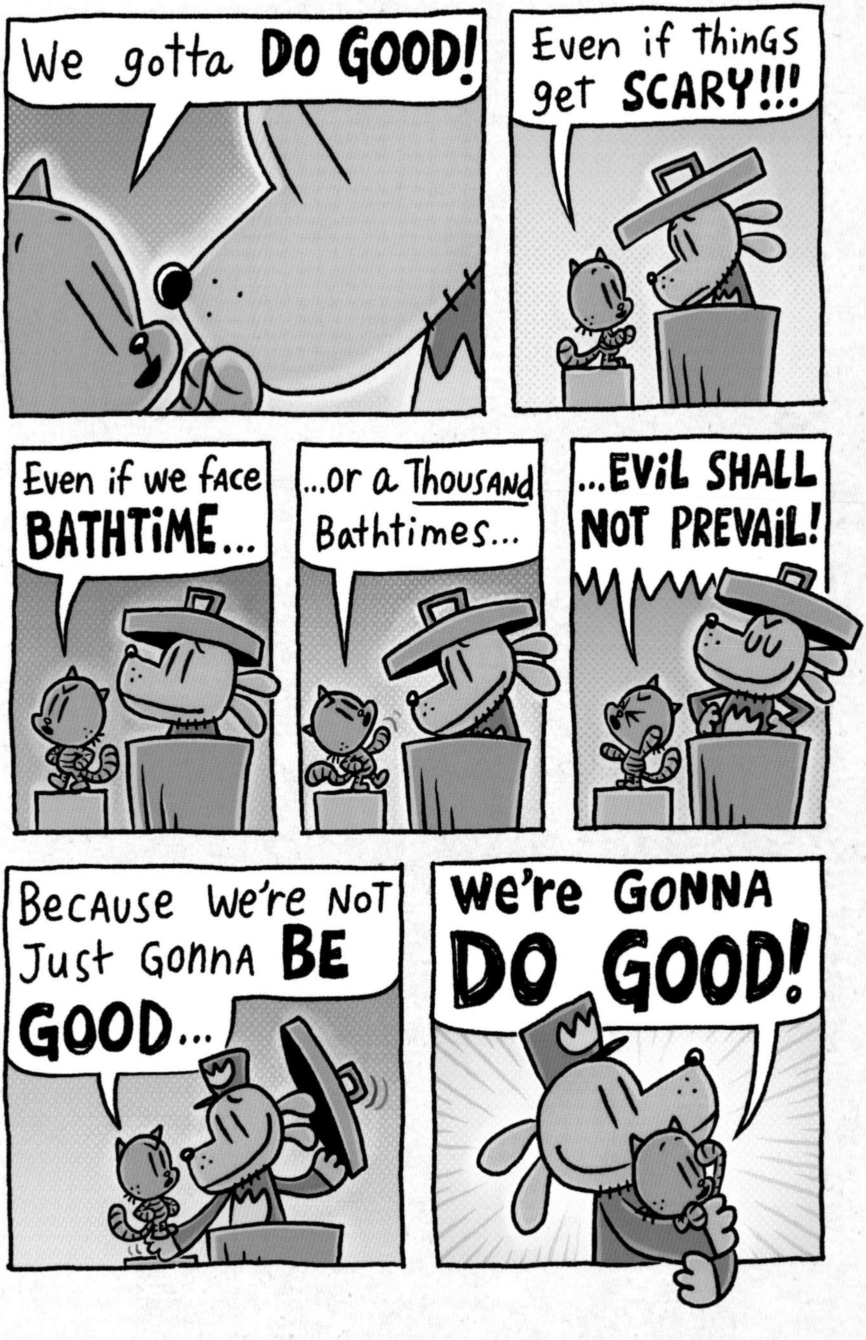
We gotta DO GOOD!
Even if things get SCARY!!!
Even if we face BATHTIME...
...or a Thousand Bathtimes...
...EVIL SHALL NOT PREVAIL!
Because We're NOT Just GONNA BE GOOD...
We're GONNA DO GOOD!

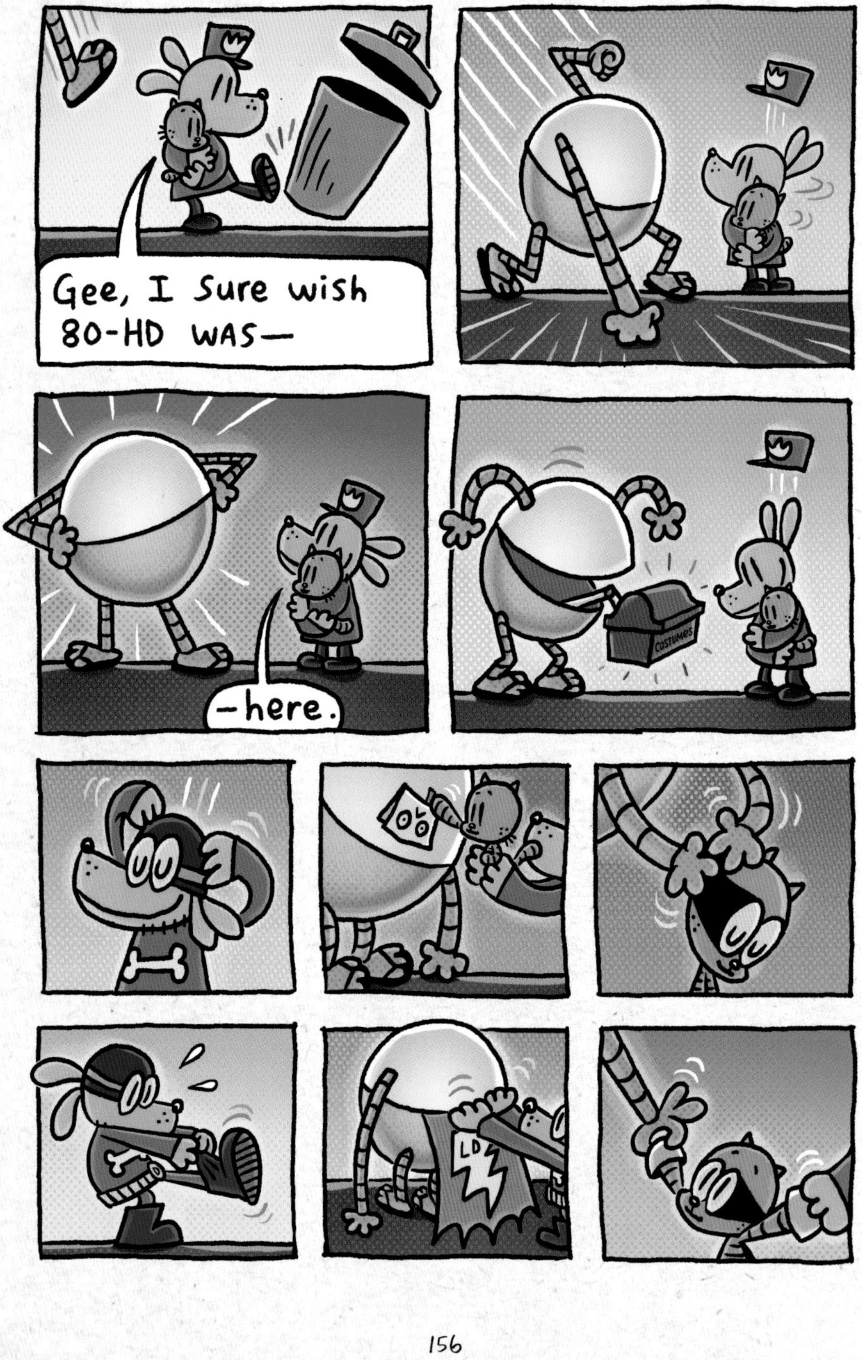
Gee, I sure wish 80-HD WAS—
—here.
COSTUMES
LD

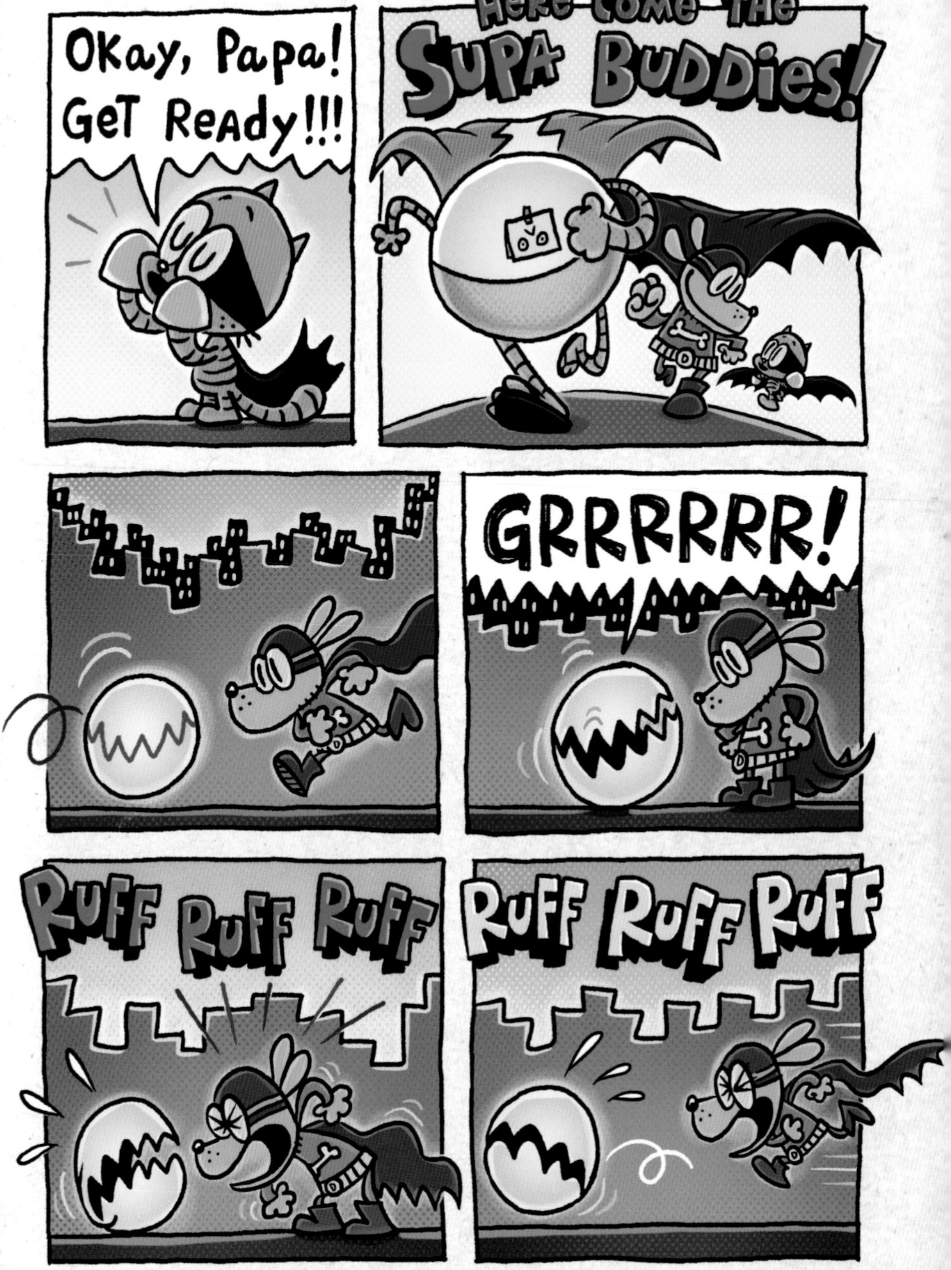
OKay, Papa! GeT Ready!!!
Here Come The
SUPA BUDDies!
GRRRRRR!
RUFF RUFF RUFF
RUFF RUFF RUFF

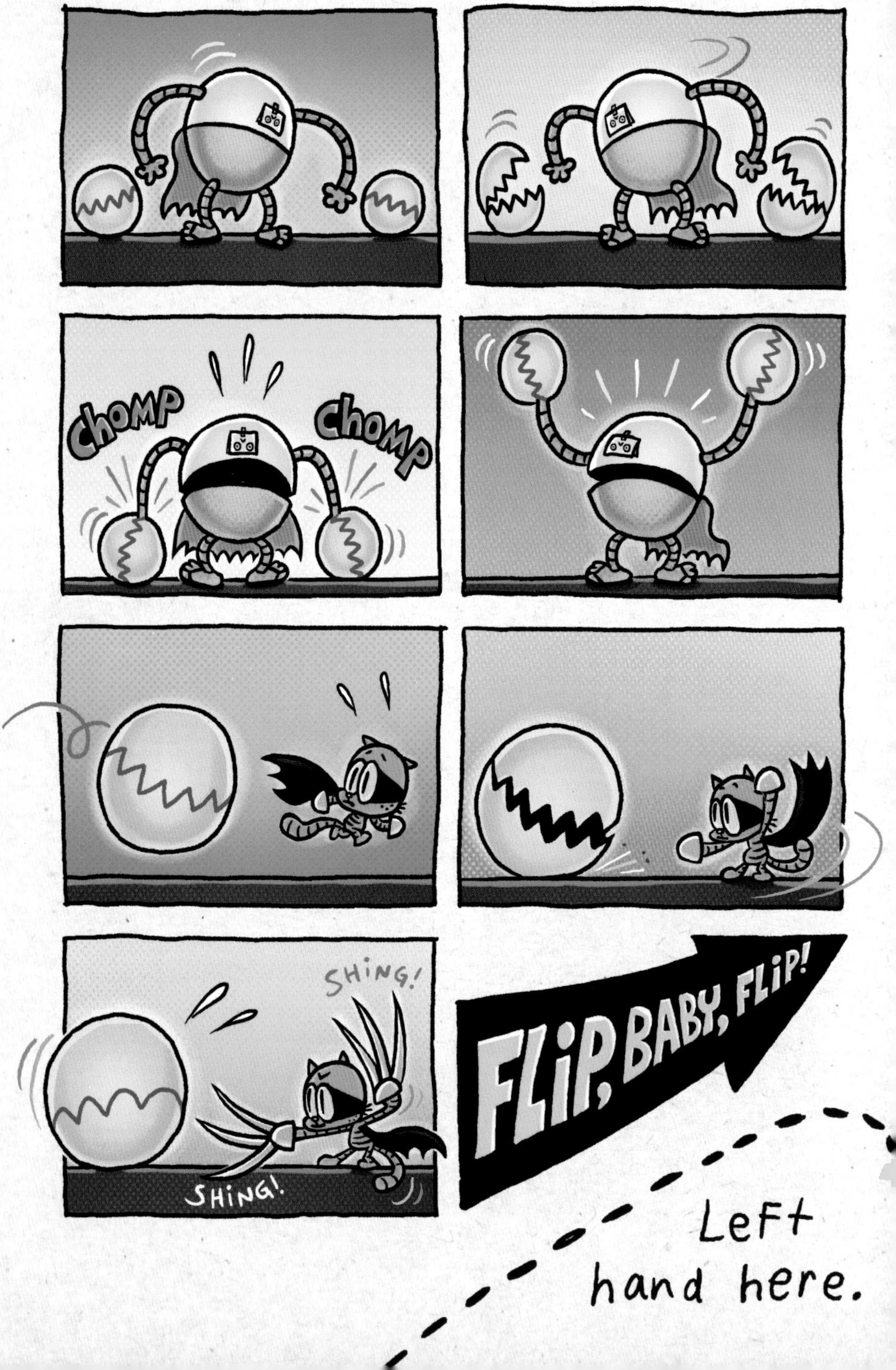
CHOMP
CHOMP
SHING!
SHING!
FLIP, BABY, FLIP!
Left hand here.

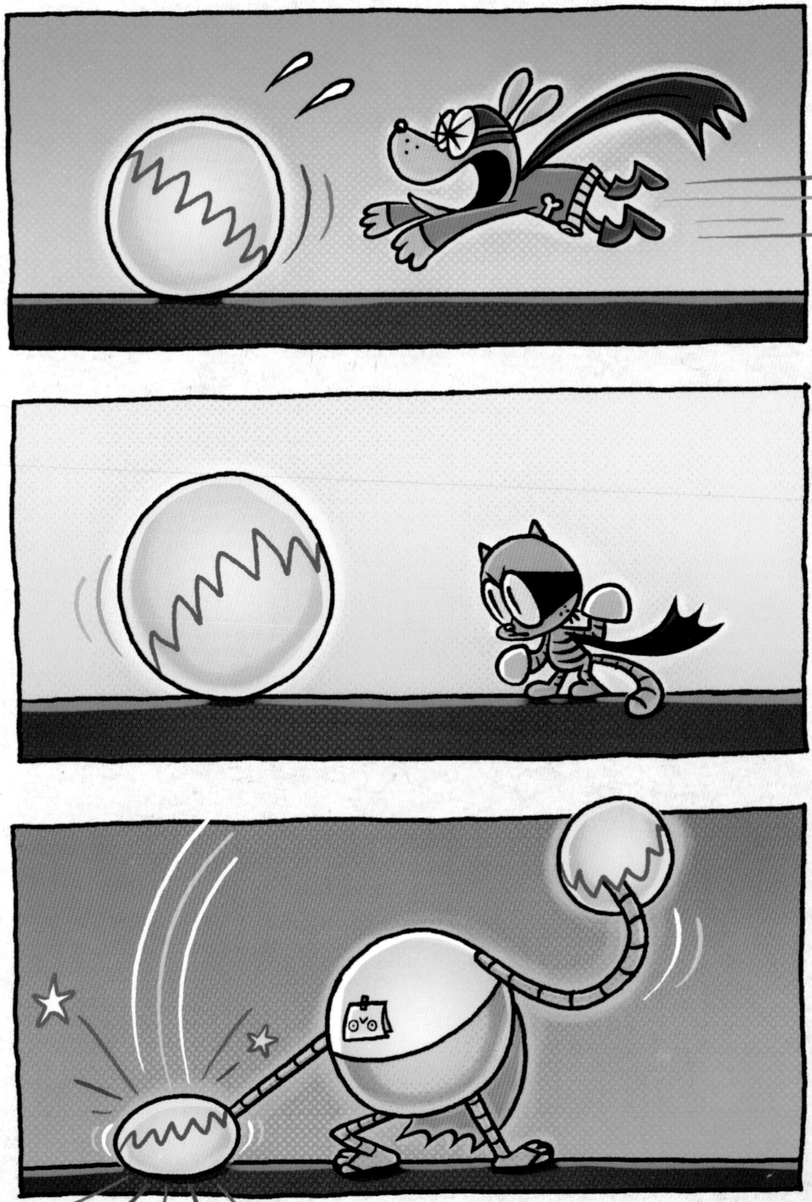

Right
Thumb
here.

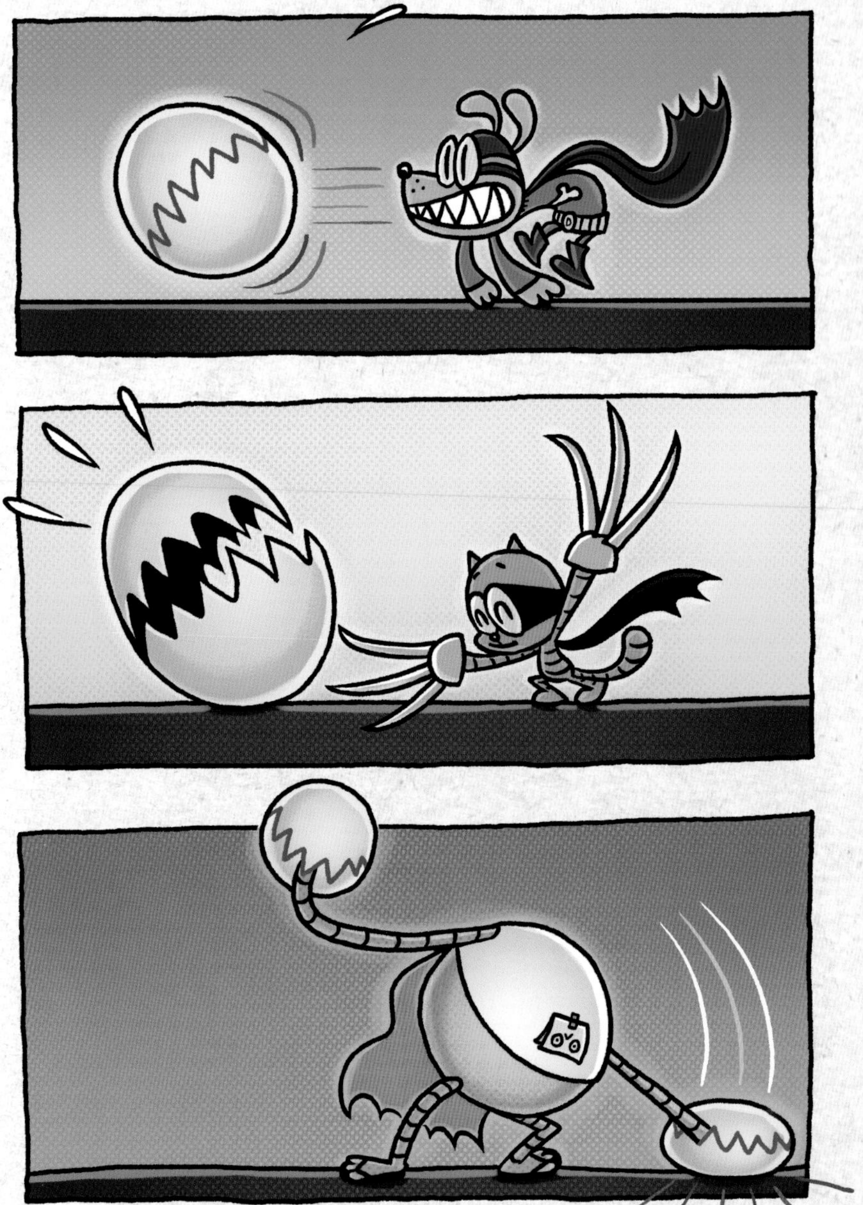

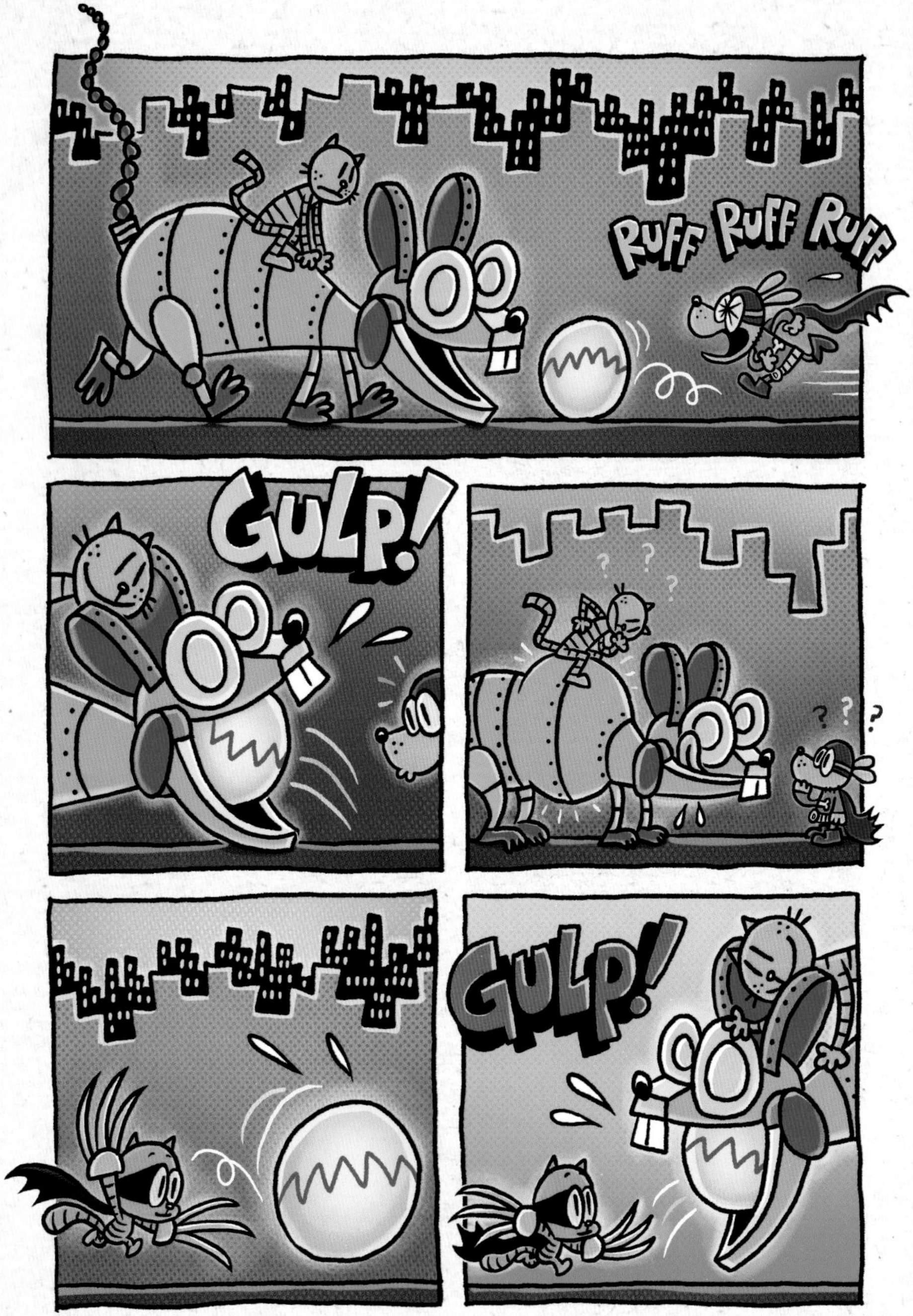
RUFF RUFF RUFF
GULP!
GULP!

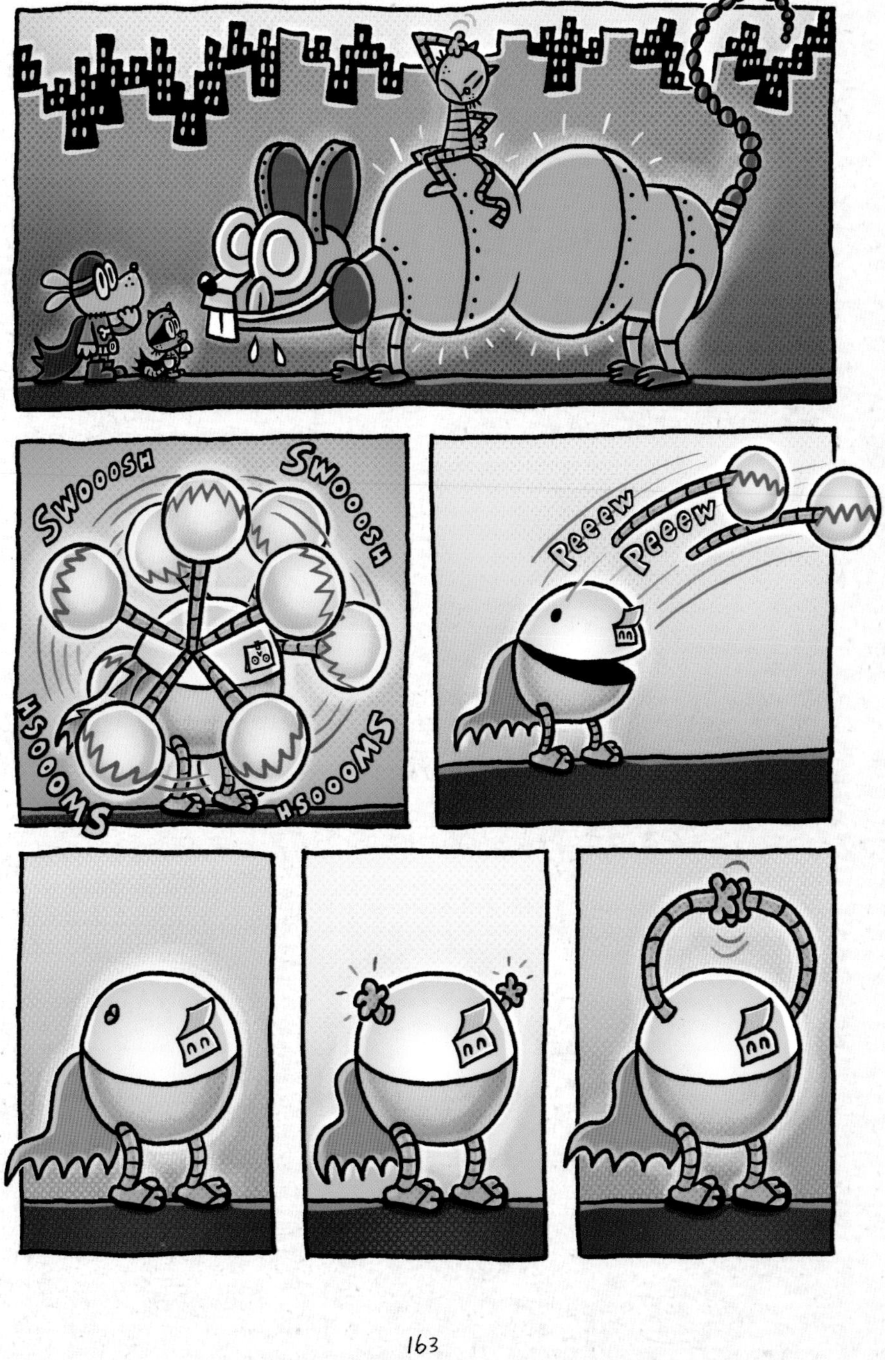
SWOOOSH
SWOOOSH
SWOOOSH
SWOOOSH
Peeew
Peeew

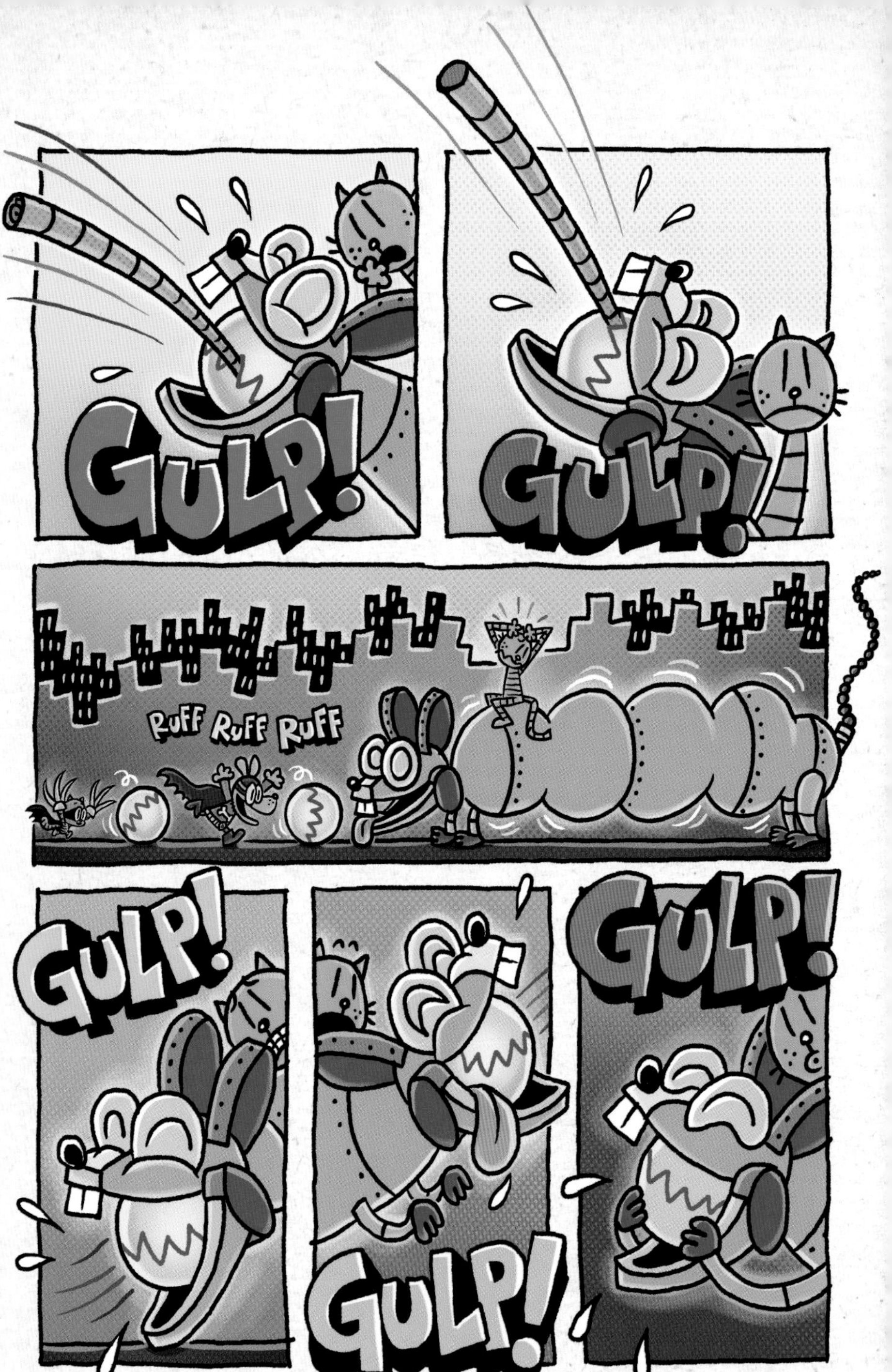
GULP!
GULP!
RUFF RUFF RUFF
GULP!
GULP!
GULP!

Tree-
House
Comix
Proudly
Presents

Chapter 11
The Very Hangry Raterpillar

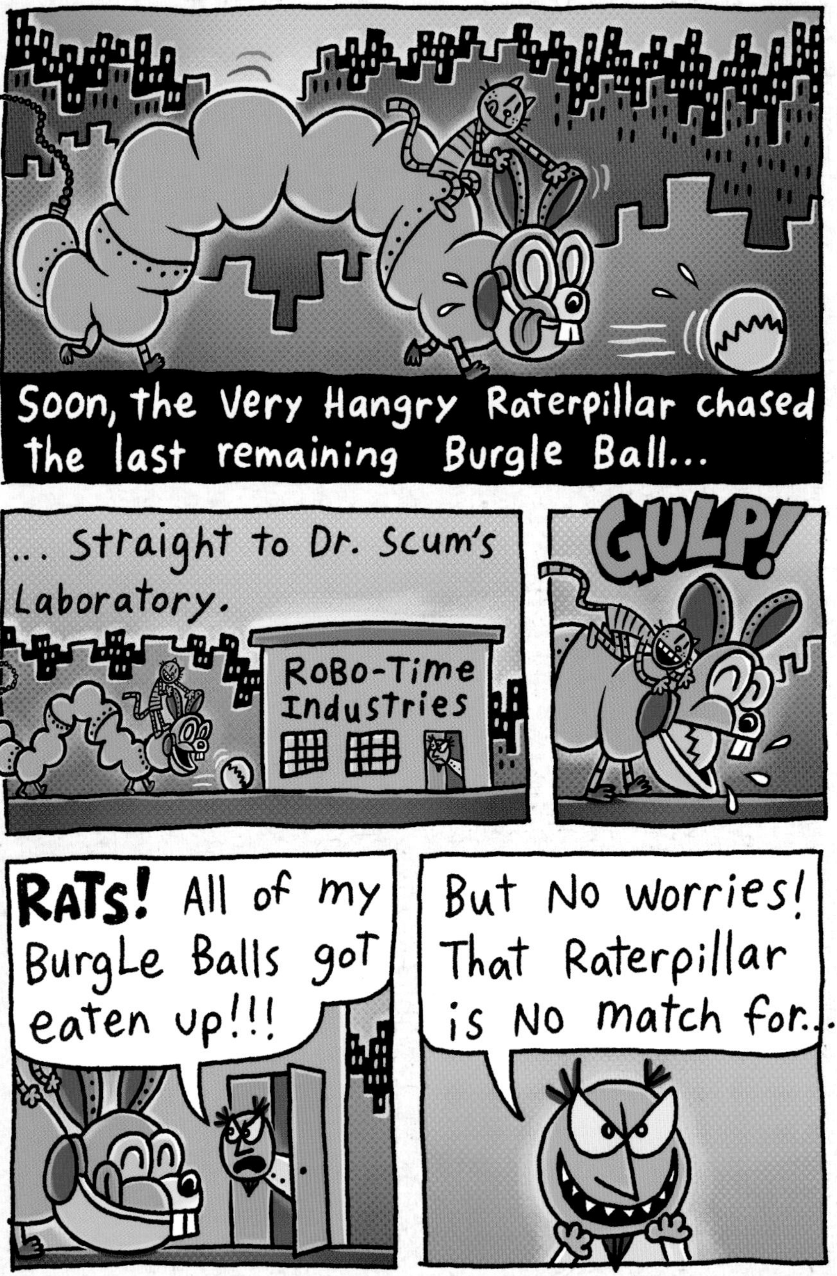
Soon, the Very Hangry Raterpillar chased the last remaining Burgle Ball...
... Straight to Dr. Scum's Laboratory.
RoBo-Time Industries
GULP!
RATS! All of my BurgLe Balls got eaten up!!!
But No worries! That Raterpillar is No match for...

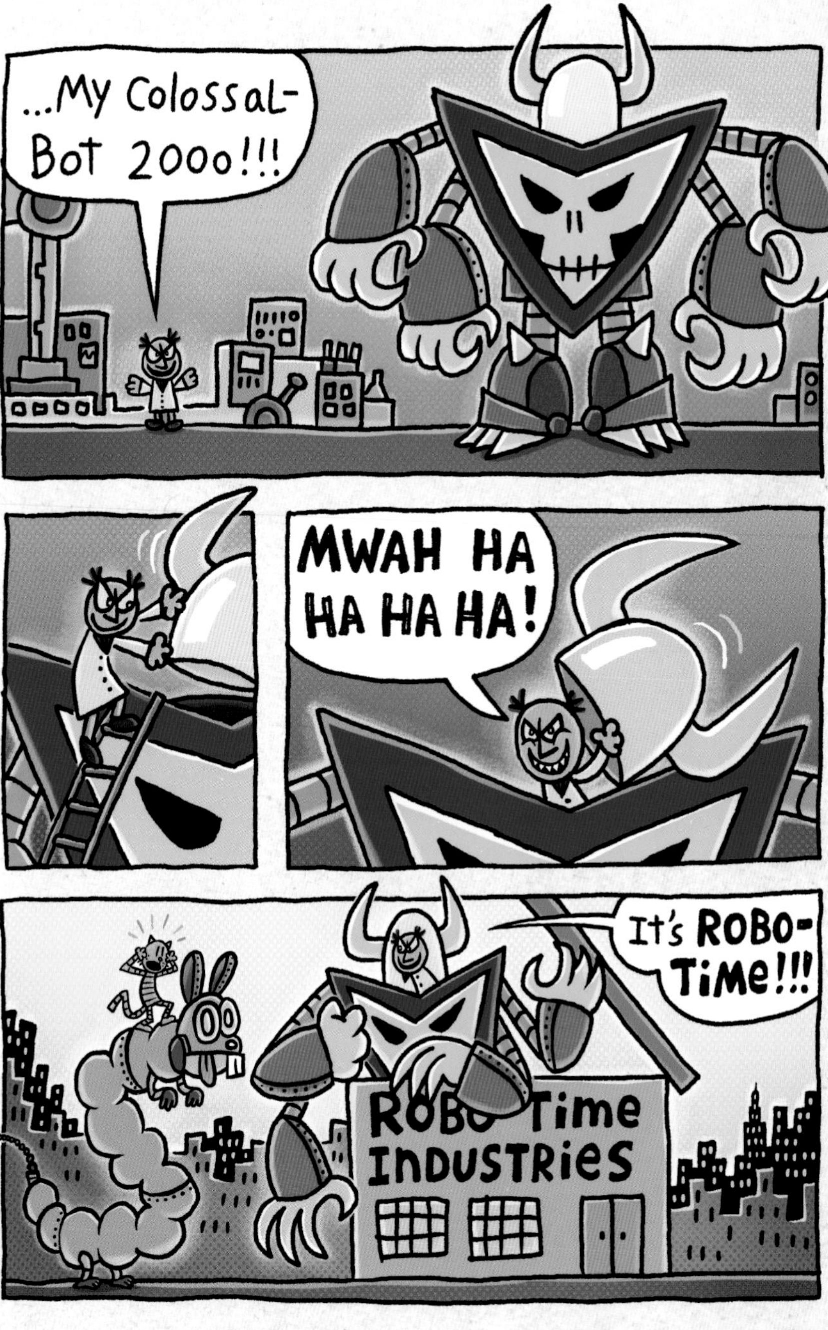

...My Colossal-Bot 2000!!!
MWAH HA HA HA HA!
It's ROBO-Time!!!
ROBO-Time Industries

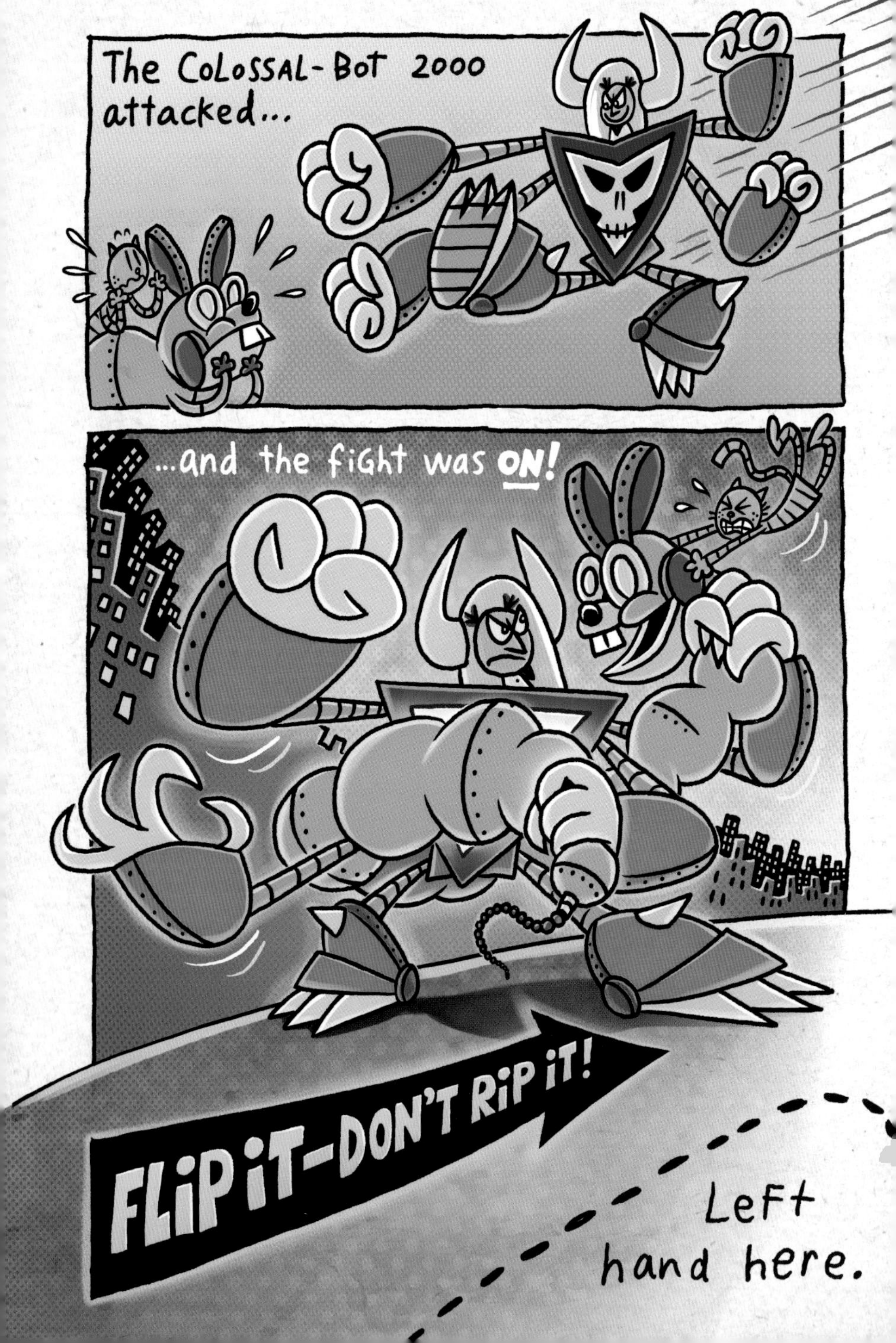
The COLOSSAL-BOT 2000 attacked...
...and the fight was ON!
FLIP IT—DON'T RIP IT!
Left hand here.

Right
Thumb
here.

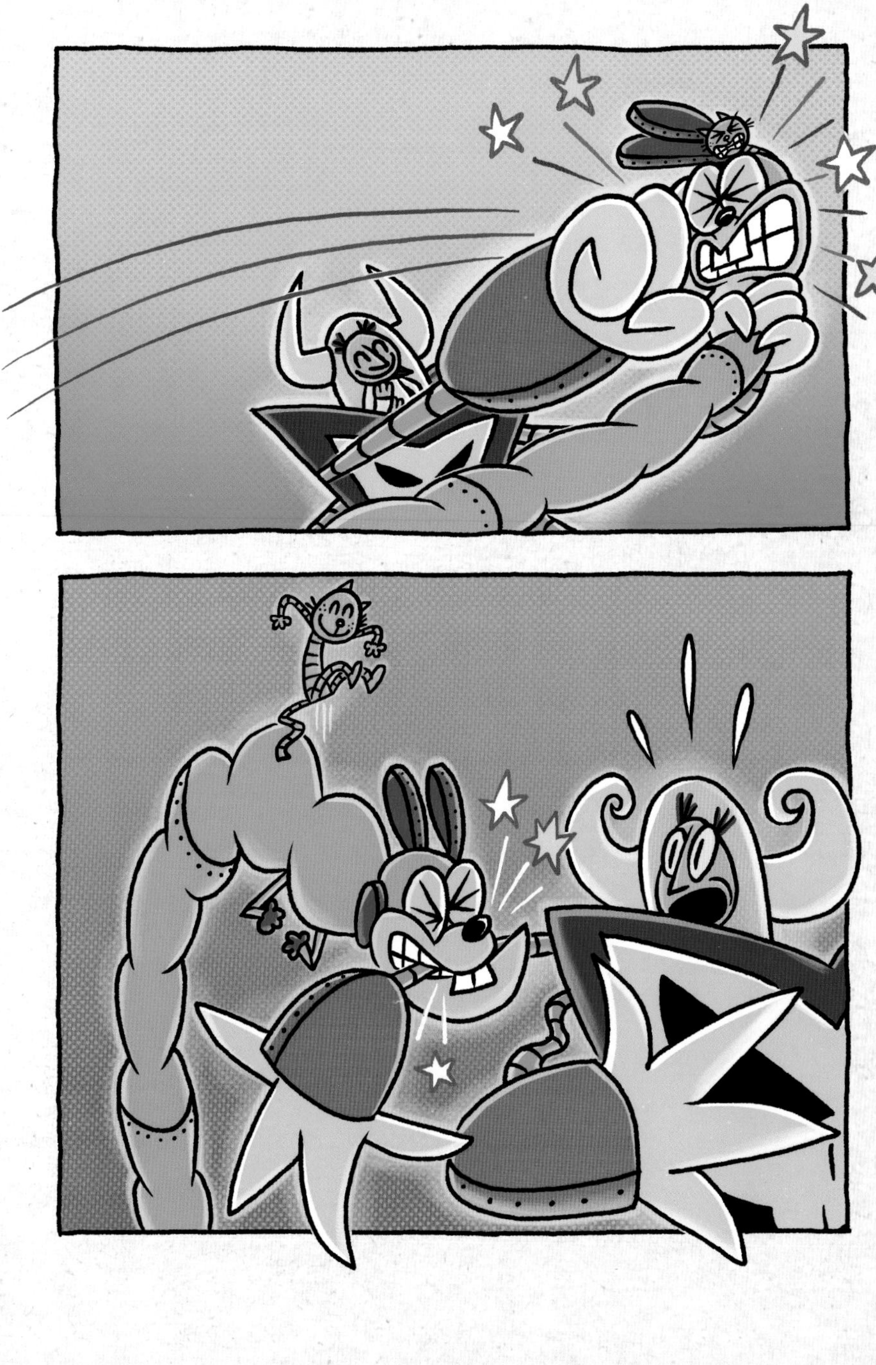

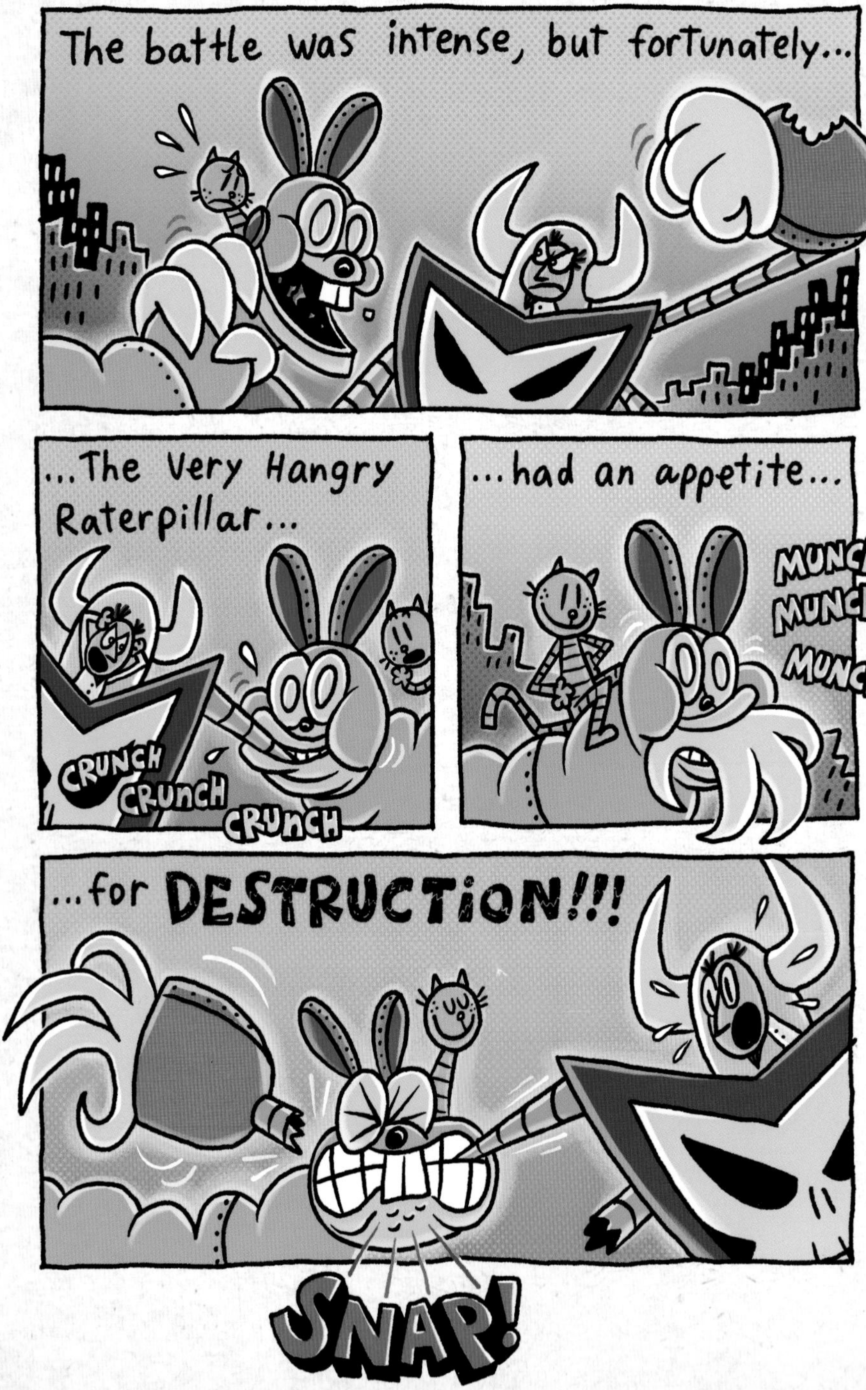
The battle was intense, but fortunately...
...The Very Hangry Raterpillar...
CRUNCH
CRUNCH
CRUNCH
...had an appetite...
MUNCH
MUNCH
MUNCH
...for DESTRUCTION!!!
SNAP!

CHAPTER 12

A Farewell to Arms

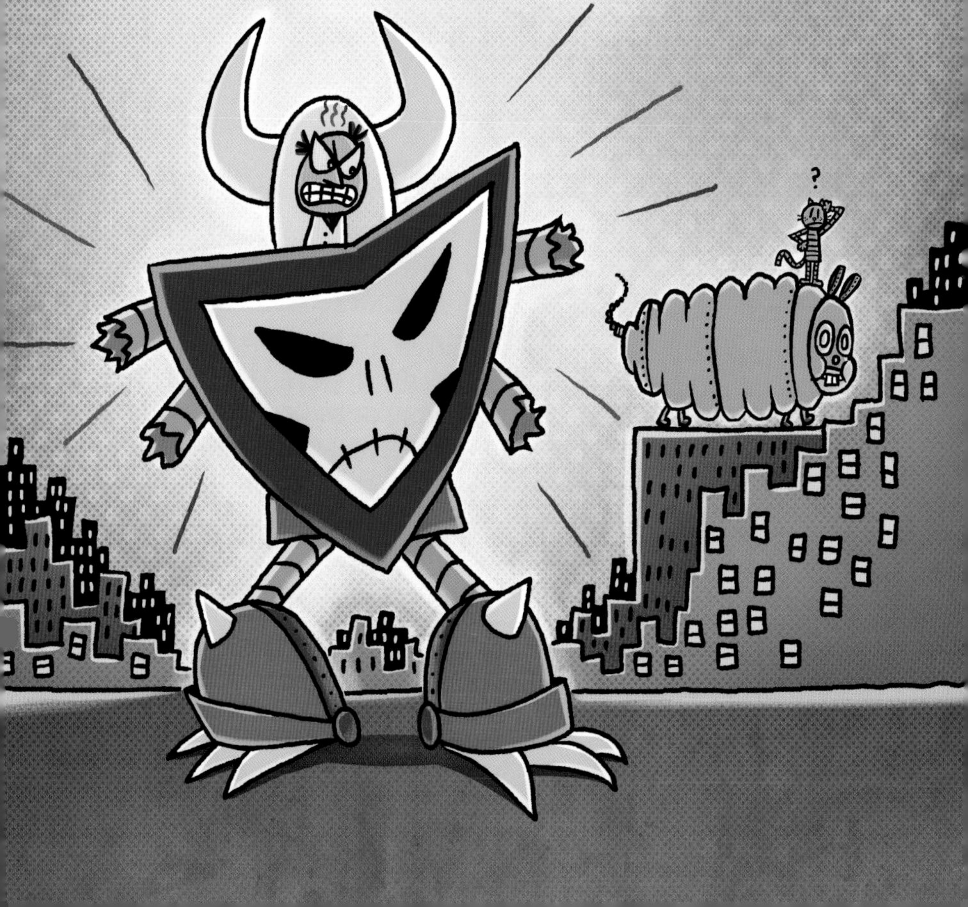

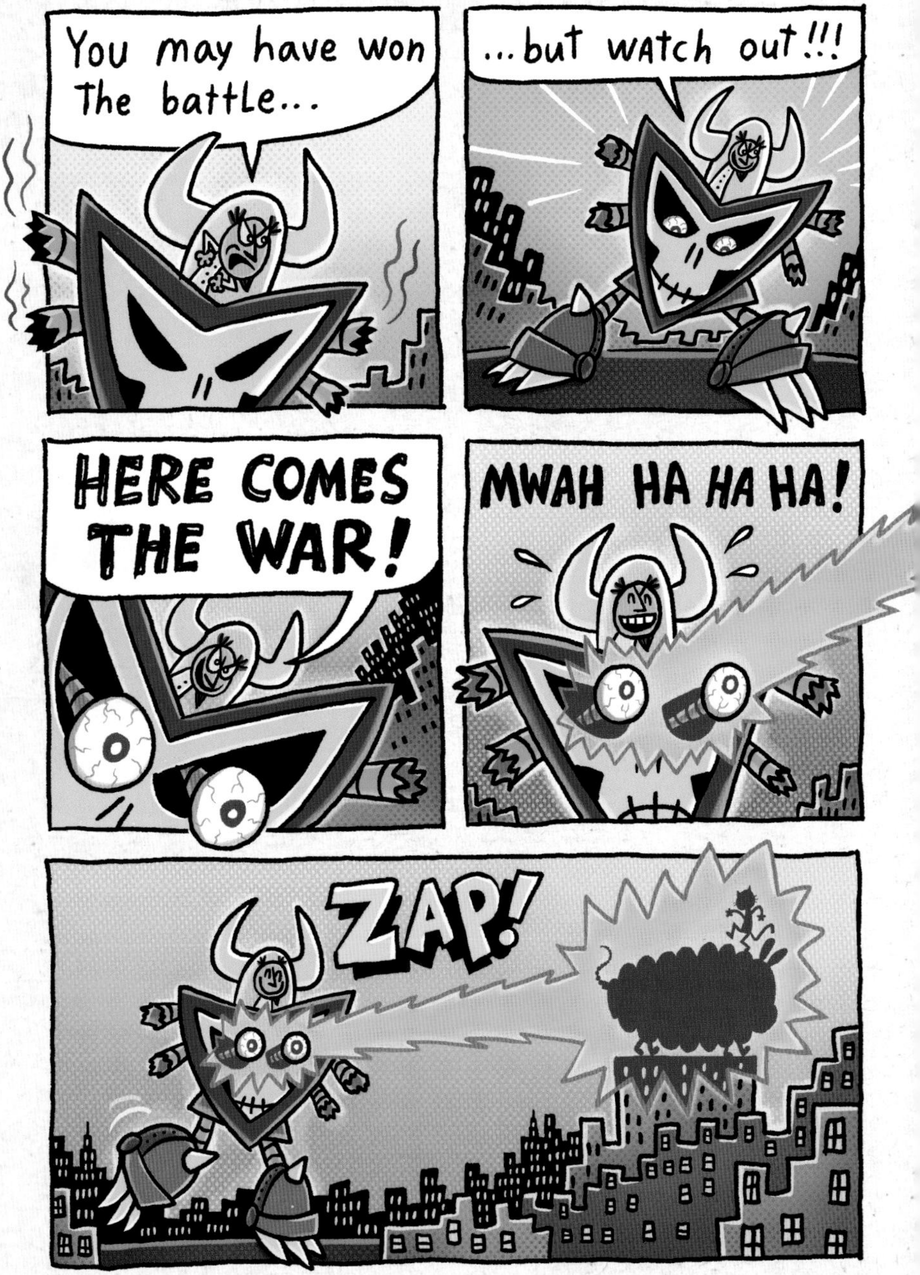
You may have won The battle...
...but WATCH out!!!
HERE COMES THE WAR!
MWAH HA HA HA!
ZAP!

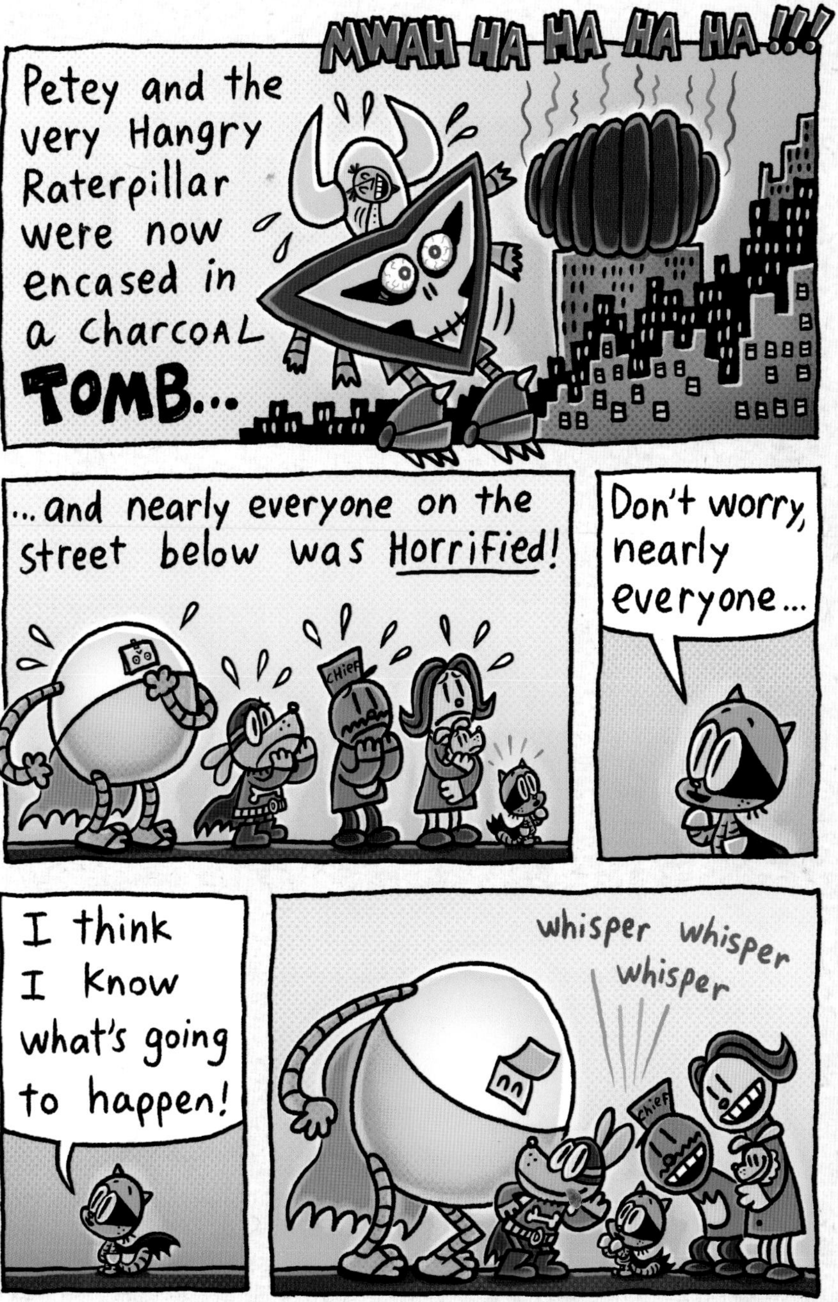
MWAH HA HA HA HA!!!
Petey and the very Hangry Raterpillar were now encased in a charcoal TOMB...
...and nearly everyone on the street below was Horrified!
Don't worry, nearly everyone...
CHIEF
I think I know what's going to happen!
whisper whisper whisper
CHIEF

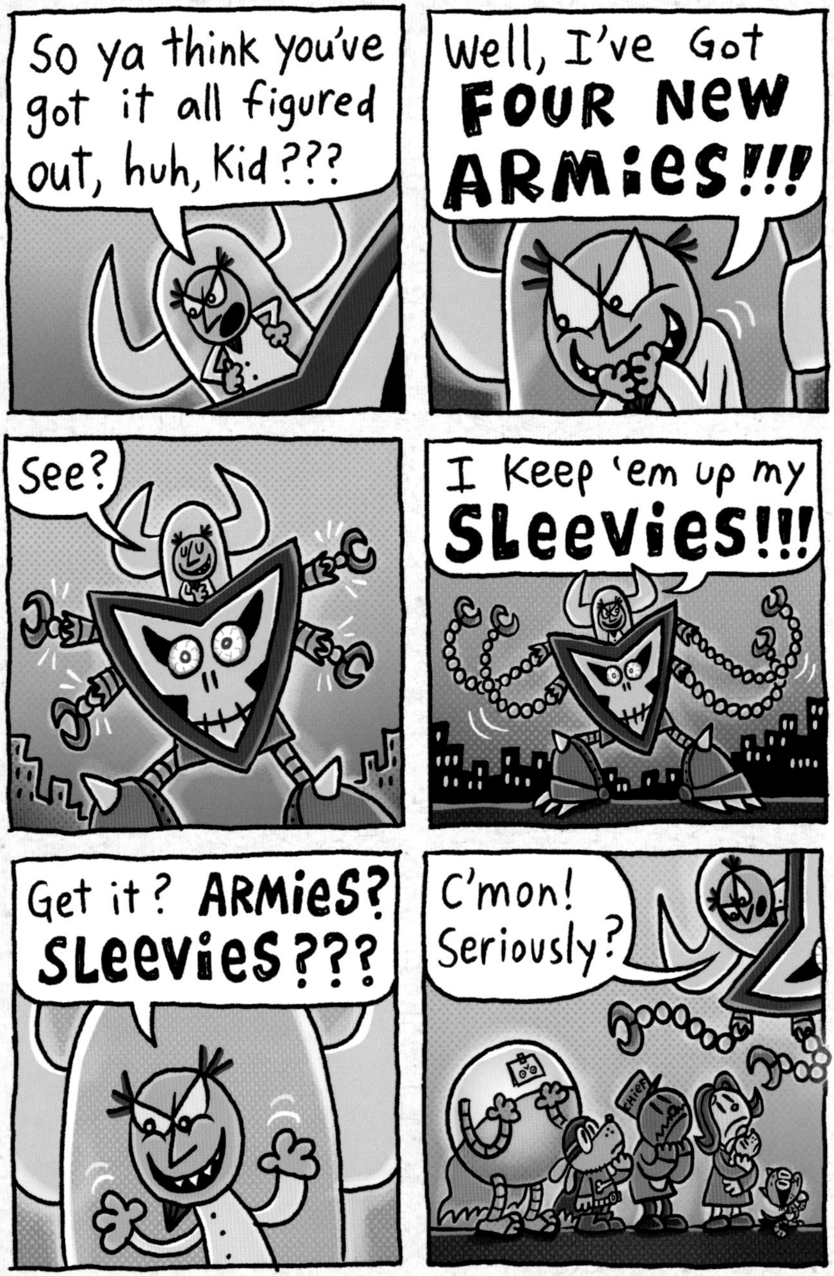

So ya think you've got it all figured out, huh, Kid???
Well, I've Got FOUR NEW ARMiES!!!
See?
I Keep 'em up my SLEEViES!!!
Get it? ARMiES? SLEEViES???
C'mon! Seriously?
CHIEF

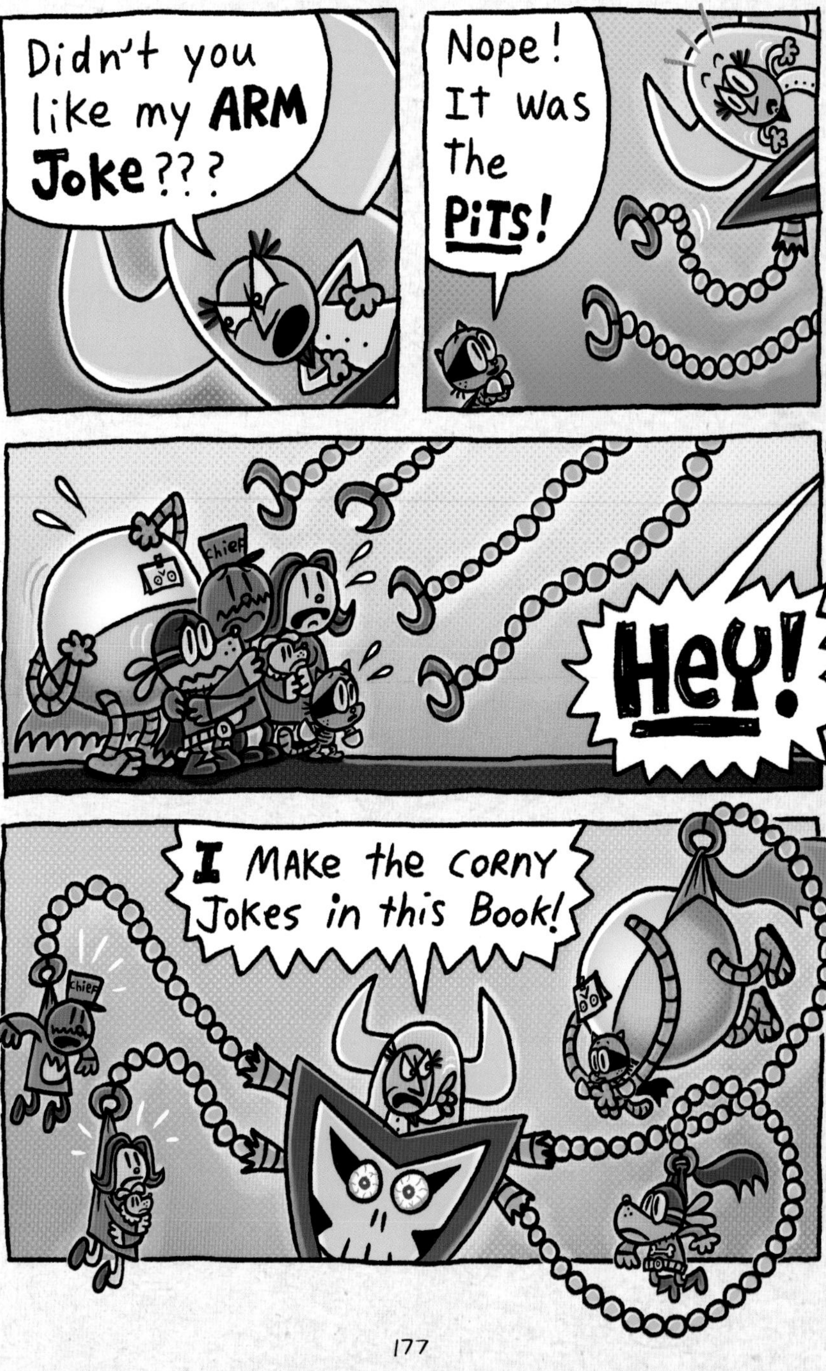
Didn't you like my ARM Joke???
Nope! It was the PiTS!
chief
HEY!
I MAKE the CORNY Jokes in this Book!
chief

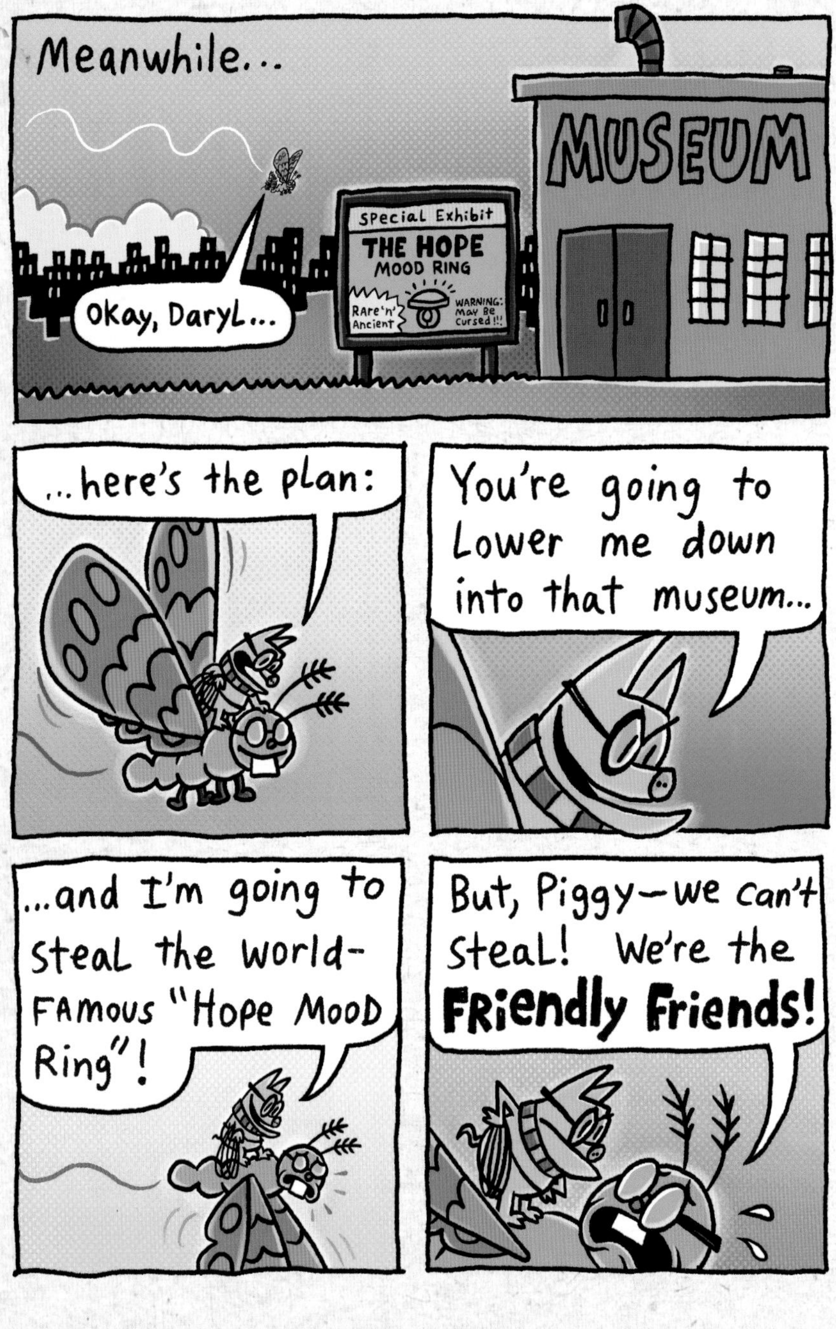
Meanwhile...
MUSEUM
Special Exhibit
THE HOPE
MOOD RING
Rare'n' Ancient
WARNING: May Be Cursed!!!
Okay, Daryl...
...here's the plan:
You're going to lower me down into that museum...
...and I'm going to steal the world-famous "Hope Mood Ring"!
But, Piggy—we can't steal! We're the **Friendly Friends!**

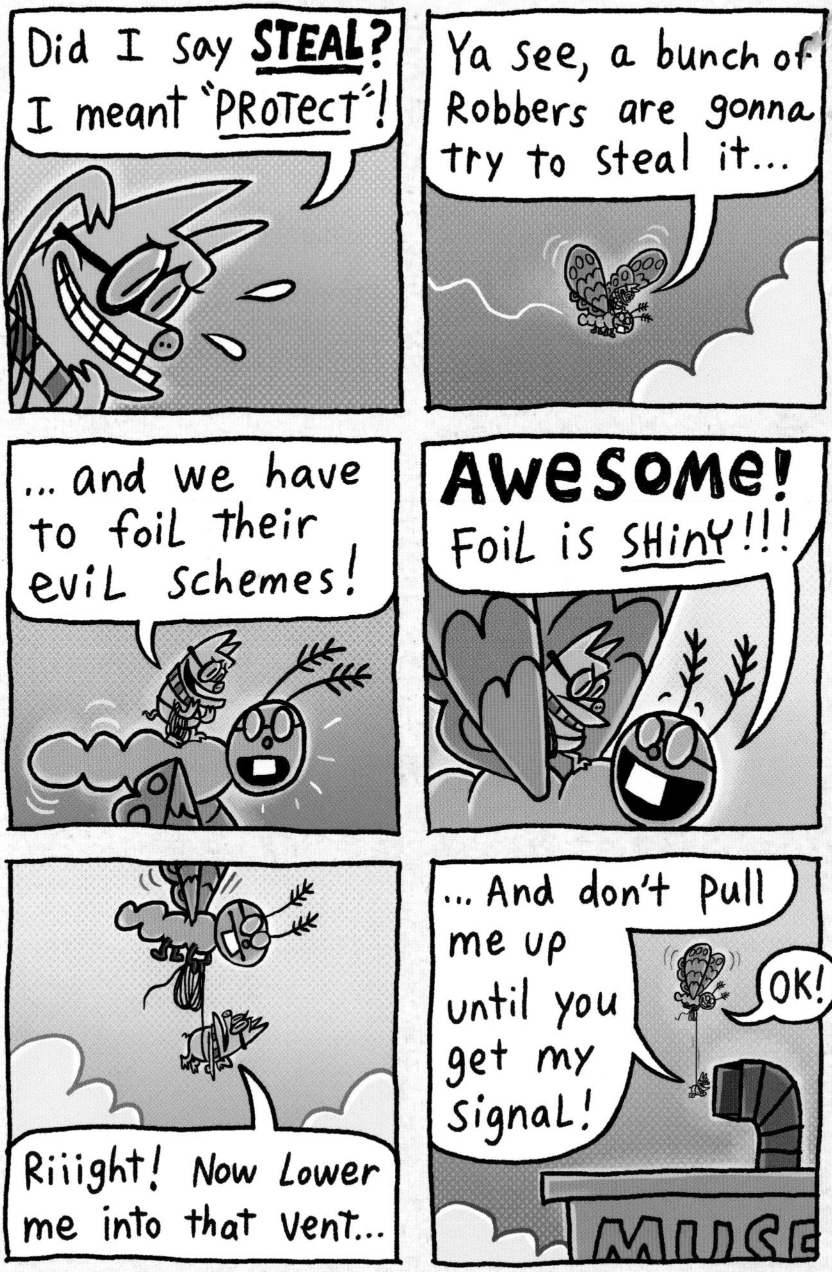
Did I say STEAL? I meant "PROTECT"!
Ya see, a bunch of Robbers are gonna try to steal it...
... and we have to foil their evil schemes!
AWESOME! Foil is SHINY!!!
Riiight! Now lower me into that vent...
... And don't pull me up until you get my signal!
OK!
MUSE

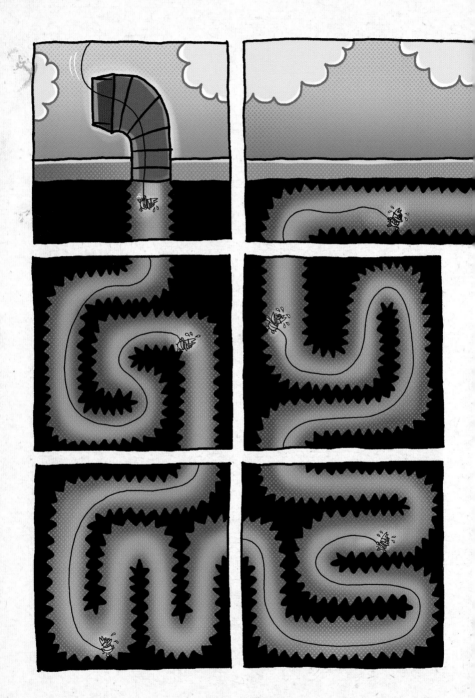

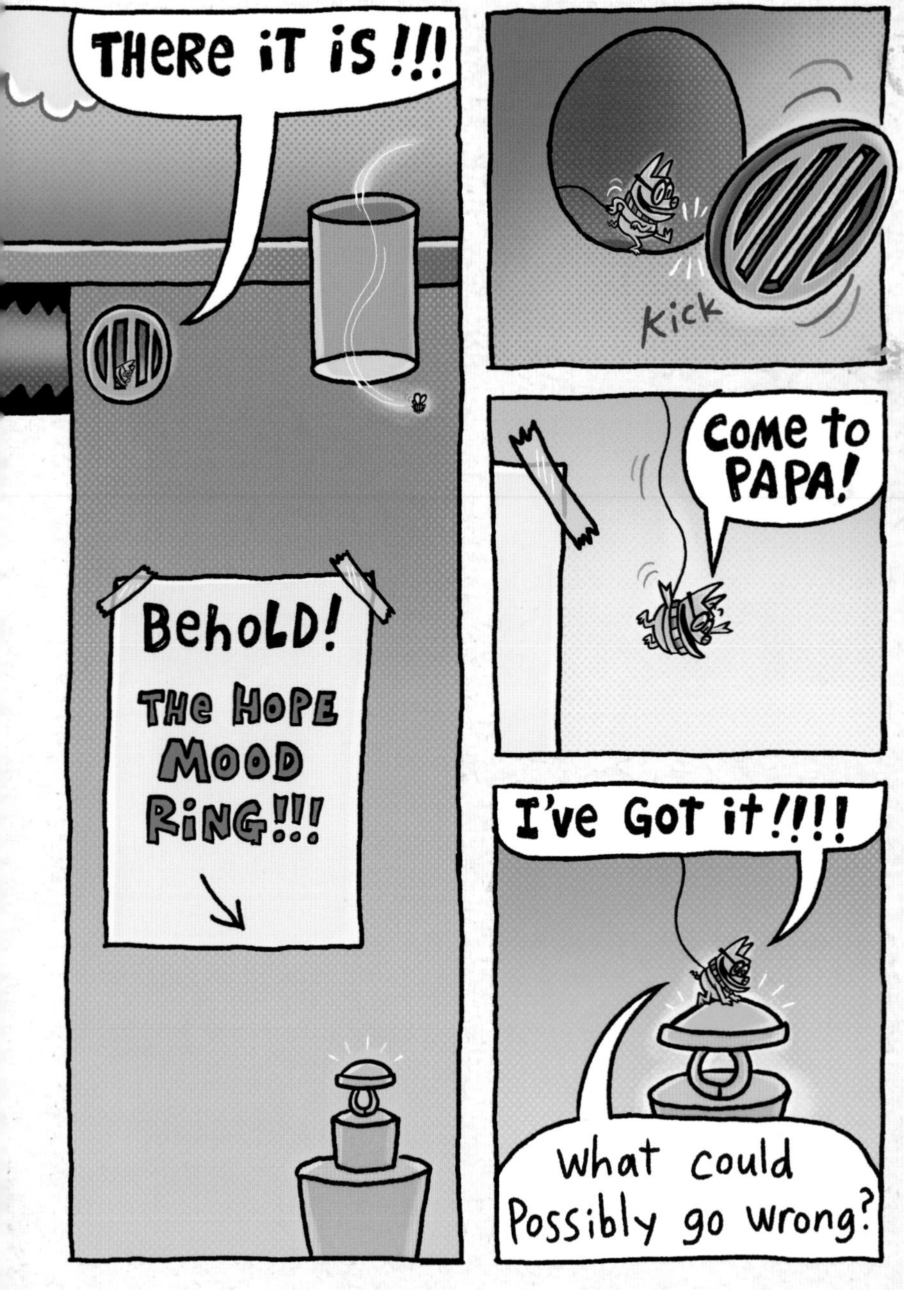
THERE iT iS!!!
BeHoLD!
THE HOPE MOOD RiNG!!!
Kick
Come to PAPA!
I've Got it!!!!
What could Possibly go wrong?

The Terrified Cries for help echoed across the rooftops...	... and fell upon the ears of a hungry, hungry hero!

CHAPTER 13

COMMANDER CUPCAKE RETURNS

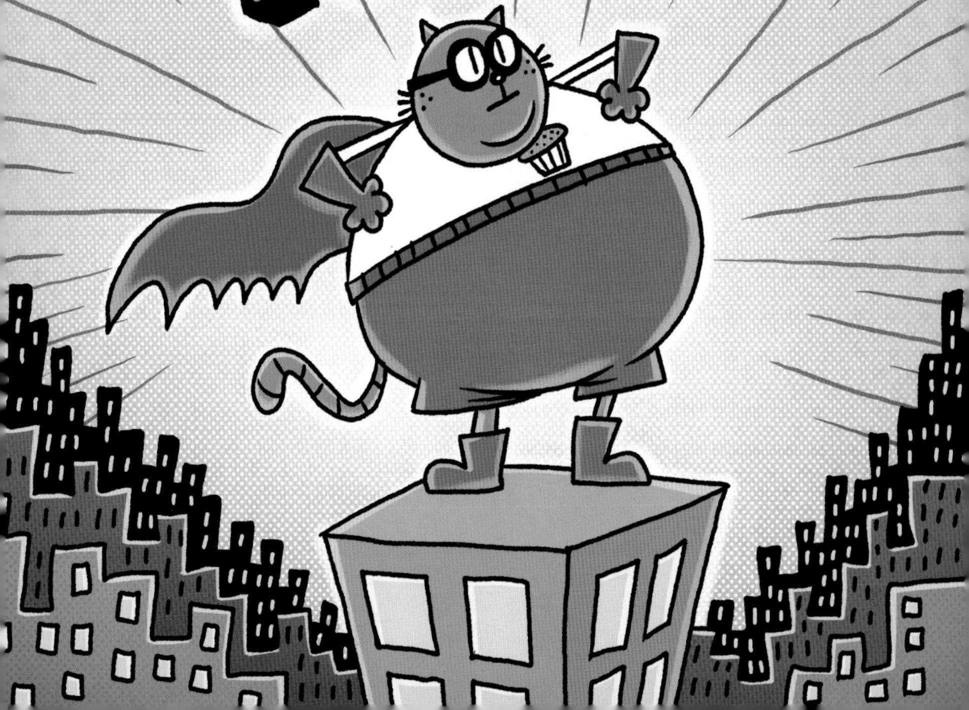

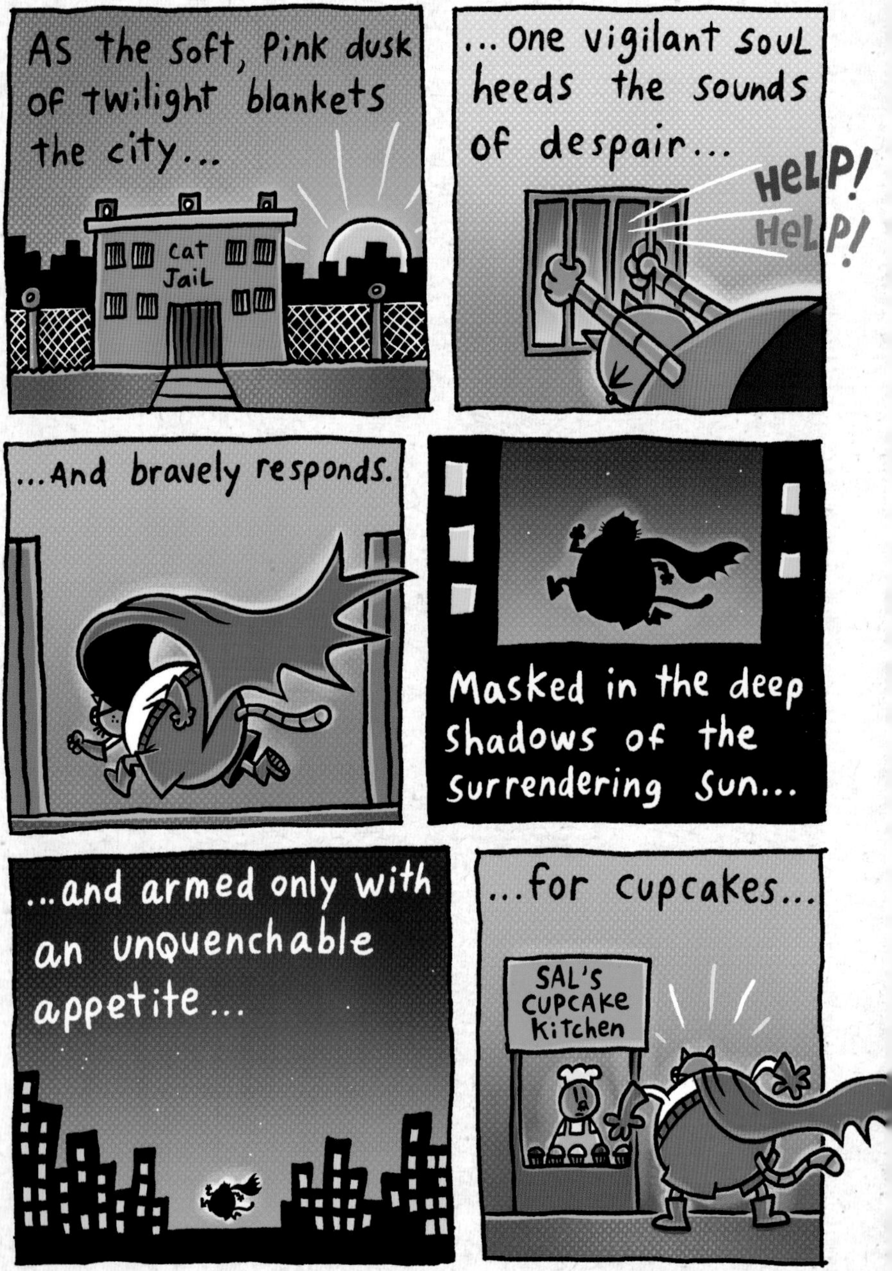

As the soft, pink dusk of twilight blankets the city...
Cat Jail
...One vigilant soul heeds the sounds of despair...
HELP!
HELP!
...And bravely responds.
Masked in the deep shadows of the surrendering sun...
...and armed only with an unquenchable appetite...
...for cupcakes...
SAL'S CUPCAKE Kitchen

...Our Spunky spartan of sprinkles barges forth where even the most Valiant fear to tiptoe!
NOM NOM
NOM NOM
CHIEF
NOM
Nom
Um — That's not really helpinG!

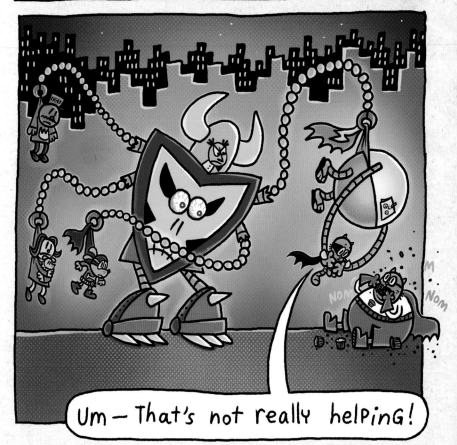

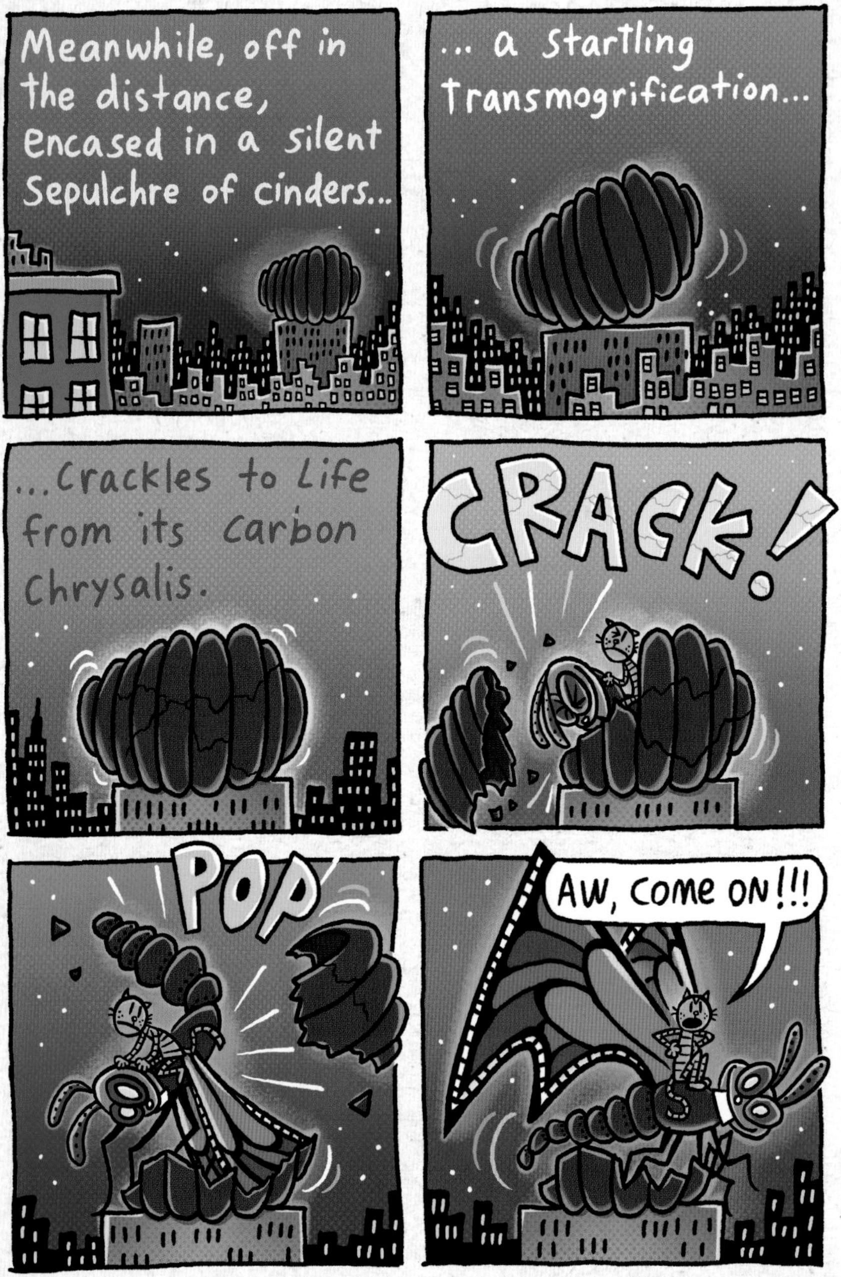
Meanwhile, off in the distance, encased in a silent sepulchre of cinders...
... a startling transmogrification...
...crackles to life from its carbon chrysalis.
CRACK!
POP
AW, COME ON!!!

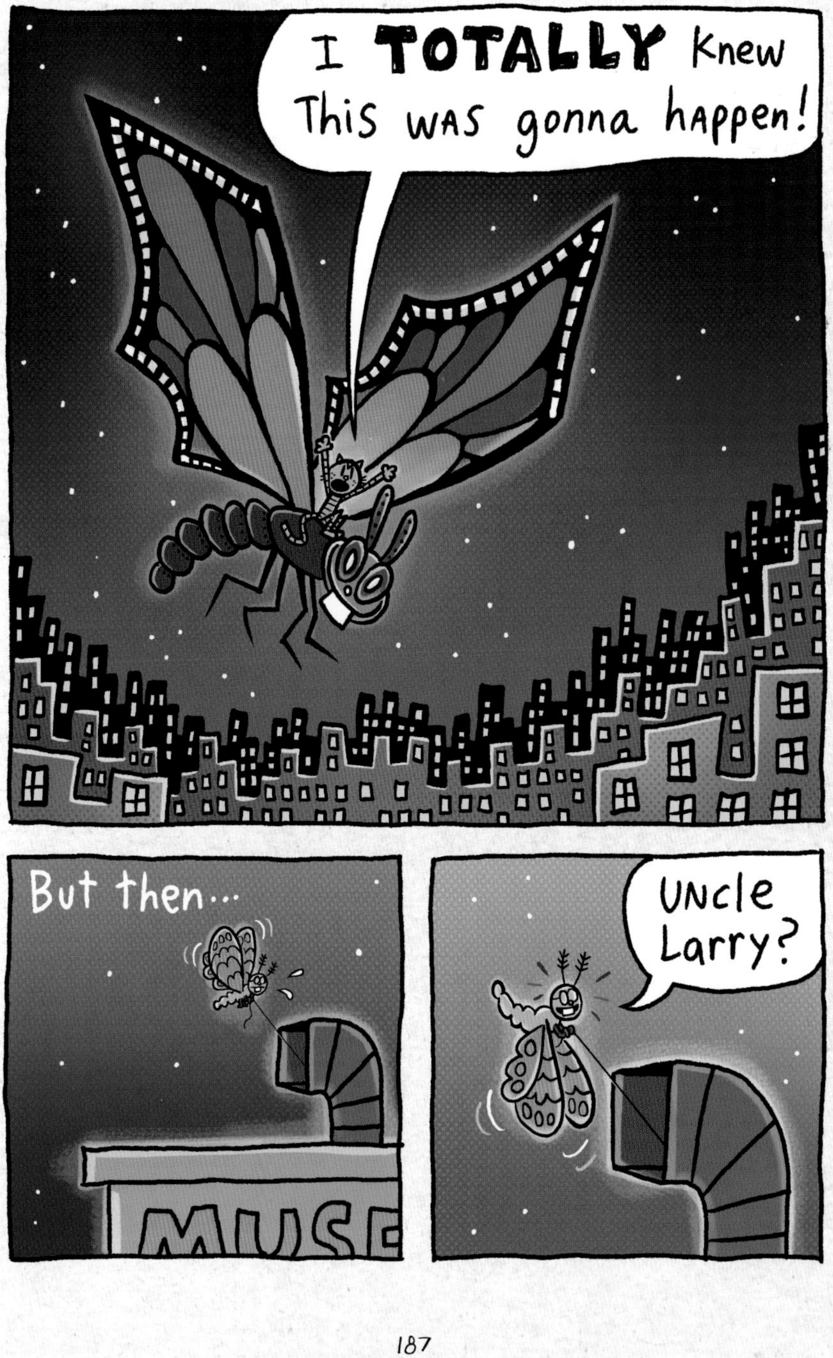
I TOTALLY Knew This WAS gonna happen!
But then...
MUSE
Uncle Larry?

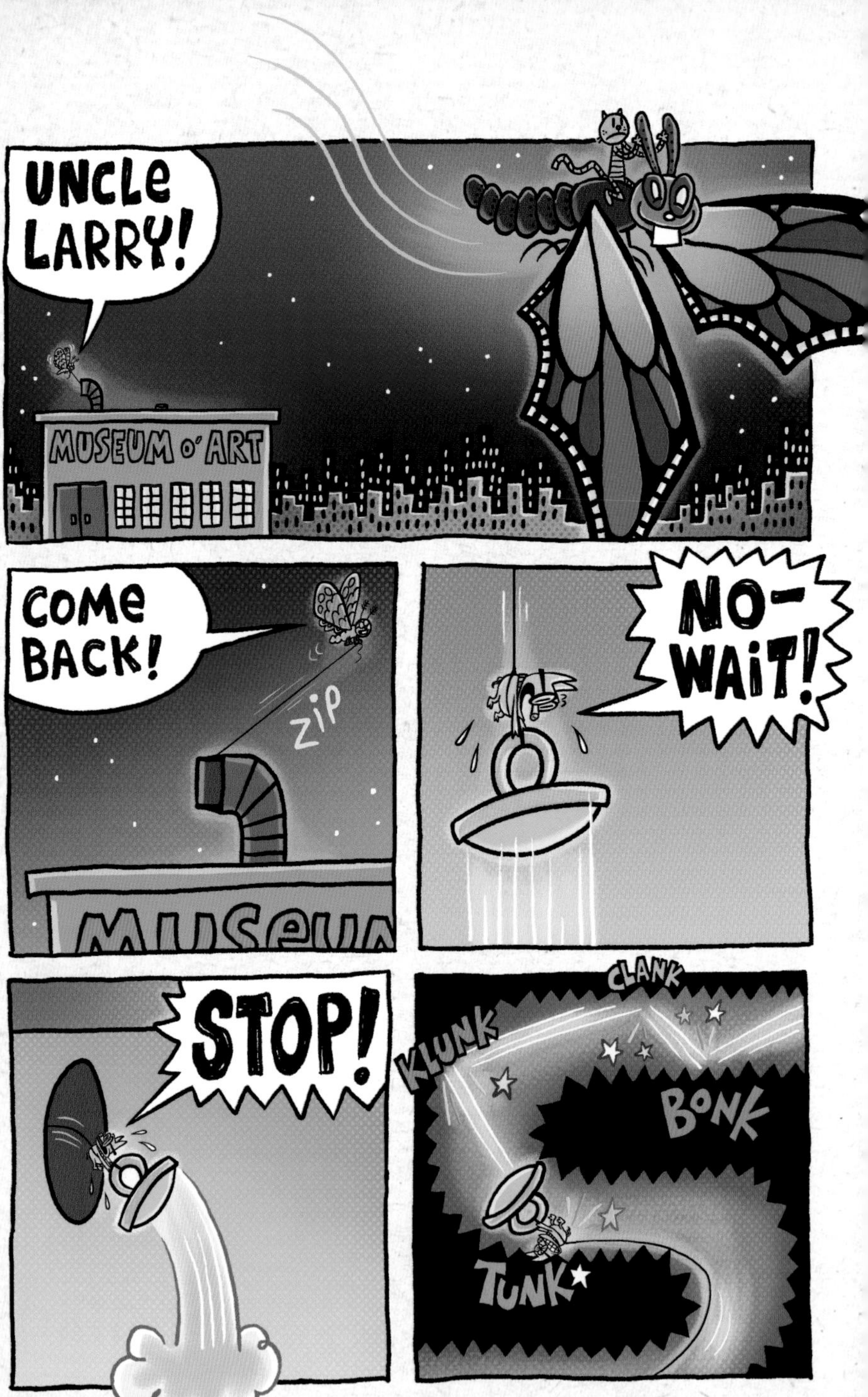
UNCLE LARRY!
MUSEUM O' ART
COME BACK!
ZIP
MUSEUM
NO- WAIT!
STOP!
CLANK
KLUNK
BONK
TUNK

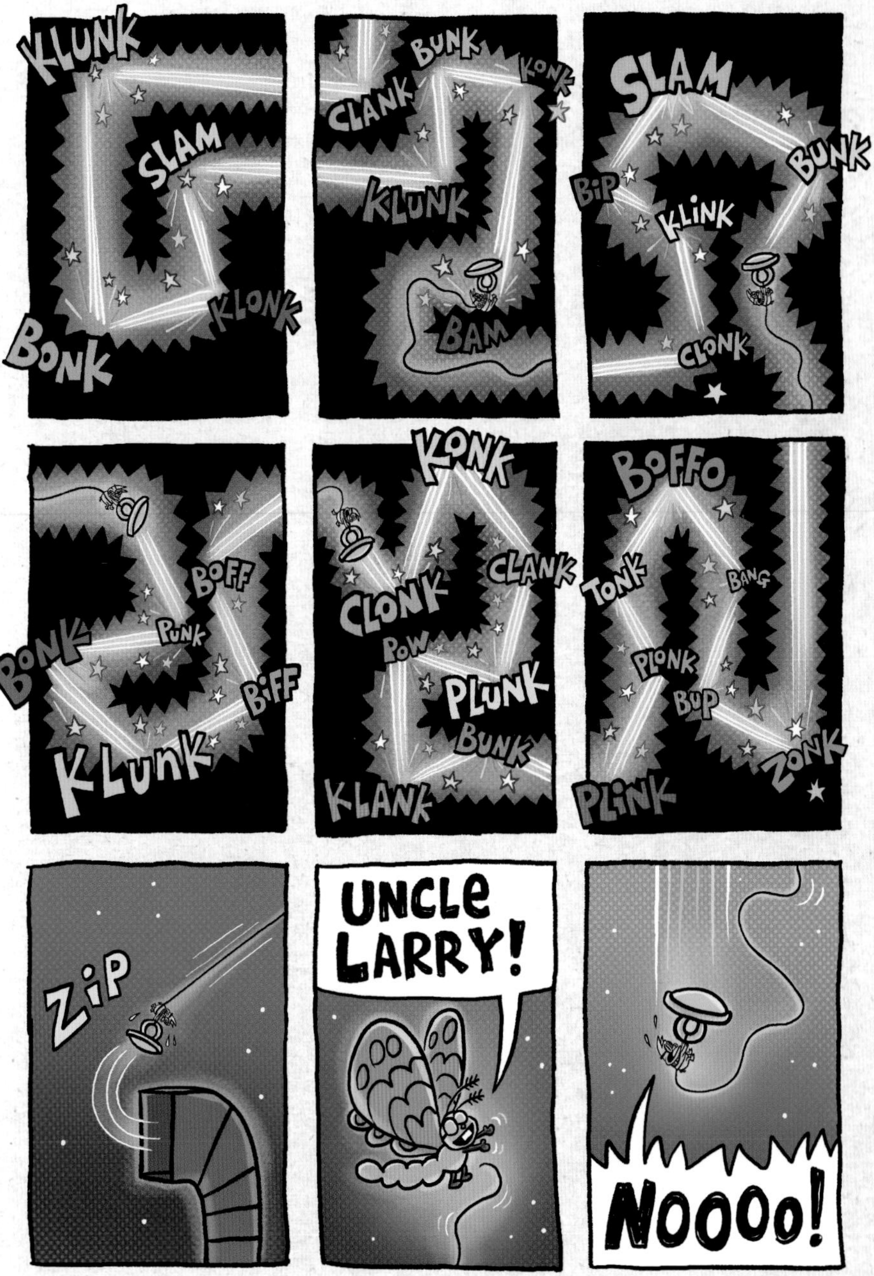
KLUNK
SLAM
KLONK
BONK
CLANK
BUNK
KONK
KLUNK
BAM
SLAM
BUNK
BIP
KLINK
CLONK
BOFF
PUNK
BONK
BIFF
KLUNK
KONK
CLANK
CLONK
POW
PLUNK
BUNK
KLANK
BOFFO
TONK
BANG
PLONK
BUP
ZONK
PLINK
ZIP
UNCLE LARRY!
NOOOo!

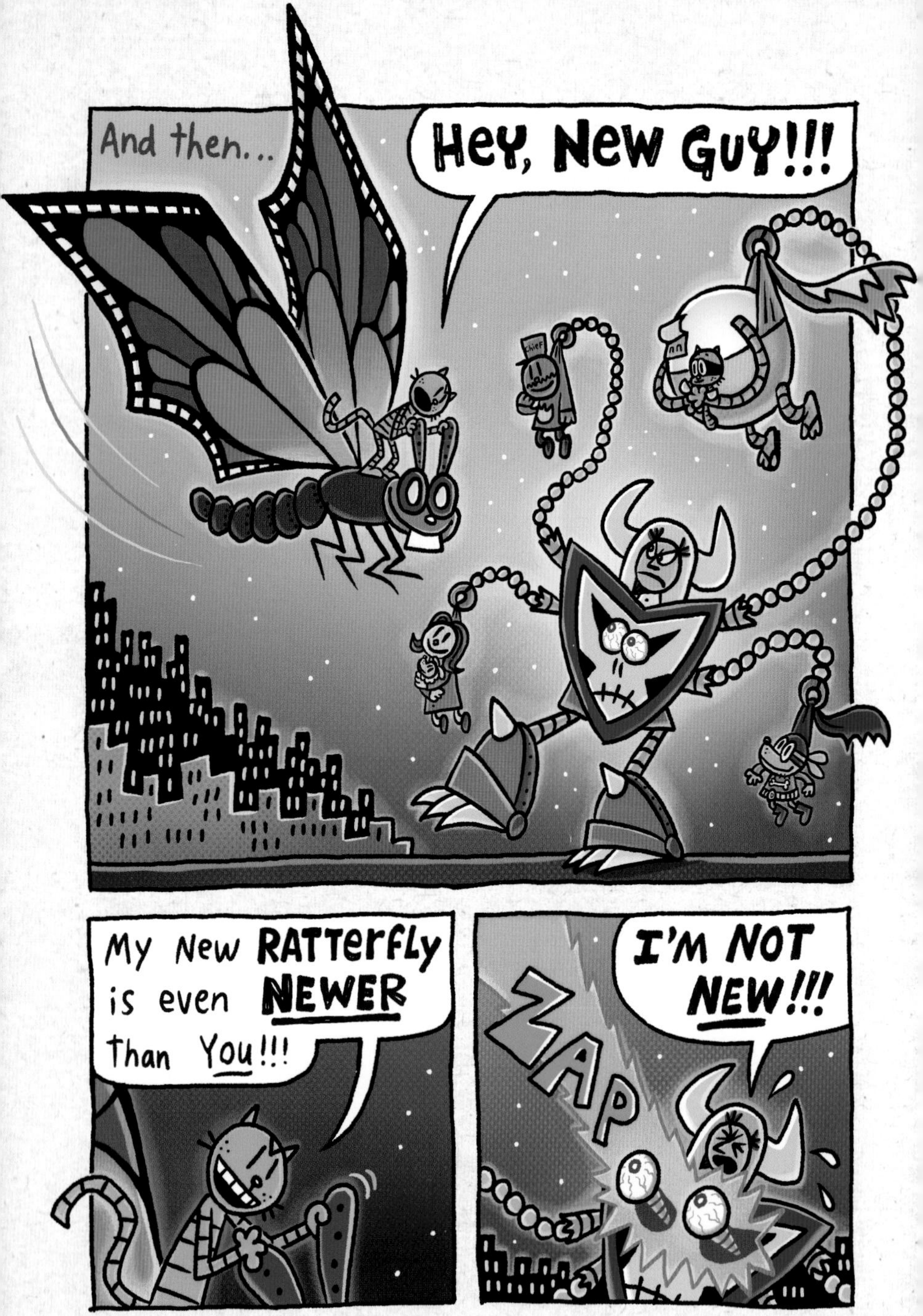
And then...
HEY, NEW GUY!!!
My New RATTerfLy is even NEWER than You!!!
ZAP
I'M NOT NEW!!!
chief

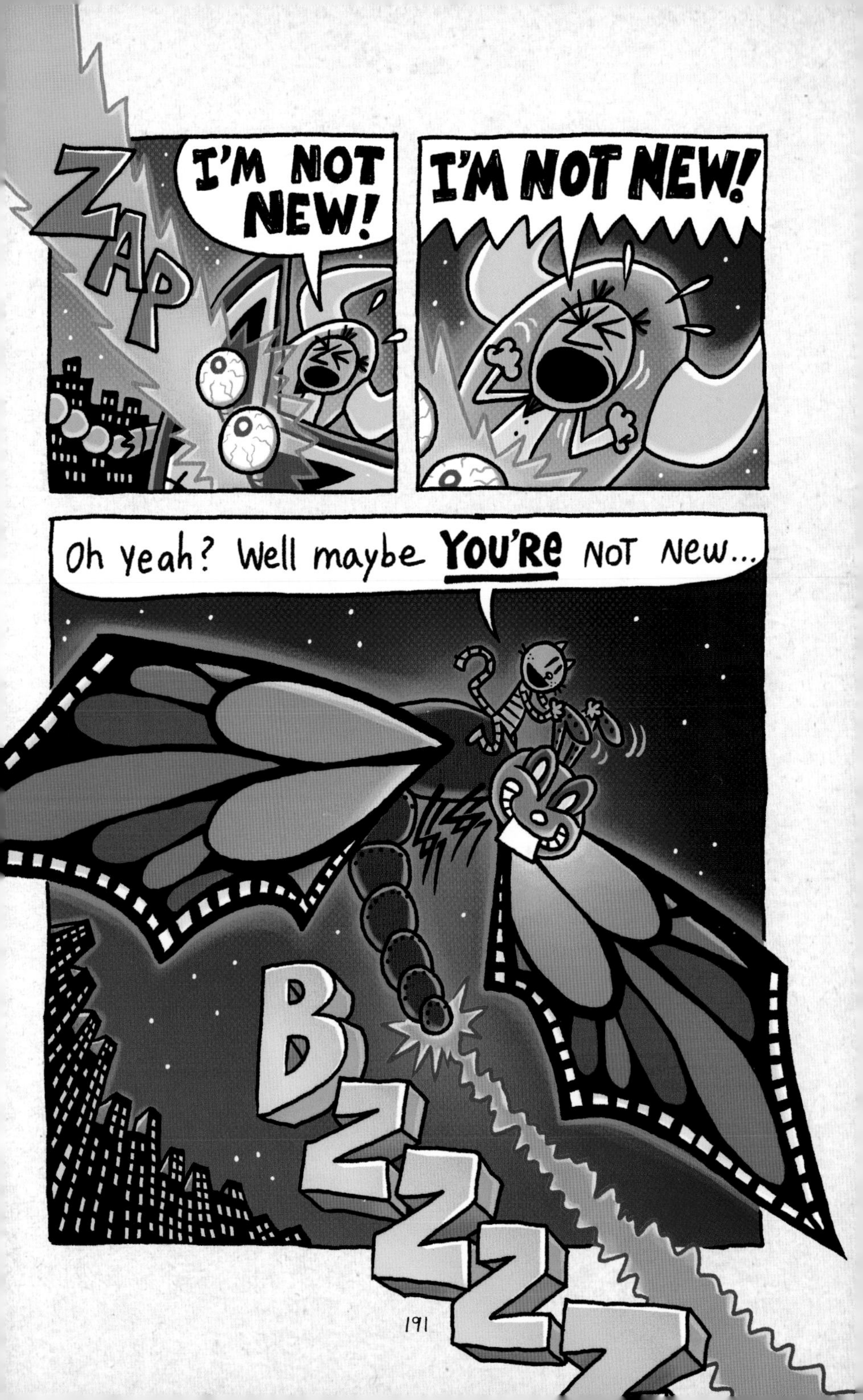
ZAP
I'M NOT NEW!
I'M NOT NEW!
Oh yeah? Well maybe YOU'RE NOT NEW...
BZZZZ

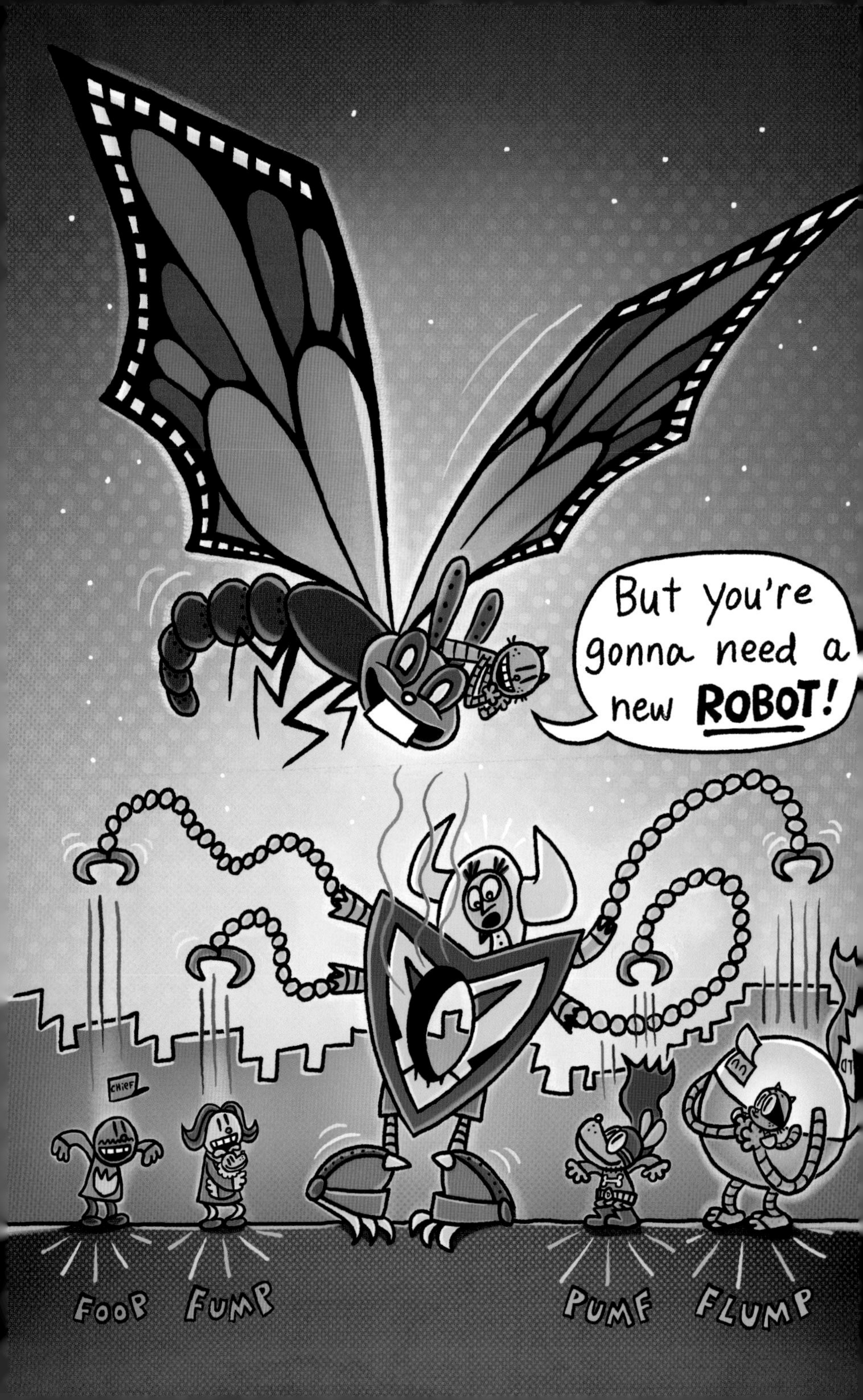
But you're gonna need a new ROBOT!
CHIEF
FOOP
FUMP
PUMF
FLUMP

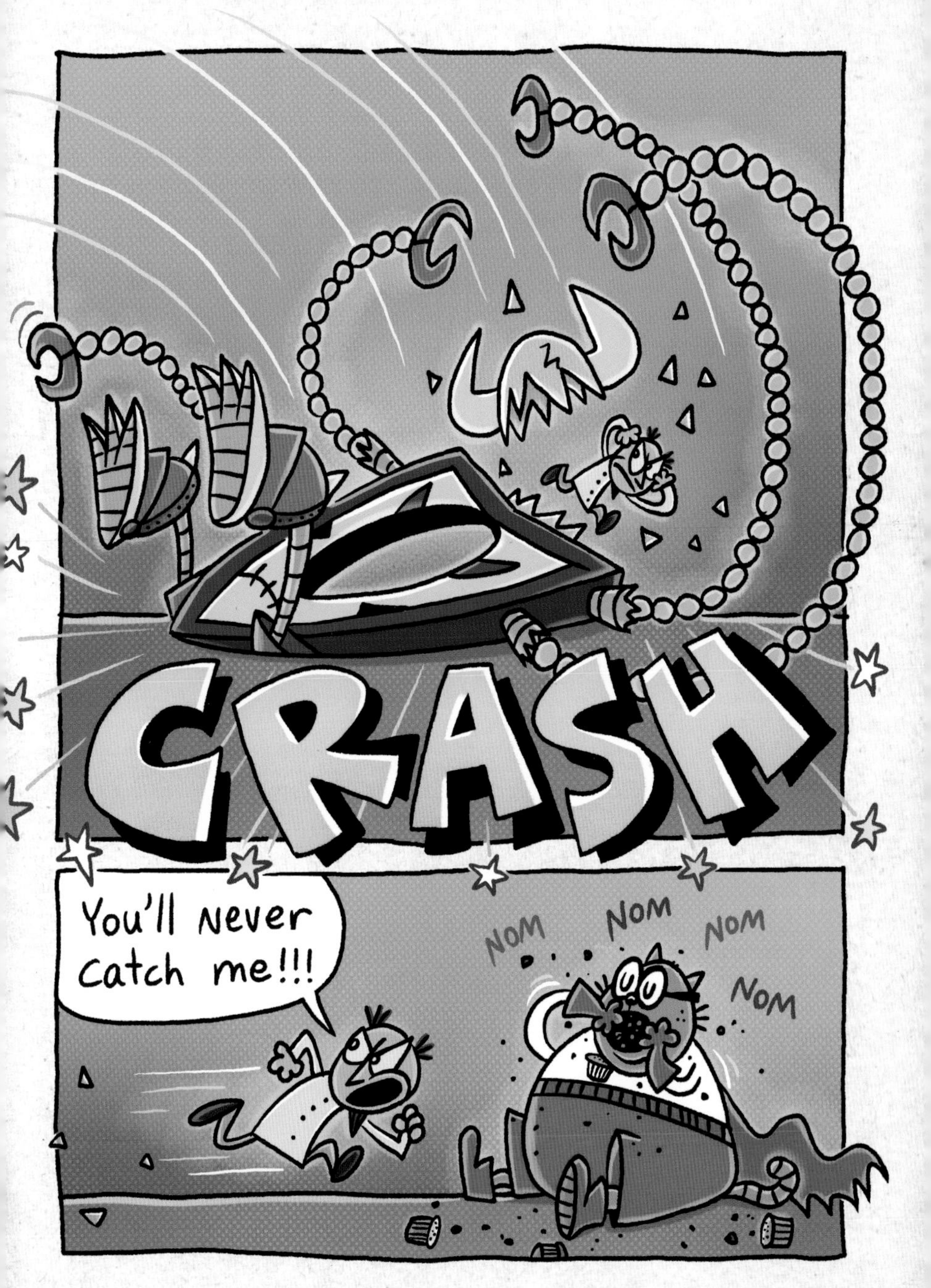
CRASH
You'll never catch me!!!
NOM
NOM
NOM
NOM

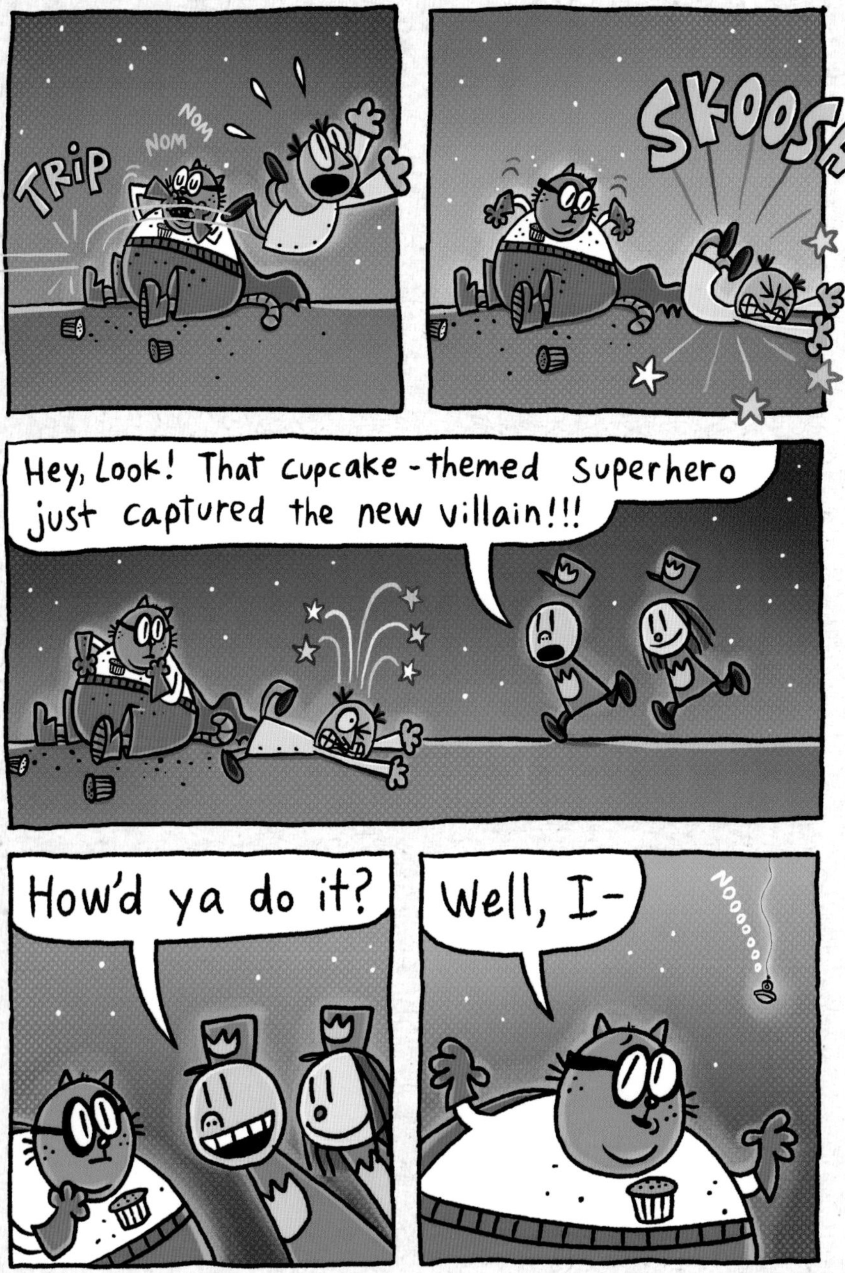
TRIP
NOM
NOM
SKOOSH
Hey, Look! That cupcake-themed superhero just captured the new villain!!!
How'd ya do it?
Well, I-
NOOOOOOOO

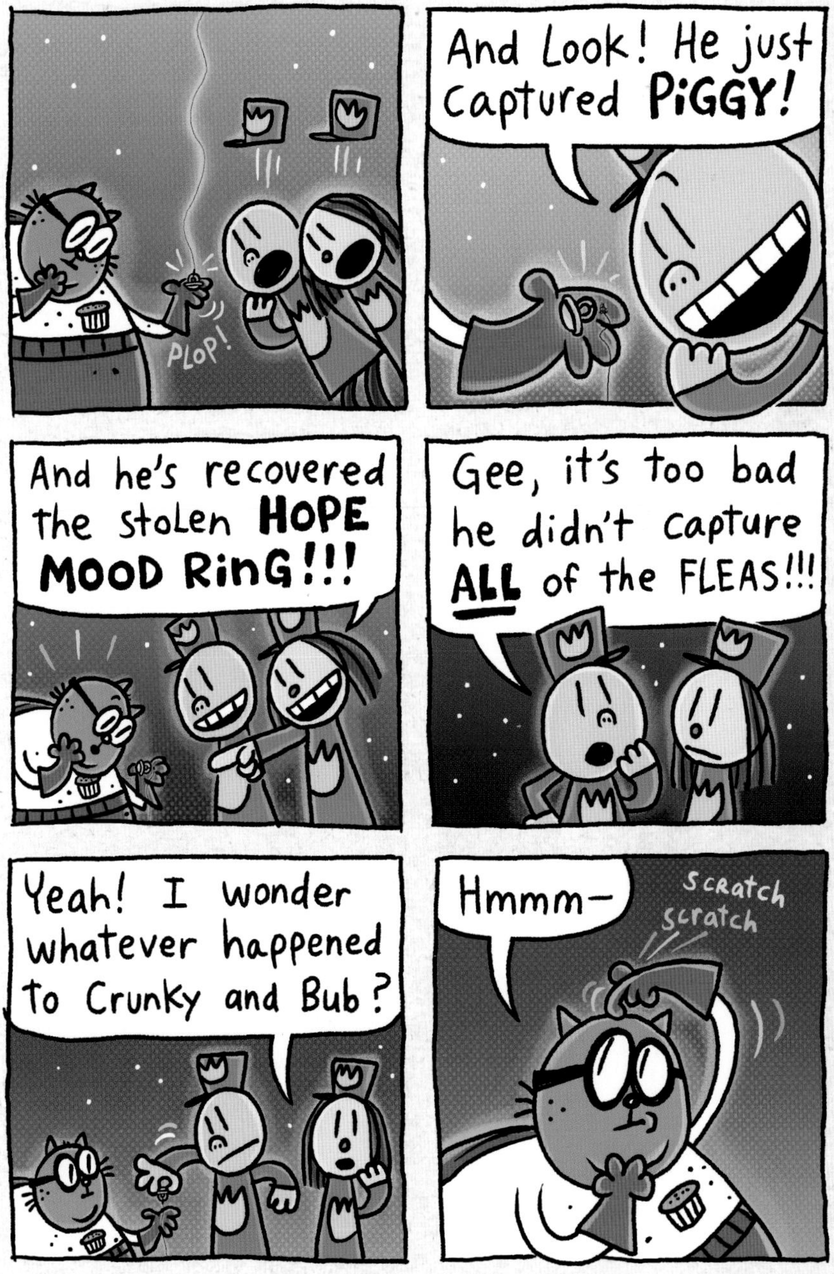
PLOP!
And Look! He just captured PiGGY!
And he's recovered the stolen HOPE MOOD RinG!!!
Gee, it's too bad he didn't capture ALL of the FLEAS!!!
Yeah! I wonder whatever happened to Crunky and Bub?
Hmmm—
scratch scratch

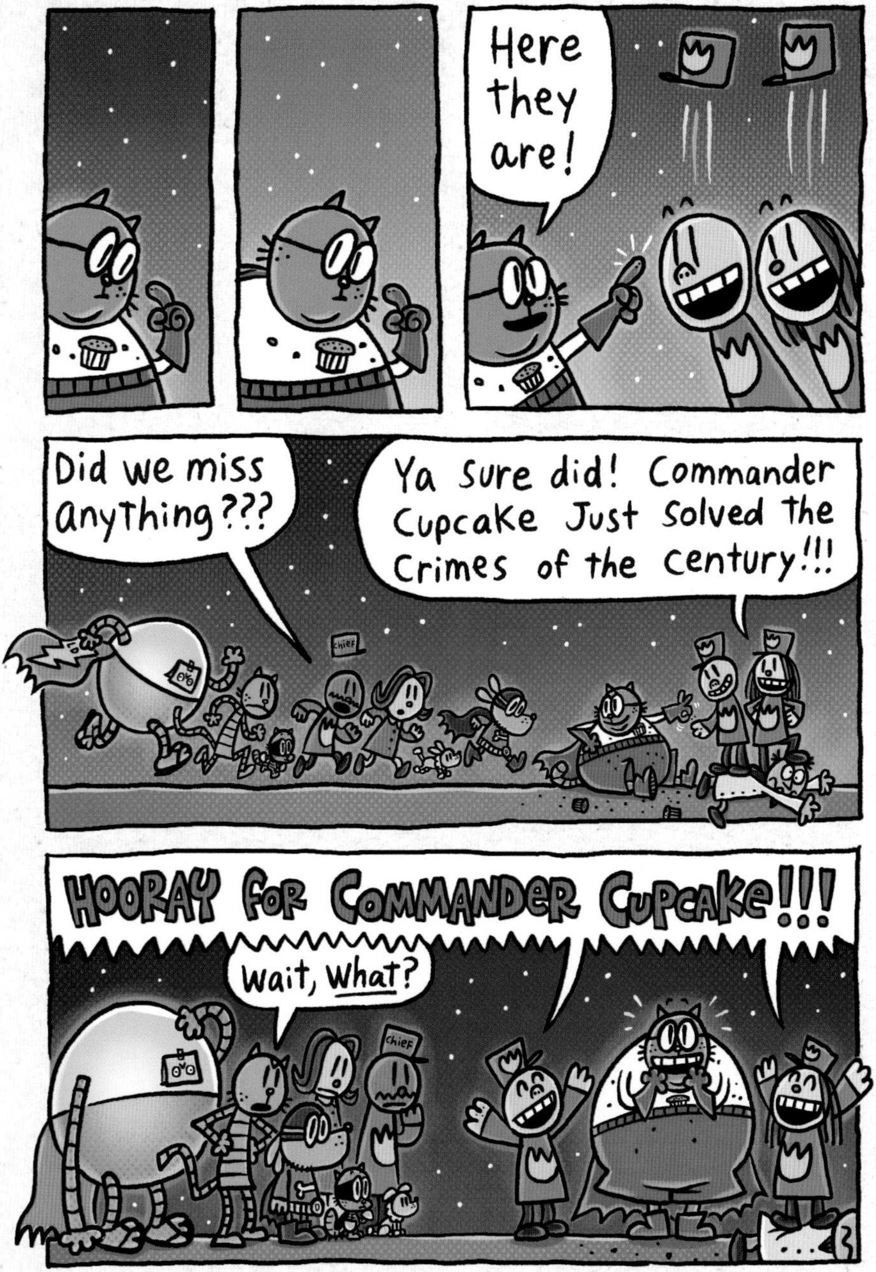
Here they are!
Did we miss anything???
Ya sure did! Commander Cupcake Just Solved the Crimes of the century!!!
HOORAY FOR COMMANDER CUPCAKE!!!
Wait, What?

CHAPTER 14

THE MUD AND THE STARS

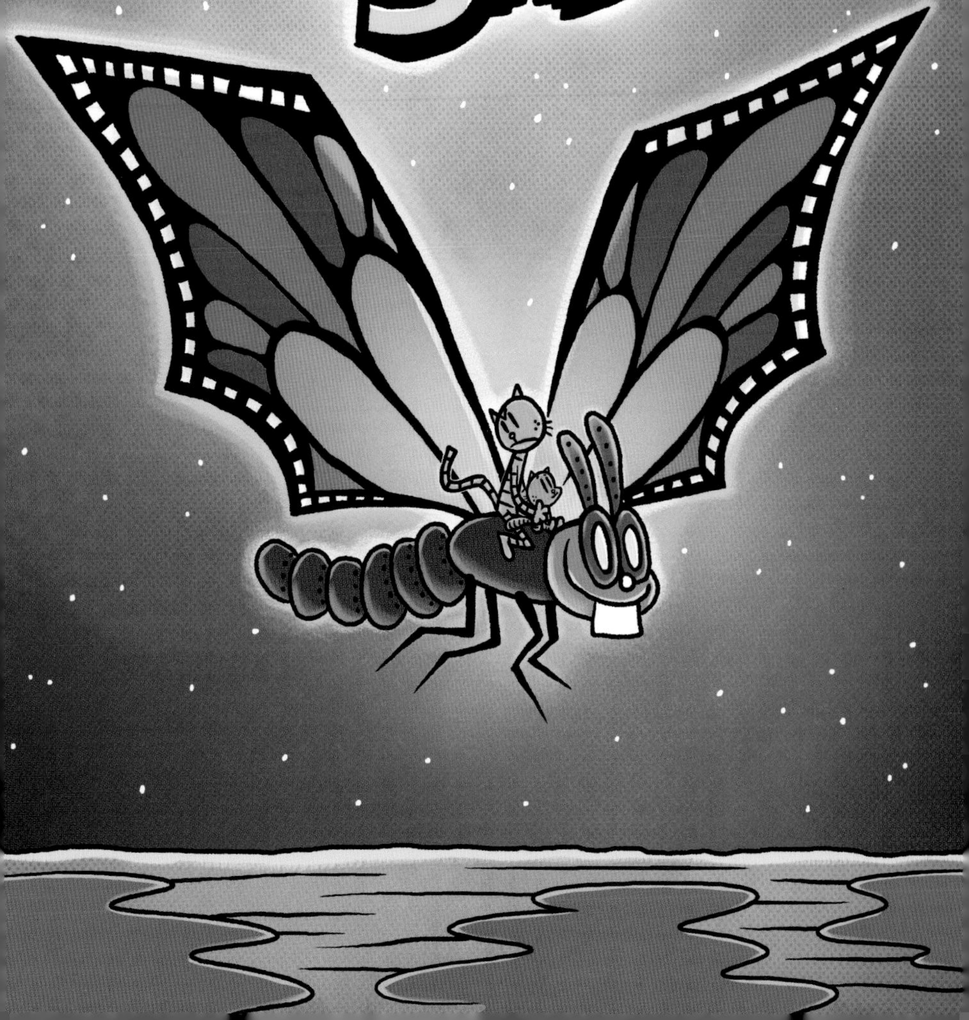

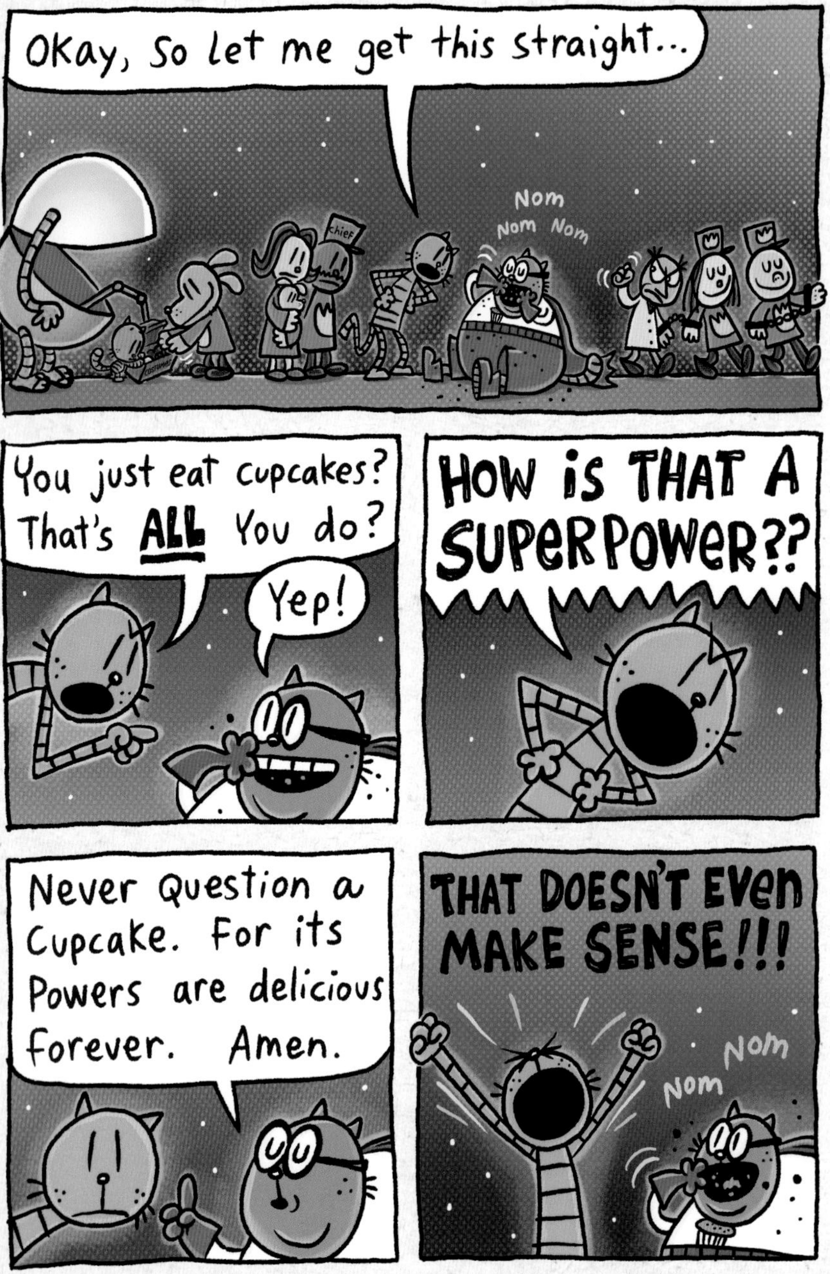
Okay, So let me get this straight...
Nom Nom Nom
You just eat cupcakes? That's ALL You do?
Yep!
HOW IS THAT A SUPERPOWER??
Never Question a Cupcake. For its Powers are delicious forever. Amen.
THAT DOESN'T EVEN MAKE SENSE!!!
Nom Nom

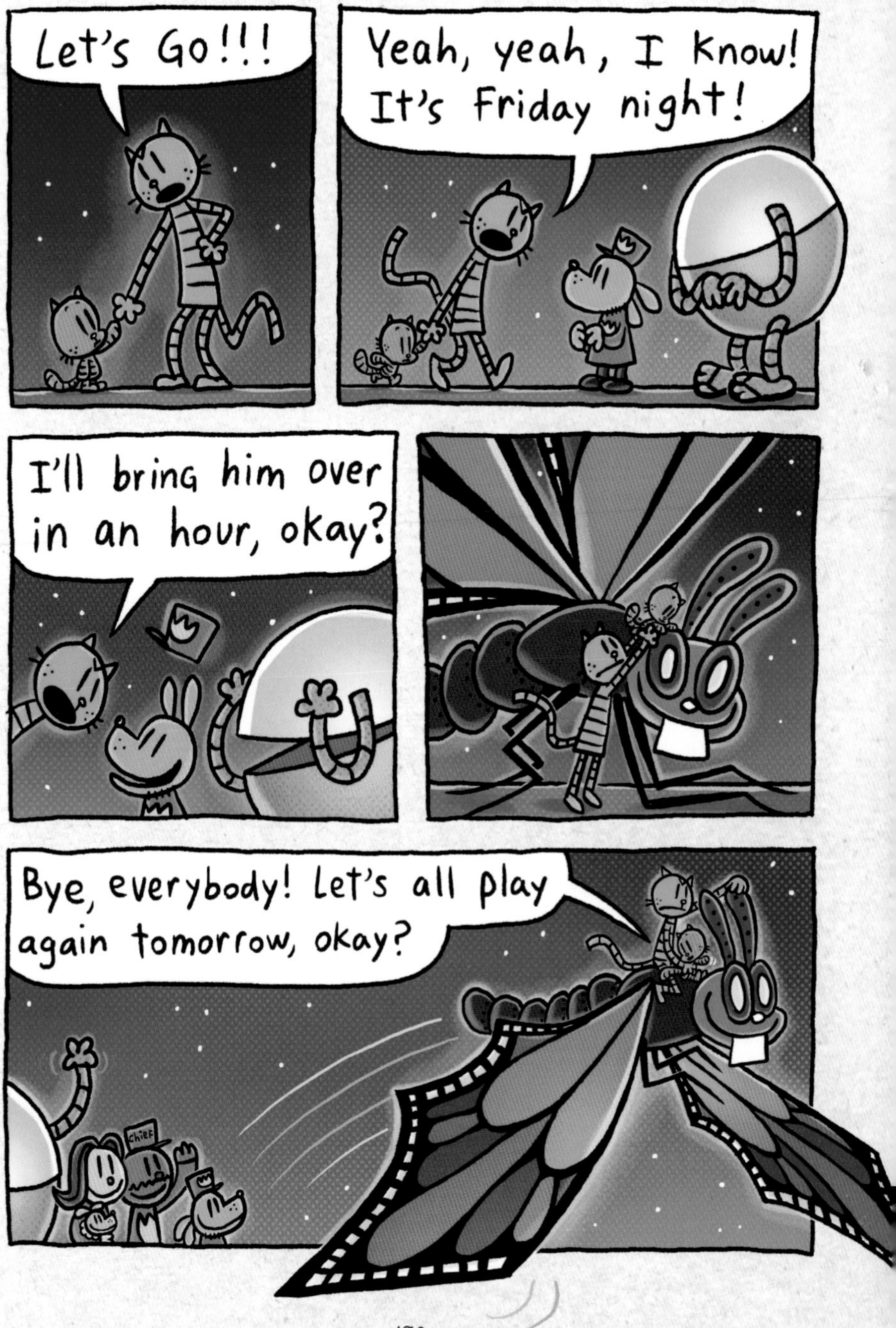
Let's Go!!!
Yeah, yeah, I Know! It's Friday night!
I'll bring him over in an hour, okay?
Bye, everybody! Let's all play again tomorrow, okay?
CHIEF

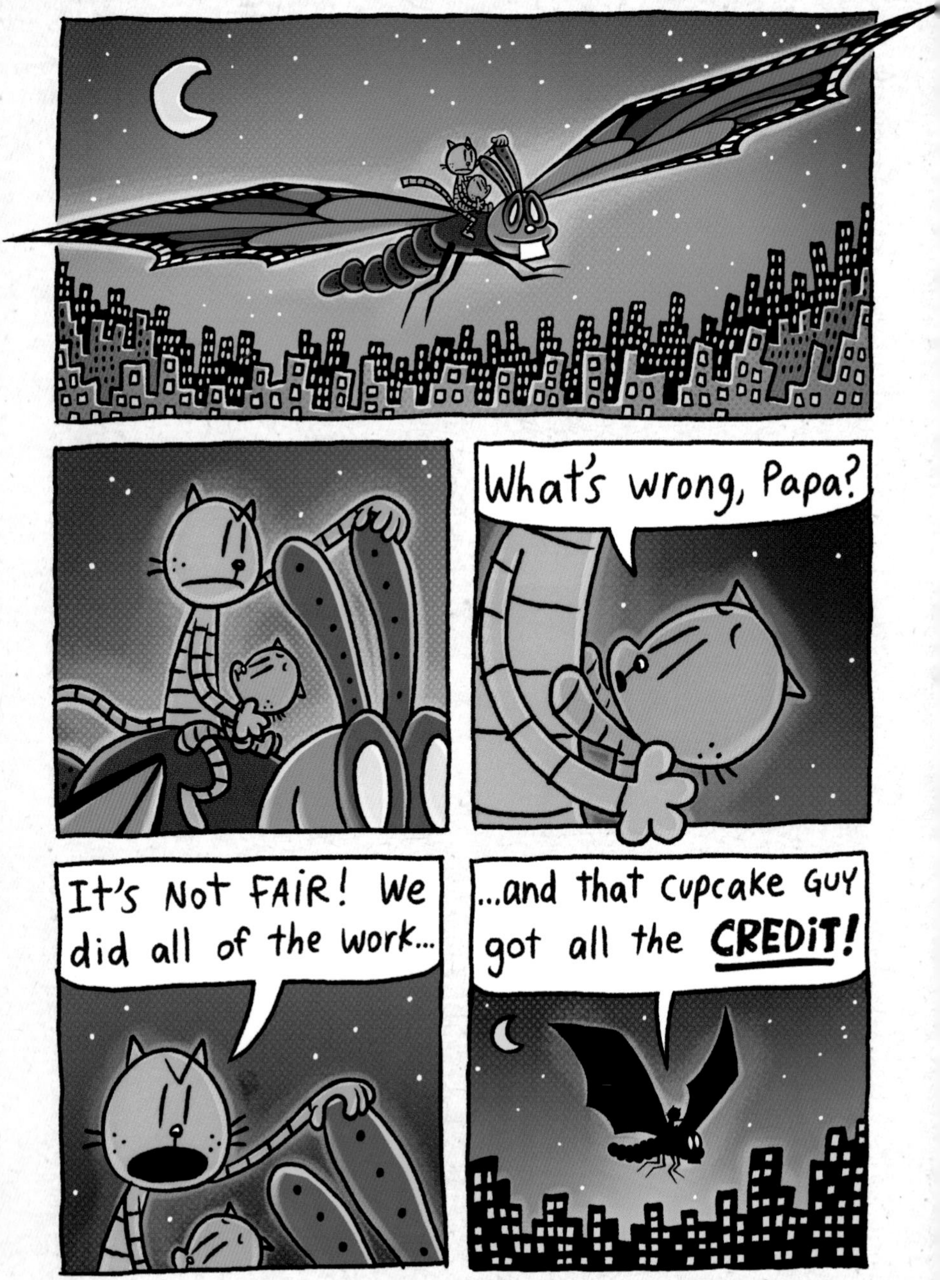
What's wrong, Papa?
It's Not FAIR! We did all of the work...
...and that cupcake GUY got all the CREDIT!

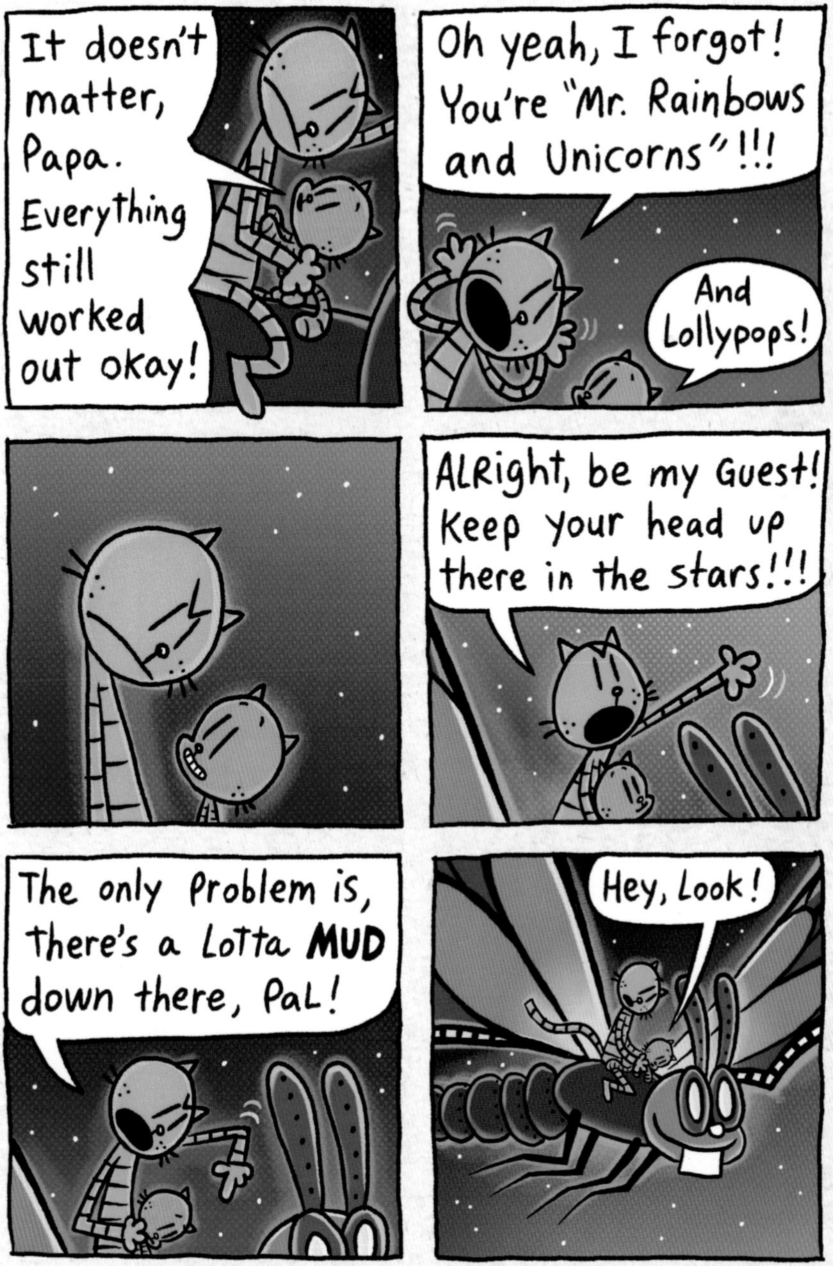
It doesn't matter, Papa. Everything still worked out okay!
Oh yeah, I forgot! You're "Mr. Rainbows and Unicorns"!!!
And Lollypops!
ALRight, be my Guest! Keep your head up there in the stars!!!
The only Problem is, there's a LoTta **MUD** down there, PaL!
Hey, Look!

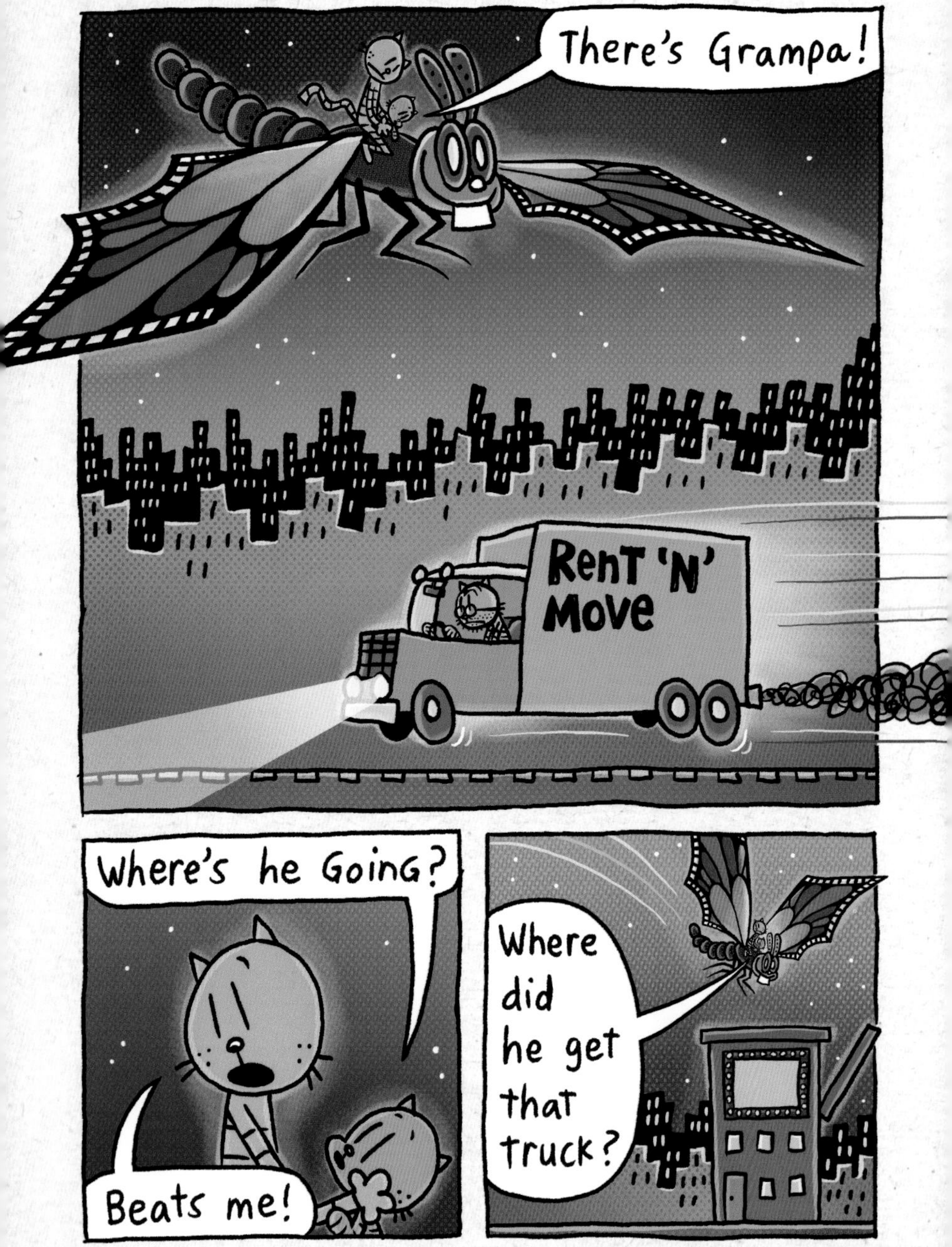
There's Grampa!
RENT 'N' MOVE
Where's he GoinG?
Beats me!
Where did he get that truck?

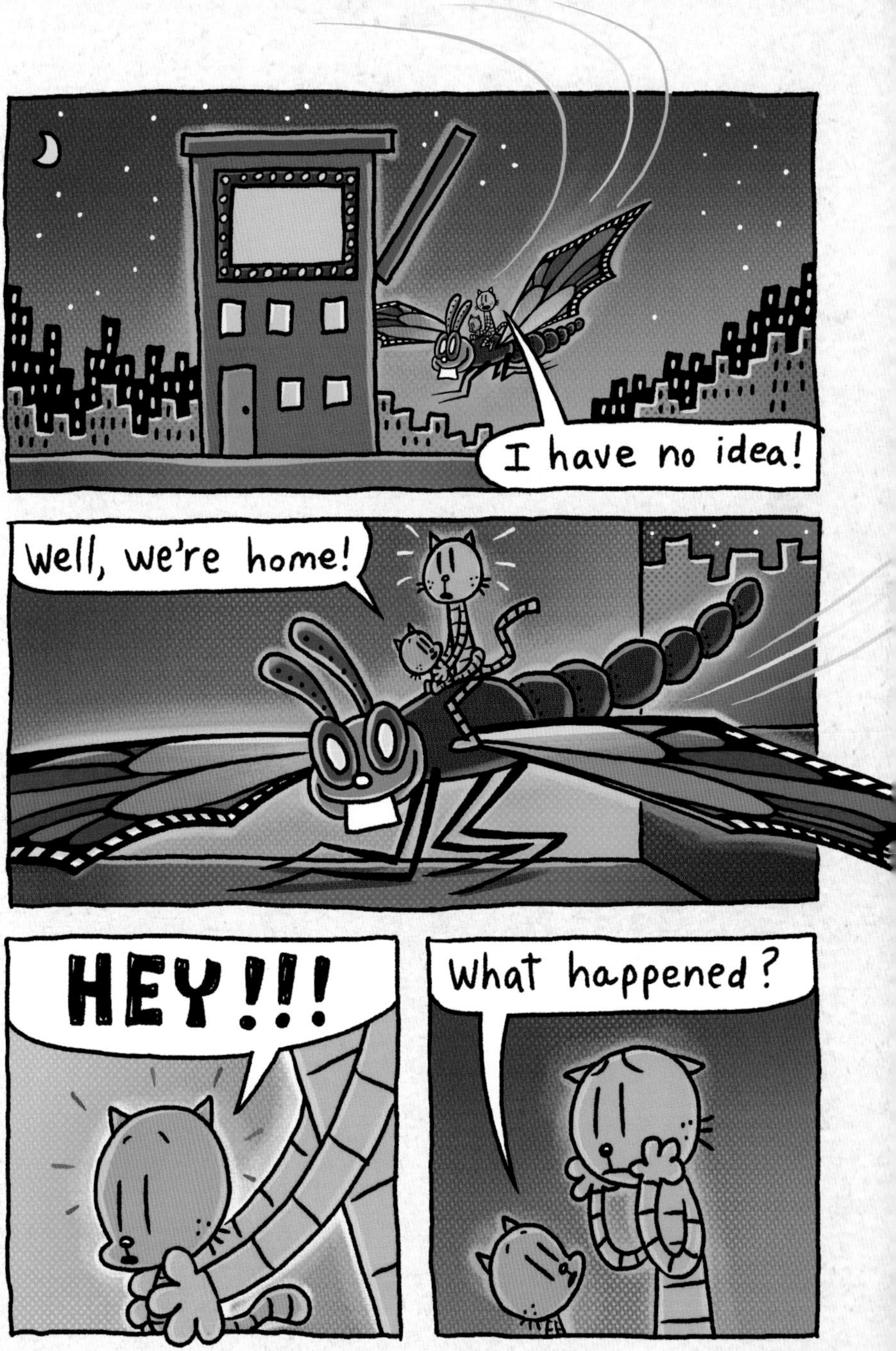
I have no idea!
Well, we're home!
HEY!!!
What happened?

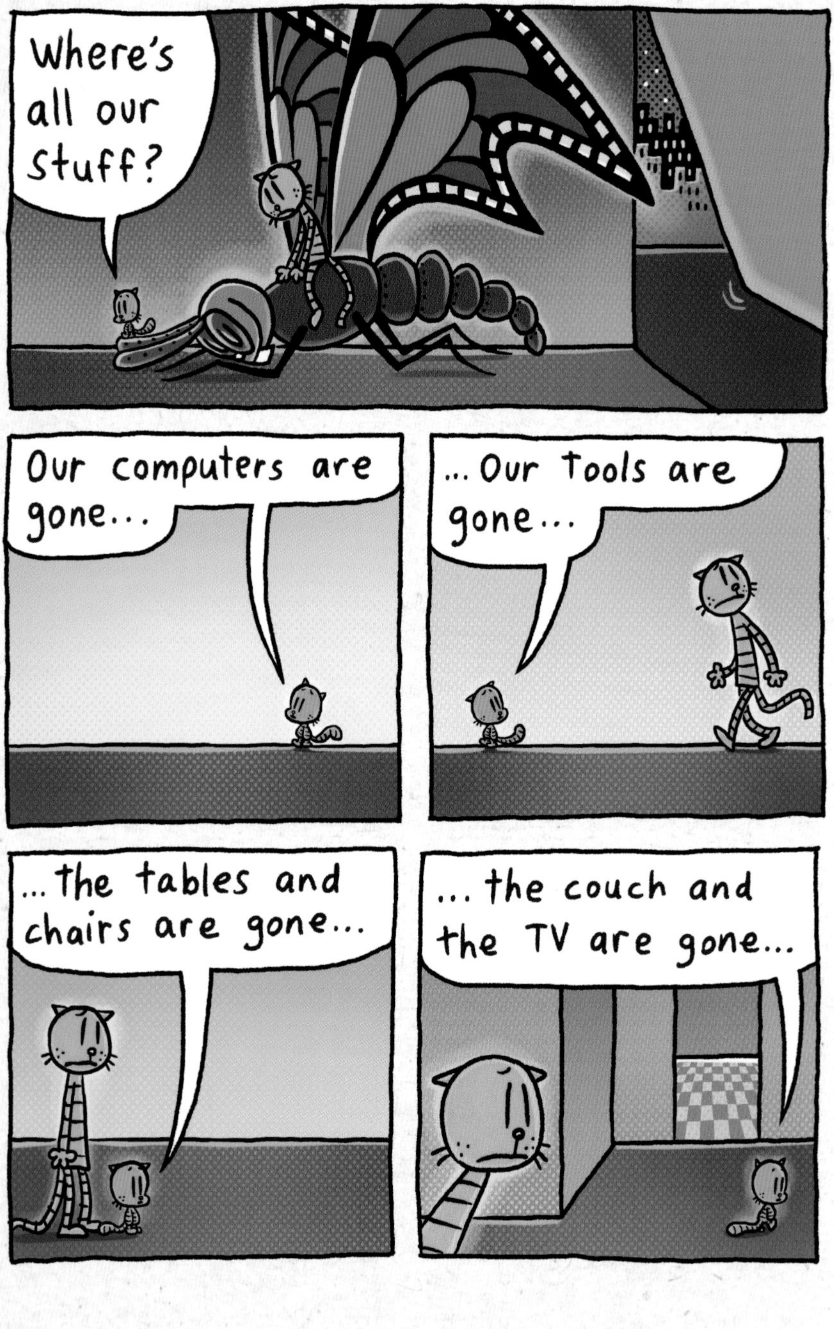
Where's all our stuff?
Our computers are gone...
...Our Tools are gone...
...the tables and chairs are gone...
...the couch and the TV are gone...

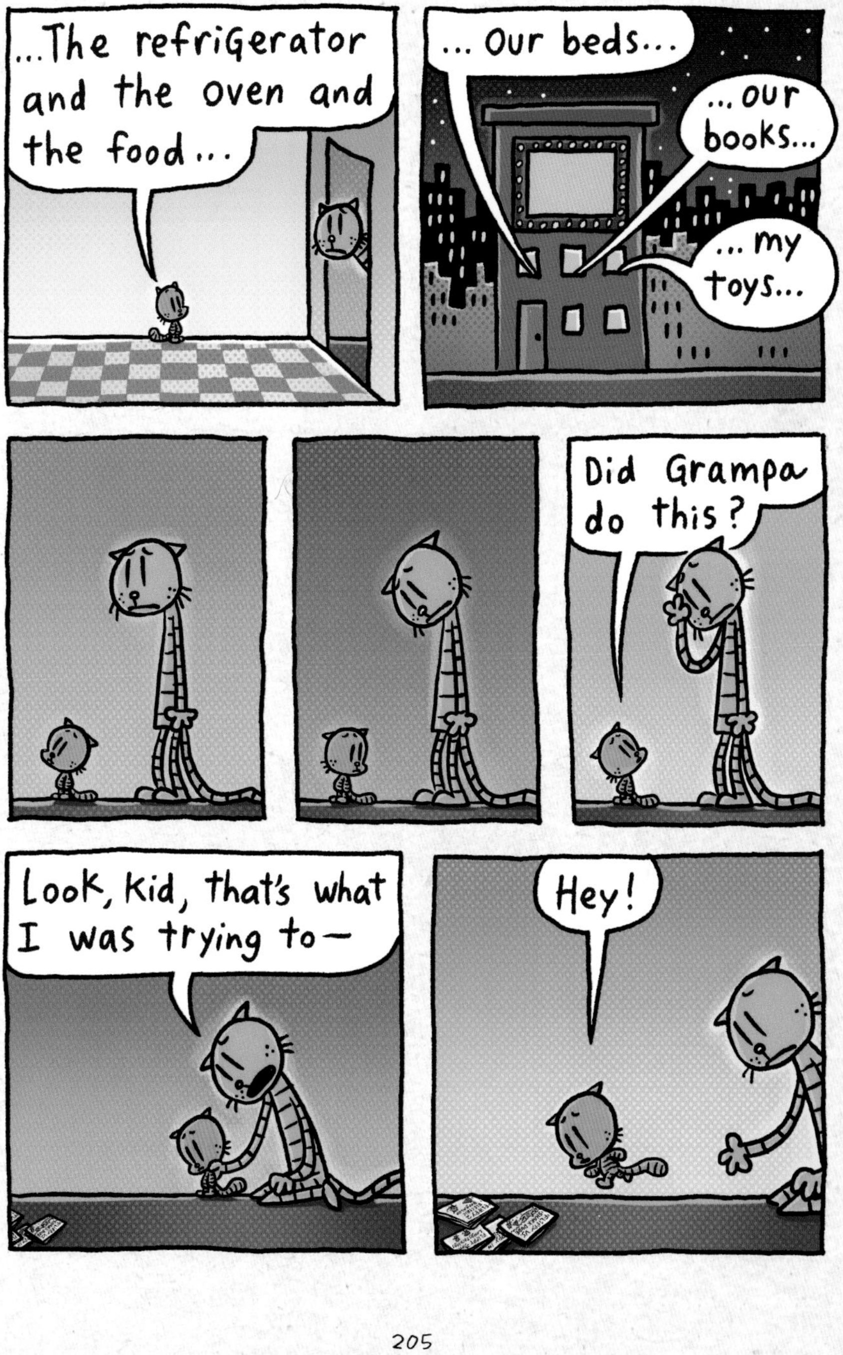
...The refriGerator and the oven and the food...
... Our beds...
... our books...
... my toys...
Did Grampa do this?
Look, kid, that's what I was trying to—
Hey!

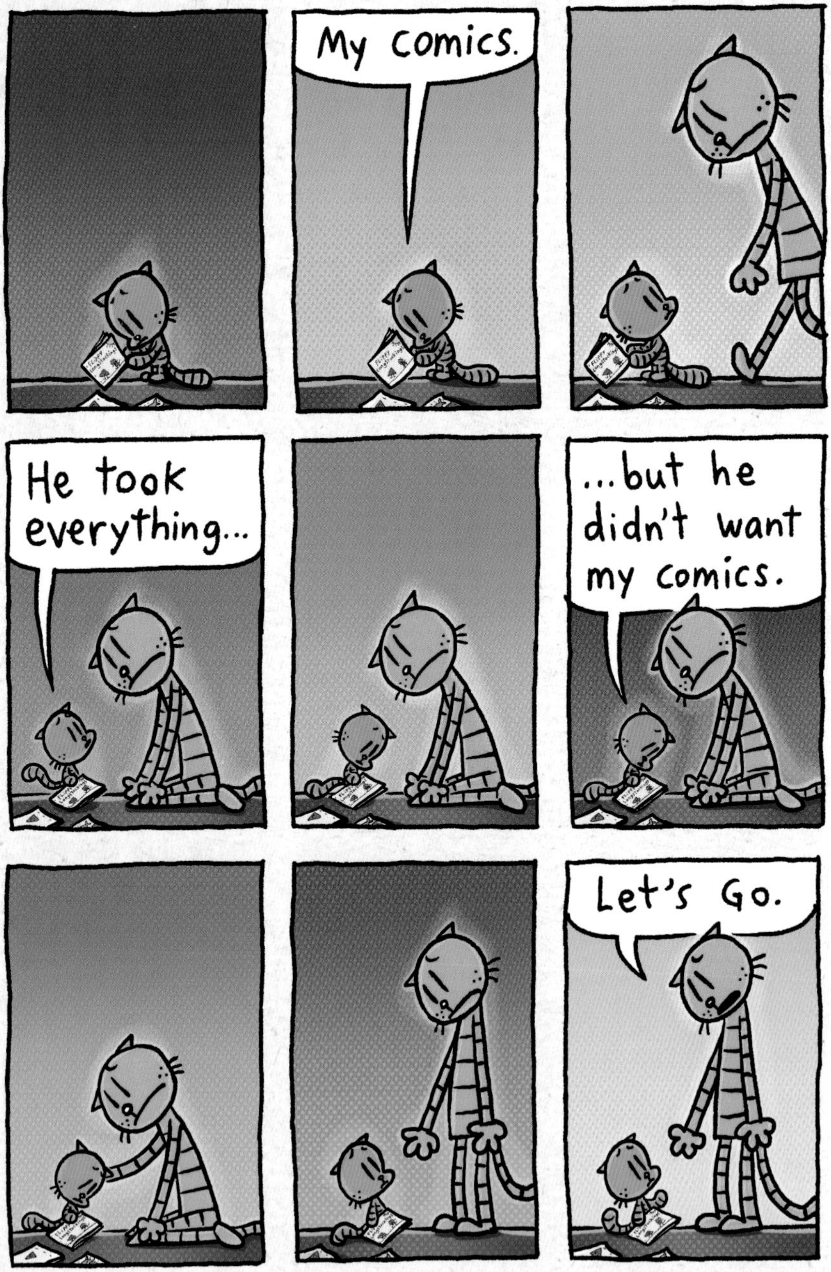
My comics.
He took everything...
...but he didn't want my comics.
Let's Go.

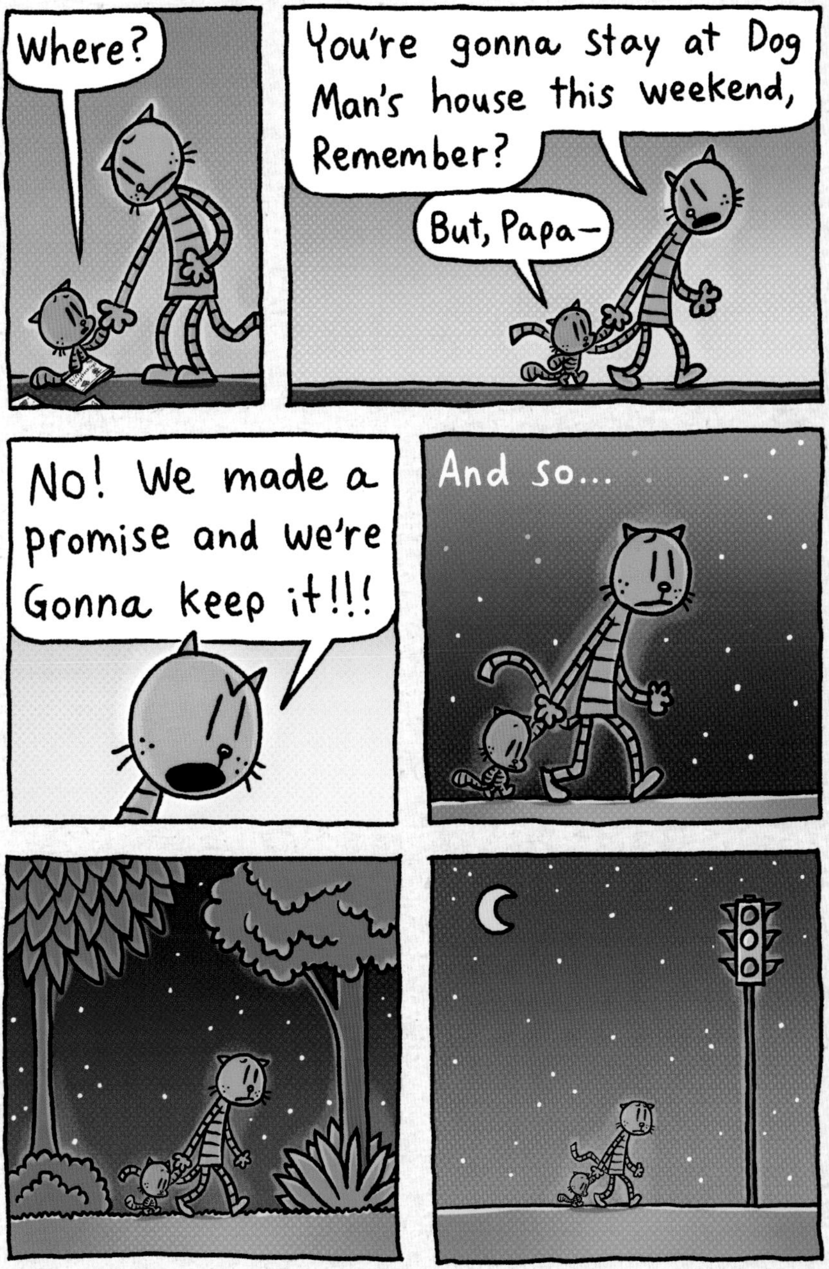
Where?
You're gonna stay at Dog Man's house this weekend, Remember?
But, Papa—
No! We made a promise and we're Gonna keep it!!!
And so...

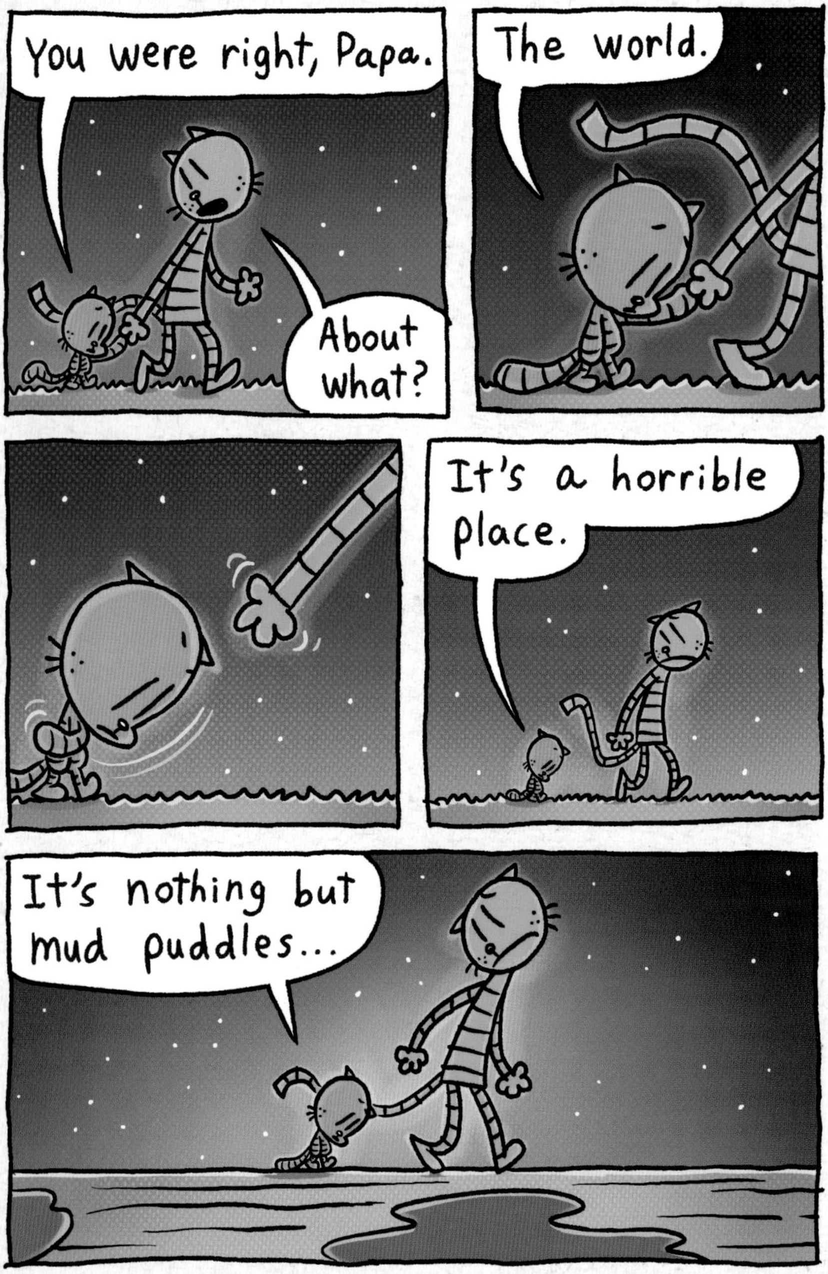
You were right, Papa.
About what?
The world.
It's a horrible place.
It's nothing but mud puddles...

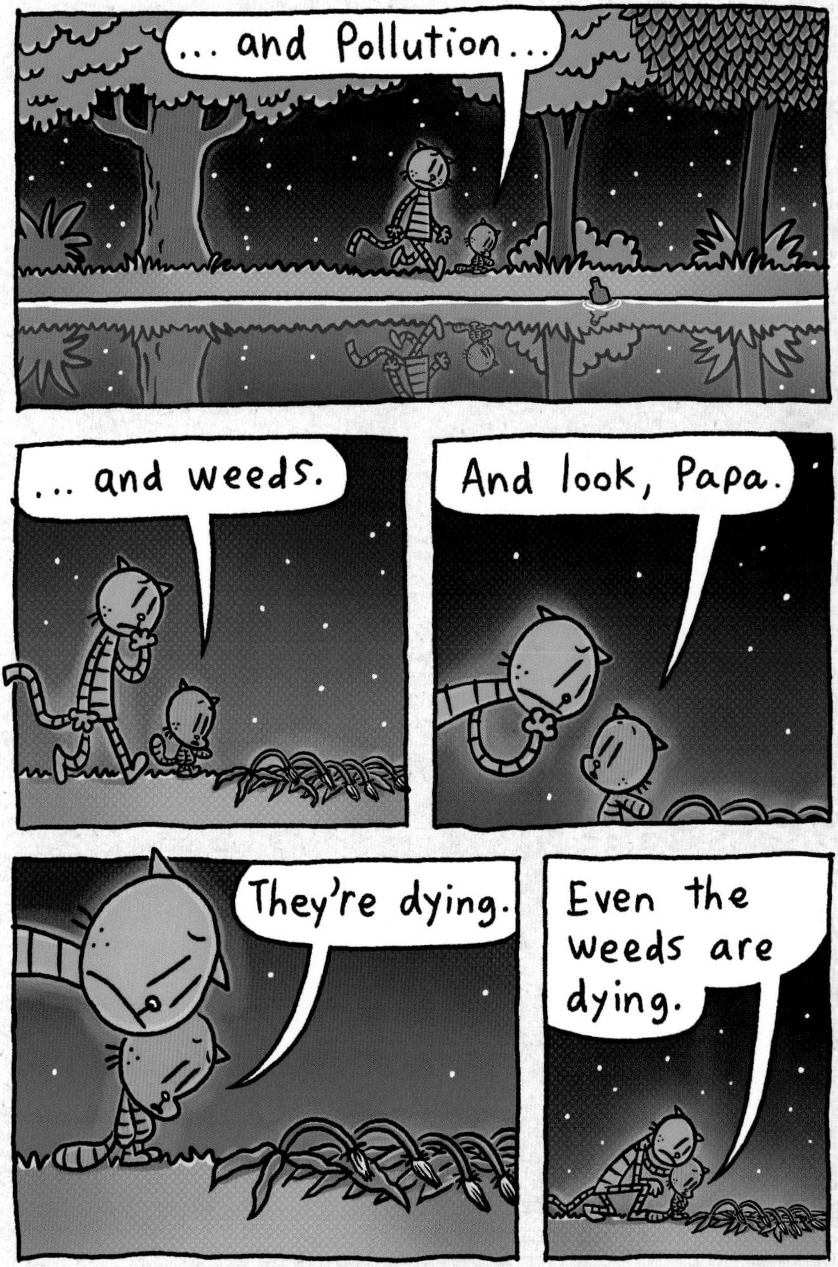
... and Pollution...
... and weeds.
And look, Papa.
They're dying.
Even the weeds are dying.

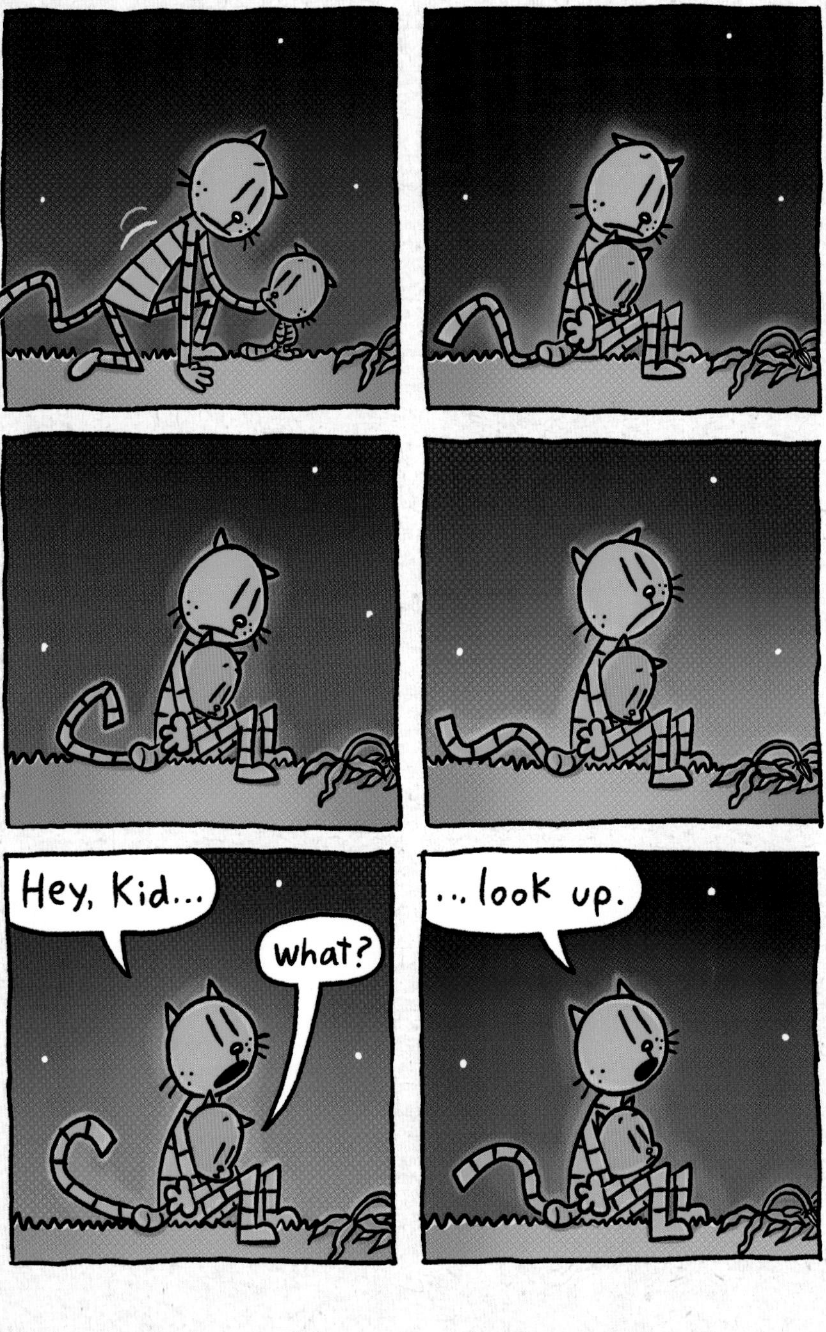
Hey, Kid...
What?
...look up.

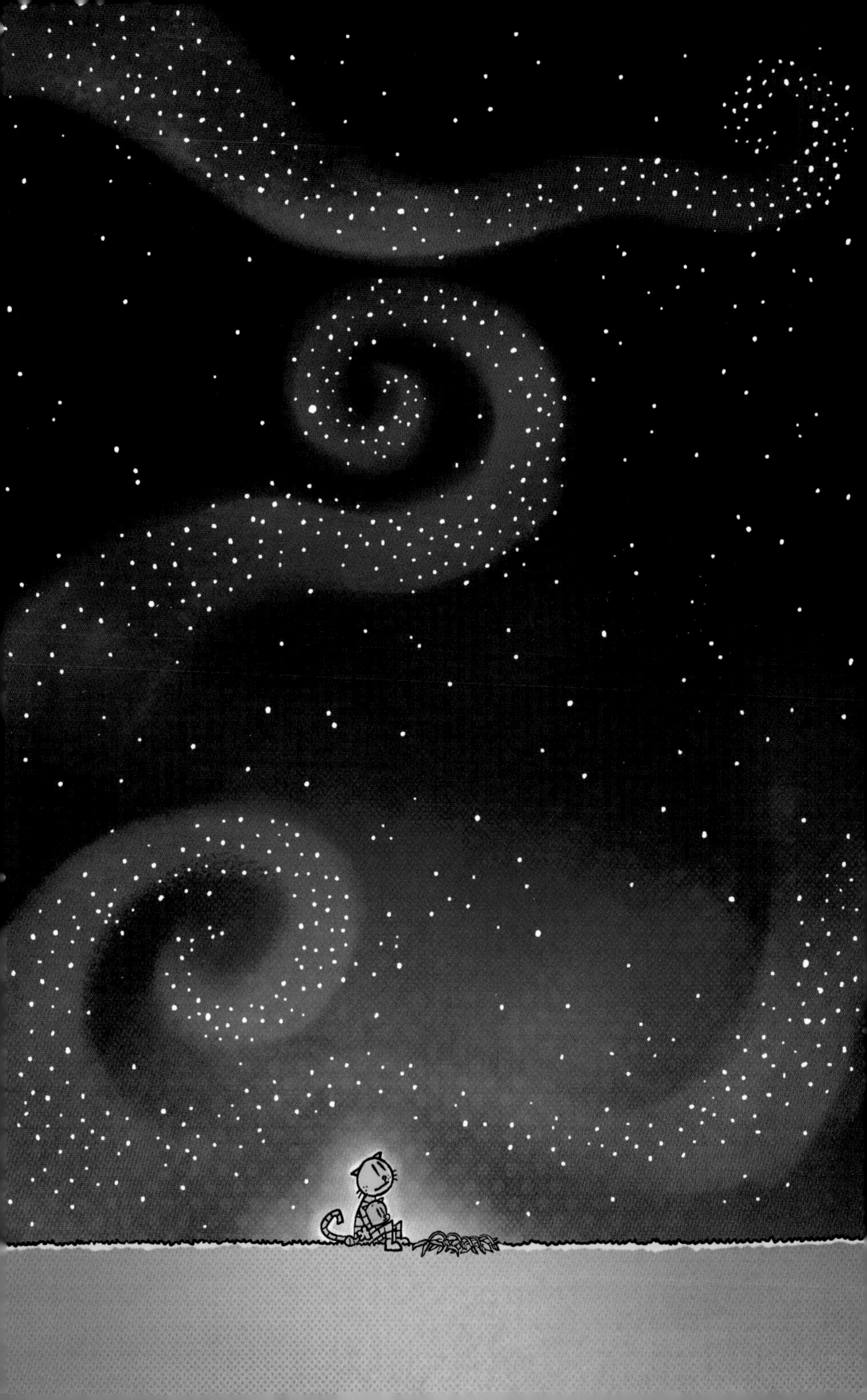

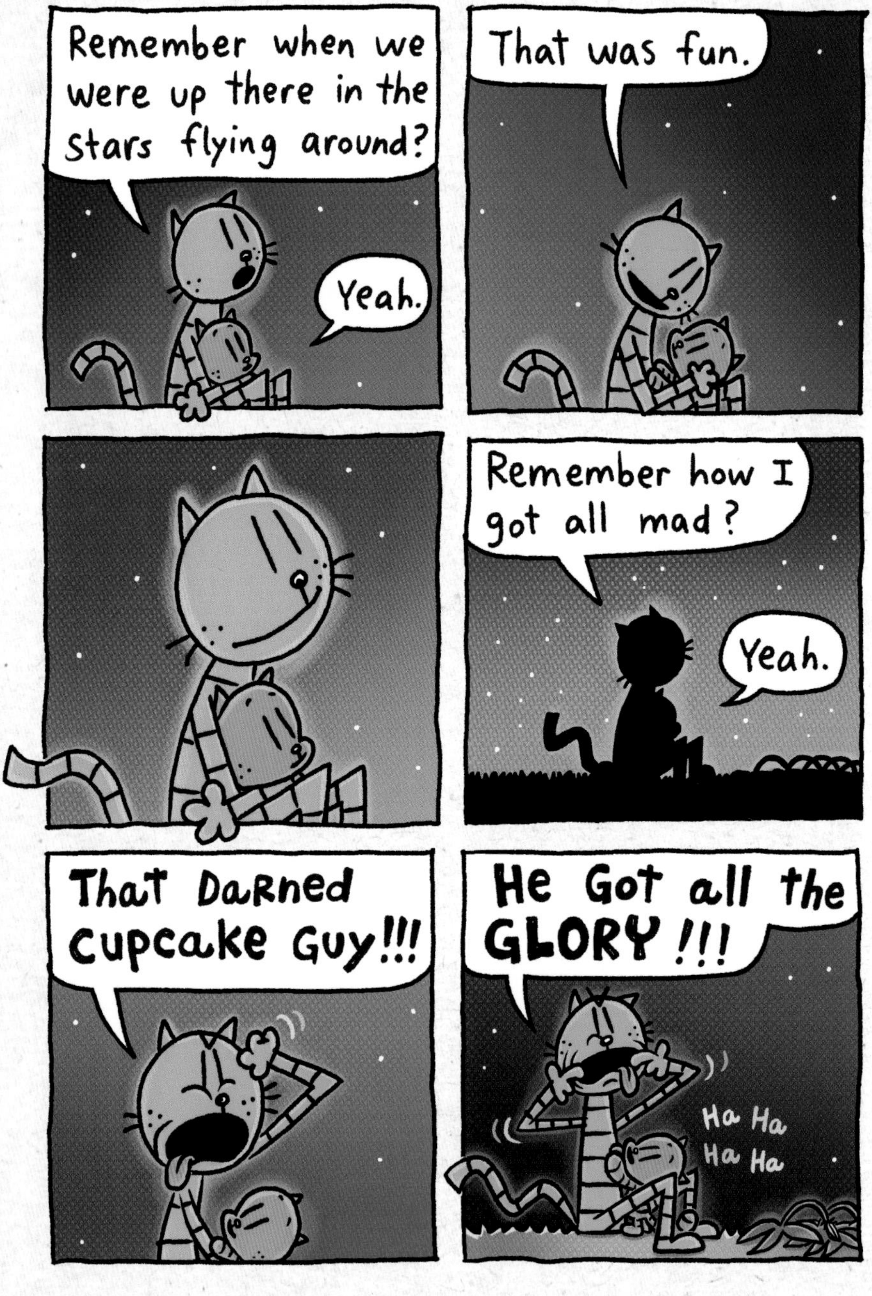
Remember when we were up there in the stars flying around?
Yeah.
That was fun.
Remember how I got all mad?
Yeah.
That Darned Cupcake Guy!!!
He Got all the GLORY!!!
Ha Ha
Ha Ha

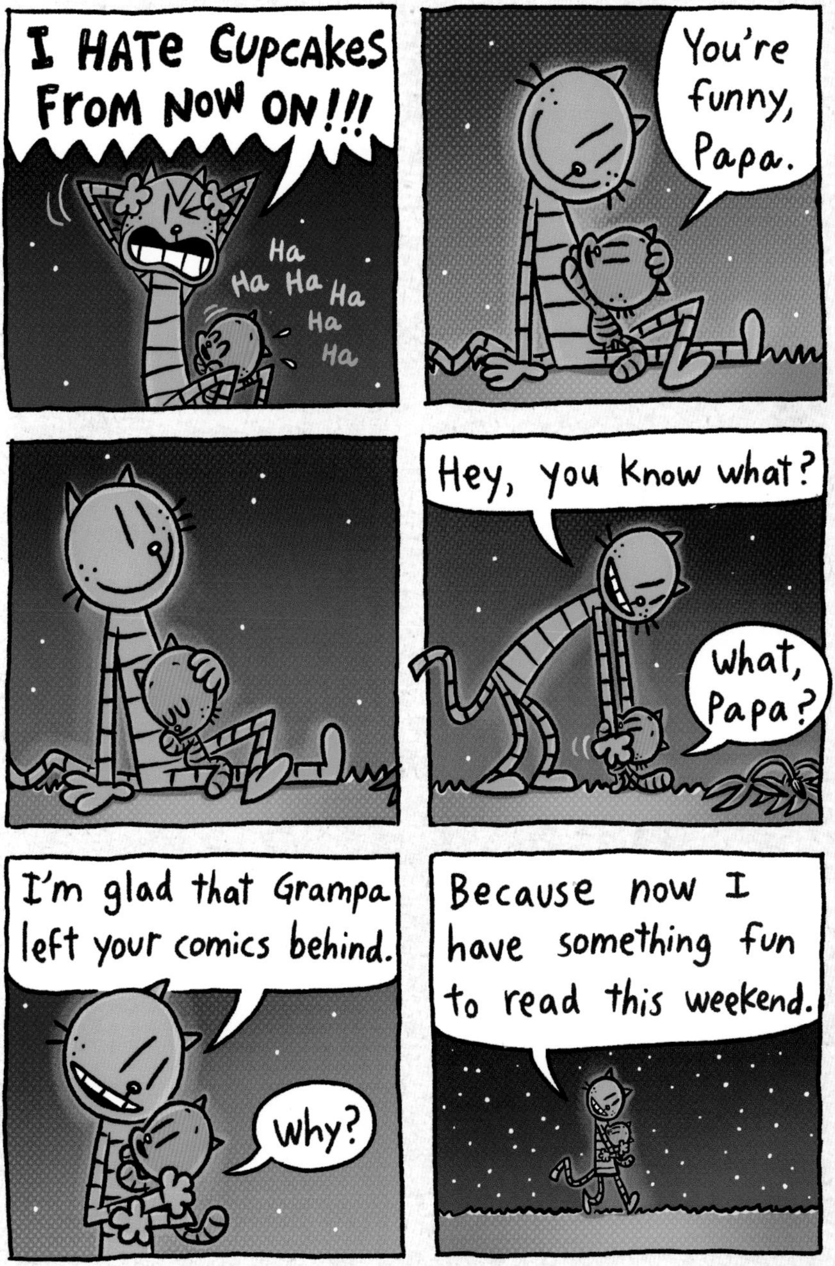
I HATE CUPCAKES FROM NOW ON!!!
Ha Ha Ha Ha Ha Ha
You're funny, Papa.
Hey, you know what?
What, Papa?
I'm glad that Grampa left your comics behind.
Why?
Because now I have something fun to read this weekend.

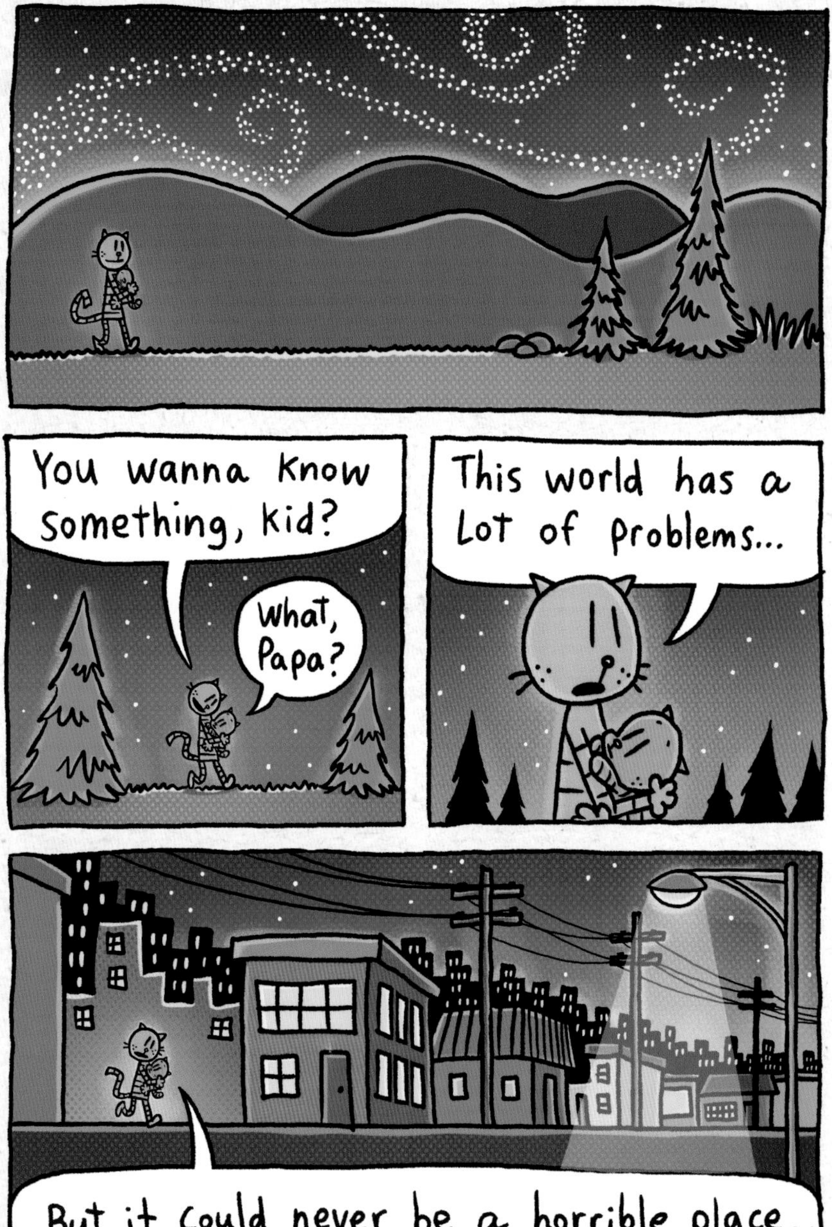
You wanna know something, kid?
What, Papa?
This world has a lot of problems...
...But it could never be a horrible place...

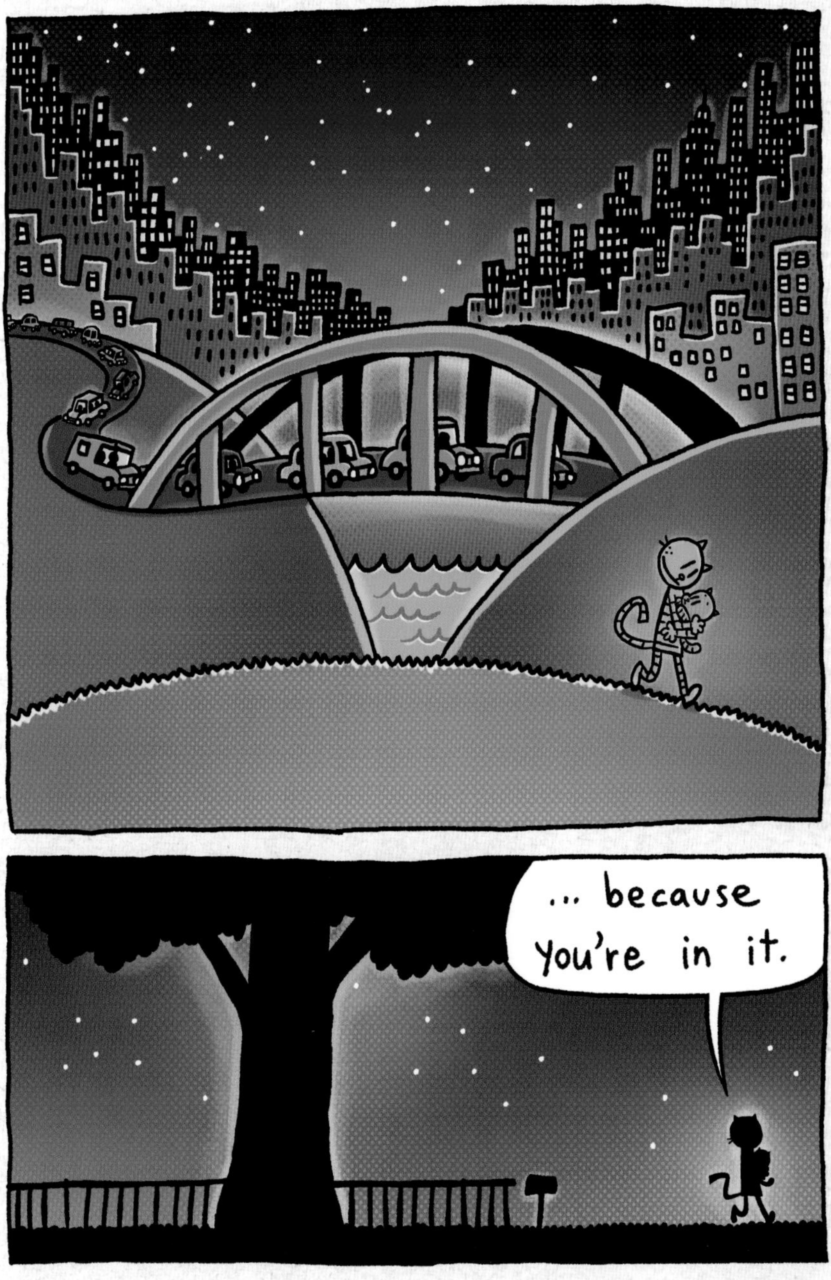
... because you're in it.

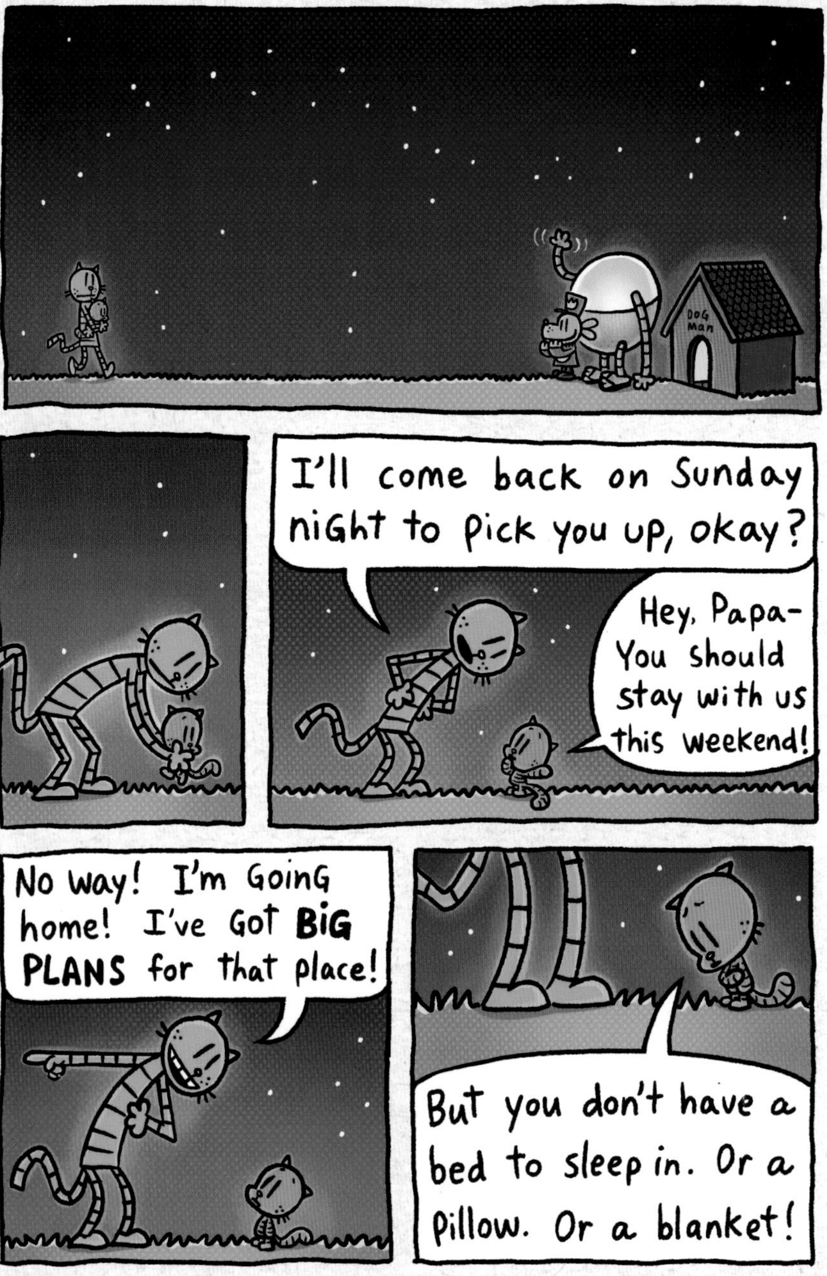
DOG Man
I'll come back on Sunday night to pick you up, okay?
Hey, Papa- You should stay with us this weekend!
No way! I'm Going home! I've Got BIG PLANS for that place!
But you don't have a bed to sleep in. Or a pillow. Or a blanket!

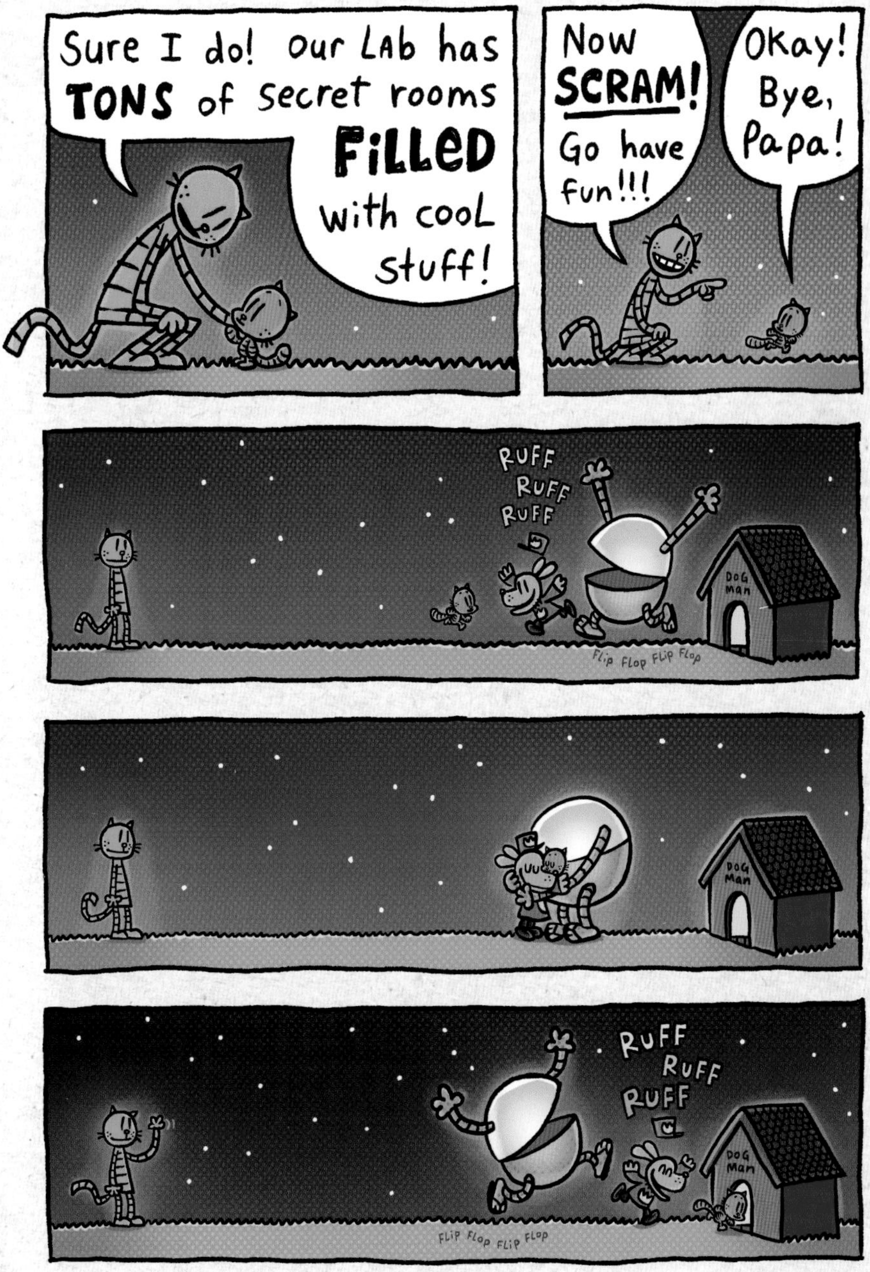
Sure I do! Our LAB has TONS of secret rooms FILLED with cool stuff!
Now SCRAM! Go have fun!!!
Okay! Bye, Papa!
RUFF RUFF RUFF
DOG MAN
Flip Flop Flip Flop
DOG MAN
RUFF RUFF RUFF
DOG MAN
FLIP FLOP FLIP FLOP

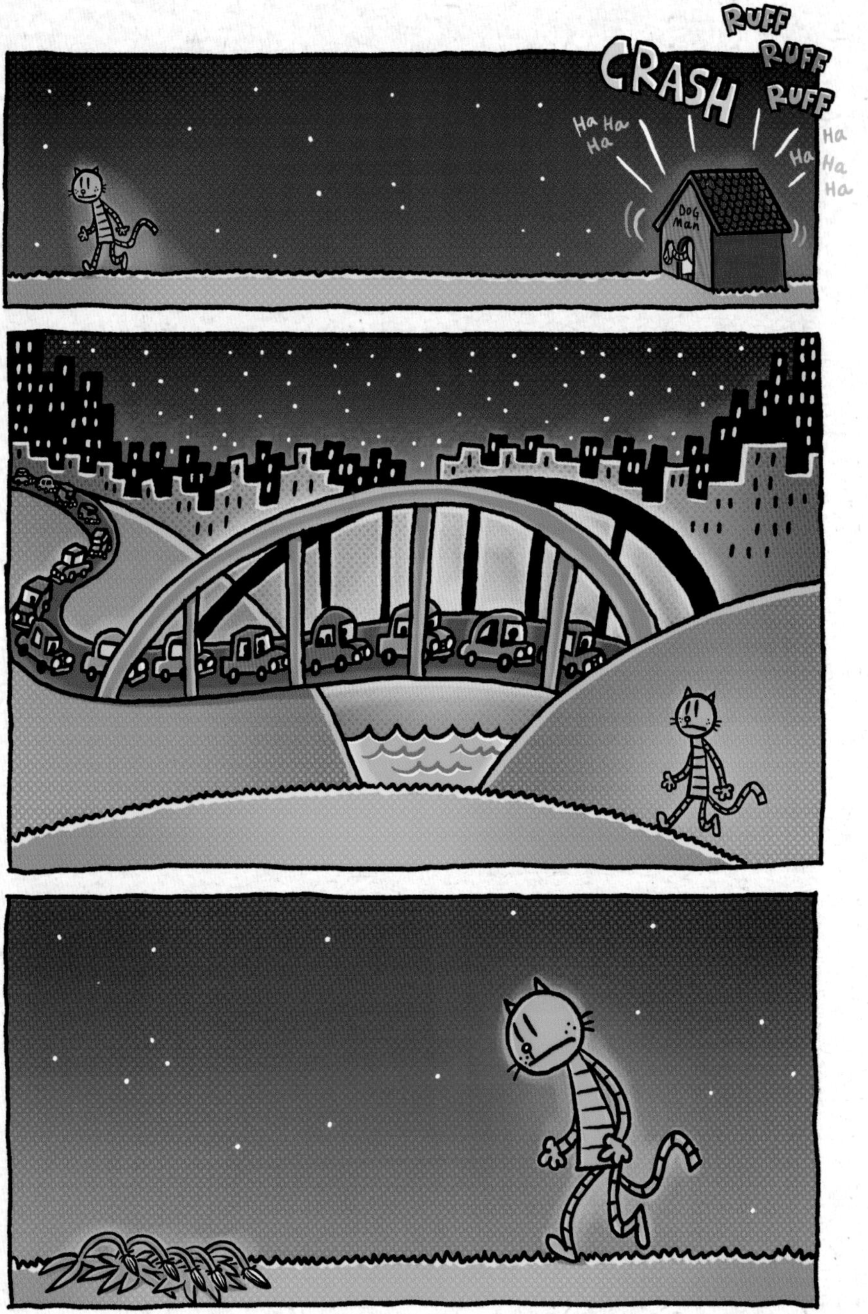
CRASH
RUFF RUFF RUFF
Ha Ha Ha
Ha Ha Ha Ha
DOG Man

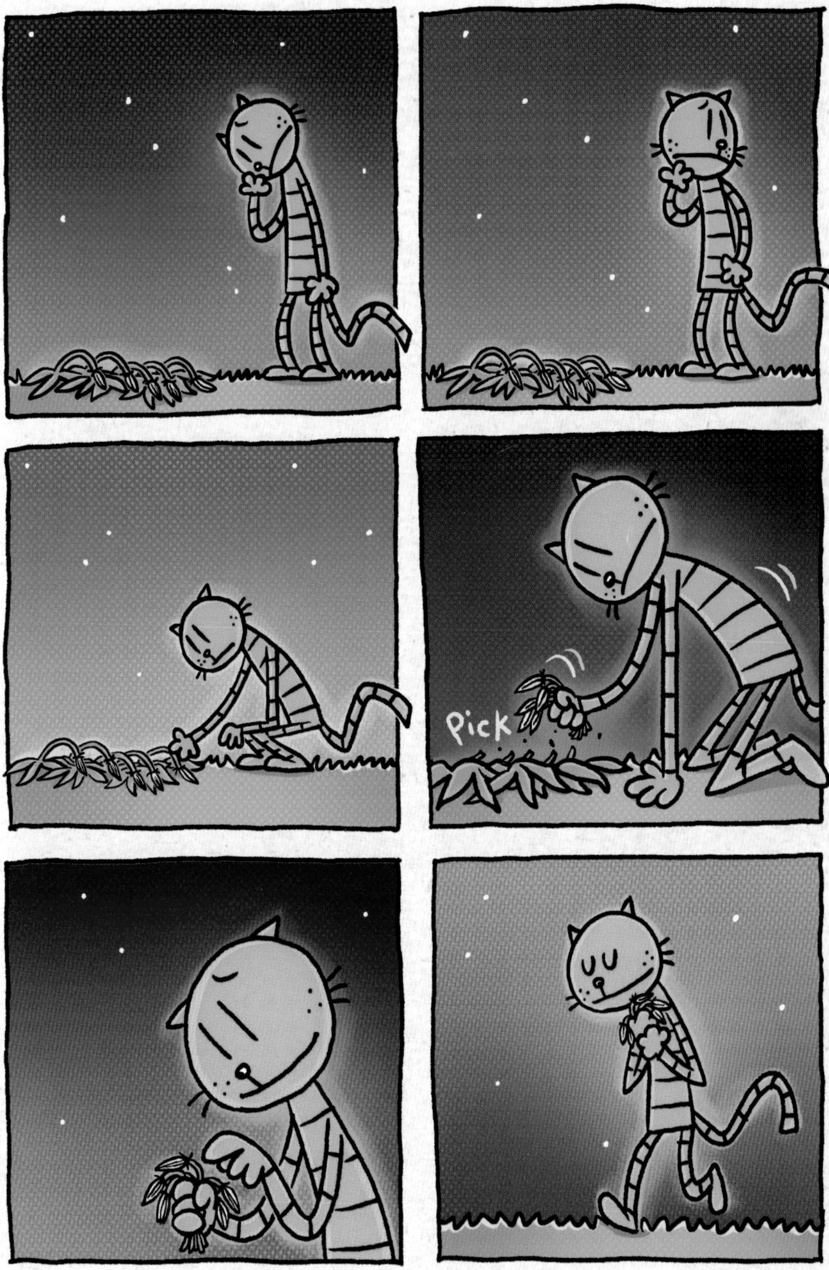
PICK

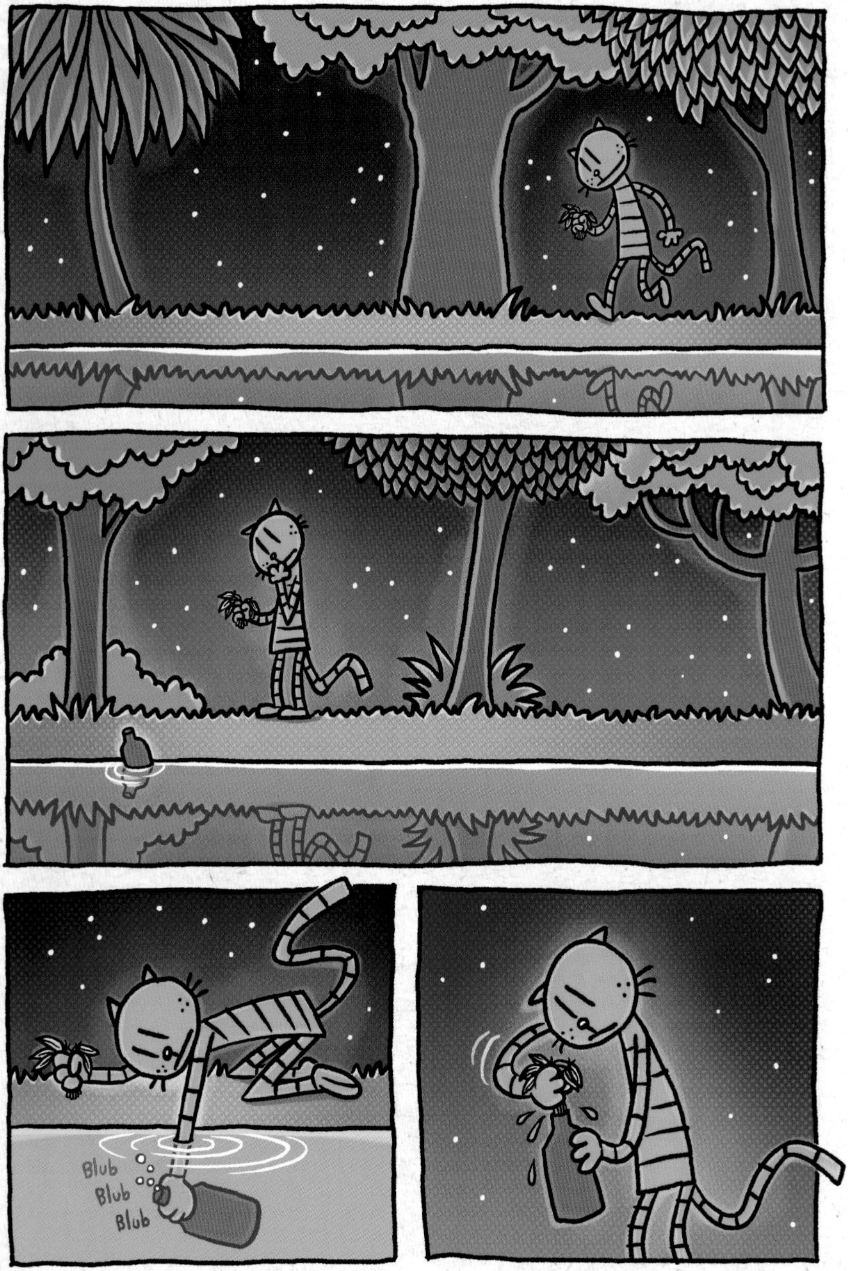
Blub
Blub
Blub

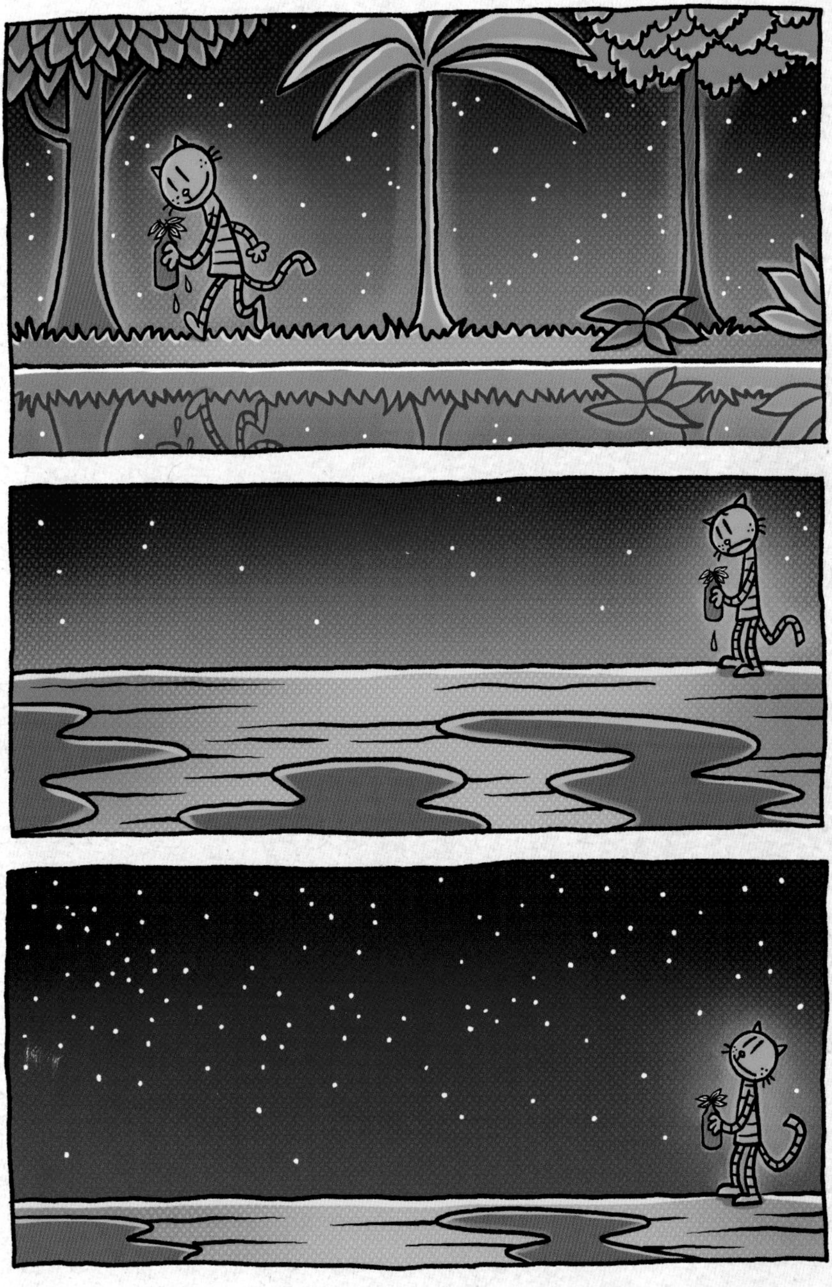

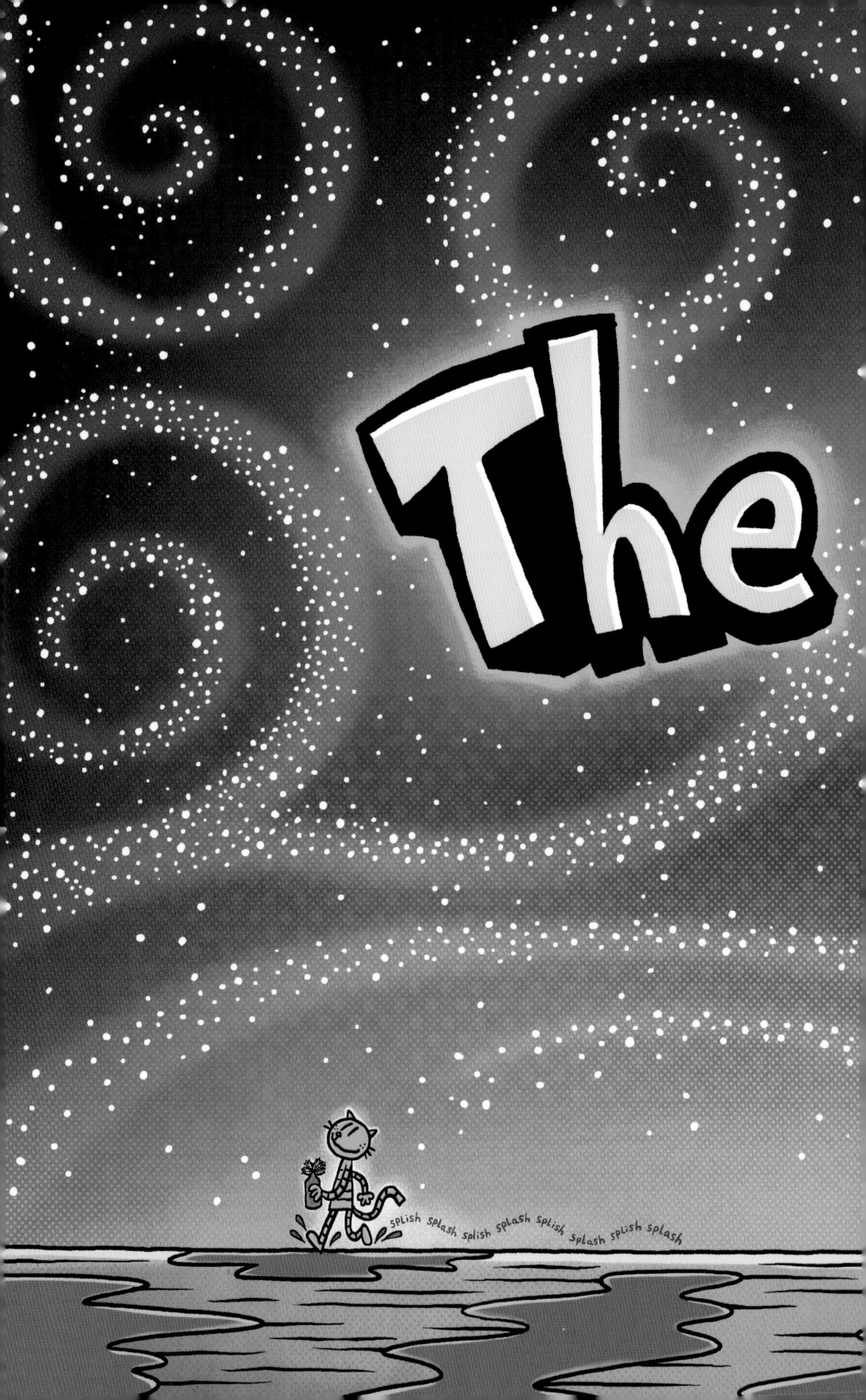
The
splish splash splish splash splish splash splish splash

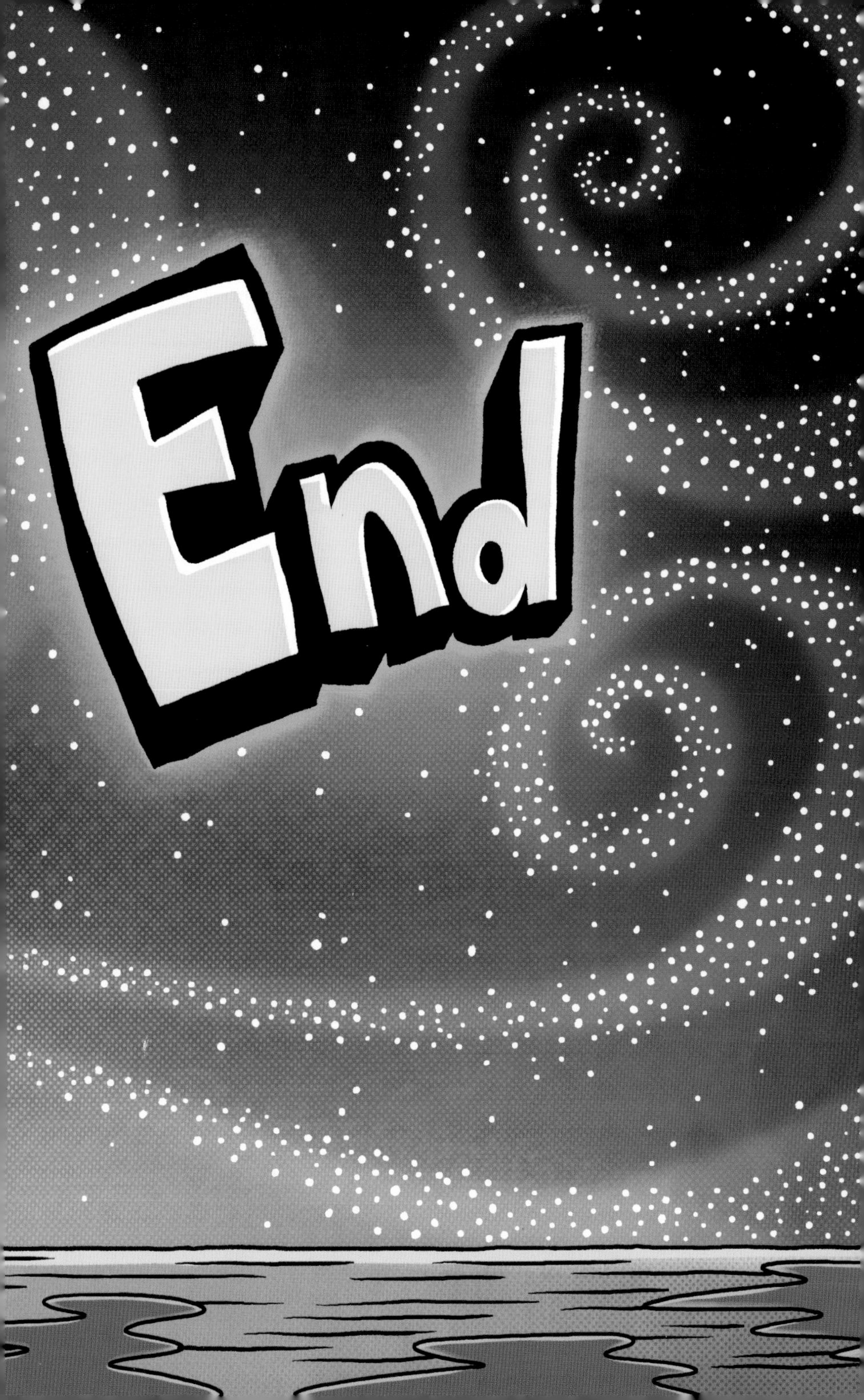
End

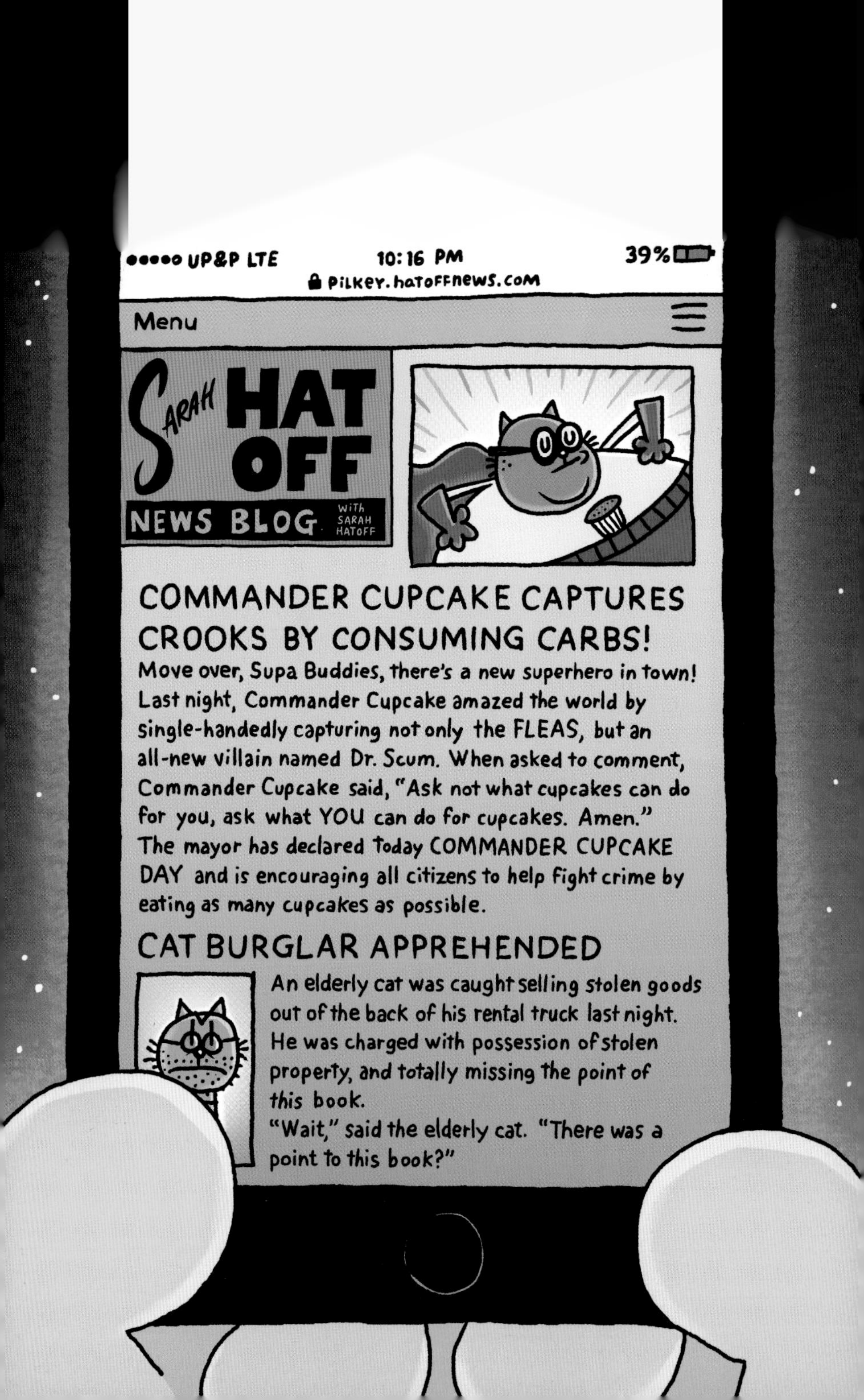
●●●●○ UP&P LTE
10:16 PM
39%
pilkey.hatoffnews.com
Menu
SARAH HAT OFF
NEWS BLOG
WITH SARAH HATOFF
COMMANDER CUPCAKE CAPTURES CROOKS BY CONSUMING CARBS!
Move over, Supa Buddies, there's a new superhero in town! Last night, Commander Cupcake amazed the world by single-handedly capturing not only the FLEAS, but an all-new villain named Dr. Scum. When asked to comment, Commander Cupcake said, "Ask not what cupcakes can do for you, ask what YOU can do for cupcakes. Amen."
The mayor has declared today COMMANDER CUPCAKE DAY and is encouraging all citizens to help fight crime by eating as many cupcakes as possible.
CAT BURGLAR APPREHENDED
An elderly cat was caught selling stolen goods out of the back of his rental truck last night. He was charged with possession of stolen property, and totally missing the point of this book.
"Wait," said the elderly cat. "There was a point to this book?"

Menu ☰

BEHIND THE BARS: AN EXCLUSIVE INTERVIEW WITH A NEW VILLAIN

This morning I got a chance to interview Dr. Scum, the newest villain ever!

Q: What's it like being a newcomer to the world of villainy?

A: I'm not new! I was in the first book!

Q. How has your newness affected your outlook on life?

New Kid in Town

A: I just said I wasn't new! What is WRONG with you??? I was in chapter 2! A LOT!!!

Q. Have you thought about returning for a SECOND shot at world domination?

A: I JUST <u>DID</u> RETURN! THAT <u>WAS</u> MY SECOND ATTEMPT! WHY DON'T YOU PEOPLE LISTEN?!!?

Q: Has the stress of your newness been a—

A: THIS INTERVIEW IS <u>OVER</u>!!!

DOG MAN IS GO!

If you thought our adventure was over, you ain't read nothin' yet! An ALL-NEW Dog Man novel is coming SOON, and it's goi... ...BEST ONE ...s, we'... ...IVE S... ...he ...the ... ...e! The... to f... a new fri... ...see and a p...l of them. SPOILER ALERT... ...at hap...ens when Flippy ...psychoki... ...wen...

Uncle Larry?

Hi, Daryl!

NOTES

by George and Harold

★ The title of this book (and the titles of Chapters 8 and 12) were inspired by the books of Ernest Hemingway.

★ Panels #2 and #3 from page 50 are direct Quotes From <u>For Whom the Bell Tolls</u> by Ernest Hemingway (who was A <u>supa</u> cat Lover).

★ The Very Hangry Raterpillar was inspired by one of our All-Time Favorite books: <u>The Very Hungry Caterpillar</u> by Eric Carle.

★ Big Jim was named after a 1970s action Figure.

★ Harold, who usually only illustrates these books, helped write the story for this one.

★ One of the themes of this book was inspired by Harold's favorite short poem:

Two men looked through prison bars.
One saw mud. The other, stars.

– author unknown (but variations are
often attributed to Dale Carnegie
and/or Reverend Frederick Langbridge)

COMMANDER CUPCAKE

in 42 Ridiculously easy steps!

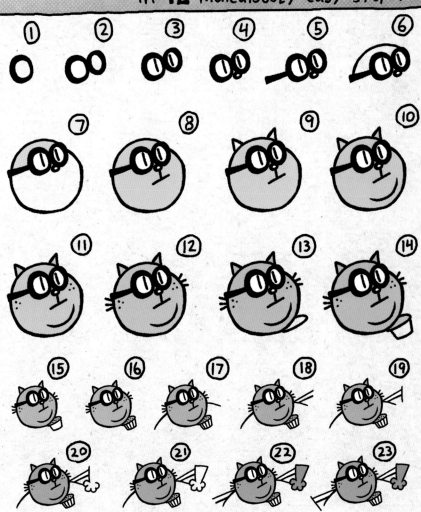

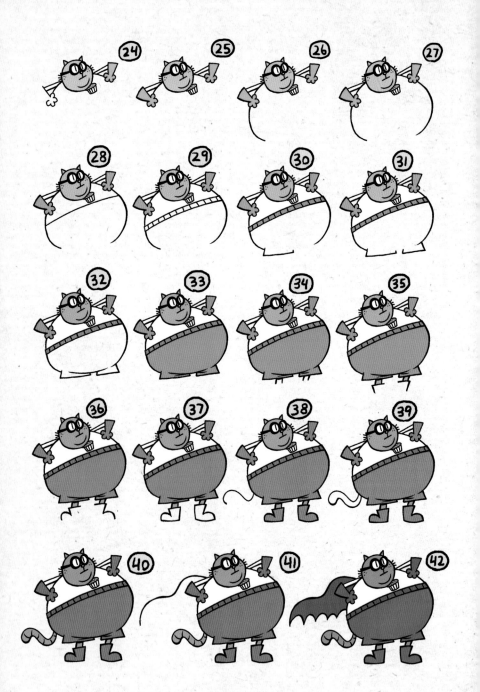

HOW 2 DRAW PAPA AND the KID

in **39** Ridiculously easy steps!!!

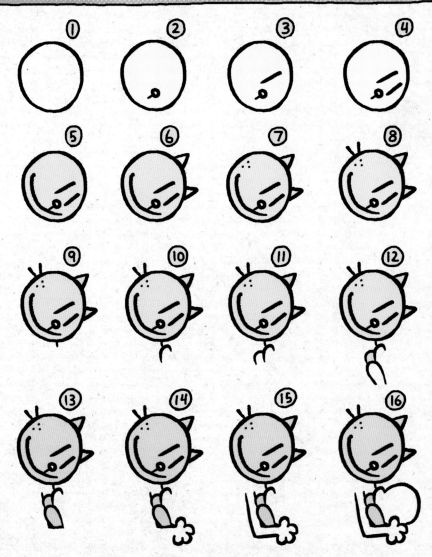

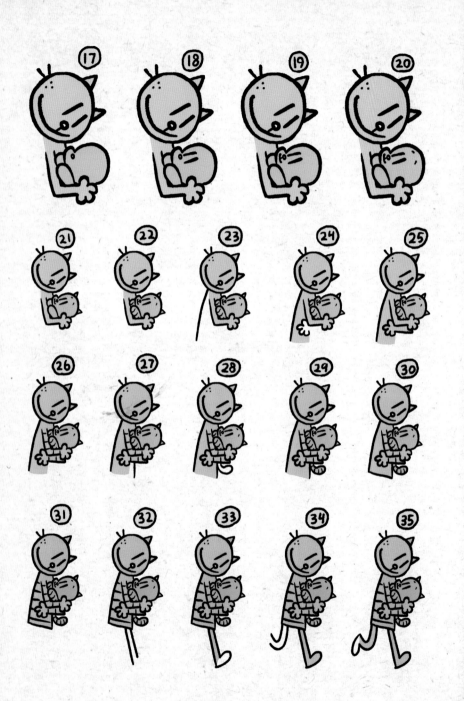

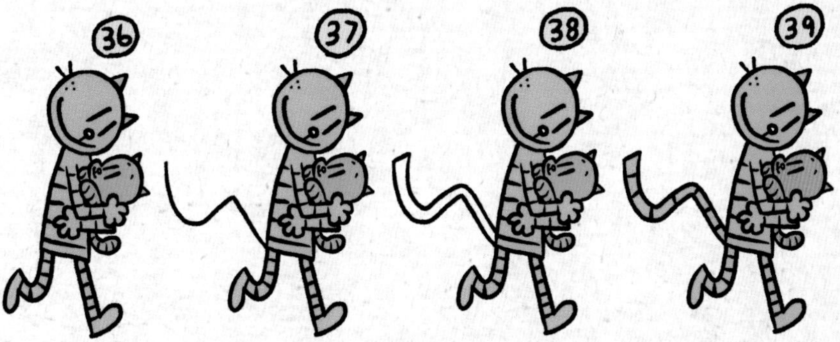
36
37
38
39

Turn the page to give these two fellas a ride on the back of a **RATTERFLY!!!**

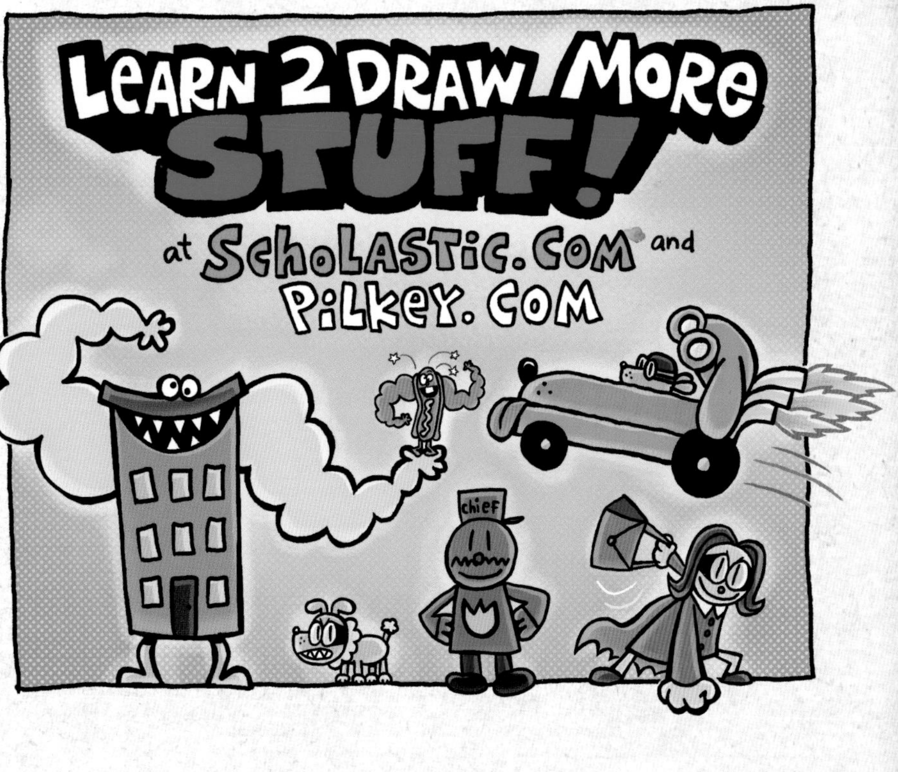
LEARN 2 DRAW MORE STUFF!
at SCHOLASTIC.COM and PILKEY.COM
chief

HOW 2 DRAW The RATTERFLY

in 38 Ridiculously easy steps!

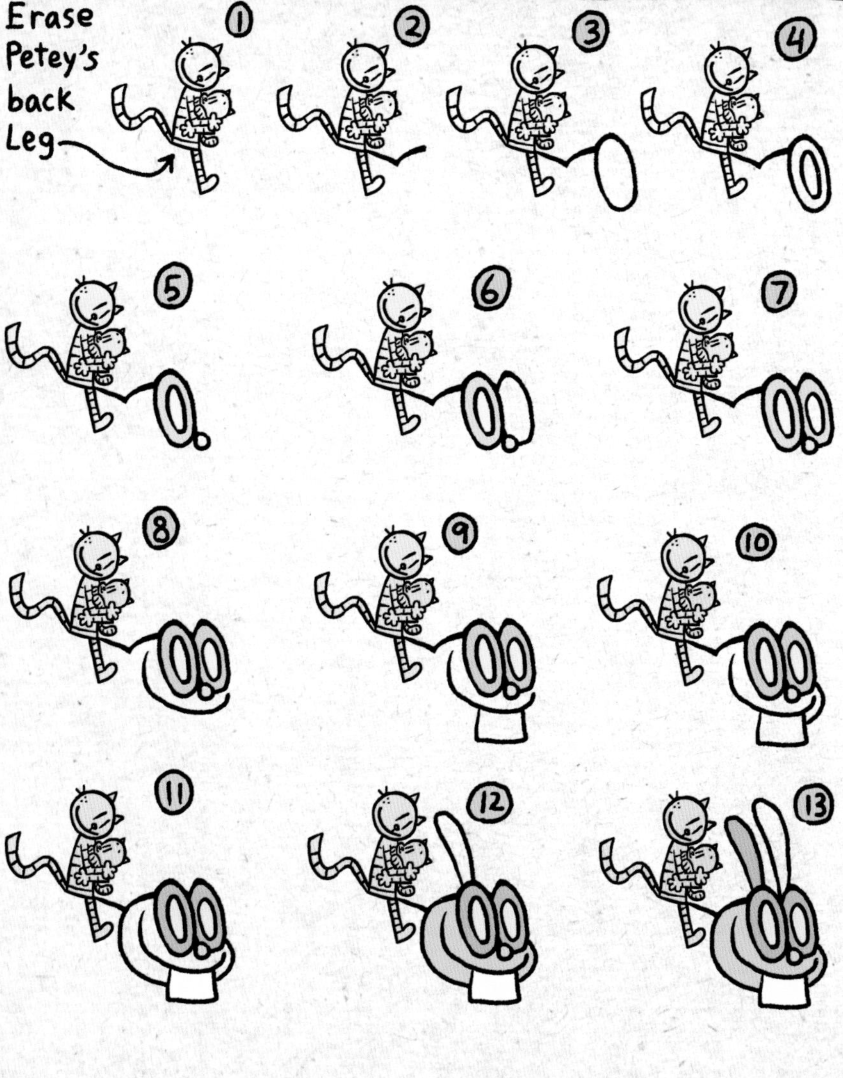
Erase Petey's back Leg
1
2
3
4
5
6
7
8
9
10
11
12
13

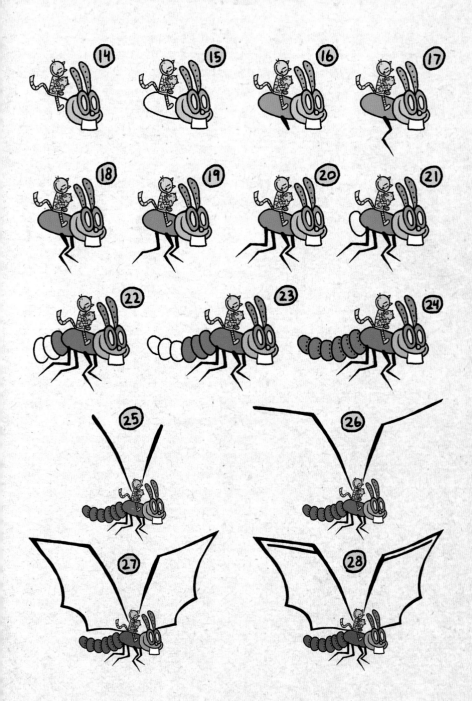

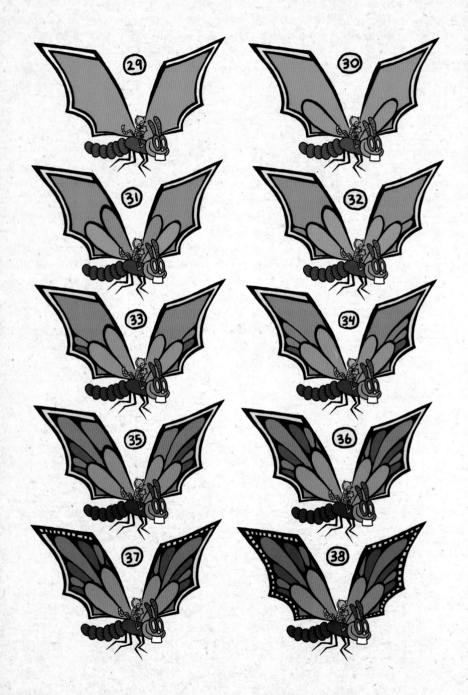

HOW 2 DRAW DOG MAN

in 26 Ridiculously easy steps!

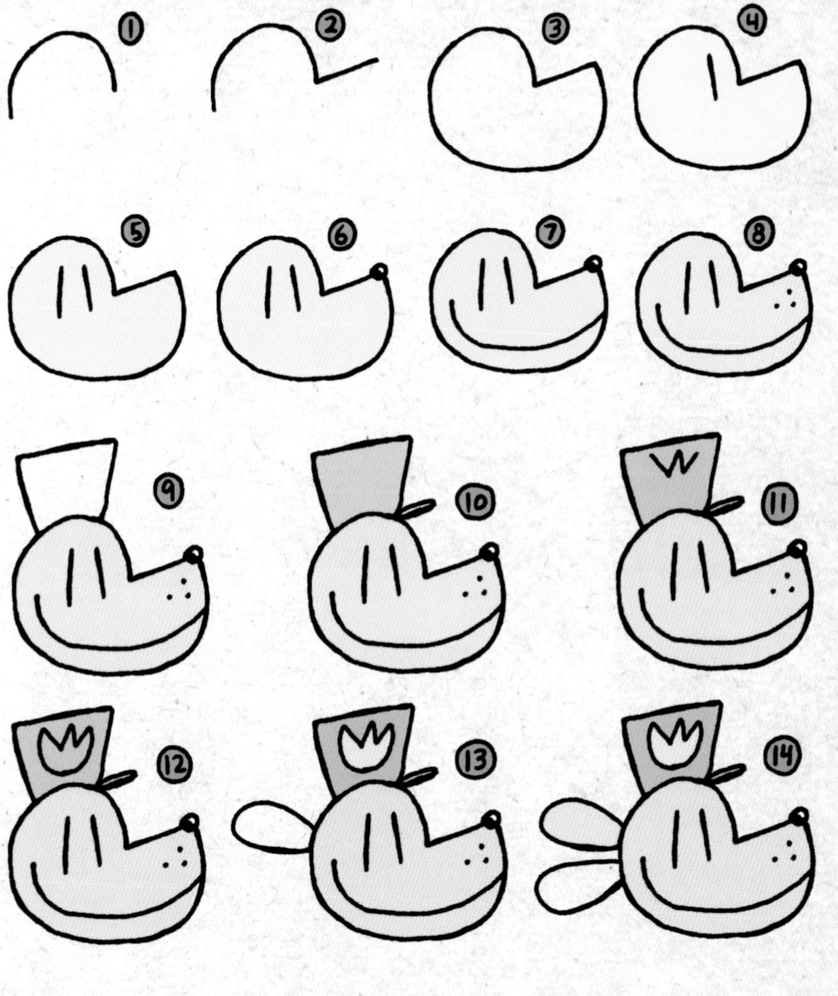
1
2
3
4
5
6
7
8
9
10
11
12
13
14

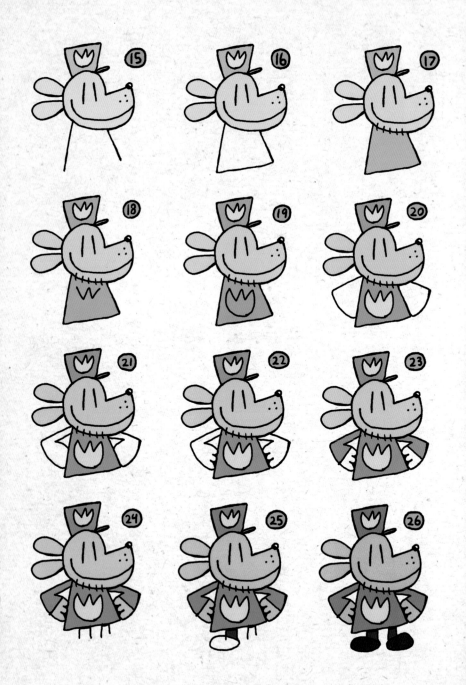

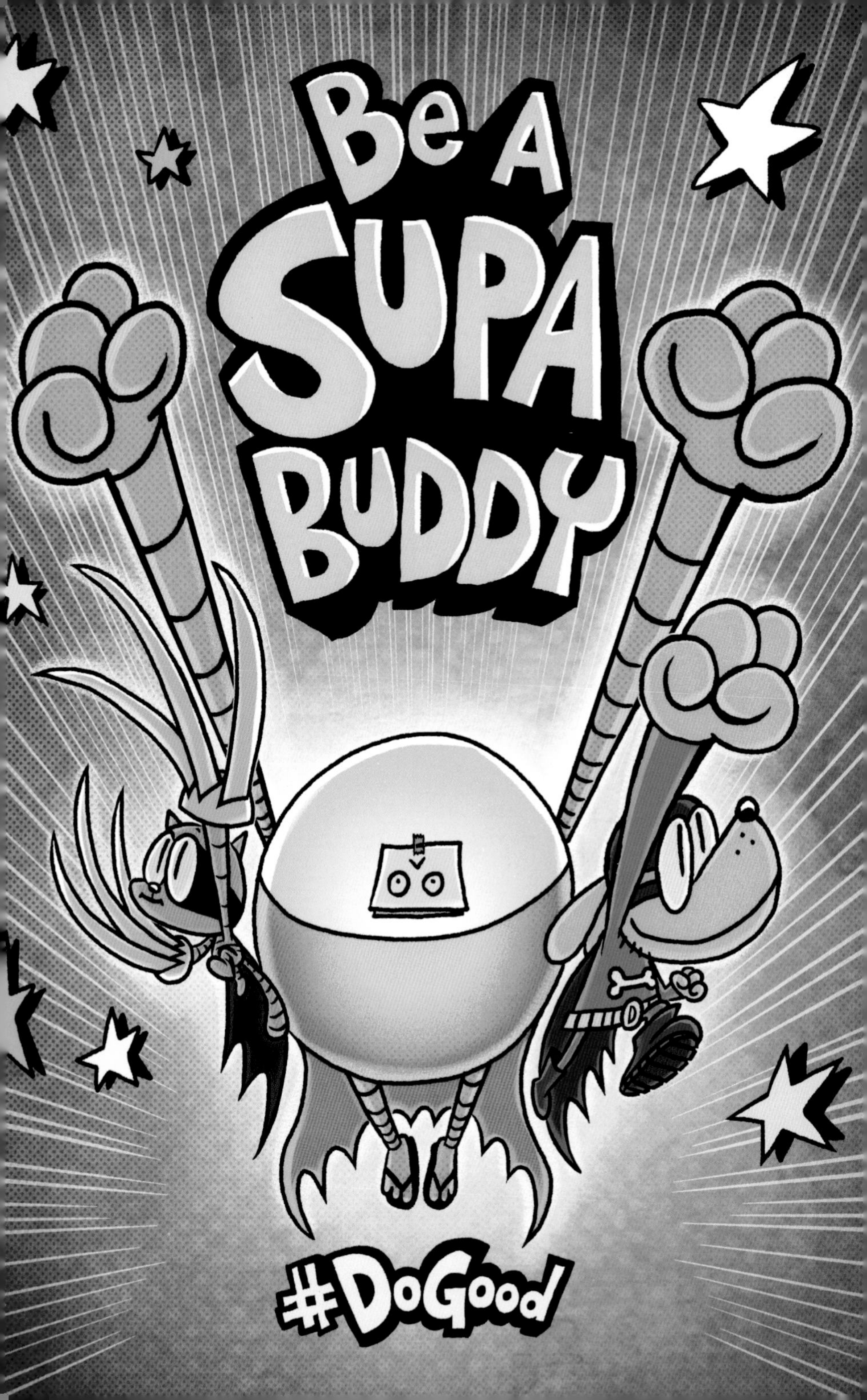
Be A
SUPA
BUDDY
#DoGood

GET READING W

TH DAV PILKEY!

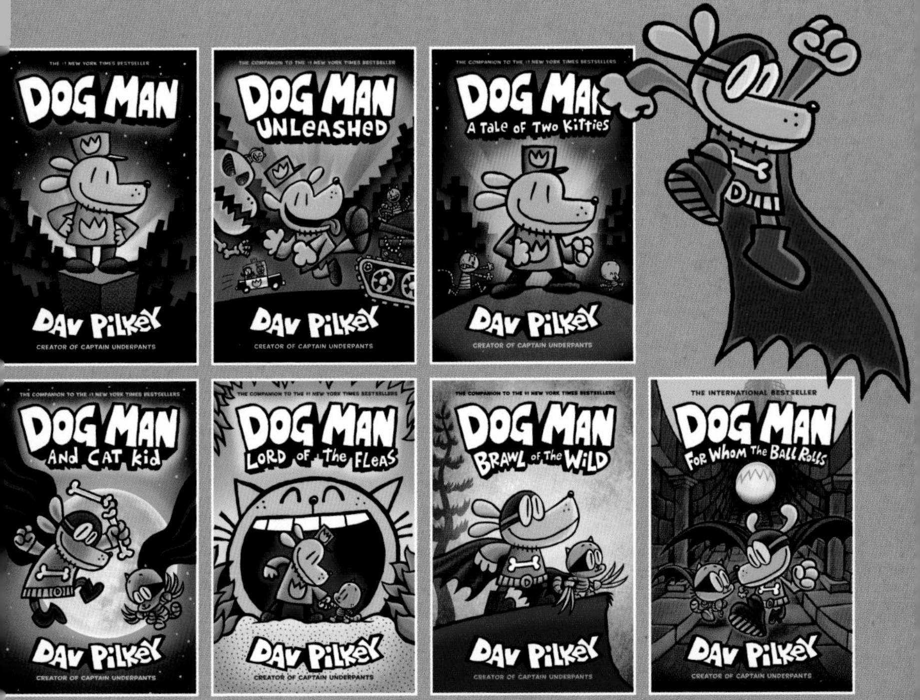
THE #1 NEW YORK TIMES BESTSELLER
DOG MAN
DAV PILKEY
CREATOR OF CAPTAIN UNDERPANTS
THE COMPANION TO THE #1 NEW YORK TIMES BESTSELLER
DOG MAN UNLEASHED
DAV PILKEY
CREATOR OF CAPTAIN UNDERPANTS
THE COMPANION TO THE #1 NEW YORK TIMES BESTSELLERS
DOG MAN A Tale of Two Kitties
DAV PILKEY
CREATOR OF CAPTAIN UNDERPANTS
THE COMPANION TO THE #1 NEW YORK TIMES BESTSELLERS
DOG MAN AND CAT KID
DAV PILKEY
CREATOR OF CAPTAIN UNDERPANTS
THE COMPANION TO THE #1 NEW YORK TIMES BESTSELLERS
DOG MAN LORD OF THE FLEAS
DAV PILKEY
CREATOR OF CAPTAIN UNDERPANTS
THE COMPANION TO THE #1 NEW YORK TIMES BESTSELLERS
DOG MAN BRAWL of The WILD
DAV PILKEY
CREATOR OF CAPTAIN UNDERPANTS
THE INTERNATIONAL BESTSELLER
DOG MAN FOR WHOM THE BALL ROLLS
DAV PILKEY
CREATOR OF CAPTAIN UNDERPANTS

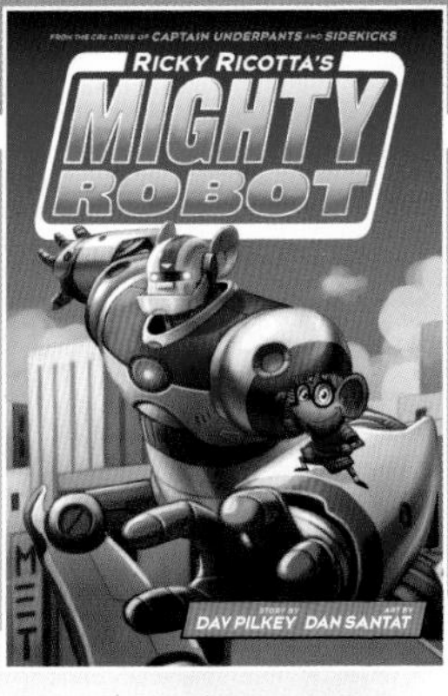
FROM THE CREATORS OF CAPTAIN UNDERPANTS AND SIDEKICKS
RICKY RICOTTA'S
MIGHTY ROBOT
STORY BY DAV PILKEY
ART BY DAN SANTAT

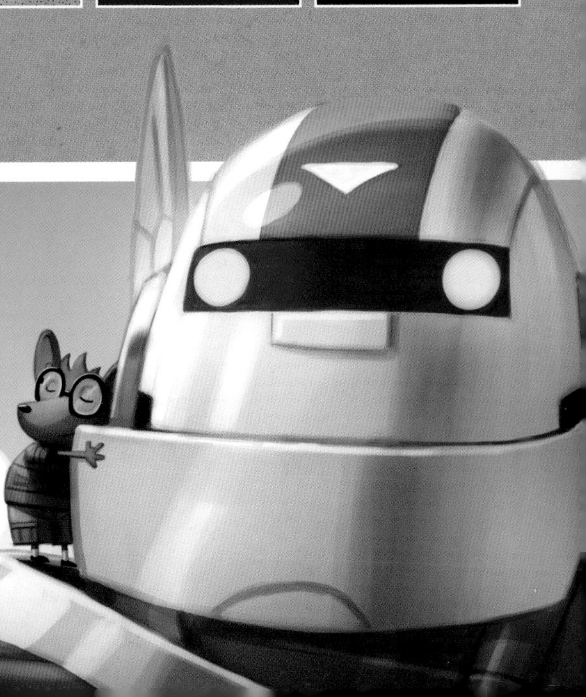

"A fun introduction to chapter books."
— *SCHOOL LIBRARY JOURNAL*

ABOUT THE AUTHOR-ILLUSTRATOR

When Dav Pilkey was a kid, he was diagnosed with ADHD, dyslexia, and behavioral problems. Dav was so disruptive in class that his teachers made him sit out in the hall every day. Luckily, Dav loved to draw and make up stories. He spent his time in the hallway creating his own original comic books.

In the second grade, Dav Pilkey made a comic book about a superhero named Captain Underpants. Since then, he has been creating bestselling books that explore fun, positive themes and inspire readers everywhere.

ABOUT THE COLORIST

Jose Garibaldi grew up on the South Side of Chicago. As a kid, he was a daydreamer and a doodler, and now it's his full-time job to do both. Jose is a professional illustrator, painter, and cartoonist who has created work for many organizations, including Nickelodeon, MAD Magazine, Cartoon Network, and Disney. He is currently working as a visual development artist on THE EPIC ADVENTURES OF CAPTAIN UNDERPANTS for DreamWorks Animation. He lives in Los Angeles, California, with his wonder dogs, Herman and Spanky.